TOUCH WOOD

TOUCH WOOD

◄o►

A MITCH MILLIGAN MURDER MYSTERY

BROCK BARRACK

iUniverse, Inc.
Bloomington

Touch Wood
A Mitch Milligan Murder Mystery

iUniverse books may be ordered through booksellers or by contacting:

iUniverse
1663 Liberty Drive
Bloomington, IN 47403
www.iuniverse.com
1-800-Authors (1-800-288-4677)

ISBN: 978-1-4502-7003-8 (sc)
ISBN: 978-1-4502-7005-2 (ebk)

Printed in the United States of America

iUniverse rev. date: 11/24/2010

Touch Wood

—◄ ◇ ►—

"I call bullshit, fagboy! Skeptical? Very." Classic Mitch Milligan rebuttal. "I don't believe that for a second."

"Man Mountain" Brody shook his head. Smiled. Unfolded the pipes. Groomed his walrus. Slid slab hands into black jeans. "Still true."

"Pork Brains?" Mitch winced. His stomach a trampoline. All morning. No thanks to the McMoney special. Still tasting it. Bad decision, hungry or not. "In cream sauce?"

CORE's best martial arts instructor spread his hands. Then his shoulder blades. Made wings. Levered himself up and off the wall. Repeat. The Hindu thing he'd tried teaching Mitch. Without success.

"Jesus," Mitch muttered a few seconds later. "That's gotta be wrong. Where'd you hear that?"

"Read it," Brophy answered. "Website. Palate Planet or... I don't know, something like that. Weird canned food. Like sandwiches. Worse. No lie."

Mitch put his hands up. Surrendered.

Brody looked over the growing crowd of agents and detectives. "Rats got nothin' on us." Deep breath. Yawn. Showed a full set of blinding enamel.

"Maybe so," Mitch replied. Rubbed grit into his eyes. "But I sure as fuck don't want to know about it this early in the morning. Especially not if it's pork-fucking-brains."

Mitch turned to his right suddenly. "Hey, Affirmative. You people eat pork brains? Where you're from?"

"No, mon," the muffled reply. Figure sat slumped in his chair, large head on larger chest. Python dreadlocks twisted down from under a yellow and green cozy. Hair barrier. Mitch nudged the closest chairleg with his foot. An eye opened, shut again. Resting your chair against the emergency exit could excite the anal. Affirmative's lookout. He didn't care. Jerked a thumb at the big, dozing Jamaican.

1

"He's never heard of it either."

Brody checked his com. "Christ," he muttered, "lets get this thing underway. I got shit to do today." Another dramatic yawn. Hindu stretch. Mitch heard the muscles pop. Mitch followed with his own routine. Less painful. "Stiff today," he acknowledged.

"Friday meetings," Brody groused. "Always a pain, even short. Like I hope this sucker is."

Door whisk. Field Detective Max Sharp rolled in. Looked chipper, the bastard.

"Hey, ho, sports fans!" An unwelcome bellow. Mitch watched him shoulder his way past a knot of men. Made it to where Mitch and his crew were gathered. "What say you all this fine, fine morning?"

A chorus of 'fuck you, cocksmoker' greeted him. Sharp couldn't have looked merrier. Group misery amused him.

"What's got you lookin' like Santa on Boxing Day?" Mitch snarled.

"Nothing," Sharp shrugged. Lips pressed together in his best shit-eating grin. "Oh, yeah. Almost forgot. Bought my tickets yesterday."

"Shit, that's right," Brody said. Leaned his head back. Despair. Closed his eyes. Exhaled slowly, as though in pain. Sharp had won the first leg of the hockey pool. He'd quickly let it be known how some of the winnings would be parlayed.

"They found the sun. It's in Cuba," Sharp gloated.

Images of sand, surf and silky skin. Mitch's hangover muscled aside. McLaughlin, three rows in, actually groaned. It caught on briefly. A morose Wilson could be seen shaking his head. Nothing worse to hear. Sharp triumphant. Again.

"When do you leave?" Anderson turned around in his chair. Fresh lidbuzz, Mitch noticed. Face still a little orangey from the tinted shit he had to wear. Undercover. Not Mitch's game at all. Something he'd read about their brown friends. They couldn't grow beards? They didn't have freckles? Vultures wouldn't eat them after they'd died? Something. Anderson had freckles, though. Couldn't be that then.

"Monday," Sharp answered. "Early." Rubbing it in.

"I heard we got a blizzard arriving then," a voice snarked. "Pearson'll be buried."

"Yeah, yeah, I don't think so," Sharp blew him off. "Monday dinnertime, I'll be sitting on a warm beach. Cold rum in one hand, hot little snack in the other."

"How much they run down there now?" somebody cracked.

"They see Max, they'll run so fast no amount of money'll get'em back," said another to laughter. Stapleton wielding needle. Mitch didn't see a cast.

Meant he'd be back in the lineup soon. Which was good. Their power play wasn't the same without him.

"Oh, I think little Miss Jean Itera will be happy to see me," Sharp countered. Winked. Pretended to count out bills.

"Packed your non-participation ribbon, princess?" Armitage. Wicked way with words. Added, "Can see the headline now. Balding eagle perishes while paragliding in paradise."

"Borrowed one," Sharp said, riding over the ripple of snorts. Sharpie. Pure Canuck. Zero interest in "exploring" the local culture. Except for paying it to bounce up and down on his stick. Beach, beer and boobs the sacred travel agenda. The famous ribbon. Told any wandering happy/clappy event organizer to shove off. Leave a man alone with his drink and doxie.

"Say hello to the Commandante du jour for me." Mitch's eyes were half closed again. Still recognized Political Bob's heavy sneer. Sharp shrugged. "Say what you like about the Commies, man, they run clean tail. They're not stupid when it comes to real money. We keep the Commies going. All they have to do is let us fuck their daughters."

Political growled something unintelligible. Mitch shook his head. Not good getting him warm this early in the day.

"Hey, I heard a good one," Sharp said. "What do you give an old hooker with hot flashes?"

Several heads moved. The clouds of pain were too thick for thinking. No offerings.

"Whoremones!" Sharp said in triumph. More silence. "Geddit? Whore… mones." A chair-rattling fart greeted the explanation. Actual laughter followed.

"Okay, okay, got another one." Sharp undeterred. "What do fags on a diet eat for breakfast?"

Conversation volume dropped. Somebody should know the answer. Or be able to ruin the joke.

Mitch tried. "Pork brains?" Sardonic applause from Brophy.

"No," Sharp responded in dismay.

"Fist and chips?" somebody offered. Grudging applause for the attempt.

"Cream of Pete?" More clapping. A couple of snorts.

"No! On a diet! No cream….well…fuck. Anyway, c'mon, give up?"

"Long ago," a voice said bitterly.

"Queerios!" Sharp barked. "Just add milk. They eat themselves!" He collapsed, giggling. Ripple of strangled laughter. Mitch smiled. Fag gags. Always funny. Unfortunately, moving anything caused brain daggers. The hangover demon had no sense of humour.

"I got one." Fender Bender—red hair, road rager—turned around in his chair. "What's the first thing 40,000 battered women in America do after they leave the shelter?" Ears perked up. F. B. could tell them. "The dishes…if they know what's good for them."

Appreciative applause. Chatter level spiked. Collective mane-shake among the forty or so agents gathered. Guys were slowly finding their feet. Battered women jokes did the rounds for a while. Then back to Sharp and his series of 'Little Johnny' stories. Mitch thought he'd already heard all the sex education ones. Then Sharp hit the punchline. "My Daddy always calls it 'the black cat with its throat cut'."

Fuck the headache. Mitch had to laugh. Sharp. Where did he get them?

Voices grew animated. By the time the suits arrived, the atmosphere had improved noticeably. Hangovers were like assholes. Everybody knew one. You just had to push past the pain. Mitch was ready. The demon, less so.

CORE admin reps entered single file. Made their way to the front. Panel of five this time. Must be important. Meeting brought to order. Some 'spurt Mitch didn't recognize was introduced. Information provided. No fucking powerpoint. Mitch happy to not see that. He forgot everything instantly anyway. Only his head and stomach held his attention. Nothing critical missed, he didn't think. The 'spurt was a bit of a droner. Like most experts. Self-admiring. Assumed everyone else was.

Then it was over. Slumped figures were roused. Several agents bolted for the can. Mitch considered it. He always felt better after a spew. A workout would accomplish the same thing. No time, though. Not sure he was up to it either, this early. Some guys could manage it. Keech, for instance. Big advocate. Sweat the toxic shit out. Mitch had tried it. Opposite of fun.

"Pissholes." O'Brien sidled up to Mitch. Joined him in the outflow of agents. Thumbed him in the ribs.

"Ow! Shit! What?" Mitch said, startled.

"Your domelights," O'Brien smirked. How do you see out of them?"

Mitch nodded. "Yeah. Fuck me. Thunderbirds are not go today. I feel like three bags a shit."

"What time'd you get in?"

"No idea. I think I drove, too. Car was there when I came out this morning anyway."

"Scandalous," the man clucked. Nil sympathy. O'Brien never bar surfed. So the face brimmed with health and good cheer. Mitch wanted to smash it. Cloud over those alert blue eyes. Leave a blood trail along the neatly razored jaw. Sadly, O'Brien was a friend. Not on, as a result.

Mitch shook his head in remorse. They rounded the corner in tandem. Swept up in agent wake. "Why, oh…fucking…why, do I drink tequila shooters?"

"Ow," O'Brien winced. Led Mitch through the seminar door, out into the corridor.

"It always hammers me. I'm so…"

"Braindead," O'Brien completed the lament.

"Fuck you," Mitch rejoined. "And I also got this killer crick in my neck." Rotated his head. Glowered. "Must have slept on it wrong."

"Water, water, water."

"Yeah," Mitch nodded.

"Seriously," O'Brien said. "For muscles, too. No quick fix for misery, but it helps."

"Yeah, I think I'm gonna need a lake for this animal. My head feels like… Christ. If I could just screw it off and leave it somewhere…"

Denis clapped him on the shoulder, smiling. "You'll be okay…in another eight or ten hours."

"Prick." Mitch gave him the evil eye.

O'Brien snickered. "Hey," he remembered suddenly, "Game's on the uni tonight. Don't forget. Lounge three. You're second in the group pool. And it's still a race, except for Sharp. Espo has an outside chance to catch you if the Rangers keep winning."

Mitch stopped with his hand on the floor exit door lever. The antique hinge variety. Safety regs. In the event of a power outage. All CORE facilities had massive backup generators in case of emergencies, of course. Still, Mitch liked a door you could touch. That didn't vanish into the wall as soon as you got near it. Comforting somehow.

Mitch's brain was cold gravy. A wet igniter. Roadkill. Thoughts surfaced briefly, then sank in the muck. Something was trying to get his attention. Couldn't focus on it. Held up his hand to keep O'Brien in place a second longer. Then he corralled it. The puzzle.

"Hey. Today. It's Friday."

"All day," Denis concurred.

"There's hockey tonight?"

"Yeah, it's one of those fucking…weird things." Denis O. furrowed his brow. Old acne craters caught light from the overheads. Whatever he'd used on them hadn't helped. At least nobody called him graterhead anymore. Especially not after word got around he was a uni Merlin. Being far from one himself, Mitch cultivated the friendship.

"I don't know. Just tonight. Once a year…in honour of Buffalo or something. But you're there, yeah?"

"Fuck, yeah." Mitch said. Death's head smile.

"Good," O'Brien said. "Good, good." Faked a slap at Mitch's head. Mitch went to bat it away. Missed by a wide margin. O'Brien laughed. Gave Mitch a final once over. Smirked. A 6'2", 110 kg slab of jangly nerves. "Don't be picking any fights today. My Mom could take you right now."

"In her dreams," Mitch replied.

"That's the spirit." O'Brien smiled. "Well, back to the mines." Peeled off to his right. Headed off to the computer wing.

Mitch wondered why he'd even bothered to attend the meeting. He wasn't department rep. Pushed through the door. Stopped on the landing. Tried to remember what floor he was on. Did he go up or down? His hangover was getting worse. That was it. No more Thursday tipple. The all-you-can-drink karaoke festival at Billy's Club. Killer. Shooters of choice for anyone willing to get up on stage. Fool's Parade. Agents elbowed each other aside for the opportunity. Dignity abandoned. Mitch's colleagues. To a man convinced they could sing. Even boozed loose, most sounded as if they were gargling razor wire.

He blew into his spacious square. Slumped onto the leather. Switched on his desk. Waited for central data link. Memory snippets percolated up. No fighting. That was good. He remembered a fall-down funny can-can number. A clutch of sluts thrown up on stage. Told to sing for their release. Somebody found "99 Leadballoons" in the archives. Fucked around with it. Speeded it up. Slowed it down. Hilarious. Everyone singing in German. Bad German. The best kind.

Op's Squad Leader Mason Eyre the master of mimicry. From Marley to Mick to Manesh, he had a roster of foreign voices he'd trot out at any time. You couldn't not laugh. But his Herman the German was tops. And his Bengali Bani bit was so good you could smell the curry.

Mitch suddenly noticed the strawberry. An angry red blotch on the palm of his right hand. Had antiseptio spray in his desk. Couldn't be bothered.

His left knee was stiff also. Then he remembered why. He'd slipped on ice in the parking lot. Banged it hard. Did his hand the same time. Tequila, Tequila. What's your name? Sheila? Mitch directed a silent curse towards the cornholing Mexican bastard who'd invented the stuff. If it was a Mexican.

The uni hummed. CORE theme song. Mitch touched the console. The holofield jumped into life. A flagged item drew his attention. He upped the window tint. Glare was strong that morning. The day's weather report appeared. Grim. Again. Overcast. Again. Like living under some homeless fucker's filthy mattress day after day. Chance of flurries, freezing rain. High of 1C. Beautiful. What had Sharp said? They found the sun…in Cuba. He believed it. Waved goodbye in October. Fucking Toronto in fucking March.

A scroll through the crim updates came next. Another body found near the lake. Female. Prolepro, most likely. Humped, stumped and dumped. Nothing to do with Mitch. The general alert did turn over the heart somewhat. He read it twice. Rubbed his nose. Felt for his smokes. Fingered the drink icon. The cooler ejected a frosty bottle of enhanced mineral water. A beer was what he needed. Popped the lid. Drained it. All the daily vitamin requirements. Better still, thirty minutes of adreno charge. He wanted that. The nap was a non-starter now.

Double-checked the feed. Event had already begun. Slight gut kick. The juice was kicking in. Mitch pushed his chair back. Dropped the uni into idle. Five seconds later, jogging down the corridor. Follow the arrows. A little Tank time. Just what the doctor ordered.

POLITICAL BOB HOLDS COURT

―◄◇►―

H e sensed he'd missed the moment a soon as he stepped into the room. Full house. Standing room only. Wall of blue. Smokers out in force. Mitch edged down the wall. Found a space. Happy faces all around. Everyone gestured at the main viewing window. Or pointed at one of several vidscreens staggered about the room. Mitch waited. Eyes adjusted to the gloom. Slowly noticed who he stood next to. "English" Matt Worcester. Nudge and nod. Nod in return. Mitch leaned in. "Drama?"

Positive head jerk from English. Though he didn't know much. Only that Political Bob was indignant. Something about the 'spect in The Chair. Mitch shot a look up at the wall Holofield. The left half display, picture of a skinhead powerplug. Face twisted in murderous fury. Draped over him, three Burlies. Yes, Mitch thought. PB looked peeved. The Burlies had their hands full. Gatemouth howl. Jawmuscles bunched, cheeks blood bloated. PB screaming something. CORE's most famous terrorgator. Ready to dismember a 'spect.

"Volume!" an agent yelled out. A PB show without sound? Thin gruel.

"Fucked!" came a reply from the back of the room. Groans, curses greeted the admission. A few laughs. Salute to honesty.

The split-screen expanded. Wide-eyed lard-loaf in The Chair. Mitch glanced at English. Shrug reply.

"Self-buttering," Mitch observed. "That's good."

Under the spots, the man's face gleamed. Dinner plate waves lapped out from his armpits. The 'spect wore street clothes. Unusual. Definitely need a shower after. And a complete change of nerves.

Political writhed and snarled. Frenzy mode. The Burlies had him well-pinned, nonetheless. The object of PB's theatrical display sat paralyzed. Mitch had to smile. Panicked hyperventilating. Like pike in a catch bucket. Sucking air hard.

Mitch cursed hangovers. They made him forgetful. Should have checked his com sooner. He hated arriving late to the party.

Full screen. Camera on Political. Rogue rage undiminished. A Burlie put a lock on his pipes. Between the three, they bulldogged him backwards. Towards the escape hatch. Forty-years old. You wouldn't have guessed it. The Burlies struggled. Even 50% acting, it put wrasslin' to shame. PB was hard as a stone. Arms like I-beams. Bank safe for a chest. Hydro tower legs. Joke was he could kick-start a Dreamliner. Perfect gentleman away from the Tank. But the man owned a live temper. CORE admin liked their suspects to survive, mostly. So Burlies tag-teamed special P.B. efforts. Mitch mused on what the gormless-looking dweeb had done. Political didn't usually do his crazyman act.

Political finally maneuvered out of the Tank. Strong he was, but no match for three Burlies. Playacting or not. To even qualify for consideration a Burlie had to be 6' 5". Bench 400 pounds. CORE ignored state-ordered quotas. Meet the standards or make coffee, mitt.

The Burlies were cautious with a guy like Political, though. Man was ex-Special Forces. Done black ops. Along the AfPak border. He'd seen the digiholo's. Sunblasted face. Full beard and puggaree. Could be any ugly Pashie going. Also Kashmir, Iraq, Iran, Turkey, some Latin American shithole. Even a stint in Burkina Faso. Which was in Africa, Mitch learned. Whispered hints of unspeakable deeds. All the more intriguing for not being spelled out. Couldn't be worse than what the UN did.

Regime change came to Washington, however. Appeasement the new black. Boomers' last gasp. Fuck everything up proper before they wheeled in the gurney. Trundled them off to be incinerated. Political, other old hands kicked to the curb. Claimed later it was God's wrath. Political's team had scored serious intel on their missions. Information they'd nicked from Al-Qa'ida. Saved New Sodom from a dozen other 9/11's. Pissed off God. He hated the place.

The ink on Political's walking papers wasn't dry before the headhunters arrived. CORE was interested. Would he consider switching teams? Insight-for-hire? Canadian snipers he'd worked with vouched for him. So the NSC's loss was CORE's gain.

Moving north, no problem. P.B. didn't fish. But the market crashes of '08 on put a hold on black bag opportunities. The retirement funds suffered. Plus, Buffalo boy hankered to work in Toronto. He accepted the offer. The rest, history. Only American ever offered a position at CORE. Hugely popular with the men, despite being a Yank. Humble, hard working, no bullshit. Knew what he was talking about. Quick to laugh. And an experienced "terrorgator." Everyone a winner.

Mitch's good fortune. Political took to him instantly. They'd hit it off during one of Mitch's first training missions. He'd been tagged to deal with a low-life perv. Liked to hang around Branksome Hall. The lech chose the wrong private girl's school to haunt. Especially with a lengthy sexcrim file. A member of the school's steering committee knew a senior CORE adviser. StateCare counselling hadn't produced any behaviour modification. The call went out. CORE went on patrol the next day.

Agent Sims spotted the creature in the shrubbery. Hunched, ratlike. The girls he hunted were taller. A perfect shorteyes. Greasy brown hair tied "ronin" style. Gave the crew a good laugh. Fashion by Sally Ann. Layered rumplewear. Zebra-striped top, soiled, navy flightpants. Combat boots, well-scuffed. Multiple zircon ear plugs. Neck tatts. Moonscape face. Street moniker—"Trick" Logan. Nickel and dime petty crime. Favoured monied crumpet. "Known" to D.P.'s. Laws prevented them from acting until he'd raped or killed someone. So they shrugged. Went back to their bearclaws.

They collared the wretch in his blind. Sims the stealth torpedo. Crept up noiselessly. Hard-sapped the weasel. Threw him into the Badger that raced up. Inside, they gave Logan the CORE welcome. No crim ever forgot it.

Nearby Moore Park Ravine the sentence venue. Mitch the designated executioner. Ten minutes of closed-fist instruction. He liked to work fast. A foolish escape attempt. Tragic error. Broken field tackle. Mitch face-planting Logan in revenge for getting his jeans dirty. Kicked the street creature onto his back. Pulled out the hose. Pissed Trick's face free of turf. Niagara spill. Steam rose off him. Still early-morning cool.

A loud gasp. Mitch turned. Two joggers had stopped to stare. He smiled. Easy wave. "Park perv," he explained. Pointed at the dripping Trick half-hidden in the mist.

"Ah, well..." the taller of the two said. Paused. Glanced at his wristcom. Resumed jogging in place.

"Yes," his partner said. Pushed a strand of blonde hair back behind an ear. Adjusted her cap. Glanced again at Mitch's member. Moistened her lips. Different circumstances? Solitgary jogging? Mitch would find a dropped biz chip after. Pertinent details for uploading. So it went. Next time.

"Carry on, I guess," the man said. Self-congratulating chuckle. Mitch offered a half-salute as they passed by. Overheard, a snatch of chatter. Something about full dockets. Overtime. Crown prosecutors from the sound of it. So no stress from them. They'd be happy to see the creep get what was coming. Seeing as it wouldn't be coming from the justice system. That much was a given.

Mitch zipped up. Waited until they were out of sight. Dropped his gaze to the quivering Logan. Snapped his fingers. Logan got up. After he was upright, Mitch spun him around. Grabbed his collar. Marched him to where the grass ended. Then deftly dropkicked him into a spiny bush. Logan screamed as frozen thorns tore into his face and neck. Cheers from the ridgeline greeted his yowls of pain. Happy endings. Always popular.

Mitch scrambled back up the slope. Loped to the parked Badger. Black doors slid away with pneumatic ease.. Hands reached out. Pulled him inside. Backslaps, vigorous handshakes. Hero's welcome. Efficient, productive savagery held in high regard among the CORE fraternity. Three long blaster growls sealed the triumph. Letting the jungle know. New lion on the prowl. Beware.

Behind the wheel, Political caught Mitch's eyes in the rear view. Nothing said. But Mitch could tell. He'd met the challenge. Drank free that night. Approving glances, shared stories. The exclusive CORE fraternity had increased by one.

So Mitch had a mentor. Got taught the inside game. The kid from the Kap happily took to the arrangement. He was a natural enforcer by nature. And a quick study. Concentrated instruction smoothed out the rough edges. Like some scrub on skates finding a new level. Inside a year, word was out. There was a new terrogating force to be reckoned with.

Political, in turn, invigorated. Mitch's larky enthusiasm and fondness for fisticuffs rubbed off. They drove and inspired each other. An affectionate competition developed. Mitch, the new gunsel. Political, the wily vet. Bragging rights at stake. Without meaning to, they started setting the pace. Jenkins, Anderson, Wills, Scapinello, McCready and the rest. Put on notice. Raise their performances or sacrifice position. Soon teary admissions of brute stupidity were commonplace. Confession success approached Japanese rates. Perfection the goal. Top floor was ecstatic. The plan was moving ahead of sched.

Of course, Political on the rampage still drew the crowds. The troops loved it. Mitch himself never tired hearing the tales. How captured terrorists begged to be shot. Or fell on their swords when permitted. It couldn't help but leave a positive impression on the younger agents. As much as he kidded around with the man, Mitch held Politcial in quiet awe. He only came up to Mitch's shoulder, but he was larger than life.

And it was Political who coined the term "terrorgator." He'd wanted to distinguish them from mere information gathers. 'Grocery clerks' in his estimation. Him for the jumper cables. As a means of opening discussions. The other tools in his arsenal were equally famous. As for the claim spread by rattled jihadists…that he engaged in cannibalism…Political was contemptuous. Dismissed it out of hand.

"C'mon," he'd argue. "Think about it. You know what they eat there? Fucking chickpeas. Morning, noon and night. I don't like chickpeas. Ask anyone. I'd juggle camel spiders before I'd gnaw Muslim. Planted lies. To discredit me in Washington."

Which didn't mean, Political reassured everyone, calculated violence was unsound practice. "Torture, in one form or another, has been used for thousands of years. All over the world. Why? Because it doesn't work? Sound logical?" No-waiting surgery, razorings, tazorings, scourings, scourgings, rack 'n roll, the Iron Toecutter, straight up, garden variety beatings—all would render positive results in time. Plus, they were fun to administer. All work and no play, the reasoning went.

The screen flickered. Regained Mitch's attention. A three-metre tall face replaced Political's. White as chalk. Suet in a suit. Miles Melling, Mitch heard. A fumblebutt, doofus jerkweed. Guy who had to check to see his pants were front to back before he left the house. Mitch took an instant dislike. No effort required.

Pointing at the greasy glob on the screen, Mitch lobbied Matt for his opinion. What might the perp's crime be? Itchy digits bookkeeper, Mitch's guess. Pew troller caught with moppets. English Matt's theory. Neither, it turned out.

Decided to find out for himself. Mitch lightly backhanded Matt on the chest. Farewell. Made his way down the amphitheatre steps to the front. Ducked low past the view wall. A few strides brought him to the debrief entrance. Slowed. The mass of agents all around still laughing at Political's mad antics.

Mitch smiled. Waved a hand at the hip-level biologic bar. Two blinks. Barrier parted. Mitch slipped inside. Instantly sideswiped by a flanking Burlie. More laughing and shouting. Mitch elbowed himself upright. Disoriented. No one had noticed. The two lead Burlies released their charge. Backed away, hands raised. Mitch up on toes behind them to watch. The bemused CORE support staff also kept their distance. A final bout of bulldog swearing. Then the clouds withdrew. The sun shone. Political burst out chortling.

Ivan, the debrief captain, frowned. "Political, Political," he groused in a thick Ukrainian accent. "You keep to be doing this crazy thing and you heart…maybe it go 'pffft' someday."

"No worry, Ivan," P.B. said. "Just cleaning out the valves. What the old man used to say." He caught the puzzled looks on a few of the subalterns.

"Combustion engines," he explained. "Exhaust buildup." Zero comprehension.

"Never mind."

"Yeah, yeah," Ivan said. Stalin eyebrows jerked up and down. Battery –powered. "Still, too much…da waving and zee energy. You are not so young no more."

"The hell you say!" Political responded, indignant. "I'm not even… forty yet," he lied. Pulled off his CORE top. Gave everyone the pocket

Hercules pose. Biceps bulged. Delts danced. Lats like gargoyle wings. The man's stomach, a freshly-plowed field. Barest hint of love handles. Otherwise, Chelios reborn. Or so Fitness Jim, CORE's head trainer, said. And he'd worked with the man before he retired from the NHL. Explained why the Burlies were cautious. Respectful. Political gave away 50kg to most of them. Even so, none took him lightly. Rehab sucked cock.

Lordly bow from Political. Acknowledging the applause. Resumed undressing. Mitch pushed past the Burlie barrier.

"What the hell was that about?" he asked, eyebrows knotted.

"Just a little personal business, is all," Political grinned. Sweat dripped from his arrowed nose. Chamberlain shimmered up. Toady on call. Handed over a sweat towel. Political dried off. Mitch closed to within a few feet. Promptly reversed course. Man radiated heat like a tire fire.

The post-mortem unfolded. The Burlies added their own accounts. Ivan chimed in with holovid angle commentary. Spirits were high.

"It's weird," Political said in conclusion. Face still pinked from hard wrestling. "You dream about something and then…when the opportunity actually arrives…" Political couldn't finish. Coughed. Mitch chucked him on the shoulder. Tight-lipped look. Murmurs of support from around the room.

"Anyway," Political said to Mitch, eyes moist. "He's primed and ready. I just couldn't…I lost it. Totally unprofessional, I know. Good thing for my blockers." Waved for beers. Raised a freshly-cracked bottle in salute. Return clinks.

"Slice'em and dice'em for me, would you? " he asked Mitch, solemn. Mitch nodded, hard-faced. The American spun around. Found and tossed Mitch a book from the cabinet behind him. No cover. Dog-eared. Possibly dog-chewed. Mitch riffed the pages with disgust. No disguising the contents. Obscene diagrams littered page after page. Mitch felt the bile rise.

"Remember," Political said, as Mitch moved to prepare himself, "what he's done to me, he's done to thousands of other innocent people. His kind… they need…."

"To know the fear of God," Mitch finished for him. "I got it brother." You can count on me. Mitch flashed on Political's revealed torments. Time to set matters right. Mitch was just thankful he could contribute. He had no love for the scum either. Rolled his shoulders. Loosened his neck muscles. The Hindu breathing routine. That bit of foreign shit he understood.

"Well, boys," Political smiled, "looks like he's accepted the mission." Smattering of laughs. PB waved Chamberlain over. Order whispered, he turned abruptly. Launched his uniform top in a sweeping arc towards the laundry basket. Far side of the room. It grazed the screened emergency light. Perfect trajectory. Found the target thirty feet away.

"Swish," said a techmonkey, forgetting his place.

Political stood stock still. "Shit!" he exclaimed. "Three-pointer! Why can't I ever do that in a game?"

Polite foot shuffling. A few coughs. Political's strengths and accomplishments were legendary. Dead of night parachute jump over hostile terrain? Hand-to-hand combat under fire? PB was your guy. Basketball? Another matter. No trampoline? No vertical jump. It was what it was.

Rueful grin and wave. Political ambled off to the showers. Chamberlain scurried after. More fetching likely. Political's post-terrorgation cool down's were well-known. The beer fridge took a beating.

Mitch finished stretching. COREwear appeared. Regular gear. Nothing too serious planned. Still, quick tear-check by Ivan's boys. Inspection passed. Mitch readied himself. Glanced at the telemonitors. Lounge still packed. Good mix. Vets, middies, some upstairs staff. CORE encouraged fraternization between all levels. Ability trumped rank. Oldies vied with turks for attention. Heavily veined beams, corduroy stomachs the norm. The unofficial "Anytime, Anybody" code made it a necessity. CORE agents had a special stride. The confident swagger of a law-giver. These were the new lords of justice. Handpicked. Collie loyal. Rottweiller mean, when provoked. And their time had come.

Mitch gave Ivan a thumbs-up. Nabbed Political's book. Stood before the hatch. Airlock hiss. The titanium door telescoped into the wall. Mitch stepped into the Tank. Inhaled, deep and deliberate. Home again. The trapped figure at the other end tensed.

"Hel-l-l-l-o-o-o-o, fuckhead!" Mitch bellowed. In the best of humour now. "Man, am I glad to see you!!"

He strode forward with purpose. Overhead spots splashed over Melling. Little piggy eyes quivered with alarm. Man was rice pudding at low voltage, Mitch thought. He decided not to adjust the blaze. Big audience today. They'd want to to see every open-mouthed howl. Every blood spray. CORESales also preferred well-illuminated revenge scenes. Made for higher quality holovids.

Mitch walked up. Kicked The Chair's frame. Reassuring heavy metal echo. The 'spect squealed. Perspiration beaded the tuber. His sky-blue button-down resembled an inkblot test. Mountain range beltline stains above banker chinos. Tasseled loafers. The Mr. Comfortable Suburb ensemble.

Mitch guessed mid-thirties. Tuft of unmotivated sawgrass on his head. Coaxed backwards. Bit like Rin-Tin. That idiot Euro cartoon kid. Only gone to seed. The doughy face spoke of sodas. Hickory stickwiches. Nearmeat microwave meals. Extra salt, cancer wanted, cracker snacker. Funeral Parlour bait.

He knew the balloon's occupation. Otherwise, he'd have guessed sub-sub-assistant manager. Canadian Tire, parts department. Sexbooth attendant, dead end of the mall. Elementary school principal.

Mitch drilled the Chair again. Steel-toed Kodiacs. It felt good to see Melling cringe. Mitch ignored the asthmatic rasp. Faker. Nowadays everyone suffered from something. The evil bastard could drown in his own lugie stew for all Mitch cared.

"Well, well. The butcher in the flesh," Mitch said. Grasped the armrests. Drew close. "You're something special, you know that?"

"Please, please," Melling begged. "There's been some kind of mistake. I'm not who…I don't know…please, you have to believe me. Something is wrong."

Mitch flared his nostrils in annoyance. Ran a hand over his face. Man's breath smelled like an alley after the bars closed.

"We know you killed her?" Mitch stated emphatically. "It took us awhile to find you. You don't fit the profile. Clever."

Raisins shook in their sockets. Reminded Mitch of fruit jellies. Tempted to pop one out. Scarf it down. In the spirit of that great Aussie standover man, Chopper Read. The old Chop Chop. Had a huge CORE following. Terrorgator par excellence. His books never long in the library.

"Always with a sense of humour, comrade," Political used to joke. That was the Chopper. Rational cruelty. With a dash of the comic.

"What?!!" Melling gawped "No! No! God, they pulled me over for…I rolled a stop sign. That's all! I swear!"

"You're not fooling anyone, Milesy," Mitch shook his head in despair. Miles Melling. Perfect name. "We have the body. After you threw it into the lake. Plus, there were witnesses. CitiTV news team. Filming the absence of spring. Caught it on digi. It'll be all over the ether soon."

"Oh, God," the man babbled. Turned his head to seek help. Nothing. Empty room. "That's imposs…you don't understand. It can't be me. I was just going to a conference downtown."

"Where were you in late February?" Mitch snarled. "Or do you have crimnesia?"

"February? When in…February?"

"April, May, June, July," Mitch mimicked. "Stop evading the question, dickwad. You know when."

"Look, there's been…there has to be a mistake. I'm an engineer. Honest to god. I work for…"

"You're…an engineer?" Mitch took a step backwards. Feigned look of surprise.

"Yes, yes, I tried to explain to the other…gentleman…officer. He just got really angry. Started…screaming at me. I'm…I'm an engineer. I design video cameras. I work for a…"

"Shut up," Mitch waved him silent. Stood with hands on hips. Close survey of the pleading Miles. Earnest, doggy sincerity.

Mitch turned. Deadpan look at the two-way. Knew the audience would be doubled over. Everybody but Melling in on the joke. Straight face essential. Mitch understood Political's difficulties. Melling was such a weed. He took a deep breath. Waited for the collapse-in-laughter urge to pass. Returned to stand over the mystified blodge.

"Let me see if I have this correct," Mitch began. Voice, holocaster direct. Melling a model of innocence. "You're not an assassin. You don't work for the terrorist organization known as "The Ovarians?"

"No, God!" Melling sputtered in horror, mouth open. "I've never even heard of them. Who?"

"You're a design engineer?"

"Yes, yes! I work for..."

"Yeah, yeah, got it," Mitch interrupted. "I heard."

Melling frowned. Confusion apparent.

"And you were visiting the 'Hot 'N Taut Venus' for a pre-conference rub and tug. Is that right?" Fishing expedition. Remote possibility Melling had been a customer of the recently found dead trull. Or another one. Who knew? Couldn't hurt to ask.

Melling started. His mouth slammed shut. Guilty. Mitch laughed to himself. No clinic in cool calculation. Mitch knew instantly what he had before him. Man was a dime-store whack off. Namby pamby burbobutt. Likely knew squat about anything remotely criminal.

"Tick tock, tick tock," Mitch said. Tapped his boot on the Chair. CORE had his story uploaded. The Life of Melling sifted. Found wanting of interest.

No way out. Melling admitted the claim. "Yes."

Mitch nodded with satisfaction. Forgot his question. "Yes, what?"

"Yes, I was...I sometimes visit that...establishment. Before work."

Mitch remembered. "Right. Now we're getting somewhere," he said. "Okay. In addition to being a lonely loser, you're a holovid camera designer?"

"Yes." Melling white as milk.

"Meaning...you'd know about, say, the Canine 430 i3Holovid?"

Political's tale of woe was well known. The trials. The frustration. The boiling fury. His i3Holovid. Unusable without years of training. He'd bend the ear of anyone who'd listen. For weeks. Mitch knew they'd be enjoying this moment in the box seats.

"Yes!" Melling responded with evident pride. "I was the lead designer!" He launched into particulars. Mitch held up his hands in mid-spill. Smirked at the mirror. Fixed Melling with the coldest look he could manage.

"You fucking worthless piece of lowlife shit!" he screamed in rage. Melling quailed under the spit barrage.

"What?"

"Do you fucking admit you helped design that camera, you fucking dimwit asshole?"

"My team and I…"

"Oh, ho!" Mitch laughed without mirth. "It's 'My team' now, is it? Jesus Christ, this has been a long time coming. Know what I mean?"

"No." Melling croaked, thoroughly befuddled.

"No, I suppose you wouldn't." Mitch shook his head. Thoughtful stroll time. Began orbiting The Chair. The bootstep echo followed close on his heels. Mitch enjoyed its effect on Melling.

He let his eyes roam the walls. Marveled at the artistry. Nothing out of place. Sleek, brushed copper. Recessed rivets. Barely visible indentations marked where sensors sat, blinking. Monitors in all corners purred left and right as he passed. Satlink lights blinked soft yellows and greens. And then there was the vast two-way mirror. It filled an entire side of the Tank. Gave the room a unique SeaWorld feel. Melling…the plump seal sunning itself on an ice shelf. Mitch…the crowd-pleasing killer whale about to dine.

Mitch's hand slammed down on the Chair's backrest. Melling looked to leap out of his skin.

Mitch rounded The Chair. "Still with me, princess?"

"What…what can I do?" Melling whimpered. "What do you want? I'll try to help."

"Oh, you'll help us alright," Mitch declared. "That much is certain. That much is an absolute fucking guarentee." He leaned in. "Listen up, penisbreath. Reality begins now. I'm going to ask you some questions. You're going to give me straight, honest answers. Failure to do that means we run you down to…the Black Block."

"The…Block? What's the Block?" Melling bleated.

"It's where we keep the…" Mitch paused. "Never mind. Pray you don't find out. What's important now…is your giving me your complete attention."

"Yes," Melling's voice broke. "Yes, yes….I have a family."

"No you don't, you liar," Mitch corrected him, laughing. "Who'd marry you? You're a fat…shitball…engineer."

Mitch cocked his thumb. Pointed his index finger at Melling's forehead. "You…and your technical writing dream team," Mitch drawled, heavy sarcasm, "put together the Canine 430 i3Holo…whatever the fuck else it's called…3-D camera, yes?"

"Yes, but…" Melling began. Mitch backhanded him. Hard. It felt good. So good, he had to do it again. And then once more. Very satisfying.

"And did you help design all those wonderful apps? In your capacity as a…fucking engineer?" Mitch sneered. Pulled Political's ruined manual from his suit. Waved it in front of Melling.

"The features," he continued, "that require…one-hundred-and-sixty-five fucking pages to explain?!!" Slapped Melling's open mouth with the book. Mouth closed. Opened again. Closed. No sound from pikeboy. Doofus catatonia. Mitch felt something akin to…pity. The man was so utterly pathetic. Then he was reminded of Political's stroke-causing grief. Not that the locker room rants weren't hilarious. Accounts of the many deranged "extras" had agents falling down. But the anguish was real all the same.

"How often does an eclipse happen?" Political would scream. "I mean, Jesus H. Christ! Who wants to see pictures of dark? Forty minutes of fucking around for that? Or I can bounce a fucking signal off a Google satellite. Then film shit falling from a giraffe's fucking butt! So fucking what? What friggin' moron would want to?"

Mitch was disgusted with himself. Wasting even a shred of sympathy for something so…worthless. Weakness.

"My partner wanted to rip your heart out. Eat it in front of you," Mitch felt it important to share. "You got no idea why, do you?"

Melling gagged. Perspiration dripped off his nose. His kind never got it, Mitch knew. He'd seen it before. Political's tale had unleashed scores of other nightmare design stories. Electronics, appliances, computers. No one was immune from inept engineering. Hard to know whether it was mere criminal stupidity or deliberate evil. Whatever the reason, it had to be stopped. The Commissioner heard the complaints. Permission given to expand the original CORE mission. In addition to crims, fuckups, shitbrain activists and the like, CORE now hunted idiot engineers. Straight out good luck handed Political his nemesis. Minor traffic violation after a pinkhouse stopover. Same pinkzone under surveillance. The trull skullings drew reluctant interest. Perfect excuse. Not that CORE needed one. Ran the vehicle chip. Vocation alert. CORE immediately notified. Political pegged for payback.

"Okay, Shakespeare," Mitch said in dead earnest. "I'm going to walk you through this. Keep your head screwed on tight and your ears open." Mitch folded his arms. Paced. "Let's examine the original crime. You wrote a 165-page operating manual." Mitch stopped. Looked directly at Melling. "What the fuck…were you thinking?"

Melling's Adam's apple bobbed. Audible swallow. Shrank further into The Chair.

Mitch continued. "This is the thing, cheese-dick. A guy like Political…" Mitch paused. Stupid error. He winced at the camera. Pointed at his chest. His miss. Too late to stop. "He's not some…waste-of-sperm digit head, right? He's human. Has a house. A family. Works hard. Plays basketball…kind of. Can even mangle a bit of towelhead talk. He doesn't fuck plastic pussies working off their passage…like some people we know." Mitch saw it hit home.

"In a nutshell, he's not a gadget-head. He's normal. But…when he buys them, he wants them to work. So…he laid out serious capital to buy your little product. Shoot the kids shaving the dog. Film his little princess doing her arena routine. He opens the box. Know what he finds?" Mitch stopped. Glared at Melling. More fish-eyed goggling.

"I'll tell ya'. He finds a spankin' new holovid…that he can't use. Why? Because it comes with a fucking phonebook list of instructions!" Mitch screamed at Melling. The surge, that wonderful adrenaline surge. Mitch's ill-will was obvious. Hatred that penetrated.

Mitch took several deep breaths. Savoured the chemical rush. His cells filling with liquid rage.

Melling looked on, frozen with terror. Mitch scratched the pulpy head with a gloved hand. "You know what I can't understand, shit-for-brains? How can you guys be…bright…and yet so…incredibly stupid at the same fucking time? I mean, how does that work? You designed a camera only another engineer can operate."

Melling mumbled an answer. Mitch cocked his ear. "Missed that."

"Yes." Melling upped the decibels.

"Yes, you can't take a piss without getting some on you?" Mitch prompted. "Yes…no!"

"Bullshit! I know you can't." Mitch pumped a fist for the two-way. The best terrorgators read people quick.

"If I could…" Melling began. He stopped. Mitch looked unreceptive.

"How many people on your team?"

Melling scrunched up his eyes. "Four…not including…"

"Yeah, yeah," Mitch cut him off in irritation. "Group effort, group incompetence."

"It wasn't all our fault," Melling said in a muted whine.

"No?" Mitch responded archly. "Whose fault was it? Climate madness? The C.I.A.? NHL management? That last I'll believe, by the way."

A shadow flickered in Melling's eyes. Mitch caught it. Didn't understand it until later. Cube eel cunning. Slithering away from responsibility. Toronto man. Corporate footstool. Chief skill, grovelling for advancement. Giving head for the chance to give more head later on.

"All right," Mitch said. Felt soiled in the man's presence. "Three little words. Ready?"

Melling never moved.

Mitch shrugged. Pinched Melling's ear until he drew blood. "Here we go. Ease. of. use."

He studied Melling's face. No evidence of a pickup. With both hands, Mitch brought Political's manual down hard on Melling's skull. Excellent echo. Did it again. Same sound. Grinned at the two-way. Something they could use in the future.

"Ease of use!" Melling squeaked.

"Repeat it, dirtbag" Mitch ordered.

"Ease of use!"

"Again!"

"Ease of use!"

"Once more!"

"Ease of use!"

"Outstanding," Mitch commended Melling. Boxed his ears to cement the lesson. "How hard was that, Microsoft-in-the-head?"

Moist, melon-sized eyes looked up at Mitch with dread.

"Next bit is tricksier, though," Mitch warned. "You'll have to concentrate with a-l-l-l-l your might." Mitch raised his open hand above Melling. "Okay?"

Electric bobblehead response.

"You want to think… in three's. Always in three's. Three's are easy. Three's are fun. Father…Holy Ghost and son."

Melling looked ready to lick Mitch's hand. Sometimes that was cool. Mitch didn't feel like it just then. Denied.

"'Ease of use', for example. That's three," he continued. "On…off…play'. These are the most important functions for any device, yes?"

"Yes, yes, abso…" Melling babbled. Mitch's expression told him to stop.

"So that's your starting point. Anything different, you're…moving away from perfection. Clear?"

He was talking to a sundae gone soft, Mitch thought. Or an overturned turtle. Abject wimpering powerlessness had a face. And it was melting. He shifted his feet. Leaned on an armrest. Fanned the manual in Melling's face. "The holy three."

"The holy three," Melling repeated.

"If you must go beyond them, 'pause' is acceptable. All else is just engineers' masturbating." Mitch air-stroked the meaning with his thumb and fore-finger. Wrinkled his nose. "Nobody likes that."

Melling nodded. Avoided Mitch's stare. Guilt and shame. Obvious.

"So you're going to swear to end this crap, right?"

"Abso…lutely," Melling promised.

"No more billion-moving-parts-one-of-which-is-fucking-designed-to-break bullshit."

"No. No more."

Mitch faked a fatherly smile of fondness. "You better not be pullin' my dick."

Bewilderment from Melling.

"On, off…" Mitch hinted.

"On, off." Melling repeated.

"…Play…"

"Play. Sorry."

"S'okay," Mitch held up a hand. "Two outta three. Better than I expected. Anyway, your mission, which you're going to accept, is to move among the other idiots you work with. As soon as one of those jerkwads comes up with a…a really stupid idea. Something sure to make life hell for people…what are you gonna do?"

Mitch cocked his fist over Melling. Double-pumped. Melling's eyes closed. His upper lip danced. Mitch had the feeling he could pull the man's tongue from his head. Wrap it around his throat. That's how pliable he was now. Mitch prayed they were getting it on digi.

"Call you?" the man-like thing mewled.

"No, you moron!" Mitch corrected him. "Look at me! You! I mean… what you have to do. Haul off and drift the pencil-neck dork. In the face. Hard as you can."

Mitch demonstrated the point. Threw an uppercut that would have taken Melling's head off had it landed. Squeak of terror from Melling. Vampires had healthier skin tone than he did at that moment.

"Don't worry. It's the best thing for them. Really. For you, I should say. For your type. Straightens them right out. Clinical studies show it. The… electrical things in your brain? An engineer's brain? They frequently misfire. So you get these, you know, really bad ideas sometimes. But a shot to the head…boom. They vanish. Like magic. Kid you not. I've seen it happen."

Melling exhaled through his nose. Mouse whinny. Tried not to look at the five-fingered anvil idling inches away. "I'll try," he moaned. "I'll really…I will."

"That's my boy," Mitch smiled. "Who's the little…well, who's the engineer that could, eh?" Mitch squeezed cheek until Melling's eyes watered. A last joy.

Final penetrating glare. The veiled-threat smile. Then the cheerful farewell wave. Flashed the CORE victory signal on his way past the screen. Brought the audience to its feet. Extended ovation. A happy Mitch bounded out of the Tank. A pleasing piece of terrorgation brought to its proper conclusion. Political would be content.

Two Trogs and a Burlie overseer saw to Melling. By the time Mitch had finished peeling off his suit, Melling was dismiss-ready. Release signed. What happened in the Tank stayed in the Tank…under penalty of neck-snapping. Or worse.

The Trogs peeled him off the Chair. Marched him into the lounge. Mitch followed behind. Third-floor showers the destination. A stop off in the Red Room after.

A roar greeted both their arrivals. Applause for Mitch. Shower of empty beer cups and boos for Melling. A gauntlet of agents lined the aisle. Bad engineering examples were shared as Melling waddled past.

"Thanks for the fuckin' Star Trek remote, brainman-shithead-cocksmoker!" a red-faced giant screamed. Aimed a kick at Melling's back.

"And my fucking microDutch, asshead!" another vet bellowed. Waved his middle finger. Punctuate the sentiment.

Others joined in. Corridor Doloroso. It nearly unmanned Melling. Mitch wondered if he'd shit himself. Peculiar gait. Like he was clutching a apple between his buttcheeks.

There was a pause in the procession. Melling wiped hork from his face. A Trog goosed him along. Finally, the upper deck landing reached. Agents swarmed him. Noodle-knee moment. More hoots and insults. Ear-splitting din now as angry men pounded on seatbacks. Theatened ugly, painful reprisals.

Then someone started in on a CORE favourite. Abruptly taken up by all. They serenaded Melling out of the room. Behind Mitch, a thundering rendition of "The Idiot Engineer (is Here)." Mitch doubled over with laughter. Added his own lusty voice to the chorus.

"The Idiot Engineer is here
The idiot engineer
He came at last
He's not so fast
The idiot engineer

The idiot engineer is here
The idiot engineer
It can't be fixed
He's out of tricks
The idiot engineer

The idiot engineer is here
The idiot engineer
You'd best stand clear
We think he's queer
The idiot engineer."

Through the door and into the stairwell. Bouncing melody echoing. Trogs hustled Melling forward. Sensed what was to come. They made three flights down. Basement level 4 the object. From above, the sound of a heavy steel door slamming against a wall.

"He's getting away!" someone yelled. "After him!"

Melling let loose a high-pitched screech. The Trog duo collapsed against each other recounting the story the next day. Both tried to mimic the sound. Mitch, Political and the rest wiped away tears. Roared with laughter.

"Fucking wide-ass bagbiter could move when he had to," Trog One chuckled. Nickname of "Pickering." Other Trog called "Bruce." Because of their huge heads. Mitch had forgotten their real names.

"The pipes were a nice touch," Trog Two added. Vicious pounding on the railings triggered Melling's second bowel mishap. An old CORE prank for departing crims. All they could do not to ruin the moment by laughing, the pair admitted.

Safety finally reached. Poured Melling into a waiting Badger. Blindfolded him. Removed it when they dropped him off. A designated Burlie repeated the standard warning. Told him he was on probation for the rest of his fag "career." Any mouth flapping, he'd get the Tobermory tour. One-way. Booted Melling out onto a crusty snowridge near where they'd picked him up. The armored crimtrans rumbled away. The passenger Trog stuck out his tongue. Gave Melling the finger. One of the fun parts of his job.

Miles M. found his Biarritz parked next to the dumpster. Behind Harvey's. Wept at the graffiti. A strange, frightening symbol keyed onto the hood as well. His com box would be full of sparks. How he would explain his day? How would he explain his new approach to engineering? What a horrible situation. He was tempted to return to the Hot 'N Taut for relief. Knew that would be death. Wept for his fallen state.

ANDREA PUTS OUT, GET'S PUT OUT

—◄○►—

Mitch rolled the rigid nipple around his mouth. Busied himself tonguing the plump, juicy baltimores. His com buzzed. Andrea stared at the night table. Groaned in dismay. Drove her enflamed tit further into Mitch's mouth.

"You're not going to answer that, are you?" she gasped.

Mitch spit out the slick silo. "Right now? Fuck, no!" he declared. "Only a moron would do that. I'm celebrating!"

He dove back to work. Vacuumed up the rigid morsel of flavour. Lay into it with lusty enthusiasm. Andrea wriggled, squirmed, sighed happily. A willing captive of delight. Mitch was spiking her pleasure meter.

Sudden change of tactics. Now a round of volley and slurp. Like a slo-mo metronome, his head rotated from one erect twizzler to the next. The owner arched her back. Moaned softly. Cupping her prodigious melons, Andrea mashed them into Mitch's face. He grabbed a handful of flank. With two fingers, he probed her ham wallet. She welcomed him with a feverish cry. Rocked forward on her knees. Impaled herself on his questing digits. Let the miners moil her greasy seam. When she reached full boil Mitch withdrew. Grabbed his throbbing funbar. Jabbed it into her stomach. Andrea giggled. Relished what she beheld—the ten and eleventh wonder of the world.

"Oh my wonderful God," she murmured as always. Corraled the hefty fire hose with both hands. "I still can't get over how ginormous it is. It must be 15" long."

"Just erect," Mitch said. Ever modest.

"Please," Andrea pleaded. Drool pooled at the corners of her mouth.

"Later," Mitch promised. "Caving time now." Flipped Andrea onto her elbows. Hunched forward. Clasped her udders. Positioned himself for entry. Released one milker to run his hand back. It came to rest on Andrea's firm, perfect rump. Sleek, proper moons. Mitch's somewhat new mattress-presser had a grade 'A' chassis. No denying it. Sweet look. Superb rack. Ass that could make a tuning fork sing. Broccoli for brains. Jackpot.

Mitch inhaled with anticipation. As the golf pros all said, there came a time to grip it and rip it. He secured his hip hold. Hoisted caber into turf. Andrea shuddered. Gutteral groans greeted the toss. Mitch jammed her face into the pillow. Faked remorse after. Force of habit. Forgot he'd had the bedroom insulated. Too many neighbour complaints. One compared it to living over the Lubyanka. Which seemed extreme. Mitch knew Africa was a slaughter zone. But he'd never killed anyone in the room.

The man from CORE gave of his best. Tunneled into Andrea's cleft with expert ease. No false starts. Mitch knew what he wanted to do. He buck-walked Andrea from headboard to hope chest. Back again. Deeper and deeper he drilled. Suddenly, a squeal of surprise. First contact. Mitch's thrust encountered resistance. Kidney or spleen? Mitch couldn't be certain. Andrea raked varnish from the night table. That usually meant he'd discovered a major organ. She fed herself handfuls of pillow. It helped muffle the screams signifying volcanic orgasms. Then she fainted.

Near-death climaxes were nothing new. Mitch availed himself of the free moment. Found her teddy on the bedpost. Toweled himself dry. Tossed it onto the floor as she came around. She always complained about him doing that. No choice, though. Slick patches were as dangerous in bed as on highways.

Mitch let her wallow in bliss for another minute. His second wind returned. Leaned over her rump. Slapped her withers. She awoke. Immediately apologized.

"I'm so sorry, Mitchikins," she purred. Chunks of sponge clung to her upper lip. Mitch bit back anger. That was the third one she'd gnawed open. His Korean seamstress was going to wear her look again. Pants were one thing. Pillowcases another.

"God, I feel like I've been fucked into another...dimension," Andrea whimpered.

"You're welcome," Mitch obliged. "But...break's over." With a practiced heave he pulled her upright. Then down onto his glistening pike. And, like the storied vole a'questing, he plashed about her fens. Andrea sucked air like a jet fighter entering space. Mitch increased the tempo of his lunges. Rocked her pocket. The antique clock on the wall ticked off the passing minutes. Still Mitch persisted. Postponed his own pleasure. Selflessly extended Andrea's. Muscles bunched in his forearms. A grid-like stitching appeared across his stomach. Good things were happening. A funfuck had evolved into a full-fledged workout.

Andrea went ragdoll. Bovine eyes gazed up at Mitch. Her tongue hung out. Golden hair loops sweatmatted her back. Saliva threads depended from a slack jaw. Mitch smiled. Waved at her. No mercy. No let up. The hammerjack assault on her boneyard continued.

And then…an eerie, warbling wolf howl. Mitch felt tingles race up his spine. Animal kingdom! And he was Steve Irwin, returned from the grave! In the old days, he'd have slapped her silent, of course. But he trusted the work done. The contractor was originally from the Sault.

So Mitch concentrated on his punchboarding. The blood-curdling banshee cries stayed inside. Bad enough being on a first name basis with most of the city's paramedics. It was the D.P. visits that annoyed him. Word had got around. They were dropping by to see who was getting nailed. Dispatch knew to ignore the complaints. The D.P.'s were just being nosy pricks. Still, no good always pissing off the neighbours. Ill-mannered, immature behaviour. Not Mitch's style.

Back to Andrea, who no longer ruled her domain. Something primitive had taken over. Mitch watched in awe as she contorted herself. Absorbed him. Half-upright, hands free, she pulled at her hair. Slapped her breasts. Beat her thighs. Mad minx on the march.

With a gymnast's lithe dexterity, she threw a free leg over Mitch's head. Spun around. Squatted above him, Thai fashion. Rippling contractions convulsed Richard's house. Mitch grimaced. It was like having his python swallowed by an anaconda. They were joined together, one crotch under God.

Shockwaves from concurrent seismic orgasms threw Mitch onto his back. Andrea rocked above him. Eyes glazed, tongue lolling from her head. To see her, Mitch was reminded of a zombie. On speed. No sooner had the thought occurred than he was swept up in a pachouli cyclone. A golden hurricane of hair fanned the air. Andrea flung her arms around her head. Rotors on a dying helicopter. Guttering candle flames threw demonic shadows over them. Mitch was quite enjoying it all.

Blood spattered Mitch's chest. Andrea had bitten through her bottom lip. No evidence of pain. Far from it. Mona Lisa smile. Her missiles were aimed straight at his face. Mitch launched himself at a cherry lifesaver. Nibbled away.

Andrea, meanwhile, seemed set to split herself. Some primal urge demanded every succulent inch of Mitch. Again and again she drew him deep into her molten valley. Once more, cosmic euphoria. She surfed into nirvana on a crest of hot, frothy spume. Dragged herself up onto the serene beach of release. Collapsed, exhausted.

Business concluded. Mitch semi-gently flung the still spastic Andrea from off his rod. She puddled on the mattress. Kitten cry of satisfaction. Ran her hand from hip to tip. Looked up at Mitch with undisguised worship.

"You're...like...Superman," she gushed.

"Jah. Octoberfest or not, I still bring the sausage," Mitch said offhand.

Andrea giggled politely. Didn't know what Octoberfest meant. Ran her middle finger into her mouth.

"Oh, I haven't forgot," Mitch assured her. "Foreplay's over. Catch your breath. Dig in." Mitch's com buzzed again. Andrea glanced at him. In the short time they'd been together she still knew he 'hated fucking interruptions'.

Mitch rolled off the bed. Watched in disbelief as his still rigid cock carelessly pushed the com off the table. Snapped his fingers. Motioned for Andrea to go find it. Wiped down again with her teddy after she bent down to look. He had a strange feeling. Something was up. Something else, that is.

"Found it!" Andrea yipped. Handed it to him. He squeezed a poont in thanks. Read the message. Exhaled. Tossed it into his work bag.

"Anything wrong, honey?" Andrea asked.

Mitch's eyebrows were knitted. She only ever saw the white scar blaze of a scar when he was troubled. Or tired. Or angry.

"Not sure," he said. "Meeting with the Commissioner. Tomorrow morning. First thing."

"Is that bad?"

"I haven't done anything lately," Mitch said. Pursed his lips in thought. "But it means a rain cheque on the rest of tonight."

"Ahhhh, Mitchy," Andrea pouted.

"Hey. I need a solid seven if I'm meeting shoulders in the AM." Mitch grabbed her jeans and top from the chair. Squashed them into her hooters.

"I have to go?" Andrea whined.

"Not until right now," Mitch confirmed. "I can't have your tits up my nose all night. And you're always flailing about. It's like sleeping beside someone on fire." He dug a thirty out of his wallet. Happy to be rid of it. Gayest bill ever. "This is enough to get you most of the way home. I'll get the rest to you...soon. Promise." Sincere. Mitch wasn't a loadie."

Andrea toed her panties under the bed. Mitch didn't notice. She scrambled into the jeans. Ran musky fingers through her hair. Under her nose. Closed her eyes in rapture.

"How do I look?" she said, a little glum.

"Wonderful," Mitch replied, examining his com. Thumbed her towards the door. "Out. I mean it. I gotta get some shuteye."

Winsome smile from Andrea. "See you this weekend?"

"Oh, you know it. For sure. For sure. Yeah," Mitch mumbled. Punched in a reply. "Bye bye."

"Ok. Thanks for...everything."

"No problem. Lock the door on your way out."

"Do you want me to…"

"Nope," Mitch cut her off. "Door close. Lasers engage. Elevator down. Taxi go."

Andrea giggled again. "Oh, Mitch. Well, see you around."

"Might be on the table," Mitch answered. Concentrating on getting his com alarm set right. His mind busy with scenarios. That incident at Billy's was old news by now. If the Commissioner had even heard about it. Raiding the kitchen that last party? Pretty sure they'd got away with that. Couldn't think of what else it could be. The terrorgations had been going great. Hadn't heard anything but good reviews.

Mitch fell into bed. Thought, fuck it. What happens, happens. Beat out Andrea's face print from his pillow. Smelled her perfume. Groaned. Too much effort to find another pillow case. Groaned again. Fucking candles. Not his idea. Rolled back out of bed. Three hearty gusts and done. Launched himself back into the sack. The big downer jobbie pulled up under his chin. Asleep in seconds.

THE DEAD DRUNK TWAT

---◄○►---

At the same time Mitch was riding Andrea into paradise, Detective Andy Herron was exiting his Tortoise. Slammed the lid shut. Enjoyed how the tinny sound irritated him. Brief pause by the door to smell the air. "Jesus, that's rank."

His partner also wrinkled his nose. Slammed his lid in the same fashion. Indifferent to the cheap construction. "Yeah. What is it? Ammonia? Sulphur?"

"Hamilton," Herron replied. Hunched down into his overcoat. "Wind's up."

The two men slithered over a crusty ridge of snow-ice. Headed towards the lake. A nearby yardlight threw weak illumination. Distant horn bleat. Cat yowl. A nasty, damp, ugly night. Both men wished they could be elsewhere. In bed. Where normal humans were.

Jameson's foot shot out following Herron down the slope. Caught himself before falling. Looked over his shoulder. Hoping to see what? Nothing. A unmemorable industrial park. He couldn't even remember the name. The Tortoise had found it through central GPS. Hard to imagine a crim out on such a shitty evening.

Herron coughed. "How's that song go? 'When the north winds come whistling'? That right?"

Jameson grunted. Non-commital. Knew the song. Wasn't sure about the lyrics. Knew it was a bitter fucking knife off the lake that night. Cleared clinging crap from his muddies. Just then noticed the line D.P. Flashlight beam highlighting surf.

"Whaddawegot?" Jameson machine-gunned the question.

The officer gestured right with his torch. They followed the brilliant arrow. Five-metres off, a mound. Semi-circled with glow balls. Water lapped close.

"Anus di Milo," the DP said. Smirking tone.

"Shit. Again?" Jameson spit in dismay. The D.P's had evidently settled on the nickname. Third time Jameson had heard it. Hoped they were wrong in this case.

Herron unholstered his own torch. Approached the spot. Gave a low whistle.

"Oh, yeah," he said. Held his nose. "Fucking disgusting." Kicked at the limbless lump. Face swollen up like his ex's ass. Exact same colour as the garlic cheese spread in his frig.

Jameson asked for and got the D.P's torch. Stepped carefully through the gluey muck. Joined Herron. "Fish do that?"

"Yeah," Herron nodded. "They snack. Probably healthier than the usual shit floating out there."

Herron gave the remains a quick once-over. Looking for signs of non-fish violence. Jameson surveilled the immediate area. Bleached sticks. Smooth, flat rocks. Dirty sand. Shiny plastic. The breeze off the lake picked up. Changed the stink. Less industrial, more raw sewage now. It burrowed under Jameson's coat collar like a wet rat. He turned away from it. Returned the maglight to the hopping Constable. Watched him secure it. Back to the two-step shuffle. Young face. Jameson caught a brief glimpse of it. Barely-shaving. Son of Aylmer sent to Sodom. Blow the dust off me, Jameson thought. Mid-fifties. Too old for mole work.

"Some cold tongue off Ontario tonight," Jameson said.

"That's the truth," the D.P. chattered back. "Hey, if you guys don't need me, mind if I wait in the car?"

Jameson shoed him away.

"Thanks," the cop said. "I been out here almost thirty minutes. I think my nuts are about froze off."

"Hold," Jameson ordered. "Mind if I have that torch back?"

"All yours," the D.P. said. Handed it off like a relay baton. Beat it back to the idling cruiser. "I need it back," he reminded Jameson over his shoulder. Scrambling up the hardpack ledge. "Department issue. I'll catch shit if I lose it."

Jameson walked a dozen metres along the shore. Both directions. Mostly to keep warm. Didn't expect to find anything. Suds and slop predominated. Dog footprints lead away from the corpse. He returned to stand near Herron.

"How long, you think?"

"Thirty minutes since the first call…plus a week feeding perch. She's looked better, I'm sure."

"No," Jameson corrected. "I mean how long 'til we're finished?"

"Soon. Can't see any obvious cause of expiry." Herron booted the torso again. The jacket refused to fall away. Clasps held firm. No bullet hole revealed. No axe gash exposed. Nothing the least bit interesting.

"Goddamn it, that's a mean wind," Jameson groused. "Let's fold this tent. Cleaners should be here any minute. Let them handle it. Job's not worth this kind of misery."

"My thinking exactly," Herron said, standing straight. One more half-hearted kick at the crypt fare. It failed to overturn. Worse, an unpleasant lack of resistance met the effort. Like trying to punt tofu. Herron cleaned the toe of his Broughdales in the sand. Ordinary lakeshore beach filth. Much to be preferred over cold Betty rub-off.

"Who found it again?" he asked.

"Don't know," came a voice from behind them. The first doughnut pro's partner joined them. Crunched his way across the frozen wrack. "Dispatch only told us location. A rough location."

"Seen anyone different in the area?" Jameson lit a cigarette. Didn't really want one. Just tired of being downwind of the Porta-Potty factory.

"No. But we'd only just started patrol when the call came in. Bad timing."

Jameson gave a knowing grunt. Report filing. Another joy of modern policing. How did that Little Village song go? "Do you want my job?" If people only knew. Brilliant strategy. De-nut police by making them do what most hated. Monitor make-work. Arresting anyone now meant a week of mindless uni input shit. The onus on police. Justify everything. Who could be bothered? So they let as much go as possible go. Which meant everything. Crims weren't long in figuring it out. So the public paid for the illusion of police protection. If the secret ever got out, they'd shut the whole joke down. Truck it to Michigan.

"Only reason she's not as God made her," Herron said. Pointed his beam at the bloat's midriff. Metal loops flashed dully. Queen street twat togs.

"What are the odds the current carried her to this spot. From…somewhere far away?" Jameson mused aloud. Herron was far more knowledgable about tides, lake business. Kept a boat somewhere, Jameson was sure he'd heard.

"You mean like from France?" Herron joked. "She's local. That's downtown hair."

"You can tell?" Jameson was intrigued.

"Yeah. My oldest wears it like that."

Jameson's eyes now adjusted. Overflow city light bounced down from the low-hanging clouds. Gauzed everything. Darkness made visible. Who said that? Shakespeare, must be. Jameson's thoughts were all over the place. Night shift. Confused the metabolism.

"You guys on lakefront often?" Jameson directed the question and the light beam left. Found the hydro tower nearby.

"Pretty often," the D.P. replied. "Transfers. Low men on the duty roster pole."

Jameson smiled to himself. The goliath had cop features. Box jaw, bunker brow, large beak. Even hunched into himself against the cold the kid was drunk squad huge. The partner was admin. bound. Clean-looking. Groomed. Alert eyes. Department spokes person. Spokesman, Jameson corrected himself in irritation. Had a backroom polish that leapt out.

Cop types like every other. Some enjoyed crushing skulls. Others wanted soft work, no stress. Pension suckholes. Christian sorts got hollowed. Too much drug and skid depravity. Irish disease took others. But big-and-ready brutal had options. No need to remain the blue monkey on a leash. Among his other services for CORE, Jameson scouted out talent. Made a mental note. Find out more about the cruiser team. The muscle stack and his sardonic partner. The organization liked a certain kind of man. And they might fit in.

The constable stamped his feet. Box stall impatience. Looked anxious to hand matters off. Get back to the warm.

"It stink like this all the time down here?" Jameson asked. Small talk. Probe the kid's personality.

"Stink like what?"

"Nothing," Jameson said. "No one else around when you arrived on the scene?"

"Nope. Sir."

"A dog," the constable corrected himself a split second later. "It was near the body when we arrived. Then it took off."

"A dog," the detective repeated. Remembered the footprints. "Good. Okay. Any description?"

"Pretty big," the officer replied. "Maybe a lab, shepherd. Something like that. Dark fur with, you know, that head that…"

Jameson held up his hand. "We'll interrogate it later. Thanks anyway."

"You gotta be done," Jameson said, looking out over the lake. Pencil-thin whitecaps rolled into shore. Black water. Prison wall overhead. Tomorrow's forecast. Same as yesterday's. Chance of flurries. Chance of freezing rain. Chance of going fucking mad because of the shit weather. Jameson hated March. Cold, sunless, drizzly, unpleasant crap day after day. You want to end immigration? Show wannbe imports a vid of T-burg in spring. Or winter. Line-ups instantly torpedoed.

Stomach growl. D.P. snickered. Too early for breakfast. But Jameson felt like getting around a proper menu order. Beat the herd. Hit the Pompeii on Bay soon as it opened. Demand the 'whitey' special—three eggs, poached.

Bacon, double order. Hash browns, double order. Whole wheat toast, real butter. Slices, four. Glass of Florida, double pulp. Two cups of Valdez-the-peon's best. Squeegee the tubes. A mild Cohista over the morning sports. Hurry home for a hot shower. Dreamland to follow.

Dream was right. Meeting elsewhere that morning. He'd be lucky to get four hours before his next shift. Negative thoughts. Long the road, etc. And goddamn hard slogging, a lot of times. But he had reason to remain where he was. Viva la counter-revolucion!

"Should have brought my gloves." Herron talking to himself. "Didn't feel this cold out…riding in the scramjet." Old joke. The Tortoise boasted the new eco heater. Meaning no heat. Still, Jameson was ready to crawl back into the deathtrap to escape the wind. Coop until sunrise.

Recalled his first cruiser. Secretly chopped. Lightning fast. Back when the 401 was more like the Indy brickyards. Their new staff car had a top speed of 70kph. Pursuit restricted to jaywalking joggers. Careless elderly tooling down sidewalks on their electric go-carts. Skaters. Chase scenes were archive holovid only.

Herron spoke again. "I hereby declare this death to be a complete fucking mystery."

"Beautiful," Jameson snorted. Someone else's business now. He prepared to leave. Took no special skill to find a gunshot wound. A knife slash. If it wasn't obvious, call forensics. Let the Cyclones suck up any evidence. Assuming they hadn't trampled it into the sand. They'd shovel the body into a rubber sack. Truck it back to the morgue. Slapdash unseaming, chops to nave. Night school coroner. Practicing for final exams. Poke, prod, digiphotos. Misfile everything. Go home. Public service.

Cases like Ms Mary Nated got forgotten, quicktime. No surprise. Dead twats were falling from the trees these days. The latest five-year crim prevention plan. Still bearing fruit. Pols and GovPress agreed. Crime levels plummeting. No one even bothered to laugh at them anymore.

Herron pulled out his holocam. Technically, trophy-keeping verboten. Herron ignored the rule. Most guys did. Everyone had their favourite pics. Herron had built up a serious collection. Turned out, death was an aphrodesiac. Some women got totally aroused. At least, the kind of women Herron talked into going home with him. Drunk women.

Over time, he grew adept at choosing the photos with foreplay power. Roadkill did nothing. Death by terrorism? Zero popularity. Lover's tiff? Gun or knife work? Body on the floor? Blood pool? Hit a bedpost on the way down? Contusions? Goodbye hospital corners. Firecracker sex. Herron's secret. One he intended to take it with him to the grave.

"Ah, shit!" Herron apologized. "False dawn." Bent down. "There is something. Analyzer picked it up." He held the cam up for Jameson, who squished his way back.

"Take a look at this. Behind her left ear there."

Jameson peered at the frozen image. Sighed. "Damn. I wondered as much when we got the call. Then it looked like we'd got lucky. Too bad."

He handed the holocam back to Herron. "Well, that puts the turd in Saturday." D.P. whickered like a horse.

Creaky-cold hands fumbled his com out. Jameson casually pointed it at Herron's cam. Signal sex. Re-routed the image. Punched in the code. Paused. Return signal. Special icon. Jameson snapped his com shut. Looked over at Herron.

"Pack it in. We're through. They've scrambled CORE. ETA in ten."

Herron was already moving towards the car at the mention of CORE. Jameson informed the D.P. Change of plans. No argument. They slopped over to the idling cruiser. The driver's side window shimmered down. Interior light. The constable slid in. His partner sat cramped against the passenger door. Grunted welcome.

"We're done here for now," Jameson said. "Thanks for your help. Specialists due." The two D.P.'s shared a questioning look. "You look ready for some caffeine." Chuckles of agreement. Jameson dug into his coat pocket. Found the gift chip he'd been saving. Passed it over. It vanished into the driver's shirt pocket.

"Appreciate it. Enough of being outside in this shit."

"Hmmf," Jameson responded. He gave the men a quick wave. Lurched into the wind. Three steps towards the tortoise, stopped, spun. The window disappeared again. Jameson fought with his flaps. Handed over the borrowed torch.

"Oh, shit. I knew I'd forget it," a voice in the dark rumbled. "Thanks."

Jameson grinned. Dipped his head. Wanted to fix the man's face in his memory. The giant's knees rested on the vehicle's inflatable face mitt. He wondered if the doughnut pro was being punished. Why else sardine him? Shit-disturber signpost. Jameson intended to follow up. His antenna quivered. The Toronto DP's oversight would be CORE's new advantage.

"Nice to meet you boys," Jameson said. Pushed off.

Back inside the car. Spread his butt cheeks. Absorb the seat's candle warmth. Herron behind the wheel. Breathing through chapped lips.

"What the desk say?"

Jameson waited a three-beat. Replied, "Send the sirens home. Come back in. If it's Ovarian work, CORE has the nod." Which is what they would have said anyway. Roughly. Had they known. CORE was rolling. Leave it be and go.

"Suits me fine," Herron nodded. He checked the digi. "Almost quitting time. You thinking of breakfast?"

"Always thinking of breakfast." Jameson said. Reached for an illegal. Sparked it. "Not today, sorry to say."

Herron spun the wheel, goosed the worthless. Front tires chewed into wheelwell buildup. Hard as concrete come March.

Found the narrow strip of pavement. Winked his lamps at the cruiser. Let the road lead them out. Solitary crate. Arrows of carbonized snow glued to it. Row of metal stanchions. Headless skeletons. Beaten bushes slid by. Sprouts of industrial weeds. Toughest plants on the planet. Survive the most toxic environments imaginable.

Jameson thought of his front yard. Pesticide-free Ontario. The years he'd spent in hand-to-hand combat with every variety of intruder. Screw the mission to Mars. Seed space with twitchgrass, dandelions, thistles. Wouldn't even have to GM them. No alien species could withstand it. The known universe would be mankind's for the taking inside a decade. Planet after planet covered in shitty-looking lawn. Good joke on God. And the killjoy-eco crowd.

Jameson slapped feeling into his hands. Whiskey. Knew where they could serve out the night. Rest their elbows. Serious consideration.

"Wonder what she did?" Herron mused. Street light standards ahead. Half dark to save money. Trees glistening. North sides sporting ice whiskers.

"Something those cunts didn't like, evidently," Jameson said. Blew a jet of smoke out a crack in the window.

"I almost wish…" Herron let the thought tail off.

"What?"

Herron shrugged. "I don't know. Sometimes it would be nice to know if the rumours were true."

"About the Ovarians?"

"No," Herron shook his head, "CORE. Do they really…you know…do the shit we hear?"

Jameson peered out the windshield. Gate posts approaching. Car beams slicing over brownfield, derelict buildings. "Don't know," he lied. "Doubt it. Be great if they did, though." Lowered his window. Jettisoned his smoke. Watched the wind catch it. Mayfly comet.

"You ever think of transferring?" Herron asked. "If you could?" Eyes aslant towards Jameson. "I mean, someone with your record…"

Jameson chuckled quietly. "Nah, they're too red ass for me." Jameson liked the Americanism. In fact, he rather admired American patriotism. As did many at CORE. Americans overdid it, of course. Like most things. But better that than the commie-faggo-bleeding-heart-nicey-nice nationalism peddled in Canada. "I'm just a glorified doughnut pro at heart. A pension hound. Like all the rest. That kind of excitement's for the younger set."

"Good, good," Herron said. "I keep hearing stories. Cops, young cops, retiring. Then word is they've turned up with that crew. We need to keep a few good ones around. Otherwise…"

Jameson laughed. "No worries, my friend. Much as I'd love to kick hell and change Canada back for the better. Too late for that." Sighed. Deliberate pessimism. Actually thought there was still a chance to save the country. Wouldn't be working two jobs if he didn't.

The Tortoise stalled out. Herron cursed it. Pushed the starter. Life again. Barely. No exhaust. No power. Nobody liked them. A sunroof on wheels. Unsafe when moving.

A monster snowflake smacked onto the windshield. Remained glued there. Jameson knew the roads would be greasy. Herron didn't notice it. Busy with dispatch. Eye flash as the the car lamps swept around the curve. Jenkins saw the outline bolt. Dog. No owner, maybe. Same witness, he wondered? Rugged night to be exploring. Then again, found a corpse. Something to tell the other mutts at breakfast. Come the future, they'd hunt it down. Extract its memories. Not a job he'd enjoy.

MITCH MEETS MAEDA

—◄ ◇ ►—

"**M**itch, think of it as a…mentoring task." Commissioner Ciccarrelli. Desert dry sense of humour. Also possessed 'The Look'. Immediate 'nad squeezer. So Mitch didn't roll his eyes. Remained at ease. Tried to appear relaxed. He was on good terms with the Commissioner. Liked him. Was liked in return. But being alone in a room with him…

Fortunately, he wasn't in trouble. His early morning doubts quickly erased. In fact, he'd just been handed his first case. Totally unexpected. Not even hoped for. Very positive moment. A reward for teeing up on Melling. (Man had already offered to work off his debt to society through CORE. Mitch would meet him in the halls every now and again over the next year. "I'm disabling such and such," he'd explain with enthusuasm. Mitch always listened politely. Hard to cut off someone who'd seen the light. Still, guy was a tiresome fatball. That wouldn't change.)

So Mitch was given his first murder investigation. He was pumped. It sounded like fun. Get to look at dead bodies whenever he wanted. Go Sherlock on people. Stomp them for info. Very holovid. Idly debated getting new clothes. Trench coat. Fedora. Look the part.

Getting saddled with some FNG was something else, though. Watered down the whiskey. Mitch knew he was luckier than most. Still, it had to be acknowledged. Not many got their cake and eat it too.

"As you know," Cicarrelli continued, "CORE is a…different kind of organization."

Mitch nodded. All-time understatement.

"Though we operate mostly under the radar," the Commissioner said, "we can and do…exploit the resources others may offer."

Why the boilerplate, Mitch wondered? He already knew all this. Everyone did. First day training. CORE was independently funded. It operated on two levels, publicly and privately. It did contract work. For some customers, it was the go-to justice system of last resort. For others, especially among national security agencies, it was a multi-purpose weapon. The Sage explained it. Western society was like the human body. It spawned it's own cancer cells. Activists, advocates, professional whiners, looters, politicians, bureaucrats, artists. War was one means of eradicating the disease. CORE designed to be the other—killer white corpuscles. Virus slayers. Scourge of bacteria. Only CORE accepted PayPal.

"There are perverse truths about Canada," the Captain intoned.

"It's enemies occupy the highest positions in government." Mitch provided the rote reply.

"And this is possible because…?"

"They are well-financed."

"They obtain…"

"…a steady source of income."

"That being?"

"Taxation," Mitch said.

"And what do they serve, knowingly or not?"

"The Cause."

"Which is?

"Pure fucking evil!"

"Exactly!" The Commissioner's mouth tightened with quiet approval. "From impotence to action to victory. Now we are developing our own resources. This is a long war. We're fighting on several fronts. So it's been decided to expand the range of our contacts."

Mitch bobbed the head. Hoped the meeting was close to over. He'd heard variations of this speech before. Wasted on him. Mitch bought in early, eagerly. It all made obvious sense. No selling necessary. Look around. But Ciccarrelli was old school. Sharp, shrewd, cautious. Like his grandfather, oldies said. Also a cop. His father too. Generations had worked construction in Hogtown. A picture of the CN Tower displayed prominently on his wall.

Mitch had taken in the other photos on previous visits. One in particular—a good-looking kid. Full hockey gear pose. Toothy smile. Fake crowd background. Team sweater hitched up a famous way. Mitch recognized the crest. Mississauga. Knew they put out quality Triple-A teams. NHL feeder system. The grandson never made it to midget. Car accident on the way to practice. Wise old delivery van jockey new to winter. Ice. Pavement. Half-tried to beat a yellow. Changed his mind. Hit the binders late. Shot through the intersection. T-barred the Honda. Two for the morgue.

No penalty to the van operator. Judge shrugged. Couldn't be helped. No snow in whatever barren fucking wasteland he once called home. Not the queue-jumper's fault. Another layer of hard added to the old man that day. Recruited to CORE not long after.

So the man's road hadn't run straight and easy. Hard to imagine the place without him. You did what he asked. Kept a civil tongue in your head. Made sure those black-holed cannon barrels didn't swivel your direction.

Mitch listened to the spiel. Nodded occasionally. Couldn't help but take in the sight. The Commissioner's bristle shock of hair, senator white. Eagle hook nose. Jaw like a carpenter's rule. Back of hands scarred, misshaped. Twisted from slugging bags, pounding bars. Early years spent working cement. Nights spent working over the next crew. For money. Mitch had at least 30 years on the man. And 30 lb's of muscle. Hadn't turtled in a hundred fights. On ice or off. And he still wouldn't bet on his chances with the guy in a scrap. Weird. Some of the old bastards. Made out of granite. If you ever hit them and they found out about it…Marciano time.

"Our goals evolve, Mitchell, to meet new conditions." Uninflected delivery. Like reading a shopping list. Rote. "Some of what we do is known to other agencies. Most is not, though it is suspected. Still, The Board believes the time has come to move beyond cooperation. Coordination is inevitable in these uncertain times. And in everyone's best interests." Mitch winced at the news.

The Commissioner was quick with an answer. "We are a private concern, and will remain so," he assured Mitch. "There is no question we will continue to operate as we have been doing. However, to fully exploit our potential, we need greater access to…information. So we have agreed to pool some…data streams with the Force. Among other agencies. In order to better facilitate… corporate communication…they have asked that we pair one of their younger members with one of ours. For a time. You were chosen."

"But I'm not even with CORE. At least officially," Mitch argued, forgetting himself.

"Better still," the Commissioner almost smiled. "You shepherd the agent around while you work. You answer what questions he may have…within reason. You will explain the more…unique aspects of your job. He is to be your…shadow."

"He's not…?"

"He is roughly your equivalent in rank. Not that you actually have any. As you've noted." Jab. "He understands your position as…an outside contractor."

"He might be here…the whole week?"

"A few months. No more, I shouldn't think."

"Months?" Mitch slumped. The Commissioner's eyes narrowed. Mitch straightened up immediately.

"It's just…I didn't realize it would be…" Mitch shuffled his feet. Gathered his thoughts. Looked at the window drapery. Distracting pattern. Like a giant bacteria war. The Commissioner never moved.

"Happy to help," Mitch said finally.

"Glad to hear it," the Captain replied. Granted Mitch the fatherly smile of approval. Looked Mitch in the eyes.

"You may also wish to learn exactly what his talents are. CORE would be interested in…his real mission. Should you learn of it during his visit."

Mitch felt the full intensity of the Commissioner's flat stare.

"I see," he said, though not entirely. "Meaning…this guy is a…?"

The Commissioner looked down at his fingers. Laced them. Back up at Mitch. Smiled. "Who knows? Upstairs has agreed to go along. If they're not worried…?"

"Okay." Mitch flashed the famous grin. "I"m on board. When do I meet him?"

"Right now," the Commissioner said. Let his hand hover over a glowing light. P.A.'s voice. Command given. Ciccarrelli leaned back in his chair. Regarded Mitch with a near-amiable look. Mitch, the Beefeater at ease. Arms behind his back. Resumed staring at the curtains. Guy was taking his sweet fucking time getting into the room. The silence seemed to grow louder by the second. Mitch could hear his heart beating. No discomfort visible from the Commissioner. Calm as a glass of water. Easter Island statues fidgeted more.

A spot just above Mitch's left testicle suddenly wanted scratching. Right then, right in the brambles. No sooner did that urge hit than the top of his ear sought attention Then the crown on his head. His left eyebrow. A spot right between his shoulder blades. Unbelievable. Places he didn't know existed wanted clawing. And the idiot PA had cranked the heat on for some reason. He could feel his pores open.

Went to the old tactic. Turned his thoughts to baseball. The Jays. Spring training. Batting practice. Shagging flies. Loping around pretending to exercise.

No change. Warning itch on his hip. Another on his neck. He thought of his grandmother. Showering. Having sex. Taking a dump. Zip relief. He'd have strangled kittens for a wire brush and a minute alone with his crotch.

The office door finally whisked wide. Mitch saw the Commissioner rise. He spun away. Buried his hand. Lighting quick harrow. Finished turning as his new workmate approached. The Commissioner waved towards Mitch. He held out his hand. Car salesman smile. Grip and pump.

"Mitch, I'd like you to meet Yasumitsu Maeda." The Commissioner beamed welcome. Mitch had never seen him so…friendly. "I hope I pronounced that correctly."

A nod from the diminutive guest. "Perfectly," he replied. Almost imperceptible bow.

"He's with the Force. Counter-terrorism. At least, that's what I was told."

Another nod. Mitch gazed down at the man. Hoped he hadn't crushed any bones. Didn't mean to go Neanderthal. Just…guy wasn't so big. An overstatement. He looked to be half Mitch's size. Might touch 70kgs…wearing scuba gear, boulders on his back. Mitch dwarfed him in every respect. It had been years since he'd worked with anyone he could pick up and throw across the room with one hand. Hard to imagine him in the Force. Musical Ride groom maybe. Door polisher. Accountant. The first question popped out without his thinking. Mitch's bewilderment genuine.

"How old are you?"

"Twenty-four," Yasumitsu looked up. Clear expression.

Mitch had only a few years on him. Even as a child, he was sure he'd never looked that young. His spirits sank. The guys were going to ride him about this. He knew it.

"Hey Mag's! Who's your little butt-buddy?

"Hey Mitch! Santa called. He wants his elf back. Christmas is coming."

From positive to negative in seconds. Life. Waits around the corner with a lead pipe for the first sign of good news.

"Wow." All Mitch could think to say.

"Yasumitsu," the Captain jumped in, "as I explained earlier, you'll be working with Mitch while you're here. He'll give you a better idea of what CORE is all about. Mitch is…something of a special member here. He's an integral part of our team, of course but…it's kind of a gray area. I'm sure you can understand that."

"No need to explain, sir," Maeda said. "I'm here to learn. If needed, I'm to assist in whatever fashion my training allows."

Mitch couldn't imagine what that situation might be. Comic relief maybe.

"Fine," the Commissioner nodded. "If you have any problems, my door is always open." Kept a straight face saying it. Mitch marveled. Caught the sidelong glance. Time to leave. Did an about face. Smoothly glided to the door. Outside and clear of the frosted glass, he stopped to exhale. Realized his itching grief was gone. Stress. Fucking nasty. That's why he liked working alone. Corporate shit made him uncomfortable.

His thoughts jumped all over now. Guide for the new guy. That meant showing him around. A pain. Plus, he should get at his new case. At least the trulls were dead. It wasn't like they were waiting to be interviewed. He'd seen a blurb in the Sun. A kind of everyday thing, finding one.. And a big game on the weekend. A lot coming in at once. Beers at Billy's. Talk it over with a few of the boys. Seemed a good plan.

Mitch nearly ran over his new partner when he backtracked suddenly. Thinking about Billy's Calgary steak sandwiches brought on a shit. Decided to deal with it there. No better time. Reversed course and came within inches of tank treading the wee lad.

"Woah, sorry," Mitch apologized. "Jesus, I forgot…"

"Yasumitsu," the man offered.

"No, no. I mean…but, yeah. That's good, too. Sorry. Once more. Your first name?"

"People in high school called me 'Yaz'."

"Wa-a-a-ay better," Mitch conceded. "Yaz it is. Okay, uh, I guess we could…yeah, show you my office. How'd that be?"

"Whatever you say," Yaz said. "I'm going to try not to…inconvenience you. I understand this partnering thing is probably…difficult."

"Orders is orders," Mitch said. Lead the way down an empty corridor. Still mulling over the idea. Working with the Force. Like playing with a winger from another team. In a weaker league. The Force was famous, of course. Although it's press wasn't anywhere near what it had been. Regular incompetence had seen to that. The Commissioner had said as much. It was coasting on rep. Long-past glories.

Among the intel community the Force was dismissed. Running joke about them and CSIS. Both had been penetrated more often than a CBC rentboy. Moscow couldn't afford to pay the number of willing leakers in the federal bureaucracy, including the Force. The Pentagon saved time. They just monitored all the electronic traffic. The Brits, the Yanks, the French, Germans, Israelis…anyone who cared had a man inside. Canadian state secrets were as numerous as penguins in the Arctic. For this reason alone, CORE kept its distance. Contagion the ever-present concern.

Yet the Commissioner was aware the Force had men who couldn't be turned. Recruiting mistakes were made. Proud patriots accidentally accepted. Once discovered, they'd be promptly shunted aside. A hidden resource CORE exploited. Poaching gems. To build the crown that was CORE. So there was some kind of double game underway.

Passed an empty meeting room. Gave Mitch an idea. He disabled the sensor. Led Yaz inside. Instant illumination. Mitch turned. Eyeballed the man. Mitch's first face-to-face Asian. Excepting his Korean needle wizard. But she never said more than, "Ten dollah. You pay now." Impatient bitch.

The guy standing before him gave away half a foot in height. Blockier than Mitch had originally thought, however. Something about him Mitch couldn't quite figure. Hair was normal. Irridescent. Preppy flavour. The way he carried himself. Flat-footed, feet apart. As though ready for trouble.

Mitch tried his let's-drop-the-gloves-and-go face. No reaction. The beardless little prick wasn't intimidated in the least. Mitch couldn't remember if Asians shaved or not. He'd played against a Six Nations guy in Junior. Cheeks smooth as a baby's butt. An ugly baby. Sharp elbows, wicked point shot.

"Got any vices?"

"What do you mean," Yaz responded. Aluminum cool.

"I smoke…a lot. I like it. If that's a problem, better let me know now." Smoking was only just enjoying a national comeback. Still a near-crime in the Big Stink. Which is why it was popular at CORE.

"I smoke, too," the man said. Guileless eyes held Mitch's.

"Really?" Mitch said. "What brand?"

"Tolson's."

Mitch rolled his eyes. Milligan family sigh. His luck. "Better than menthols, I guess. They'll do in an emergency." He gave Yaz another rapid once-over.

"Anything else I should know about? Methhead? Gambler? You spend Thursday nights at the Y playing 'Drop the Soap'? Moonie? That kind a shit."

No immediate reply. A hearty laugh from someone nearby penetrated the walls.

"I appreciate that this…my being here…is probably an unwelcome development. It's not my choice. But it's clear this situation aggravates you. I suggest we speak to your superior. I'm willing to work with someone else."

"Whoa, whoa. Slow down, tiger," Mitch said, slightly concerned. Hands up to dampen the governors. Prevent an exit. The Commissioner would not be pleased.

"Nobody said anything about bailing. I'm just trying to…you know…get a ballpark idea on what's what. That's all. I mean…different organizations and shit. You might be observing some unusual things here. I just needed to know where you were coming from. What might be a shock for you to see." Mitch gestured again, calming. "Didn't mean to say anything…un-PC, okay?"

"I'm not politically correct," Yaz responded sharply. First sign of emotion Mitch had seen. "I despise totalitarian thinking. It's intellectually shallow… and lazy."

Mitch did a rapid reappraisal. Guy talked smart. Step careful.

"That's great! I mean…yeah, great! That shit does not fly around here. No lie." He calculated for a second. "Okay, look…uh…let's go to my cave. I show you the playbook. Sound good?"

Yaz nodded. Face still unreadable. Mitch did recognize the practiced office half-smile. Scout motion for Yaz to follow him. Into the corridor. Mitch took a hard right into the first washroom they saw. Time out. Back in five, moving fast.

"Better haul ass," he advised Yaz. "That thing had legs. Two flushes might not have killed it."

First door to the left. Company policy. Stairs unless an emergency. No exceptions. They'd no sooner hit the fourth floor landing than a voice cried out. Bouncing off the walls urgent.

"Pseudo-agent Milligan! Hold up!" A man rounded the stairs from above. Stopped, hand on the railing. Yaz gazed up in alarm. Rectangular head. Silvery slash of hair. Sine wave widows peak. Black eyes blazing. "Cheeks warped inward, as though the man was malnourished.

T. "Mort" Dalrymple. Mort short for mortuary, Mitch explained later. CORE's chief medical officer. And sometime coroner. Laser intellect. He looked displeased. Buttoned his labcoat. Glared down at Mitch and Yaz.

"Hey, Doc," Mitch smiled. "What can I do you for?"

"Were you involved?" The accusation hurled like a javelin. The doctor's index finger stabbed toward Mitch as he descended the steps at a measured pace. Yaz sensed artifice. Behind the indignation, amusement.

Mitch took a step back. Released the door handle. The doctor stepped level. Same height as Mitch. He bored in, unsmiling.

Mitch's jaw muscles worked. Controlling a laugh, Yaz thought. Most curious. Finally replied, "In what?"

"You know damn well what," the doctor snapped. "I had a recruit class coming through the lab just then. Two of them threw up after."

Mitch. Mister Innocent. "News to me, doc. Honest. What happened?"

The doctor's eyes narrowed. He snorted. Suddenly noticed Yaz. Looked back at Mitch "Who's this?"

"New man," Mitch replied. "From the Force."

Those famous eagle eyebrows met at his nose. "Some clown…" the doctor gritted over Mitch's shoulder, "…or clowns…decided to turn my cadaver into Cape Canaveral. They inserted various…fireworks…illegal fireworks…into the body's…nether orifice."

Mitch bit his lip.

Yaz had only a vague idea of what was going on.

"The…devices left a crater where his ass used to be. You created a munitions dump in that poor bastard's butt."

Mitch could feel tears coming.

"I've still got bottle rocket spears sticking out of my ceiling."

Mitch let his eyes wander up the cool green wall. Concentrated on the two-fer he'd just dropped in the can. How much lighter he felt now.

"If that road flare was CORE issue, somebody better have signed for it. They're not cheap. Where you got the cherry bombs, sparklers and that Roman Candle…I don't wish to know. Not in Toronto. Perhaps our friend from Buffalo?"

A high whine escaped from between Mitch's pressed-white lips.

"Mistreating the dead, even if they were only homeless, is an inefficient use of resources."

Mitch refused to break. The doctor turned. Spoke to Yaz.

"Let's just say…had there been anything inflammatory in my lab at the time…well, you wouldn't have lugnut here for a partner now. I'm be using his carcass as my new training display."

The man half--spun on his heel as though to leave. Yaz suddenly realized why he looked familiar. If a crane could graduate from medical school, he'd look like the doctor did.

Mitch received a firm finger in the sternum. "How'd you do it? Tell me. Upstairs will never here of it."

Mitch spread his hands. Dared not speak or he'd lose it.

"Well, he blowed up real good. You should be proud."

Mitch ready to piss himself hearing the classic line. Yaz still looked mildly perplexed.

The doctor peered at Mitch from under heavy lids. "Pass the word, Loki. Happens again? I'll put whoever's responsible on my table. When I'm finished, they'll be hitting high notes at karaoke from then on. Clear?"

"Crystal, sir," Mitch replied through his teeth. Couldn't resist adding, "Some people. Never grow up."

Dalrymple squinched an eye. Sideways glance at both Mitch and Yaz. After an emphatic "Hmph!" he blew through the door into the Science Wing.

Mitch waved Yaz down the steps. Didn't speak until they were a full floor away. Far enough from the moment he could collapse. Not necessary.

"Pretty funny," he chortled. Pulled on the door. "The Gerbers got an eyeful. But we forgot about there being gas or shit in the air. He's right. The whole place could a gone up. Last time for that gag, I guess. Too bad."

Seconds later, seated in Mitch's office. Cotton batting bumped against the window. Depressing. He punched in heavy tint. Flurries forecast for the rest of the week. Wrist-slitter info. Fucking weatherman fuckers.

The smoke-eater appeared. Sleek, pencil-thin. It rose soundlessly from the far end of the uni. Mitch gestured at Yaz's shirt pocket. "Smoke'em if you got'em."

Grateful nod from Yaz. Mitch sparked one immediately after. Blew a stream that arced back to his desk. Just what he needed. Felt his shoulders relax.

Cheering chimes. Mitch sat up straight. Fingered the holomail icon. Read it. His face darkened. Looked at Yaz.

"Well, you picked the right day to get traded. We've got action in the Tank. I'll fill you in on the way. Let's go."

They clipped and saved the rest of their illegals. Popped them into their packages. Quick-trot departed.

RAMADAN MAN

---⊰◇⊱---

Mitch dropped Yaz off in a seat nearest the debrief room door. Twenty minutes later, the Tank boasted two occupants. Comic wave for Yaz. The new pumpkin-orange shell suit made him feel mountain large. He twisted his torso. No constrictions. Lots of give in the material. In-house design. Instantly popular with CORE terrorgators. Lightweight, flexible, tough. Blade and blood proof, according to the book. Tankwork perfect.

"Dragger" Vasco had prepped him. Normal account. Local Islame-o-loon wanted to destroy Western civilization. Convinced Toronto represented the apex of Canadian society. Irony thick as peanut butter. Had no idea the best part of the city had long since pulled stakes. Drove off in disgust. Fags, hepniks, looters and imports all that remained. Consensus in the rest of the country. Blowing the place up? Best thing for everybody.

Man and group bankrolled by some branch of AQ. Bomb materials purchased all over Brampton. Receipt trail a Down's baby could follow. Network rolled up the day before Armageddon. Story leaked to the web. Dinosaur press couldn't bury it. Everyone knew. Everyone laughed.

Mugged by media weepers in the past, Metro DP sidestepped them. Released their chief suspect. The rest to follow. Cited 'lack of evidence'. The secret of every con. Find out what the mark wants. Pretend to give it to him. City council elated. Unlimited immigration advocates ecstatic. A relieved GovPress dropped all mention of the arrests, aborted attack. Big win for Team multi-culti. Or so they assumed.

A CORE recovery team found "Afghan Stan" later that day. Chained to a cement pillar. Garden District hotel parking garage. Popular drop zone of late. Conveniently close to a CORE dispatch centre.

They ferried bomber boy to CORE HQ. Bad news for him. Great news for Mitch. Totally unexpected. Nothing on the day chart said he was up for something high-level like this.

"Goldsworthy has the flu," Dragger explained. "Political's somewhere in…upper New York state. Giving a lecture to the O'Brien Group."

"Oh, yeah?" Mitch couldn't see himself ever being invited to give a speech anywhere.

"Stapleton took a slapshot off his ankle last night."

"Again?" Mitch sighed. "Shit. So much for the power play."

"Yeah. He's on crutches for at least a week. As for Saunders…we can't get him on his com."

"Gash attack," Mitch smirked.

"Probably," Dragger concurred. "Ivan's not happy about it. He was told to stay hot. We've got shelved agents."

"What about Feral?"

"Fucked off to Cuba with Sharpie. The slick prick."

"Oh, yeah, right," Mitch nodded. Image of palm trees sprang to mind. Bathwater warm ocean. Naked nymphs splashing in the surf. Accidental moan. Feral Cyril and Sharp would be having the time of their lives. Cheap Montecristos. Cheap rum. Cheap Cuban quim. The Canadian trifecta.

"Vanderspank? Cranston?"

"Healthy scratches," Dragger said. He burrowed a finger into at an acne gulley on his lower jaw. "Coach thinks your game is ready. This is major league stuff today."

"No argument here," Mitch said. "I'm making shit headway on my case. Might as well be doing something useful."

Dragger pursed his lips. Checked his holopad for updates. "Double pay for this one, by the way. Ciccarrelli's word."

"Beauty," Mitch joked. Unconsciously straightened his spine at mention of the Commissioner.

"How's the Gringolet?" Dragger asked. He loved Mitch's car. Thought it was the sexiest cushion ever.

"Runs like a top," Mitch gloated. "Loves the cold."

Dragger winced. "It's not right."

"Who's working 'tronics?" Mitch asked. Did a slow yoga shoulder roll.

"Shef and…" Dragger scrolled down the pad, "…Forbes."

"Iron Lungs?" Mitch frowned. "He's out already?"

Dragger nodded. "Doctors say he's okay. Sort of. Should cut back to two packs a day, though. Docs told him to keep a loaf of rye bread handy. His lungs looked ready to eat."

"Hmmm," Mitch said. "The Mohawk boys won't be happy to hear that. Forbsie keeps that reserve going all by himself."

He zipped up. Beat his chest. Breathed deeply. Held it. Exhaled through his nose. Glanced at the monitors.

"Raptors crowd out there," he said. Pointed at the deserted lounge. "Shellack's birthday party upstairs."

"Oh, yeah. Shit," Mitch cursed to himself. "Forgot that was on. Oh well… maybe if I get done early…" He nodded to Dragger. "Time to drop the puck."

Dragger gave him a thumbs up. Looked at the nearby Trog. The hatch seal hissed open. Mitch rolled into the Tank. Looked good, felt great.

What met him surprised him. The holoshots Dragger had pulled up were deceptive. Even from a distance, the 'spect clamped into The Chair looked really young. Too young to be a terrorist. The file said twenty-six. Mitch would have pegged him at sixteen, tops. Smooth forehead. No pits, zits or infant tits. The scraggly beard added a few years. Enough so he could probably buy booze without I.D. Supposing he drank. Shaved, people would guess he was just some sandbagger on a homestay.

Mitch grabbed the remote from the wall. Dimmed the lights. Studied the figure. All terrorgations were livecapture. Some were for sale. Others, no. The counter-intel cases were interesting, but not financially lucrative. Some of the 'spects were thick as bricks. Others mad. Broken, deranged, delirious. Useless. A few were snaky smart. The one sitting quietly in his chair didn't fit any types Mitch had studied that day. No fidgeting. No sweating. He didn't crane his neck around in wonder. Not the first time he'd seen walls before. Though not lead-imbedded ones, probably. Mirrored. Nearly imgregnable.

And Dragger claimed he hadn't once hollered for Allah. No infidel this. No Mother-of-all-Hellfire that. Small mercies. Mitch was grateful.

Mitch drew closer. Still pondering tactics. Tarmac black eyes followed him. No emotion, no concern. Wary interest only. Mitch took a deep breath. Inspiration arrived.

"Hey, Mistah Ramadan! Tally me bananas," Mitch sang. "Daylight come and me want fuck goat." Became an instant CORE tagline. Someone was sure to utter it whenever a market exploded in the M.E. Fit the moment perfectly.

Mitch reggae shuffled up to the chair. "Abu Imam? And how are you being today? Better is it we be talking now, yes?" Mitch stopped. Wrong accent. He was doing that guy in front of Union station. The Dogwagon CEO from Bangadrum. Tried to think of a famous Arab. Drew a blank. Aborted the gag.

"It says here," Mitch waved Dragger's borrowed holopad, "you're twenty-eight years old. Sorry, twenty-six years old." Mitch peered down at the young man. "Bullshit! What grade are you in?"

Seconds passed. Zero lip action. The man refused to meet Mitch's gaze.

"Talkative prick, aren't you, Ashur?" Mitch said. Slight eyelid twitch. Old trick. Introduce something true. Watch for a reaction.

"That's right," Mitch nodded. "We know your real name, Boo-boo. But we can call you something else, if you like? How about 'Ashur bin Adick'? Or...'Ashur bin Afukup'? Ashur Needajob'. Which one works best for you?"

Rock still. Man never budged. Fizzy black hair tied back in a bun. CORE regs. Tan complexion. Dark, magic marker eyebrows. Slender beak, knife edge. Pink rind hiding teeth. Normal-looking. Way less ugly than the last Islame-o they'd worked on. Mitch grinned to himself at the memory. Asteroid boy. Face had taken some serious collisions. Double-plus sub-species. Political opened the man up like a can of soup. Said real Pashtun's wouldn't have let the guy clean their latrines. That stupid. Barrel-bottom Al-Qaeda. Mitch's new project didn't leave that impression.

"Oh, hey!" Mitch palmed his forehead in mock forgetfulness. "You like political cartoons? Hang on." Winked broadly. Touched the bookmark. "Ah, Dragger. Lord of the files. An a one...an a two..." Mitch held the holopad up for Ashur to see. "Check these out. Oldies but goodies, yeah?"

Ashur glanced at the images. Album display. New ones appeared every three seconds. Slight jaw clench. Otherwise, Ashur looked unmoved. Didn't fool Mitch. He knew when he was holding dynamite.

"C'mon!" Mitch exclaimed. "The one where Mo's wearing a bomb hat? That's pretty damn funny." He spun the device around. Reviewed it again. Barked a laugh. It really was hilarious. Double meaning in Danish, the apple reference. Mitch forgot what.

"Oh, shit, this one's a classic, too!" Mitch said, high with enthusiasm. "Look, look! All these martyr fucks are lined up to get into heaven. Saint... Intifada has to turn'em all down. Big run on virgins. Heaven's out." Mitch slapped his thigh. Roared. Ashur would only stare past Mitch at the wall.

"Seriously," Mitch continued. "A billion people went apeshit over these? Over fucking cartoons. Does that make sense to you?"

Nothing.

"Now...'Burn a Koran Day'...'Draw Mohammed Day'...'Free a Goat Day'...I can see where that might twist your pricks a bit." Low chuckle. "Comin' up in September again. Looks like you're going to miss this year's celebration, though. Too bad. We're having a weenie fest near the river that night. All-pork dogs. Yum, yum."

Quick blink. The man had received training. Mitch recognized the posture from films. He spun away. Flashed the signal. Techmonkey monitors dimmed the hatch light twice. Message received.

Mitch debated options for a second. Reached a decision. Placed Dragger's holopad on the table. Thank you wave. Knew the guy would be watching close. No fucking the dog with 9/11 types.

Back in front of Ashur. Blazing smile. Sincere as he could fake it.

"Hey," he began warmly, "I hope you don't mind but…you know, there's some things that have…really…puzzled a bunch of us over the years. Ummm…now that we got someone…a real 'spurt, maybe, who…probably knows the answers, well…shit…hate to waste the opportunity." Ashur looked Mitch in the eye for the first time.

"Okay…," Mitch rolled on, encouraged. "So…let's say you or…a bunch a your Al-Tard-o buddies blow yourselves up on a bus, right? Or…or in a nightclub? Kindergarten? Wherever you can find infidels. As good terrorists, you get…Fed-Exed straight to heaven. You walk in the door and Allah, like… cuts you seventy-two of the tastiest clam canals you've never seen. Fresh out of the pot. Horny like…the heights of horny. That right?"

Nostrils flared. A flush spread over Ashur's cheeks. Eyes returned to the wall. Mitch readied the lash.

"My first question then. When you're inspecting your virgins, are they, you know…naked? Or are they wearing those burlap…HAZMAT things you see around town these days? Mitch thought he heard teeth grinding. A milky film glazed Ashur's eyes. All to the good. As Political reminded everyone. No point putting the needle in if you don't work it around.

"Also," Mitch rode on, "why seventy-two? Is that, like, some kind a magic Islamic number? Nine times eight, can't think straight? Cause…we were thinking…shit, at first that sounds like a lot. Yeah? Seventy-two snackin' sweet flytrap's. Hoo-ee! Ding, dong, chow's on."

"But then you think…hey…hang on. For eternity? That's a fuck of a long time. I don't know about you but…I'm not so old. I've plowed WAY more than that already. Frankly, seventy-two doesn't sound near enough. Know what I'm saying?"

Mitch gave Ashur the all-ears-listening pose. Tar dark expression. No comment from bomber boy.

"I mean…we're just looking out for you guys, is all. We think you're getting hosed. Shit, I'm Catholic and…I'm tellin' ya. The Vatican had Islam's game plan? And me a frontline priest? Shit, man. I'd get a spanking new boytoy breakfast, lunch and dinner. Forever. No questions asked. The rest of us? They'd promise head from God's wife for a guaranteed win. Seventy-two virgin fish dinners you can get down at Troglodykes any night a the week."

"And…" Mitch was suddenly reminded, "I also read that the whole virgin thing might be a fucking typo. You weren't promised virgins. You were promised…raisins!" Mitch had to stop for a second. Hearty laugh at the con. "No shit. I read that somewhere. You stick dynamite up your butt. Explode yourself for Allah. The prick only gives you raisins? I don't know. That doesn't seem right. Christ, they might not even be raisins! He just said they were raisins. Actually, he could be fobbing off hamster shit on you. Just for laughs.

Think about it. You're expecting a squad of smokin' bone polishers. Instead, you get handed a bowl a rodent turds. The tricky Old Fuck," Mitch sputtered. "I bet that's what happens." Wiped away a tear of mirth.

Ashur now stared hard at Mitch. "I have the right to see a lawyer."

Radical topic change. But a good sign. Mitch leaned forward. Cracked a croquinole take out with his middle finger. Right in the centre of Ashur's forehead. Got exactly the response he wanted. Ashur jerked his head back. Curled his lip. Glowered at Mitch. Never failed. Schoolyard shit always got under crim skin.

"Ash...baby," Mitch said. Looked concerned. Terrorgators deserved their own acting awards night, Mitch thought. He enjoyed it. "I want to be straight with you. I ask a question. You answer the question. That's the way it works. I don't know how they do it in your country. I don't care."

"And n-o-o-o, you 'think' you have the right to see a lawyer. But this is a...special place. No dogs or lawyers allowed."

Mitch strolled to the table. "Besides, most 'liars' aren't your kind a desert people anyway. If you catch me drift, boyo." Mitch did a passable bog Irish. Not as good as Mason's. Hollywood wink. "Hebes, man! Yeah? Jews. From Israel. Jews...Israel...Jews...Israel...Jews...Jews...Jews..." Big smile. Which triggered a sudden yawn.

Ashur's forehead. A wormy vein curled down from his hairline to the bridge of his nose. Above his eyebrows, a pushstart welt glowed red. Done right, the finger snap could really hurt. Mitch was pleased. Not as easy to do perfect as it looked.

Mitch wouldn't have been surprised to know what Ashur was thinking. That he was in the clutches of the CIA. That Mitch was mere muscle. A hired thuggee. That his probable death would mean martyrdom. And eternal salvation.

Ashur's thoughts were also occupied with betrayal. His capture mystified him. Their plan was foolproof. How had it been discovered? He suspected the Somalians. They'd been turned. He'd never trusted them. Omar argued no true Muslim left the path of jihad. Ashur wasn't so certain. AQCan polls showed only 30-35% of Canadians would lift a finger to defend themselves. Or their country. That much was known. The rest would genuflect in a second. Beg for mercy as the sword descended. Die crying, pleading for their sad, pathetic lives. Cloven-hoofed dhimmi. Nothing more.

Only the long-forgotten Crusader Bush had dared raise his hand against Islam. The hordes of Midian soon brushed away his Jewboss White House. Installed a Muslim-loving government immediately after. The Dar el Islam was nearly realized. It needed but a baby's breath to flower fully. Mohammed's everlasting peace was at hand. Ashur yearned with his entire being for that ultimate commendation.

Still, some Americans remained determined. Their army famously riddled with Christians. Whoever had kidnapped him was like the mesmerized fox in the fable. A tool of the Pentagon. Allah would eliminate them when the time was right. Until then, he would endure. His trials in Afghanistan strengthened his resolve. The training had been very taxing. The beds hard. The food unappealing. It was unbearably cold in the mountains. Hiking over rough terrain exhausted everyone. Explosives and weapons instuction beyond dangerous. Even deadly. Poor Khadr. His hands blown off. His "Canadian" brothers abandoned to their fate.

But adversity bred determination. Assam Assad, his spiritual guide, insisted upon it. The Americans had drones. Muslims had faith. Faith to expect the impossible. To believe that however long the war, victory was inevitable. Machines broke. Evil ran its course. Spirits borne on the wings of certainty were indomitable.

Ashur felt his confidence return. He offered a short prayer to Allah. Was again thankful for the blessing. To see his older brother and father a last time. Witness his mother's quiet joy. Both parents shyly pleased with his embrace of jihad. His mother cherished thoughts of neighbourhood esteem. His death would see her status rise immeasurably within the community. How everyone would celebrate in the new land they had come to hate so completely. And his father would have one less mouth to feed. Everyone would be overjoyed at his passing.

And then, shame. Ashur found his pure train of thought derailed by an ignoble craving. Suddenly, hovering in his mind's eye, an Arby's lunch menu. The roast chicken fillet sandwich, extra mayo, homestyle fries and a strawberry shake. The combo floated before him. A temptation sent by Shaitan. It had been a favourite among his fellow jihadists during their Brampton training sessions. He salivated. He knew of no Arby's in Muslim lands. Perhaps some imam could be bribed into providing a dispensation. Under a global Caliphate, the chain would provide menial labour opportunities for dhimmi's.

"Insha' Allah," Ashur murmured.

"Yeah, and your mother swims after troopships, Stan," Mitch countered. His back was to Ashur. "You spent time in Bramladesh, yeah?"

"My family moved to Canada when I was eleven years old," Ashur lied.

"From Syria." Mitch lied.

"Yes," Ashur lied. His parent's deep involvement with Egypt's Muslim Brotherhood a closely guarded secret.

Mitch returned to stand in front of Ashur. Backhanded him without warning. Full blow. It caught the terrorist by surprise. Blood soon trickled from his nose. His eyes watered. Mitch watched him regroup. Hands secured, he was helpless. A shiny spatter pattern appeared on Ashur's suit front. Mitch rested a hand on The Chair's tubular armrest. Put his face inches from Ashur's. Bobbed and weaved to meet Ashur's darting eyes.

"I don't like to do that," Mitch lied. It would get a few laughs later. Blood continued to slow drip from Ashur's chin. He made no more attempts to free his hands. Mitch regarded him with dispassion. Something tickled at the back of his mind. He dropped his eyes. Searched for it. It had to do with the topic at hand. But whatever it was skittered away. He knew to let it alone. When it was ready, it would surface.

Thinking it might jog his memory, Mitch hit Ashur again. Straight jab to the mouth. A wake up more than anything. Ashur took it well. Bit off a groan. Now his lip bled. Mitch was suspicious. Guy cut easy. He hadn't hit him that hard for all the blood he was leaking.

"You're in trouble," Mitch said. Time to refocus the man. "My job…look at me, fuckwit! My job is to find out who you really are? How you found your associates? Why you thought blowing up…" Mitch raised his eyes to the ceiling, shook his head, snorted in disbelief, "…Ontario Place…was a good plan? Who paid for all the fertilizer? Who pulls your strings? And so on and so forth. You will provide answers to all these questions. The alternative? I hammer them out of you. Your choice."

Ashur moved his lips. Praying, Mitch suspected. He'd seen it on newsfeeds. And the rocking thing. A bad thought flashed. What if the little prick was holding? He'd passed through security. The sensors would register explosive chemical signatures. Still, doubt crept in. If he'd buried a secret bowel bomb…? The tank would be okay. As for the ol' Mitchster? A fine red vapour. Paper towel casket.

Fuck it, the thought. Stood tall. Gloved up. Ivan kept reminding him. Crims carried the worst diseases. Mitch fixed the heavy rubber seals into place. Deliberate elastic snap. Found the proper footing. Then drilled Ashur a third time. Punch quick as lightning. Ashur's nose collapsed. Blood exploded from both sides of Mitch's fist. This time Ashur yowled like a cat tossed onto a ready barbecue. Face scrunched up. Mouth wide. Cries echoed off the ceiling.

"What I promised you," Mitch hissed. "Blood, sweat, tears and…trouble. So tell me what I want to know. You don't? They ship you back to whatever open sewer you came from. And you'll spend the rest of your days riding around on some camel without teeth." Mitch paused. Looked down at his boots. Shook his head in irritation. Ashur gave out another keening howl. Mitch pulled his thumb out of the cratered nose cavity. Wiped his fingers on Ashur's shoulder.

"You, not the camel," he corrected himself. "YOU won't have any teeth!"

Ashur continued to blow and squeal. Mitch enjoyed his handiwork. Abstract the guys face. Or so the Sage described it. Not sure what it meant. Just liked the sound of it.

"Hurt?" Mitch smirked. "You think this is bad? This is nothing. Back in your shithole country they'd be ass-raping you so regular you'd think you were a Metropolitan usher. And when they're done with you, they feed your legs into a fucking chipper or something. That could still happen, yeah? We rendezvous your butt back into that prison over there. Where Saddam did all his shit. Aba-tibi. No. Aba…Aba-dabba do. Whatever the fuck it's called."

Mitch slapped Ashur on the side of his head. "You know the one I mean? The Americans took it over way back. It was famous. That Army gash embarrassed you guys all to hell. Made you wear her panties. Remember that? On your heads." Mitch 'haw haw-ed' with real feeling.

"Muslims will never forget the indignities! Those sons of pigs! What they inflicted on our brothers at Abu Graib…" Ashur squawked. Nasal echo. Mitch was pleased. Ashur looked to be chewing leather as he spoke. His breath caught several times. Mitch was very pleased. Weeping meant progress.

"Oh, right," Mitch played along. "A-bu Gra-i-bu." He folded his arms. "That whole torture bullshit? I think you guys need to get away from the, uh…the livestock for a bit. I mean…I get wood just thinking about Tankgirl pulling my package. Say what you like about the cooz. She was no worse looking than a lot a those babushka's you got over there. Seriously. What's with the 'stache on some of'em? Coyote ugle, guy. Know what I'm sayin'?"

Ashur glared ahead. Mitch patted him on the cheek. "There, there, goat-boy. I'm just fucking with you, is all."

Mitch slid back to the table. Step two to be got underway. Hooked a toe under the lid of the daycare yellow carryall. Pulled it out from under. Opened it. Inside, beautiful tools of the terrorgator trade. Political's well-worn jumper cables. The sight instantly cheered him. He rummaged about. Ball gags, leather harnesses, titanium cuffs, carbon fiber straightjackets. Not today. Homemade nunchuks…with corkscrew ends! Somebody had a hobby. And the ol' bullwhip. Thick as his dick. Snake supple. Smell of linseed oil rose to his nose. Tempting. Tempting. Mitch wished he was better with it. Anderson was the master.

Several other perplexing implements got shoved aside. Mitch knew what he wanted. Finally spied it. Snugged under a machine shop manufactured mini-beartrap. Snagged it. Transferred it to his left hand as he turned. Hid it from Ashur.

"Game time!" Mitch grinned. Approached again. "Close your eyes."

Ashur refused.

"Do it!" Mitch ordered. Loomed over the ashen-faced terrorist. "C'mon.

Don't worry. I'm not going to hurt you…more….yet." Ashur took a breath. Gave himself up to fate. Mitch found the laces. Stifled a giggle. Held the football near where Ashur's nose should have been.

"Okay…I know it ain't so easy but…try taking a whiff. Stop! Don't open your eyes yet!" Mitch waited a three count. He couldn't tell if Ashur had breathed in that glorious aroma or not. "Tell me what you smell."

Ashur mumbled something. Mitch craned to hear. He waved the ball under Ashur's nose several times. "C'mon! You can't smell that?" Mitch was disappointed. It looked like he'd ruined his own gag by destroying Ashur's face. "So you can't guess what it is?" One last attempt to milk the joke.

"I don't know," Ashur replied. Sound of the world's worst head cold.

"Shit," Mitch swore. "Alright. Open your eyes."

Ashur did. Recoiled in horror.

"That's right!" Mitch laughed. Cheerful again. He spun the ball into the air with practised ease. "Wrong season, I know. And don't feel bad about missing the answer. You got a pretty good excuse."

Mitch brought the football up to his own nose. Breathed in deep. Eyes shut, ear-to-ear smile. "God, I love that smell in the morning…that bacon-y smell. It smells like…breakfast!"

Ashur's eyes began to roll back in his head.

Mitch groaned. "Oh, fucking relax, would you? Bacon tastes good, pork chops taste good. Remember that old movie?"

Mitch stopped. Were Muslims allowed to even watch movies? He'd never thought about it. Guy might not even know what he was talking about. Back to the main topic.

"Pig. Pig. C'mon. Say it. Pig. It's a magical animal, dontchaknow? Jesus…" Mock grimace. "Oops. Sorry. Said the J. word. Don't catch on fire or anything."

Ashur swallowed loudly.

Mitch two-pointed the ball into the carryall. Muscle pose for Dragger's benefit. Walked over. Found his next prop after a quick search.

"O-k-a-a-a-y…" Mitch stopped to yawn. "For my next trick…" A snatch of classical music suddenly burst out of the Tank speakers. Mitch stopped. Swelling horns and violins. He actually recognized the melody. Then it ended.

"Sorry," a voice apologized.

"No problem," Mitch replied. "It was good. Heard it before." Finished digging in the container. Returned to Ashur.

"Close your eyes again."

Ashur hesitated.

"Oh, for…" Mitch complained. "I promise I won't do anything. Just for a second."

Ashur complied. It was no great demand. His eyes had nearly swelled shut anyway. Mitch closed the distance between them. Pulled his right hand out from behind his back. Held the item aloft. Money shot coming.

"Surprise!" he shouted.

Ashur opened his eyes carefully. Instantly recognized the Holiest of holy books. Blind rage consumed him.

"Do what you wish to me," he begged, "but do not despoil this sacred text."

Mitch's eyes twinkled with mischief. "So it's true. You guys really do get knotted up about this shit?"

Mitch glanced at the book. Back at Ashur. Arched an eyebrow. A brainstorm. He jogged back to the carryall. When he arrived back in front, Ashur guessed his intent. A cloud of mortal terror descended. What infidel would consider such a profane act?

Mitch was that infidel. "You know," he said with a huge smile, "what we have here is one of those unity in diversity moments…if I've got that right?" He bounced the football in his right hand. Did a scales of justice routine. Ashur looked on in shock.

"Sheepskin…meet pigskin." Mitch rubbed the two together.

"N-o-o-o-o-o-o-o-o-o!!" Ashur moaned in animated anguish.

"Y-e-s-s-s-s-s-s-s-s-s!!" Mitch laughed. "Oh-h-h-h, I think they like each other. Look, look! They're kis-sing. They're fuck-ing." Mitch humped the football up and down on the textcover. Made obscene smooching sounds. Ran his tongue over his lips. Went "mmm…mmmm." Really milking it.

Ashur lost control. Screamed for a full ten seconds. Began to lunge against the restraints. Tears streamed down his ruined face. Vivid colours inflamed the wounds. Aged him. For a second, Mitch feared convulsions. Ashur seemed to vibrate with fury. His head lashed from side to side. He moaned and cursed.

Mitch's developing terrorgator sense kicked in. No medical emergency. Just crim drama. Nothing to get exercised about.

"Oi, oi!" Mitch said. He booted the Chair. "Enough of that, melonbrain. I'm just goofin' on ya', you idiot."

Ashur slowed the thrashing. From under puffy lids he beamed undying hatred. Mitch's cue. He'd found the stressor buttons. Easy. Same for Ashur as for a billion others. Mitch sky-hooked the football towards the carryall. Political rim shot. Bounced under the table.

Turned to Ashur with the book. The man stiffened. Mitch brought the prop up to his face. He riffed the pages and inhaled.

"Ah," he sighed, "re-freshing."

Mitch changed tack. Came over all camp councillor. Captain Goodhumour.

"You know what, little buddy? I'm really not a bad guy. No shit. I just have to…figure out if you're a …threat? Or a headcase? So, like, how do you spend your days? When you're not plotting terror attacks, I mean? And how do you guys all get fucking pogey? No wonder you have time to riot. You never have jobs. I don't get it."

Mitch really was puzzled. East coast fishermen? Different story. Ten weeks work. You put your feet up. Job well done. Thanks Ontario. But ten years off the boat? Somebody was filling in the wrong forms.

Ashur's eyes locked on Mitch's. His face had ballooned nicely. Though confident he had the man close to unhinged, Mitch felt more priming was due. He reached over. Gave Ashur a fatherly pat on the head.

"Look, you don't believe this but…I'm in your corner. Really. In fact, I want to put you at ease. You look…tense. Very. So I'm gonna pretend to be one of your, uh…" Mitch snapped his fingers. Looked around in irritation. "Fuck. Now I forget what you call those chuckleheads. You know…" Mitch mimed holding a mic, haranguing a crowd. Held his fist in the air. "Those guys. The ones with, like, dogdishes on their heads. C'mon, help me out here."

Ashur chose not to.

"Well, anyway," Mitch said, "I'm going to read some stuff. From your… holy…non-Bible book. I want you to listen carefully. Take it to heart. That way, you stop being a fuckwit."

He radiated goodwill. Loved how much it obviously grated on Ashur. Vowed not to break character and laugh.

Mitch leafed through the book. Made a pretense of finding a suitable passage.

"Oh," he suddenly exclaimed. "Here's the…suture I want." Mitch privately delighted. He'd remembered the right word. And pronunciation. He could speak Arab!

"Now, listen up. Got a little dune scripture comin' at ya'."

Mitch cleared his throat. Held the book up, chest high. "I, Allah…" Mitch stopped. Looked at Ashur. Man paying crazed attention. "…do hereby declare that…fertilizer is for farmer's fields. Not carbombs. That's bad. I'm serious."

Mitch pursed his lips. Let his eyes drift up. Made as if pondering the meaning. "Straight from the shoulder shit there. I like it."

Raised his forefinger. Mr. Televangelist himself. "And for those of you, my beloved sand-dwellers, who move to a country with sieve-like borders…" Mitch editorialized, "verily, thou shalt keep thy heads down. Do not go among the people ruining things. No one invited you. If you left, no one would weep. Remember you're a guest. Try to get along. Learn how to walk on their streets. Take your hats off when you enter a room. Go easy on the curry.

Or at least don't open your windows. Most important…show a little gratitude. Count your blessings. You could still belong to some tribe with a flag. Bakin' in the desert." Mitch stopped to laugh. Accidentally made a funny.

"Hey, geddit?" he broke from his address. "Bakin' in the desert? Hot. Bacon…oink, oink. Pork."

Shrugged. Jihadi types. Comedy went right over their heads.

Mitch resumed paging through the book.

"Holy Christ!" Solemn whistle. "Oh, yeah. This is solid. Yes,…yes, that's so true."

Cocked an eyebrow at Ashur. The man was shaking. Looked ready to sink his teeth into something. Perfect.

"This next piece of wisdom should be tattooed on your brains," Mitch declared. "Ready? 'Also, no father shall stab, drown, poison…shoot…run over…or otherwise murder his daughter for…for going on dates, wearing lipstick…combing her hair…not wearing one of those bur…bur…burberry things'. No. Shit. Wait, I know it! Burlap! Ah, fuck! No, that's wrong, too."

Mitch pursed his lips, disappointed in himself. Picked up the thread again. "'Anyway, let'em wear what they want in public, etc. It makes us look sort of…whacko when you kill one of your own like that'."

"One last thing," Mitch intoned. Developing a pretty decent Voice of Doom. "By my command, thou shalt not go into the streets in large groups yelling…'Death to…' anybody. It embarrasses me. Stop doing it. If you've got time to stand around in the fucking hot sun all day chanting shit, burning flags, wanting to kill…Jews or Americans or…Danes, for fucks sakes, you've got time to look for work. O-r-r-r…you could even, like, start up a business or something, yeah?"

"And while we're at it. Get a fucking sense of humour for once! Jesus H. Christ. All murder bombing and no yuks makes Ahab a nutjob."

Mitch turned to the last page. Regarded Ashur with affected affection. Continued, "Right. Off you go. And mind what I just said. Allah has spoken. And I ain't jokin'." Mitch waited a three count. Brought the book up to his mouth. Ran his tongue over the cover. Smacked his lips.

Ashur's mouth dropped in disbelief.

"Infidel!" he screamed. "Infidel, infidel! Die, die, die! Die a thousand times!" Bright red bubbles shone in the corner of Ashur's mouth. Now he was screaming in another language. Dog, for all Mitch could tell. But the empty bluster put Mitch right on the floor, laughing his ass off.

When he recovered, he waved Ashur quiet. The man was still blubbering with fury. "Oh, Shut up, fuckface!" Mitch finally bellowed.

Brought the book in front of Ashur.

"It's a fake, you moron. Look." Mitch fanned the pages. Political's useless holovidcam manual. Uncracked, basically. He ripped off the front cover. Third floor's work. They'd rigged up something that might pass for a Koran. From a distance. Worm trails pasted on the front. Knowing the clowns on third, it was a recipe for curried camel. But as props went, Bob's your uncle.

Yaz had followed the exchange closely. In minutes, Mitch had managed to enrage his charge. To deftly push him out of his comfort zone. Yaz was impressed. As he reviewed Mitch's approach, company arrived. A barrel-chested giant collapsed in the seat next to him. Deliberate. The lounge remained empty.

The man smiled down. Yaz steeled himself. Smiled back. Pineapple-sized biceps unfolded. The man pointed at the screen.

"Whaddya' think?" Yaz had heard the term 'smokers voice'. Fully appreciated it now. Sound resembled fresh cement sluicing down a metal feeder. Yaz's future, he suddenly wondered? Vowed to cut back. Better safe than sorry.

"Very interesting," Yaz said. Vague was best. He had no idea who the man was. It paid to be tight-lipped.

"He's good, our Mitch, eh? Always a laugh. Or three." Accent. Yaz couldn't place it. Not from the West. East Coast?

Yaz cleared his throat in preparation for a question. "The suspect...?"

"The terrorist, yeah?"

Yaz took the correction in stride. "After today...?

"Back downtown. There'll be a cover story. Not that anyone will ask. He'll have his lines given to him."

"Is this common practice?" Yaz said, pointing at the Chair. Mitch continued circling it, talking.

"Getting more common all the time. Cops know it's hopeless. Revolving door system. Pissant judges can't wait to let them out again. After apologizing for profiling their guilty asses. So now we get first dibs. When it looks important."

Yaz nodded. He'd heard similar complaints from Force members. As suddenly as he arrived, the man pushed up out of his seat. Towered above Yaz. Lowered a drawbridge. "Lars Vorblen."

Yaz clasped the hand. Waited for his bones to be ground to dust. "Yasu... Yaz Maeda."

"Yaz. Pleasure." The man released Yaz's hand unharmed. Glanced at the screen. Ghost of a smile. Yaz took a discreet look. Guessed his age in the upper forties. Huge but fit. Green shirt tucked in flat against his belly. Tan slacks weren't stressed to destruction."

"Heard Mitch had a new sidekick. I kind of supervise this part of the wing. When I'm in the building."

"Which isn't often," a voice sniggered. The agent assisting Mitch earlier. His eyes never left the monitor.

Lars jerked his thumb at Dragger. "Pay no attention. Everyday insubordination. Why he's down here. No one wants anything to do with him."

"I only mingle with my peers. Since I have no peers, I mingle with no one." The classic O'Reilly comeback. Never left off concentrating on the Tank readouts.

"Lot of bad apples around here," Lars confided to Yaz. Noticed him focused on Dragger. "Buddy system. Make sure nothing goes wrong."

Slapped Yaz on the knee. "You give me a shout you need anything. And don't let that one in there give you too much trouble. These young studs today…" Shook his head. "No patience. Attack, attack, attack. Too much of this," he said. Grabbed his crotch. Ambled over to burly Dragger, hands on the controls. A brief conference followed. Clapped the TankMaster on the shoulder. Drifted out. Room seemed bigger again. Yaz had grown accustomed to working with oak tree-sized white men in the Force. If anything, CORE agents were an order larger again.

Dragger looked over at Yaz for a second. Read his mind. Wise smile. Refocused on his Tank business. Looked to make a minor image adjustment. Expletive. Hammered the wall with an open palm. Lime-green LCD face wash. Startled expression.

"Machines," he explained to Yaz. "Stick sometimes.

Yaz returned to Mitch's interview. Watched as a big paw got laid on Ashur's shoulder. Heard him say, "You ready? 'Cause there's more to come, Mortimer."

Ashur's nose throbbed. He'd been prepared for physical punishment. They all assumed they might not escape capture after the explosions. Martyrdom was the goal in any case. And much to be desired. What Ashur hadn't expected was contempt and humiliation. To be held in such low regard. To be openly mocked, laughed at. It was unendurable. His jihad training was incomplete. Nothing had been said about insolent taunting. Only about certain victory.

"Doctor…Fadl?" Mitch said beside Ashur. Dragger's holopad was a lifesaver. Mitch would never have remembered all the pertinent names.

"I get that pronunciation right? Fadl…as in go fadl a canoe? Close?"

Mitch kicked The Chair.

"He is a great man. Our spiritual guide." Ashur lisped. Tongue swell the problem. And trying to speak with lips big as truck tires.

"He's also a prisoner. In Egypt. You know that?"

"He seeks martyrdom."

"Hope he succeeds. The Egyptians aren't namby-pambies like us when it comes to terrorists. They bring it."

Mitch slid his hand across the bronzed Chair back. Not a burr or nick to be found. Beautifully tooled device.

"Al-Zawahiri? Ever meet him?"

Mitch missed the fleeting smile. "I am…was not important enough. He is also a martyr."

"You're well informed," Mitch conceded. "He got his ass handed to him. Predator missile. Big loss to humanity."

The muscles around Ashur's face twitched again. Uplifting sight for Mitch.

"Next name. What about…Christ…Scrabble time…Say-yid…yid!…Q-u-t-b?" Mitch carefully sounded out the surname. Twice. "Jesus. All your oil money, you think you could afford more vowels."

Ashur repeated the name with obvious reverence. Hundred years of trying. Mitch knew he'd never duplicate the pronunciation. His eyes narrowed. He peered at Ashur. So that was a blissed-out look. It annoyed him.

"So…you're familiar with this clown?"

Ashur tilted his head. Black eyes on Mitch. "He is the…fountainhead of jihad, the first mujahid. A great leader. A great mind. A great Muslim."

"And a great hanging, apparently," Mitch jabbed. "Meet anyone else in Pakistan or Afghanistan we should know about? Any Khadr's? Whole pack of 'em learning the trade then."

Ashur looked away.

Mitch took a deep breath. Held his arms up over his head. Brought them level. Rotated a half-dozen times. Clockwise, then counter-clockwise. His muscles had felt tight all day. He'd have paid good money for a little time on a rack. Have someone crank the kinks out.

"Toute la France divedroma Muselmane," Ashur muttered. Loud enough for Mitch to overhear.

"Ohh, la, la," Mitch stopped in mid-stretch. "Look who can speaka da lingo. You should run for Prime Minister. You'd probably win. All the 905 asswipes'd love ya'."

"The whole world will fall to Islam," Ashur stated. Quiet certainty. "First Europe. Then the rightful homelands of Mohammed. Finally, wherever a Muslim stands is Muslim land."

"Good luck with China," Mitch smirked. Wondered if Andrea was scheduled that day. He might need a massage. A real one.

"Or India. A billion Hindu's might have something to say about that. But who knows? It didn't take you guys long to fuck up our country. Give you another twenty years? Shit. We'll all be boiling bark for breakfast. And after, we get to smell the neighbour's butt five times a day. Won't that be fun?"

Ashur offered no reaction. The pain focused his mind. Assam was correct. The peace of Islam makes you free. Surrender to the teachings of the last, great prophet. Never know fear again.

"Hey," Mitch said. Stifled another yawn. "I'm not saying you guys haven't got some, you know, quality ideas. I mean, that NPOT bitch what's-her-face wouldn't last an hour if Canada was all Muslim-ed up. You'd have her on a skewer, onion in her mouth, slow roasting over hot coals. I admire that."

"Islam protects and cherishes women. They are revered as the heart of the family. Public display is undignified. Why should they wish to behave as men? To look like uncovered meat?" It hurt to speak so much. But Ashur was duty-bound to convert all who would hear him.

Mitch thought about some of the dead slut photos in his flash drive. Uncovered meat about captured it. He shrugged.

"Well, I don't know about that. Nobody likes our jaw-flapping ballbusters. You could do with them what you want. No arguments from most of us. Regular women, though. Different story. Naked is good. Banging women is good. Better than goats, not that I'd know."

Mitch tried to imagine it again. Just didn't do anything for him. Except the no talking part. Partly a hygiene concern, he knew. He'd read goats ate anything and everything. That couldn't be too clean at either end. No dookie on Mitch's noodle. Not right.

"And," Mitch said, continuing the conversation, "I have to say…a lot of us like how you handle your crims. No dicking around." Mitch hacked at his wrist. Grinned with aapproval. Went to shoot a confirming look at the two-way. Remembered the theatre was empty.

"And that whole business about dropping brick walls on the grab-ass contingent?" Mitch popped a thumbs-up. "I know lots of places that'd go over in a big way. Christ, you could probably sell tickets. Not so much in Big T, of course. This is Queerville, Canada. Probably guessed that already."

Mitch froze. The tumblers clicked and fell. That something nagging him. It finally slipped into view. He bolted to the table. Ashur watched with dulled interest. Assumed he was about to be strangled to death. Felt relief he had shaved his genitals. He would meet his virgins in purified form.

Blocking Ashur's view, Mitch crosschecked target addresses on the holopad. Could have kicked himself. Needed to be more observant. S-o-o-o-o-o-o obvious. Fortunately, no one else had caught it either. At least he had that going for him. Read an alert. Slapped the table in delight.

"Hey, one of your buddies got whacked in Gaza," Mitch shared, triumphant. "Israelis put a missile up his Hamas. Took out three other crazies and a couple a breeders. Sorry."

Yaz watched Mitch's performance in fascination. So intense his concentration he missed the flashing light. Suddenly, drunken roaring. He looked up. The second tier rapidly filled with agents. Boisterous shouts echoed around the room. Yaz had no idea what was happening. Other than that a party had arrived.

Mitch stood erect. Flashed the two-minute warning signal at the camera. Dragger responded immediately. LCD bars turned yellow. Clasps snapped open. Magnets disabled.

Mitch joined Ashur. Took a second to savour his work. The left side of the terrorist's face looked like a burst tomato. Both eyes were nearly closed. Plums in strawberry pudding. The broken stump of nose had bled out. Gouts of dried blood clung to his mouth and chin. Vampire with weak feeding manners. Even a goat might shy seeing that coming at him, Mitch thought. Score one for animal lovers everywhere.

Mitch knew the damage looked worse than it was. A CORE medic would have Ashur public ready in twenty minutes. Old hat for those guys. Like New Orleans' ER teams and gunshot victims. Plenty of practice made perfect. But for the next month, at least, Afghan Stan would be reminded of their meeting every time he looked in the mirror. If Muslims could have mirrors. Mitch wasn't sure. Thought to ask. Then realized he didn't give a fuck one way or t'other.

Instead, he pointed at Ashur's face. Joked, "That beak is a sight. Looks like you took an RPG round square." Grinned to show no hard feelings.

Ashur's composure returned. The head throbbing calmed him. He stared over Mitch's shoulder. Waited for the final blow.

"Okay," Mitch said, all business. "You saw me at the toy there. We've just had an update. It appears we got your group all wrong. Our mistake. A thousand salami's."

Ashur didn't immediately register the news. He made no sound.

"Yeah," Mitch said. Did his sheepish look. "Again. Real sorry. We thought you were, you know, dangerous. A threat to national security. I mean…we did find all those Bin Hidin' training videos in your bedroom. The shotguns, rifles, fuses, schematics, circuit boards, triggers, chemicals…city maps, targets circled…times, days, etc. You can appreciate that…looked suspicious. At first." Mitch held his arms out. What-would-YOU-think? pose.

"And then…telling Metro DP you needed five tons of sodium nitrate? To start a farm? What were you gonna do? Grow grenades?" Mitch couldn't help snort. Pictured Ashur or his mates on a tractor. Ridiculous. None of them would last a day doing manual labour. Typical malcontents. Better at jawing than doing.

"Basically, our…agency…has reached a new conclusion. You're all too stupid to do any damage. Except maybe to yourselves. They're now convinced you boneheads couldn't blow up a balloon. You're just…normal, everyday loserfucks. And we're too busy to waste more time on you."

Ashur's mouth fell ajar. He couldn't believe what he was hearing.

"Oh, yeah," Mitch added, holding up the holopad. "We phoned your Mom. You're not dead. So you're in trouble now. No playing with dynamite for a week. She'll pick you up at the Bathhurst GO station this afternoon. After we process your goat-humping ass."

Mitch stabbed at the holopad. For show. Took a deep breath. Final muscle-cracking yawn. Cheery wave for Ashur. "You're done, cameldriver. I'm outta here. B-o-o-o-o-r-ring. Bor-ing. Bor-ing. Bor-ing." Sang the refrain all the way out of the Tank.

Through the hatch without a second look. Burst out laughing as soon as the Station Trog secured the cover. Dragger stood nearby. Stunned expression. The techmonkeys concentrated on their uni's. Minions and Toadies drifted around. Tried to look busy. Ears up.

"Wait, wait," Mitch held up his hand. "Catch my breath." Explained everything a minute later. Dragger still confused. Mitch punched up the primary addresses. The map appeared. Dragger studied it. Looked at Mitch, who pointed at the main target.

"Read it again."

"Box 500, station A…" Dragger paused. "Yeah. That sounds familiar. Why?"

Mitch made the sign. Dragger's eyebrows shot up.

"Really? FMCC? That's their address?"

Mitch nodded. Cheshire cat grin. "Faggo media command central, bro. Ground Zero. If we're lucky."

Dragger gave a low whistle. He pointed at another map balloon. "I've seen this one too. Actually, both of these." He let his finger hover over the icon. The 3-D image told the tale. "Shit," was all he could say.

"Didn't you guys run a check on all these places?" Mitch wondered.

Dragger shrugged. "I just do Tank prep. I never even thought about it. But the whole theatre district…?"

"And…" Mitch gooBUTnecked his wrist, pointed his toe.

"Swish, too?" Dragger goggled.

"Bingo."

Dragger laughed. "Yeah, okay. I see where you're going with this. It's brilliant. And all these other locations…?"

Mitch rubbed his hands together, chortling. "They actually wrote it down. Hardcopy. Their…'plan'? Wipe out Toronto's…'cultural centres'…"

Mitch had trouble containing the giggles. "Thereby eliminating all of their supporters." Wall-pounding time.

"What a group a morons," Dragger said. Lit a Delhi Maximum. Blew a cloud out over a cringing techie.

"Isn't it, though?" Mitch agreed. "Win-win. For us...and the country."

"What were they thinking?" Dragger asked, mystified.

Mitch rolled his eyes. "Fuck, who knows? Not."

Dragger snorted. "Christ, people'd be dancing in the goddamn streets, they succeeded."

"Exactly," Mitch agreed, eyes narrowed. "Trick is, we can't let them know that. "Which is why we need to play this sharp. You think you can get their fertilizer back to them? They're gonna need it. Whatever else they could use, we may have to provide as well. I don't know. We're not dealing with brainiacs here. They can probably brush their teeth without cutting themselves. Beyond that...?"

"Yeah, I'll look into it," Dragger said. Peered off into space for a three-count. Scratched his chin. Ran his fingers through dark weave. Snapped his fingers. "Yeah, yeah, I know some guys in, uh....anyway, definitely doable. CORE has corporate seats at the ACC. Throw in a couple cases. Senators are in town soon. Yeah, shouldn't be a problem."

"Beautiful," Mitch said. "Okay, let me know if there's any obstacles. I'll square expenses with accounting later. You probably heard. I-got-a-bit-a-pull now," Mitch said, mocking himself.

The hatch whisked open behind them. The Burlie summoned earlier emerged. Pushed a blindfolded Ashur inside. The terrorist took tentative baby steps. One of Ivan's junior assistants made out as if to trip him. Mitch threw up a paw.

"Funny, I know," he explained to the crestfallen man. "But this little shit is utterly harmless. If he takes a fall, we'll be accused of unnecessary brutality. Wouldn't want that, would we?"

"No, sir," the Toady and assistant chorused together.

Mitch hadn't grasped how short Ashur was. The Burlie propped him up against the wall. The squirt didn't look more than 5' 5". Movie star tall. Mitch wished he had a beer. Guy's head was the perfect height. Rest one elbow while bending the other. Decided to goof around with him instead. Grabbed a heavy plastic towel bag. Lowered it over Ashur's head. Snugged it around his neck.

"Ash, baby," he said. "How many fingers I got in your face?"

Everyone roared.

"Oh, look, look! It's Mo. Hey, Mo! He just came by to say hello. What? Ya' gotta go? Oh, no! Too bad. Ashur, you missed him. The B-i-i-i-g Fella was here. And you with a bag on your head. Wanker."

Guys helpless now. Hammering walls. Kicking chairs.

Ashur was utterly disoriented. Sweat ran into his eyes. Soaked the blindfold. Stung his scored face. He had trouble breathing. The plastic smell filled him with terror. Meanwhile, the laughter rained down. The cruel baiting. To make him suffer. Yet all he could think of was release. They said they were letting him go. Was it a trap? A game?

He was ashamed by his failure. He knew his father would be embarrassed. His mother, stricken. They had hoped to cheer his corpse as it passed in the parade. Wave along with delirious mourners. Accept the congratulations of envious neighbours. And to pocket the martyr moolah. No small thing. There were many mouths to feed. Some of them in Canada. Sitting across from him again. Watching him eat their pita. That wasn't part of the plan. Their heartfelt contempt at his being alive would be difficult to bear.

Bear it he would, though. There, in the midst of humiliation, he resolved to re-embrace jihad. He would not abandon his mentors. The goal remained the same. Sacrifice the country's cultural touchstones on the altar of Islam. Destroy their national treasures. Bring the infidels to their knees in grief. Compel them to see the light.

"Fuck! Stop!" Mitch ordered. He pointed at the Tank monitor. The Burlie spun, squinted, sighed. Headed back into the bay.

Mitch cleared up the mystery for everyone. "Bombie left his…uh…Arafat thing…hat, scarf, whatever…on the floor. Behind the Chair."

Dragger glanced again at the holovid. "Oh, right."

Burlie gone, Mitch removed the plastic bag. The muffler was returned shortly after. Mitch snaked it around Ashur's head. Stood back. Whistled.

"Boys," he said, "I just created the world's first shit toque. You're witnesses."

No one could deny it. The resemblance to a coiled dump was startling.

"You know, Ash," Mitch said, musing aloud. "I cut you a grill, you're half-way to one of those Afghan beekeeper things. Fuck me if I can remember the name," he whispered an aside to Dragger. "It's on the tip of my tongue, but then…"

"Think of the old figure skater. First name Sylvia," Dragger said. "Sage's idea. Works."

Mitch filed the suggestion. Punch it into the uni when he had a chance.

Turned back to Ashur. Grabbed his Adam's apple. Warbled. "You know what that is?" he asked. "That's your Mom. She's saying…'shish kabobs for din-din! Sorry about your goat'."

The Burlie promptly doubled over. Broad smiles elsewhere. Mitch killed them.

Dragger interrupted the hilarity. Pointed at his com. Clock flash. "Sorry for the shitrain but…I'm booked again in thirty minutes."

Mitch prayer-clasped his hands. Apology bow. Snapped his fingers at

Ashur. Realized he couldn't see anything. Loosened the swaddling. Made him an almond-shaped aperture. Very Arab, in Mitch's opinion.

He and the Burlie propelled the runt exitward. Dragger followed them out. Together they marched into a room full of raging drunks. A mighty cheer erupted.

"What the…" Mitch stopped. Looked back at Dragger.

"The gang's all here," Dragger grinned. "I thought they might slide down. Catch the last bit."

They continued into the theatre. Mitch raised a hand, doubling the decibel level. Peer worship. Nothing more satisfying.

For Ashur, raw abuse. No one knew he was being released. Just as well. Impromptu lynchings caused problems. Boys would be boys. And a righteous hanging did wonders for morale. Still, legal got skittish about it. Mitch laughed to himself. If things did get out of hand, Ashur might come to miss the Tank.

Mitch kicked him up a step. Another roar of support. He actually did it to avoid hork spray. Liquid comets flew through the air. Glued themselves to Ashur's head. Their tails looped around the black and white shithat. A smoker's lungbow of colours—greenish-brown, grayish-brown, brown—clung to Ashur's suit. He knew he must look like every other failed Islame-o terrorist. Comical. A deserving object of scorn and derision. He was filled with dismay.

Fortunately, a leather-lunged mocker started in to sing. The old Septic parody number. Perfect timing. No better homage to Ashur.

Mitch was ready. Yelled up, "Join in, little buddy. This'll be great."

Booze woozy they may have been. Everyone still knew what had transpired. Another masterful terrorgation. It cheered them no end. And so they happily sang the terrorist manque out of the hall.

Ashur staggered forward. Around him, a full-scale riot. Smoke, jeering infidels, alcohol-fanned madness. White giants bellowing some anthem. Their hate stares had vanished. Now pointing and laughing only. Mad singing underway. He feared for his sanity. The enemy was nothing like they'd been painted. Ashur convinced they were all insane. Victory was inevitable, yes. But the prize? Did Mohammed know? Should he be warned?

"Who can take gelignite?" Mitch contributed with enthusiasm. Natural baritone. Fists working in counterpoint. Bruce Lee punched Ashur out the door.

"…Pack it in a vest
Hump it to a kindergarten
And you know the rest
The Taliba-a-a-a-n
The Taliban can

The Taliban can
Cause they manufacture bombs
To kill the infidels

Who can climb a mountain?
Hide inside his coat?
Disappear for days or weeks
Because it's so remote?
The Taliba-a-a-a-n
The Taliban can.

The Taliban hates
Never educates
Women 'cause they're only cattle
Saddle up, it's time for battle
Fix me up a fresh falafel!

Who can take a statue?
Blast it into dust
Dance about the rubble
Cause in ignorance they trust
The Taliba-a-a-a-n
The Taliban can

The Taliban rates
Then eradicates
Those who won't obey their wishes
Get inside and do the dishes
Otherwise you'll sleep with fishes"

Ashur dispatched, Mitch accepted kudos in the gym. Fellow agents dropped by. On their way from the courts or to the weight room. Turning Ashur loose shocked many. Mitch taking a risk. No way of knowing a fanatic's future plans. Ashur and the Chickpea Tribe. Might do more than eliminate CORE's culture vulture enemies. Innocent people could suffer. The whole 'collateral damage' thing.

Mitch acknowledged the gamble. Felt shit balanced out at the end of the day. Top floor agreed. Bonus for taking aggressive action. Penciling out the poofter posse. An unexpected benefit.

Another facilities tour finished. Science wing. Day done, though. Yaz found Mitch in the locker room. Waited until until Mitch was alone. Popped the question his superiors would want asked. "They're all free to go? After having…all those explosives? They've all admitted planning the attack."

Mitch removed his flexnets. Folded them. Adjusted his junk.

"Depends," he finally said. Which didn't make sense. "I mean. Normally, no. You'd jail their asses for life and a day. Or try." Rolled his eyes. The national reaction at mention of the pantywaist Canadian courts. "Our justice system is catch and release these days. We pat their heads. Pat our backs. Blame it on the Americans. Smile like moppet munchers on confirmation day."

"But these bulletheads…if they keep to their agenda, they could end up doing more good than harm. Line decision, basically." Mitch shrugged. "We'll see. If it goes south, we say they're Muslims. Nothing we could do. They can't be touched. Media'll lap it up."

A stacked ShowerBabe swiveled up. Full refreshment tray. Yaz declined. Mitch grabbed a lemon-flavoured caffeine bomb. Drank it down. Gritted his teeth. Immediate impact. Felt his eyeballs expand. Whistled approval. Ran his fingers around the Babe's sequined baltimores as a thank you. Gave her a rump thump as she wiggled off.

"Thing is," he said, back to business, "in this age of tolerance you can't jump to conclusions." Yaz heard sarcastic snorts from nearby listeners.

"Seriously," Mitch said, almost not smiling. "I mean…were those desert rats really going to start a farm? Fuck no. You ever see where they come from? Rocks, sand and sun. Scorpions big as dogs. Shit, I wouldn't let them near a garden. Hand them a robotiller. They wouldn't know what to do next. You'd find it an hour later dug halfway to China."

"You look at their countries on the vid? I can't figure out what they fucking eat? Which is why they end up here. They heard we had food." Chuckles greeted this statement of wisdom. Yaz looked unconvinced.

"Okay," Mitch sighed. "Truth? I did run a bit close to the rail on this. But I've seen the research. Well…Dragger told me after. Most of these bozos talk big. That's it. All bun, no weiner."

Yaz nodded. He thought he understood. It did make a kind of twisted sense. "Inter-agency rendition."

Mitch looked left, then right. No one near his cubicle to explain things. "Once more. It sounds painful."

Yaz repeated himself. Mitch pondered it for another few seconds.

"Two agencies working together. You mentioned how the MetroPolice turned him over to you. They've given up on regular channels?"

"Yeah," Mitch said. Placed gear in his locker as he spoke. "More or less.

Out of necessity, mostly." He pulled on his Martens. Locked them. "How many degrees you got again?"

Yaz glanced around. Conversation had quieted.

"Sorry. Joking." Mitch didn't mean to embarrass the guy. "It's just… apart from myself, not too many mental wizards here." Boos, catcalls, feigned outrage bounced around them.

Mitch put a hand to his ear. Laughing. Told Yaz to ignore the peanut gallery.

"Too many ten dollar words, people go gorilla here. All I'm saying," he finished once the abuse had died off.

Yaz wore a cryptic smile. His first impression of his new partner had been less than positive. He'd been steadily revising it since.

"Okay." Mitch stood straight. Tucked his shirt in. Belted up. Grabbed the horsehide. Shoved his watch cap into the pocket. "Home for some curvy pie. Catch up with y'all tomorra', rawht?"

Yaz nodded. "Thanks for seeing to the tours."

"No problem. This place is so big I get lost sometimes. Better you have a guide who knows where he's going."

Mitch did a final checkover. Said, "You find your own way out?"

"If I'm to be a detective, I should learn how."

"I hear that." User salute to the remaining agents. Mitch loped to the door and out. Yaz felt the eyes of other agents turn to him. He nodded politely. Followed Mitch's example. Exited.

Mitch correct. CORE's main complex was, indeed, considerably larger than estimated. Yaz had already estimated, memorized the rough dimensions of the departments visited. His findings would surprise people. He thought he could retrieve the building schematics. It would take some time. The next task was of greater importance to his superiors. CORE's primary funding sources. Public, private, self-generated? How much of a threat did it pose to Force funding? The institution was deeply worried about proposed operating cutbacks. The competition for scarce resources growing intense.

OVARIANS REVEALED

—◄ ○ ►—

"Ovarians," Mitch explained. They neared the seminar room. Joined the queue. "Also known as 'The Sisterhood'. 'Club DykoBitch' to the rest of us."

Yaz had trouble adjusting to the total absence of political correctness among CORE agents. People spoke their minds. Candour demanded. For a West Coaster, born and bred, it was shocking, disconcerting. In Vancouver, mealy-mouthed bowing to accepted viewpoints the norm. What not to say, most important. Avoid giving offense. Meaning avoid the truth. Truth was pain. His father laughed when Yaz idly mentioned it one day. Said the Japanese had been doing it that way for centuries.

The Force, too, expected similar restraints on public utterances. Yaz debated sharing this information. The freedom to speak his mind. It made him uncomfortable. And yet is was singularly bracing to hear others speak what they thought. Intoxicating. Not an approach the Force would likely foster.

"Feminists?" Yaz asked Mitch. Seeking target clarity.

"What I just say? Yeah, fucking femmes."

Little more abrupt than Mitch intended. He peered over the heads in front. The wave dispersed as they entered through the large plate glass doors. He pointed to a spot. Middle row, aisle seats. Proceeded to steer around blocks of chatting agents. Mitch traded barbed comments here and there. Arrived and sat. He stretched his legs under the seat in front. Both knees stiff. Barometer drop. And hockey blowback. The old man warned him. You pay for the fame and glory. Mitch adjusted the chair for maximum legroom. Marginal swivel. Still, nap comfortable. Work of a moment to lie back and grab eyeshut.

"Let's just say," he said, picking up the thread, "these horrorshows are… beyond your normal fembots. When it comes to crazy. Started in California, late 60's. Bra-burning psycho-dykos. Infected universities down there. Moved north to B.C.…." Mitch stopped. Fixed Yaz with an incriminating stare. "…your neck a the woods, yeah?"

Yaz gave a measured nod. Undeniable.

"Early 70's," Mitch said. Kicked at an agent passing by. Received a friendly middle finger salute in return. "So the research says. Worked east. Like a virus. Cunty students became cunty professors. Moved up the chain. Got control. Working to destroy everything."

Yaz turned to look at Mitch. Half-shrug response.

"Teaching weird shit. Super weird. Castrate all men. Torpedo the family. Governments should control everything. Corner store abortions. 7/11 slice and dice. Farm-slave camps. North-fucking-Korea, thank you very much. Batshit-crazy. Every one of'em."

Yaz sat, deeply disturbed. "Is this…true? I've read nothing about them."

"You won't. The fix is in. Faggo press won't touch it. They're in on it. Only blogworld has the details. You have to know where to look."

Lights flashed at the front of the room. A holoscreen shimmered into existence. The new aquamarine shade. Nice. Very ocean-y. Mitch had never seen the ocean. Wondered if it was like in that holoflick? With that famous actor guy?

"What do they want?" Yaz askd.

"Us dead." Mitch snorted. "But not just that. It's…" Mitch ran a paddle hand over his lower jaw.

"I don't really get it," he admitted. "They're women, but…they're more fucked in the head than usual. Mostly 'cause they're not getting fucked period."

Mitch elbowed Yaz after a few seconds. "That's just my opinion. Experience. Women go off the deep-end like this? They're not getting enough. Or any. This is why they're pissed. But they can't say that. So they change the subject. Typical."

Mitch shifted in his seat. Massaged his left knee. "As far as I can make out, they just want to…turn everything upside down. They hate men. They hate women who like men. They hate sex. Unless it's half-humans having it. And they hate babies. I mean really, really hate them."

"Babies? Why?"

"'Babies remind them they're women, for one thing." Mitch stopped. That was good. He'd have to remember it.

"And babies become people. Men, even," Mitch said. "They grow up, marry, start families. Fathers get jobs, start businesses. Buy food, clothes, lawnmowers. Fembots hate that. The whole 'circle of life' bit."

Mitch paused. Frowned. "Shit. I think I just figured it out. That's what they hate most. Normal. Normal shit. Mother, father, children, school, work… whatever's normal, they hate. Bossy iron-britches. Our ancestors knew what to do with that type. Burn'em. Or make'em librarians."

Pocket patdown. Time for a butt. "'Mitch Milligan!" he whispered in falsetto. "'Sit down. Stop picking on Harold. Other people are trying to read'." He lit up. Exhaled. "Fucking librarians. What a cunt she was."

The room had filled with agents. Muted conversation. Still early in the day. Hangovers in evidence. Pained looks. Puffy eyes. Shaky hands. Mitch noticed Stapleton had his cast off. Waved congratulations. Their line would be back together for the next game. Stap's the ace point shot. Mitch the deflection king. Goal machine when they were in synch.

He snapped his fingers. Glanced down at Yaz. "Oh, yeah. I just remembered. They're all fucking commies, too. Ovarians. They hate…money. No. They hate that they don't have money. And they hate you if you do. So they live to steal it. Legally. For the people," Mitch said, chuckling in derision." A few of that type in the Kap. Maybe everywhere. His old man had no time for them, union or not.

Yaz listened with quiet intensity. The Force must surely know of such an organization. Still, any information he could pick up, relay.

"Sports….barbecues…pickup trucks….drinking…lawns." Mitch casually ticking off other femme hates.

Yaz looked skeptical.

Mitch nodded. "Yeah, I know. I forget the idiot reasons." Scratched his throat. Patch the Braunsaw missed.

"Oh, yeah. And they fucking hate, hate Christmas." Now his head was itchy. Contagious. Like in the Commissioner's office.

Yaz thought about lawns. Far more in Toronto than Vancouver, he'd been told. Hadn't seen any yet. Still under snow.

"Christmas presents, Christmas trees, Christmas decorations," Mitch said, half to himself. Counted them off on his fingers. "Chistmas songs, Christmas school festivals…they despise those. Santa Claus, Santa's…those dwarves he uses. What are they?"

"Elves?"

"Yeah, right." That was the word he wanted when he first met Yaz.

"Reindeer, sleighs, sleighbells, chestnuts…you name it, those grim bitches hate it."

"Why?"

"Because…they're horrible…unhappy hags. Most of them. No man wants them. So they attack us to get even."

Yaz remained troubled by the answer. Mitch held his hands out. What could you do.

"Part of it is…the Bible makes the faggo set feel guilty. And despicable. There's a pretty clear thumbs down from God about guy-on-guy shit. No specific mention about blowing strangers in a public toilet, but it's…you know…pretty clear that…it makes the species look ridiculous."

Mitch lowered his voice. "Actually, I didn't even know there was anything in the Bible about bum-daggers. That business got skipped in my Sunday school classes. All we got taught was how that…" Mitch stopped to cough. Apologized. "Sorry. Not enough smoke in my lungs." Took another drag for therapy's sake.

"Yeah, anyway, the usual stuff got peddled. You probably don't know any of it. Something about demons in pigs. I remember that. But nothing about cornholing. We weren't hard-core Catholic."

Mitch dropped his finished cigarette into the chair arm's recessed cup. A blue ray vaporized it. Flash of light. Vanishimo. Always liked that. Shiny.

Activity up front. But no hint the meeting was imminent. He rotated his right ankle. Winced. The ache in his knee spiked. Twisted it in a rut on the ice. Minor discomfort. Mitch had long ago learned to deal with those kind of body complaints. Let his mind wander. Retraced his morning routine.

He'd arrived early for a change. Read his spark-mail. No attachments. No GUM. Coffee and smoke over the sports. Hit the john. Beached a Bruno. Queen's crown wraparound. Bowlbots whining into action. Worked to lever that substantial turd into the surf. Courtesy, previous night's cabbage rolls. Firm and spicy. Just the way he liked his rolls. His shits often came out the same way. Cabbage fibre. You had to love it. Always left the tunnels nice and clean.

Mitch checked his face in the mirror. Fingered a scrape. Not weeping any more. Andrea, a tigress the night before. Clawed him up up some. He'd almost drifted her one. Break the spell. Out of her head with blind, ravening lust. Finally managed to fuck her unconscious. Normal night's work.

Break over. Uni case research for almost thirty minutes. Every account dull. Most mattresses weren't reported as missing for months. Leads went cold. Pavement scum were unreliable sources anyway. Not to mention disgusting to be around. That made proper identities difficult to come by.

His own merry Magdelene might have had a dozen different street names. Every local dirty was a "Sally the Sausage Grinder" or "Boneyard Betty." Plus, Jezzies didn't keep in touch with family much. What decent mother wanted to know where her bad seed slut of a daughter did business?

The hard data Mitch had to work with. What you'd expect. Back alley fashion. Tit tatts. Knock off TrudGear—shoulder bags, purses. Empty. The other corpses found had similar effects. Nameless. Faceless, frequently. Beaten. Eaten by fish.

The guy at MetFor threw up his hands. No budget for special tech. Gay tolerance seminars devoured all the money. Told Mitch he'd grown to hate the waste of money. And he was ultra-gay himself. Always worked extra hard to please Mitch. Hoping against hope for the impossible.

Still the bodies popped up. Averaging two a week. Mostly in Lake Ontario. But other spots, too. The Ravine. Two McMac dumpsters. And one got left in the far corner seat at the 24/7 Starbucks on Younge. Two days before anyone noticed her. Big surprise. The one-armed stinky Kitty wasn't binging on OxyCont. How were regular customers supposed to know that?

Best one, though. Dead trull rolled under a doughnut truck making deliveries. Mitch smiled to picture the look on the driver's face after he'd backed over a leg. Make a great story over beers.

So the thing looked like it could actually be a challenge. That day's meeting might provide ideas, info. Plus, he'd only been working the case a short while. Second thoughts had surfaced, however. To begin with, puzzles weren't his strong suit. Murdered slots? Who cared? He didn't. No one he knew did. Career choice. Sell your ass, take your chances. Snowboarders got avalanched regularly out west. Never lost a night's sleep feeling bad about it. Not his fault.

He supposed if you operated a pink palace there'd be concern. Yet most of the dead trulls were garden variety filth. The rub and tugs, like where they nabbed Melling, got supplied from Asia or East Europe. Hard to see how their business was threatened. If anything, a falloff in home-grown sluttage would play into their hands. Judges, lawyers, teachers, journalists and other trolling lowlife would be forced to take their custom inside. No more drive-by rentboy blowjobs on the way to a day on the bench.

And another thing. Suck parlours had secret cameras. Perfect for blackmail. One more angle to consider. Mitch groaned. Detecting was hard.

Worse for Mitch. He'd already asked around. No reason could be divined for the crimes. The locations seemed randomly chosen. No evidence left behind.

Also confusing, if interesting. All the trulls had been mutilated. Head, shoulders, knees, toes. Eyes, ears, mouth, nose. One useful part or another tended to be missing. So whoever was responsible liked their trophies.

Nothing internal had been scooped out. Black market organ traffic unlikely. Besides pigsynth was cheaper. Everybody carried them. Amazon, Shopper's. Home Hardware sold a self-installation kit. There were good points to living in the near future. Mitch had to admit it.

Mitch had watched enough holovid drama. A serial killer might be operating. Which would be dead cool if true. Still, hard for anyone to get too excited. A message beyond normal trull-disgust? No one knew what it might be. Leaving Mitch with two choices. He could get worked up about it. Or he could get his skates looked at. No brainer.

Mitch returned to the Goodfellow link. Weird that CounterIntel was following the case. Mitch didn't know what it meant. But help was help.

He scrolled down the list of contacts. CORE-approved contacts, Goodfellow claimed. Used them all the time. Mitch didn't recognize anyone. Why would he? New to the business.

Topping the roll call, STD specialist Dr. Bruce Selosis. University of Guelph. Trulls were known disease trolleys. Mitch knew that much. And their caring government catered to carbuncles. So there might be a database somewhere.

Next up, Professor Barney Kull. Head of the Ontario Oceanographic Institute. Hard guy to get a hold of, Goodfellow warned.

Toronto Port Authority rep. Steve Dore. U of T. biologist Jean Poole. Sue Nami, Great Lakes tidal movements. Ballistics expert, Rick O'Shea. And so on. All people who might have knowledge he could use. None who answered their coms or had listed offices. Mitch put his head on the uni surface. Thought about lunch.

Booing shattered Mitch's dreamless snooze. The holovid image winked and shimmered. Momentary confusion, then recall. Ovarian meeting. Update stuff. Shouts of revulsion from agents all around Mitch. A face glared out at them. Mitch recognized it. June Eldritch. Head heifer, Status of Slatterns. Also known as "The Beast from the East" and "The Thing that Ate Ottawa." Of course she would be an Ovarian. Mitch averted his eyes. Too much ugly, too soon.

Lights raised. 'Spurts and uniforms left the room. No ceremony at CORE. Mitch swallowed a yawn. Scrunched around in his chair. Adjusted his tackle. Kind of satisfying. He'd missed another meeting.

"Shit," he muttered. Something about group gatherings. Or libraries, churches, cars in April…they put Mitch to sleep faster than a Friday night fuck. "Anyone notice?"

Yaz looked over, faintly amused. Mitch felt a poke in his back. Turned.

"Late night?" Dave Fraser, big smile. Relaxed into the recently vacated chair behind Mitch. Orillia boy. CORE old-timer. A Mitch mentor, along with Political. Bluff and outgoing. Smile that lapped up to his eyes. Workout madman, despite pushing forty. Also owned the best pushbroom 'stache ever.

"Maytag," Mitch confessed.

"Perfect," Fraser patted him on the shoulder. Everyone needed a quality washing machine. "She the one you talked about before?"

"Yeah," Mitch threw an arm over the chair back. "I told you that story?"

"Just a bit. On the rowing machine. Last week maybe."

"Right," Mitch remembered. "Yeah, same one. Fireball. I had thoughts about kicking her to the curb but…that mouth. What can you do? Service with a smile."

Fraser laughed. Glanced at his com. Raised the eyebrow. Nodded to Yaz. Left. Mitch noted the flash of curiosity. Man had dropped by to take a closer look at Yaz. The Commissioner was playing his cards close. No general announcement. Meaning? Mitch didn't know. Have to catch the man up on everything next time in the gym.

The room emptied. Mitch never rushed for exits. Saving five minutes had no appeal. All it meant was getting back to the desk sooner. Who needed it? He had a case that might end up causing him grief. Better to sit back. Talk hockey with the stragglers. Compare pool selections. Mitch was looking good this year. The Canadian teams were coming through for him. Montreal mathematically eliminated in December. Again. Satisfying development. And the Cup was staying home for certain. Could be the Leafs once more. Martel had a lock on his third Adams if Stanley returned to its rightful home. The Oil looked strong. Canucks and Flames, in the mix. Hamilton and Halifax? Not out of the race.

Yaz started to look anxious. Mitch pushed off the wall. Leg was coming around. The nap helped. They ran into Stevens on the way out.

"We watch anything interesting?" Mitch asked out the side of his mouth.

"Yeah, actually," Stevens replied, bushytail cheerful. "Undercover shit. CORE has someone inside the Ovarians."

Mitch shivered. "Jesus, don't say it like that."

"Sorry," Stevens laughed. "Yeah. Anyway, these bitches…where to begin?" They entered the corridor. Turned left towards the main offices.

"Long distance sat-recon," Stevens continued, leading the way. "Also, mic traps at targeted meets. Captured some creepy shit."

Mitch looked at him. Stevens nodded, serious. Agents peeled off as they encountered corridor intersections.

"Universities, public schools, government, media…everywhere."

Mitch pursed his lips in thought. "And they really have something to do with our morgue backlog?"

"Seems that way. Fingerprints. Femmes of a feather."

A CORE MassageMinx met them. Heading for the Health wing. Shift change. Mitch recognized her. Raised a hand in greeting. Friendly look. Returned, along with wicked lip licking. She twinkled her eyes. Spotted

Stevens. Let her guns rise. Past, trailing a heavenly scent. Triggered fond memories on Mitch's part. A great little galloper. Saw Stevens grin. Punched him in the tit.

"And?"

Stevens firmed the face again. "They have this…revolutionary manifesto. They want to…they plan to erect a new system of government. YKS. Means…"

Mitch looked at him, eyes wide. Listening. Waiting.

"Sorry. The pronunciation is…hard. YKS. Yodok…Kibbutz Scheme."

Mitch looked at Yaz.

"Yodok Kibbutz is perhaps what…he meant to say."

"Yeah!" Stevens agreed. "That!"

Mitch shrugged. "No idea. Never heard of it. YKS?"

Stevens nodded. "I guess…basically…the country becomes this…giant daycare centre from Hell. For adults. The queen Ovarian runs it."

Mitch rolled his eyes. "Anything else?"

Motioned everyone against the wall. A troop of Trogs trudged past. Training exercise. Mitch recalled yesterday's uni-spark. Some black op coming up. Trog bulwark needed.

Stevens ran a taped hand over a full mouth. Bad shaving, lower jaw bruising almost kept him being good looking. "No, that's about it." Pregnant pause.

Mitch came to a full stop. Hawk eyes on Stevens. "What else?"

"Just…stuff about dancing."

"Dancing? What fucking dancing?"

Yaz also intrigued. Listened closely.

"Surveillance cam. I forget which park. They were having one of their… events."

Mitch glanced at Yaz. Back to Stevens. "And…and?"

Stevens shrugged. "Just…a bunch of women in these…white robes. All slit up the sides. Dancing around a fire."

Mitch saucer-eyed. "Recently?" he gaped. Even feminists wouldn't be stupid enough to traipse around in a bedsheet at this time of year.

"No, no, back in September. It's some festival they have. Four times a year. Something to do with the moon…goddess. I forget."

"That's it?"

"Well, yeah," Stevens grinned, nervous. "Until…you know…they started…stripping down."

Mitch, a statue of disbelief. "Stripping? What do you mean?"

"Their clothes. It's an…initiation. For new members. That's what analysts think. The elders remove the new members'…robes. Then they…shave them."

Mitch's jaw bounced off his chest. "I can't believe I never heard about this!" he croaked. "How many? How old?"

"Thirty or forty, maybe. From Humber, York, U of T. Late teens, early twenties. Gorgeous…"

Mitch closed his eyes. Slapped his forehead. "You're torturing me."

"These old, used-up dykos sit around in what's called a…Circle of Crones. Clapping…playing these…weird-looking instruments."

"Like mutant squash? Split down the middle? With strings?" Mitch asked, keen look.

"Yeah, yeah," Stevens said. "And after that, it was…you know, full-on… lesbo action. Until the moon came up."

Mitch was rocked. Heart racing. Breathing through his nose. Could only get out a strangled, "Jesus."

Stevens' composure cracked just the slightest. The sight of Mitch, legendary prankster, slack-jawed with lust. Priceless.

It was enough. Mitch guessed that he'd been had. Spun on Yaz. "Fuck! You in on this?"

"No!" Yaz shook his head. Looked at Stevens, mouth clenched shut. He hadn't followed Stevens' explanation at all. He'd never heard the phrase, 'claque of Danvers'. Though Mitch clearly had. Nor had there been mention of lesbians in the presentation. From what he could tell, it was taken as read. The Ovarians. What else would they be?

Seconds later, second-year man Stevens, pride of Brooks, Alta, found himself pasted up against the wall. Forearm on his throat. 215 lbs dangled off the floor. Mitch was fast when provoked. Not to mention someone who didn't really know his own strength. Yaz moved from harm's way. Deserted corridor just then. No witnesses. Yaz wasn't sure if that was good or not.

"What were you going to tell me next?" Mitch growled. "That they had horses? Horny white stallions?"

"Yes." Stevens managed to get out. He knew the stories. Mitch had famously righted several kitten charmers in his career. Hearing about a coven of wild lesbians so close by? In dire need of his celebrated cockwork? Of course he'd be disappointed. Opportunity missed. Mitch would put himself up against any horse. He smoked DuMaurier's. He didn't take lessons from them when it came to drilling women.

"No fucking way I wouldn't a heard about this shit before," Mitch said. It was the first time Stevens had seen Mitch's death-mask smile. He was impressed. Pretty scary. He started to feel light-headed, though. Mitch was crushing his windpipe. He raised his eyebrows. Puppy dog sympathy plea. Worked on women. They spread like butter after.

Mitch finally chuckled. Sighed. Dropped him. Can't stay pissed at a puppy.

"Well, ya' got me, ya' little prick," he admitted. Glanced at Yaz. Started to laugh at the man's worried expression. And then both he and Stevens were into it. Great gales of genuine hilarity. The very thought of it.

"Gorgeous Ovarians," Stevens choked out. Another minute of hysterics. Yaz looked on in wonder. Two desk pilots passed by. Shared puzzled looks as the two agents risked injury punching painted cement.

"Ah, Christ," Mitch gasped. "What was I thinking?"

"Naked bo's and bonfires?" Stevens offered.

"I yam a sucker for them thar sce-NAH-rios," Mitch drawled. Wiped the back of his hand across his forehead. "Porn lizzies versus real lizzies. Different kettle a fish."

"Different herd of water buffaloes, more like it," Stevens said. "You missed the mug parade."

"Hmm…" Mitch pondered the image. "So… there really isn't any secret vid?" he asked. Playfully cuffed Stevens on the shoulder. They resumed walking.

Stevens wince-grinned. Like catching a three-wood right in the meat. Arm would be dead for an hour.

"No. But they do have someone…attached to the group somehow. Hush, hush, though."

"Just as well," Mitch shuddered. "Christ, any vid with…real Ovarians dancing. Ai, yi. Give you nightmares to last the rest of your life."

They turned the corner. Mitch already planning his afternoon. He looked over to Stevens. That big, square face. Happy-go-lucky smile. Blonde bristles tinted black and orange. Menacing build.

"What's on your sched today?"

"Weapons and explosives. Until 3:00. Practice and game after."

"Oh, yeah. Firefags?"

"Yep."

"Alright," Mitch said, picking up the pace. "Well, fuck off, okay. And don't blow yourself up."

"Roger, that," Stevens said smartly.

"And don't be going around telling everyone how you played me, either," Mitch ordered. "I'll be ringing passes off your ankles tonight otherwise."

"Yes, sir," Stevens replied. Dead serious pose. Not a hint Stevens enjoyed the moment. Good actor. Mitch wondered if there was a terrorgator future for the man. Knew it would be all over the clubhouse before he rolled in. Regardless of his demand. Such was life. Live by the sword, catch it in the back one day.

Stevens waved. Peeled off.

"Never a dull moment around here," Mitch said to Yaz, who fell in behind. With Mitch's stride, Yaz hopped to keep up. Handed a cold beer seconds after entering Mitch's office. Mitch put his down in one go.

"Jesus, I needed that. Alcohol hydration. Underrated. Plus, meetings dry me right out."

"You can drink during work?" Yaz was dumbfounded.

"Yeah, why not?" Mitch took it for granted now. Forgot it wasn't the norm elsewhere.

"It's just..." Yaz trailed away. He took a tentative taste. It was good. He didn't drink beer as a rule.

"Essential perk," Mitch declared. Raised a fresh can in a toast. "Kifaya!" Took another healthy pull. Smacked his lips.

"Joke," he explained. "Kind of sums up what CORE is about, though. Their, our...what's the word I want? Mission plan? No. That's the same thing. CORE..." Mitch looked at the ceiling. Let his eyes run around the room. Past the trophy rack. Past the walldigi. Flashing classic moments from his life. Every three seconds. No repeats for hours. He'd been lucky. What else could you say?

Skip over to the glass-walled trophy shrine. The hockey memorabilia secured inside. Championship pucks on their little gold stands. The multiple awards. Testament to consistent on-ice greatness.

"Nope," he admitted. "Nothing. Whatever it's called, they cut out a lotta corporate...crap. All the dork-designed bullshit rules. It just follows from CORE's original purpose. We want a free society back. Stuff the lawyers, stuff the socialists, stuff the fucking feminists. In a dumpster, preferably," Mitch added. "Kick'em all into the lake. Enough, man. Enough."

Mitch took another satisfying swig. On a roll. Furthering Yaz's education. What the commissioner wanted.

"The time for hoping someone acts is over. The nanny state is here. Getting worse. If we don't do something, who will? If not now, when? Cry freedom. Like in olden times. Ya' gotta believe it can happen."

Mitch saluted the building. Tossed his empty into the desk repository. Muffled grinding sound. "More flak jackets," Mitch grinned. "Now tell me you still have stress."

"It is...very good," Yaz agreed. The one thing the Force and CORE had in common he could see. Beer drinking was highly-regarded. "What is it?"

"Special product," Mitch said. Winked. Put his finger against his nose "We get these delivered as payment for...services rendered. If you know what I mean. Side business. And getting bigger."

Drifted to the uni. Entered a request.

"I've got some local micro brews that should be ready soon. Excellent flavour. There's some great shit made in Ontario these days. A lot of it on the sly. Avoid taxes."

Sing-sang, "Homebrew…..sounds good to me. Homebrew, that's the way it should be." Belched with feeling. "Not that mass produced…fucking horse urine. Short shelf life?" Mitch belched again. "Not a problem. Never around long enough to go bad."

Big laugh. Cleared his throat. Offered Yaz another can. Declined. The conversation stayed on homebrewing. They sat, got comfortable. Yaz did know something about it. His uncle's family once made rice vodka. Talked about marketing. Brewing problems. Alcohol percentage. Mitch described drinking genuine Tennessee hootch once. 180 proof. An ounce of pure white lightning in a 16 ounce Mickey Mouse glass. Mixed with Coke, he was ashamed to admit. Still nearly put him on the floor.

"But that's about it," Yaz concluded his story. "I'm not much of a beer drinker."

"Whiskey? Scotch? Vodka?"

"Wine only," Yaz confessed. Mitch grimaced. Yaz filed the information. "You?"

"No. I can get one down to be polite. In a panty-peeler situation. But it's like pickle juice to me. I don't know shit about it. Care even less. Watch out for that ice wine stuff from Niagara Falls, though. Fuck-ing pri-cey. I went to buy some once and…h-o-o-o-o-ly Christ!"

Yaz said he'd never tried it. Preferred Bulgarian varieties. Which made Mitch laugh. Explained why. Yaz wasn't aware of the rivalry.

A pause. Each man lit up again. Smoked in silence. Yaz covertly took in the office. Large by Force standards. Usual bells and tech gimcrack. Sleek unidesk. Large window. View of office windows opposite. Green-grey building. Like the sky.

Bird warble. Yaz sat forward. Mitch held up a finger. Waved his hand over the uni corner. The door slicked open. A polished gruntdome appeared.

"You busy?" Speaker filled the doorway. Tartan yellow corduroy shirt, sleeves rolled up. Popeye forearms, boulder shoulders. Broad, sculpted face. Softened by chipmunk cheeks.

Yaz stared at the buffed, hairless skull. Skin pulled tight. Like a bandit mask.

"Yes and no," Mitch said. "What's new, Stew?"

"Goodfellow send you anything yet?" Mischief in his tone.

"Yeah," Mitch nodded. "Before. Why?"

"Juicy has the details. Ask her." A smirk and he was gone.

Mitch brought up the attachment again. Wrinkled his brow. "Well, I guess it's a lead." Glanced at Yaz. "Of sorts."

Yaz waited, expectant.

"I'm to contact this…Dr. Talia over at Sunnyside. Apparently she has something hot. Or is something hot," Mitch amended. McMichael's manner suspicious. They worked out together occasionally. Friendly rivalry. With bite. Jimmy M. the top martial arts wizard. Brazilian jujitsu. Mossad commando shit. But Mitch had bumped him on the staff chart. Rumours McMichaels had been passed over for the terrorgator opening in favour of Mitch. An outsider. Didn't sit well with some guys at first.

Mitch found that out goofing around in the locker room one afternoon. Jimmy M demonstrating an escape move. Pinned on his stomach. Mitch leaned in at the wrong time. Never saw it coming. Accident. Mostly. Staggered him. Right eye ballooned. Spent the week hearing people tell him to watch the high sticks. Stop walking into doors. Stop cheating on his girlfriend. The usual high comedy routines.

In addition to the injury, though, Mitch sensed more than a few spectators enjoyed seeing the insult given. New guy takes one. How it should be. Mitch kept his head straight. Worked hard. Eventually, the guys warmed up. And things had gone well ever since.

Still, McMichaels had a joker rep to rival Mitch's. Leaned more towards the razor-blades-in-your-gym-socks variety. No shortage of the type at CORE. Mitch's hands not clean in that regard. Imagined past triumphs. Chuckled to himself. Mort's corpse. Anderson and a few others in on that. Then there was the time back in mid-December. He and a few of the boys iced down the AGO stairs and railings one evening. So-called Pride thing being held inside. Art faggos blowing each other's horns.

Mitch and team, camped out in a parked Grinder. Stones throw from the bottom of the steps. Music cranked. Night binocs, box of beer on hand. Ready for the show.

Sure enough, out the pillow-biters poured. Excellent display of acrobatics to follow as the place emptied. First wave did the top step can-can. Then the hippy-dippy shake and shuffle. Dancing Nancies everywhere, dipping, diving, plunging. Then brutal bounce and slide across cold cement teeth.

Lemming charge. Cliff sighted. Can't stop. Frantic clutching, shrieking. Brilliant banana peel backflips. Hysterically funny. Grinder shaking side to side.

Area paramedics pooled donations. Covered Mitch's beer outlay. Early alert. Arrived in time to witness the follies. Grateful for the overtime. And the free giggles.

So suspicions triggered. Hoped there wasn't a burning bag of shit in his future. Or formedehyde sandwiches. Not with a new guy tagging along.

Mitch noticed Yaz's expression. Explained.

"I hate doctors is all." Scratched his nose. "Have to introduce you to Juicy sometime, though. I share her with another couple of agents. She's kind of the office…goddess. She's…great. Great guns, great ass, great face, great personality. The only not-great thing. She's married. And that's MFS."

Yaz leaned forward. No expression change. Mitch guessed puzzled.

"MFS…male figure skater," Mitch said, rising. "Cockney for sucks penis."

Pocketed his smokes. Ran his hand over the uni. Cursed under his breath. Tapped impatiently on the surface. The holo changed colours. Flickered out. Came on again. Mitch sighed. Brought his fist down on the laminate surface. Hard.

"C'mon! Work right, for fuck sakes!"

The image winked out altogether. Appeared suddenly above the desk's opposite corner. Mitch slumped in despair. "Fuck me. Made-in-fucking-Bhutan software."

He checked his com time against the uni's. Same. Rolled his shoulders. Always tightened up when tech went toilet.

"Shit. I don't have time to finesse this thing right now. Not and give you the dime tour. Plus rendezvous with some labcoat."

Mitch gave Yaz the hopeful gaze. "You wouldn't be a uni moonie, would ya'?"

Yaz cocked his head to the side. Rotated his right hand. Prayed Mitch didn't check his background. UBC wasn't Waterloo. But a degree in computer science still read that way. One thing he didn't need was an albatross reputation.

Mitch took a deep breath. Held it. Zen mind control. Played his fingers about the black top. No change. "I swear…I generate some kind of…electrical charge. You'd think it worked for the government the way it stops for no reason."

The Milligan hard-done-by sigh. "Guess I could call in Tex Savvy again. I like my way better. Keep hitting until it self-corrects. You'd be surprised how often that works. And not just with computers."

Mitch hammered his fist on the transparent aluminum. Mostly for Yaz's benefit. Incredibly, the holoimage sprang back into place. Big and bold. Mitch, fist pump of joy.

"There you go!" he exclaimed. "Command presence. Let'em know who's boss. They straighten up and fly right."

"Congratulations." Yaz slid his finished cigarette into the annihilator.

"Yeah, well, we'll see," Mitch said. Made a face. "Been acting twitchy lately. Must have spring fever. I know I do. Thought I smelled green this morning, you know?"

Words no sooner out of his mouth then Mitch saw the reflection. Dark shadows. Turned to the window. Groaned.

"Great! Fucking snow again!" Watched the sodden flakes sink past. Hit the blocker. Enough of that depressing shit.

"Get much snow in China?"

Yaz paused before answering. "Not sure. Hardly any in Vancouver, as a rule."

"Oh, yeah. You said you lived there."

"There was one year where we got a fair bit, but usually…"

"Not during the Olympics, ha, ha," Mitch needled.

Yaz missed the reference. "Lots of snow in the mountains. Have you visited Whistler?"

Mitch shook his head. "Nah. Changed planes once in Vancouver. To get to L.A. Been to Calgary. Relatives. That's it for the West. Had a buddy in high school who went out there one year. Became a cowboy."

"Calgary?"

"No, B.C., believe it or not. Guess there's some big-ass ranches out there. Somewhere. He went to…Cowboy U." Mitch paused to marvel at the concept.

"Made it through. Can't imagine the final exam. Rope ten cows in ten minutes or something."

Mitch tood. Pulled winter gloves from a wall compartment.

"Anyway, he 'graduated,'" Mitch said. Made quote marks in the air. "Went right out. Bought a gun, a pickup, a horse and a hat. So he's a cowboy. Sent me a digi of him on one once. Up in the mountains, I guess. Up to its ass in snow. Go, Dougie. Rope them dogies."

Leaving prep. Yaz watching, silent.

"So…you can speak Chinese, yeah?" Mitch asked. Leaned against the door jamb. Putting off his assignment.

Yaz paused again. Replied, "I'm afraid not."

"Too bad," Mitch said.

"Would that help in this job?"

"Not really," Mitch answered. "At least, not now. But who knows in the future? They're probably taking over someday. Wouldn't hurt to know a few words. Sure as hell more use than French."

"Actually…" Yaz began. Mitch held up his hand. Launched into a coughing jag. Apologized. "Shit. Sorry. Don't know where that came from."

"I can speak a little Japanese," Yaz continued. "Not enough to…do more than get around, order food, ask directions. That kind of stuff."

Mitch realized what Yaz was saying. Searched for anything he knew about Japan. Nothing.

"You like teriyaki?" he asked.

"Love it," Yaz said.

"Beautiful," Mitch clapped his hands together. "I know a great place. But it's way the fuck out in Bramladesh. Yoshi's. Excellent food. Big portions. Not today, though." Glanced at his wall digi. "We're too late. It'll be packed by now. Firefags and meatchariot crews. Always get in first. Fucking locusts. But when we get the chance, definitely get you out there. The owner's a real Japanese guy. Like, from Japan. Maybe you know him."

Yaz offered the barest hint of a smile.

Mitch laughed. "I'm kidding, kidding. Yoshi's great, though. Super friendly. You'll like him."

"Sounds good. I haven't had a chance to…find my way around Toronto yet. I'm still…"

"I understand," Mitch nodded. "Get squared away. After, I'll have one of the girls whip up a list of places near wherever you live. CORE believes in eating well. Crap food, crap body. That kind of thing." Scratched his cheeks again. Duty called. No getting away from it. Alphonsed Yaz out of his office.

THE DIME TOUR

"Okay." Mitch bounced on his feet. "Let's do this thing proper. Show you your locker. Look in on some people you should meet. Then we shut her down early. Flock off. Sound like a plan?"

Yaz was ready. Followed Mitch like they were roped together. Mitch struck again. Seeing him walk in the glass reflection. Guy seemed to float over the nap. Rolled on his feet. Good balance. Mitch wondered if a test was in order. See what they taught over at the Force. Commissioner might be interested. Knew Political and a few others would be. See how the kid functioned in the world. Might be some laughs in it, too. Always an important consideration.

Mitch wanted to close shop early for another reason. The mule nose had promised him a bang-up dinner. Mitch wasn't letting her off the hook. She better be slaving over a hot Weber. He'd know why not otherwise.

So a majestic slab of beef with all the fixin's would be sizzlin' under the lid. Five pounds of lip-smacking glory. Free. Help a butcher, help yourself. Man had even provided the brick. Neatly knotted into a pillow case. The former son-in-law would drink from a straw for months. Maybe forever. Mitch's knuckles untouched. Win-win contract.

Walking the hallway, Mitch imagined himself entering the condo. He could smell that beautiful roast. Pictured it on its pedestal. Proud. A stringbound tower. Bulldog squat and solid. Its tender flesh riddled with garlic spears. Mesquite briquets flaring and flaming. Making succulent the meat. Shiny sweat trickling slowly down its browning flanks. Filling the pan below. Gravy, baby, gravy.

Salvage the drippings. Gently stir in flour as the meat meditates. Butt slap the chef should she get sloppy. Care required. Ladle result into porcelain boat. Rescue shelled spuds, onions and carrots. Place on table beside resting roast.

Steamed broccoli. (Nod to Andrea's figure.) Basket of buttered Scotch baps. Cold Corona standing guard. Mitch salivated. Grandmother's customary prayer of gratitude. That Burns offering. 'Lord bethankit' something. Then… the royal moment—carve, serve, devour. Bliss.

Gorge concluded, hit the leather. Watch the Leafs crush…whoever. Give Andrea time to scrub the kitchen clean. Hit the sack after the hot stove shutdown. Reward the little strumpet with an hour of ecstasy. Straight-ahead, no frills pronging that Andrea, like all of her kind, needed more than air. Follow up his glorious performance with seven hours of the dreamless.

Mitch and Yaz approached the admin. area. Fast pace. Sensors registered their collarc chips. Access granted. No luscious lap ladies on view. Row of blue lights over the main conference room. Something on. Mitch hestitated. Decided not to announce himself in the usual fashion. House behaviour wasn't for outsiders. And Yaz was a guest with a secret agenda. Detour in order. Head-wave left.

"Changed my mind," Mitch said. "Suits. Always best to avoid them. No good ever comes from meeting them." Shepherded Yaz up the next set of stairs. Opaque walls. Pounding music. Grunts and curses. The weight room. Mitch buzzed them in.

Pretty busy for the afternoon. Virtual boxing unit occupied. Gord dealing with Sonny Liston. Full sweat on. Swinging hard.

"Not landing many, there," Mitch yelled as they passed. Third round, man had registered only two hits.

"Fucker won't stand still," came the tortured reply.

Mitch smiled. Through and on. Recognized most of the guys. Polite nods. Pointed out the obvious for Yaz. Flashing monitors. Sleek metal machines. Racks of protein mix, organic 'roid bars. Muscle bulkup underway.

Two graybeards worked the botmasters. Mitch raised a hand. In the corner, an agent he hadn't talked to in ages. Headed over, Yaz behind.

"Anders!" Mitch shouted. Dutch blood-thrash seeped out from silvery earpeas. The man stopped in mid-crunch. Grizzly big. Eyes as bad. Squinted, plowed brow. Offered a large grin when he finally scoped out his visitor. Paused the sound. Sweat-toweled a face mis-hacked from granite. All rough edges and hard right angles. Gave the CORE sign to Mitch. Took in Yaz with placid, cobalt blue eyes.

"Don't stop on my account, guy," Mitch said. "Saw you and…thought I'd do a quick intro is all."

"No worries," the man said. A voice unlike any Yaz had ever heard. Paper shredder.

He rose up from the bench. Shook hands with Mitch. Yaz stared at a CORE tattoo. Middle bicep. Same height as he was. Meaning the pyramid must be over 200 cm tall. Mitch confirmed the guess later. Anders "Cliff" Salming. 6'10", 350 lbs. Yaz had met enormous men at various Force gatherings. None were bigger than the sunblocker chatting with Mitch.

Greet complete, Mitch ran through Yaz's folder. A minute of jocktalk followed. Then Mitch slapped the man on the shoulder. Nodded his head at Yaz. They moved away.

"Flexercise suit," Mitch said in answer to Yaz's question. "Just in. First I've seen it. Me want."

They moved swiftly. Small talk. Murders, mayhem, promotions. The corridor opened up. An atrium appeared. Artificial sunlight filled the room. Yaz blinked at brightness. Not harsh. Gentle, intensely yellow illumination. Note for the report. Mini reactor powerplant in evidence.

Great vines hung from grid rafters above. A forest of plant life visible everywhere. The rich smell of turned loam rode up to them. Wet. Vancouver. Yaz had to breath in.

Mitch saw it. Smiled. "Yeah, I do that too." Pointed at a row of box gardens attached to the far facing. Yaz arched his eyebrows in surprise. Plump, still green tomatoes hung off cyclone-shaped metal cyclinders braced every few feet.

"Beefsteaks," Mitch said, reading his mind. "Over there…" he stopped. Eyes directed further down.

"Corn?" Yaz said, confounded. "In winter?"

"CORE labs. Hydroponics. GM, of course. Dedicated radiation. We got lettuce, cabbage, potatoes, cucs. Power veggies. You name it, we grow it. Quality shit, too. Lots a trace minerals. Even the zucchini isn't bad. And I always hated it."

Yaz had questions. Too late. Mitch was moving again. Momentum carried them through peculiar domed areas. Mitch wasn't forthcoming on their purpose.

"Fucking huge, eh? That guy?" Topic jump. Yaz agreed, half-jogging to keep up. White walls, shaded windows passed by. Yaz committed as much as possible to memory. Theatres, halls, analyst dens. Science wing came and went. Remembered it. Intriguing chemical smells. Cordite, bleach, magnetized air, spent electron vapour. Weapon testing facilities. Quartermasters, legal affairs, communications…Yaz worked to keep everything straight. The place was a hive of activity. Force estimates as to CORE personnel levels were well off, Yaz realized. They had an army.

"If I told you what that guy's regular job is," Mitch said over his shoulder, "you wouldn't believe me." Mitch slowed. A bar light winked. They stopped in front of a large, semi-transparent door. Milky white. When it slid aside, they entered. Yaz was now perspiring from the pace.

"Accountant." Talking about the goliath again. "No shit," Mitch asserted. "Now. Not before. I mean, if you need someone to pound on OMG's? Angels, Bandidos, Choice, Mongols, Machine? He's your man. Just loves it. But his day job is fucking accounting."

Yaz's handler wanted to specific intel about CORE interests. Crime and justice emphasized. This certainly qualified, in Yaz's mind. "You…he disciplines renegade motorcycle gang members?"

Mitch laughed. "'Disciplines'. I like that. Good word. 'Renegade'. Another. Ah, no. More just…kicks their heads in. Keep'em in line. Used to do it for fun. Before he joined us. He just liked going around to bars. Pick fights with bikers."

Mitch's eyes lit up. He ran his lips over his tongue. Yaz saw the neon light. Guessed this was another in-house bar. Saw Mitch calculating. Slowed but didn't stop.

"His parents are, like, Mormons. Or Mennonites. Something like that. Out west. Saskatchewan, I think. Family problems. Old man went rogue. Became this area hell-raiser. He'd take his sons to the local Bucket o' Blood. Or an Indian bar. Whatever. They'd all get drunk. Start chirpin'. Before you know it, fight's on. And they'd clean the place out. Just the four of them. Great fun. Wish I could a seen it."

Mitch paused. Leaned against an exposed post. Let a clutch of labcoats chatter past. Deep in conversation. No one even looked up from their holopads. Ducks, Mitch thought. Amazing how they never ran into each other.

"It sounds like he's…" Yaz struggled for a polite description.

"Dangerous?" Mitch finished up. "A scout recruited him. CORE paid for his psych rehab. Didn't take much. Turns out, he has a talent for tabulating. Calculator brain. CORE put him through M.I.T. Now he churns out graphs and shit. The two-agents-in-one guy. Can push in your face or help you avoid taxes. In his head."

They entered another high-ceilinged room. Natural light mirrored in this time. Rows of lounge chairs. Several suspended holovids. Nobody in the place. Yaz guessed a general lounge. One of many.

"I overheard somebody being called 'Quazi,'" Yaz said. Crucial keyword identifiers. Possible passwords. Imperative to match them with member's names. At the same time, Yaz was distracted by a tantalizing aroma. Cooking smells flowed over them.

"Yeah," Mitch laughed. "Short for Quasimodo. That giant snowman. You'll hear lots of others. 'Pooch,' 'Political', 'Chemo', 'Scurvy'." The last always made Mitch laugh. "Inside baseball. Let's others know his specialty. Also good for mission security."

Retro French doors next. A warm, yeasty breeze enveloped them. Yaz nearly brought to his kness. Fresh, oven-baked bread. Unmistakeable. Coffee, lemon, onion. Soup! Yaz liked his soup very much. Clear soup. Corn soup. Spicy noodle. Potato and cabbage. Soup was life. Yaz's mother could make the best-tasting soups in the world. Pictured their dining room table at lunchtime. Bamboo place mat. Glass of oolong. Whiff of heavenly miso. The cucumber slices. Delight mingled with yearning. He missed the mountains. The sight of the sun setting. Toronto had no sun. Just a washed out disc one rarely saw. Like Vancouver in December.

Yaz came around. Realized he was standing in a cafeteria. Currents of spicy scents ran under his nose. The room was large yet inviting. More like a private members club. Which it was, in a way.

"What's your nickname?" Yaz asked, trying to focus. They slid past set tables, chairs leaning up, retired.

"Tell you later," Mitch said. Gestured at the walls. "Notice the lighting?"

Yaz quickly scanned the room.

"Muted. No more eating in prison. They had some professional design it," Mitch explained. He stamped his feet. "Parquet flooring. Data archives are right below us. Wait'll you see that fucking place. They'll tell you to the penny how much your parents have parked in the bank."

It took a second for Yaz to catch the drift. "That's private information."

"You wish," Mitch snorted. "Nothing you can't get out of the fed files. Child can do it."

He waved at the table they were skirting. "Fresh flowers on every table. Every day. Red, yellow, white. Pretty. CORE did some florist a favour. This is the reward."

"It's quiet," Yaz observed.

Mitch took that in. Checked his com. "Yeah, you're right. It's almost lunchtime. Should be some kind a action here. Must a missed the memo." Grinned at Yaz. "Been known to happen." Peered under the raylamps. Empty kitchen.

Mitch pushed the door wide. Put his head in. No answer to his hallo. On the stove, several pots. Magnets fired. Mitch's turn to inhale with pleasure. Choice moment. Alone in the larder. Mitch rubbed his hands together. Couldn't resist a chortle. Buzzed inside.

To his right along the wall, condiment trays. Fully prepped. Bone-white crockery in its aluminum warmer. Ready for the charge.

To his left, a matte black expanse. Helo stovework. Spotless. As were the fanhoods. Oven fronts gleamed. Whisker clean countertops. Scrupulous military attention paid to the work environment. Hallmark of CORE's kitchen dictator. The culinary king, Anatole Verron. Highest-paid man in the firm. No arguments. Man could turn out a gravy make workboot leather taste like filet. Mitch would have given up a kidney to ensure dining rights. He worshipped the man…as a god.

Mitch gazed into a massive ceramic tureen. Nearly wept. Inside, whole onions jostled each other, lightly simmering. Carrots surfaced to battle celery sticks. A gauzy steam lifted from the roiling mass. Bathed his face. Mitch sighed. The wonder of bubbling minestrone. Glory.

He waved Yaz close. "Stay here for a sec. I'm gonna check out the back. They can't be far. Shit's still on the boil."

Back in less than a minute. "Staff meeting. Over soon. We can look around till then." Boy-in-gamer-heaven grin.

"It smells…fantastic," Yaz said. His daily lunch diet since moving. Cup Noodle. A station hot dog on occasion. 7-11 calorie bag. The scent of real food a shock. His body physically longed to absorb the goodness.

"Top notch grub," Mitch said. "Really." He opened a freezer door. Did the necessary check. "Soups, chilis, spag, chops…that kind a stuff. They even do a meat loaf your mother'd sign off on. That good. Vegetables, like I said. Lot of fruit, too. Cover the bases. Even the healthy shit tastes not bad. Pretty much. Sometimes you get some scary crap. Eggplant. Ever heard of it? It's fuckin' purple. On the outside."

Yaz nodded. "Sure."

Mitch didn't detect revulsion. The name alone put him off. Egg. Plant. Two words that didn't belong together. God having an off day.

Solitary guffaw from the rear of the kitchen. Mitch scuffed at a brown stain marring the otherwise spotless, lava-red tile. His eyes strayed over the ranks of neo-platinum freezers. Crabs, lobsters, scallops, tuna, salmon packed within.

In the walk-in cooler, hanging sides of beef. Great smoked hams rested on miniature wooden skids. Chickens and turkeys, plump, scrumptious. A plucked duck strung up for unknown crimes. Where the eye landed, delicious dining awaited.

Upright refridgerators sparkled under the overheads. Mitch could only dream of the tasty desserts within. Anatole was famous throughout the organization. No one turned out food like he did. And this cafeteria was his base of operations. He ran all CORE's restaurants and tuck shops from this location. So it was odd the place was on holiday. Something special going on elsewhere, Mitch guessed. That conference had the look of trouble.

Mitch spied the soup bowls. Demon whisper. Closed his ears. Mitch shuddered to think of being blackballed. Anatole got hot about poaching. Unless fish was involved.

Mitch checked the salamanders. No toasted goodie overlooked. Considered guilting Anatole into having a sous chef whip up some clubs to go. Nixed the idea. Better plan surfaced.

Yaz held up a folded sheet of laminated paper. "Is this a menu?" Handed it over to Mitch, who examined it.

"Yeah. This week's. Check it out." Mitch mumbled his way down the list. Skipped the appetizers. "Okay...from tomorrow, I'm guessing. For lunch...we got orgo pork roast medallions stuffed with sage dressing. Always delicious. Baked orgo spuds...herb and garlic butter. Orgo green beans almond... something or other. And fucking orgo carrots in an orgo honey glaze."

Mitch read on. "For dessert. Three kinds of pie, including...yes!! Strawberry-rhubarb! Baby! Ho-ho, ha ha, hey, hey. They're coming to take me away..." Mitch caught Yaz's expression. Misunderstood.

"Yeah, I know. Outta season. Anatole gets all this organic shit from some greenhouse guy in Tillson...something. Or is that the spuds. I forget. Guy from CORE did a an op. for his family. Something the courts went gay on. Payback delivered. So he sets stuff aside in summer. Fast freezes it. Fall delivery. Anatole springs it on us over winter. Genius, yeah?"

Mitch folded the menu back up. Tossed it on the counter. "So...now you got some idea of the grub we get. And this is just one of lunch areas. There's a bunch others. Some we can go to. Some are for the Stars only." Mitch looked up to indicate Command. "Plus the Tank viewing area has a very decent little tuck shop thing going. Sandwiches, great fries, Westerns...Jesus. I'm making myself crazy. What say we pull stakes?"

Yaz held up the menu. "Keep this?"

Mitch shrugged. "Yeah, shit. Why not?"

A door banged open. Excited voices reached where Mitch and Yaz stood. Mitch made the exit gesture. Yaz nodded acknowledgement. Let Mitch lead. They popped into the dishwashing bay. Dishsquid absent. Mitch usually brought him a beer when he visited. A twelve for the cooks every now and then didn't hurt either. It all circled around. One back scratches the other, as Sheridan always said.

They slid out the side door. Mitch glanced at the beer as they passed by. Cases stacked to the ceiling. Sighed. Kept going. Leave the banditry for another day.

They neared the main corridor. Mitch stopped. "You still hungry?"

"I could eat," a ravenous Yaz replied.

"I got this sudden craving myself," Mitch said. Checked his com. "Tell you what. Meet me down front. Five minutes. Lunch, my buy."

"Sounds good," Yaz said.

Mitch skipped through to the stairs. Yaz pulled out his com. Set the camera. On the wall before him, the entire floor map. Click, save, click, save. Backpedaled into the dishpit. Pan vid everything. Into the storeroom. Then the walk-in freezer. Shelves groaned with goods. Armageddon posed no threat. Enough food for a battalion.

His superiors had told him to shoot anything and everything. They'd edit out the irrelevant. Yaz complied. Encrypted the file. Inserted into the building's outgoing signal. No one the wiser.

Two minutes later, flew down the stairs. Mentally reviewed his position in the building. Figured to be at the main entrance exactly on time. No coat, though. Unfortunate oversight. Lobby to carseat. Ignore the weather. Felt his stomach flip with excitement. Realized he rather enjoyed spying. A good deal more exciting than puzzling out firewall flaws or reverse programming.

Mitch waiting in a CORE transpo. And good as his word. The steaks were excellent. Better still, free.

Detect, Inspect, Destroy

——⊷⟨○⟩⊷——

The lounge was half-full of CORE agents by the time Mitch arrived. Yaz in tow, eyes peeled. Sports coats, jeans, gridrunners. The garb of common choice. Leather for the underground crawlers. Corduroy for those sentenced to the commie faculty circuit.

Mitch dressed for the outdoors. Heavy weave plaid shirt, red and black. Straight cut denims, natural fade. Scuffed-up, steel-toed loadie launchers. Cutting wood or cutting up. Mitch ready for anything.

Yaz still had a touch of the prep about him. Felt the scorn. No Hunting World slacks or deck shoes next time.

Tables stocked with beer attracted the thirsty. (Hard liquor banned. Brawling problems. The damages after CORE's first week in existence nearly sank the effort. The lone accountant ready to walk.) A group of CORE vets waved them over. Mitch and Yaz made their way to the back.

Mitch took the frosty Corona. Saluted all. Knew he'd be the only one drinking foreign brew. The oldies still preferred mass-produced backwash. The only thing Mitch envied them was the bottle. Stubbies back in fashion. Everybody loved them. Mitch included. Some things from the past couldn't be topped.

"A question for you, young Milligan." The speaker's eyes alive with high humour. "Bandy" MacDonald. Quip draw artist. Known and feared needler. And a joker. That special January "feast" at his club he invited Mitch and a bunch of rooks to years back. The songs were okay. But when they brought out that stuffed sheep's stomach. Described the contents. Then cut it open. Mitch nearly puked on the spot. Did later anyway. All that goddamned toasting.

"Y-e-a-a-h," Mitch said, on guard.

"Would you ever drink camel piss?"

Mitch heard the snickers. MacDonald setting the gag hook. Craggy gambler face. Bluff, hearty, gave away nothing. Mitch paused to consider his answer. It seemed simple enough. So there had to be a catch.

"Probably not," he admitted. "Unless it's at least 5% alcohol. Why? Got some?"

"No, no," the big man replied. Neighbours shook with silent amusement. "No, Jack here claims that our friends with all the oil have been known to indulge, is all. So we've been doin' a little survey to find out who'd try it."

O' Ryan, a husky bruiser, cauliflour ears, explained. "Like I said before, there's a whole group of people that drink piss. For their health. It's like a... secret...society."

Mitch looked on in disbelief. "Holy shit," he cried. "First pork brains, now camel piss. What the fuck is goin' on?"

"Whaddya' mean?" A bemused Wills glanced around. No one looked any wiser.

"Not a week ago I had Brophy telling me all about people who eat weird shit. You guys must troll through the same sites."

Ben Hogg cut through the laughter. "Long ago people in...desert situations would...drink the piss of whatever animal they were riding. Or driving. No choice. They ran out of water. Hit a dry oasis. Whatever. Piss is mostly water. If you're thirsty enough...you'll drink it."

Angry protestations from the group. Half claiming they'd die first. The other half looking to take bets. See how much someone would take to try it. Then, as often happened, the conversation slid off the rails. Speculation about the worst tasting piss? Best tasting? Chilled or room temperature? How much is too much?

"I'd do it for ten grand. Hell, yeah." Clarkie. Big grin looked like a wheel track in the three day growth of beard. Mitch knew he wasn't bullshitting. Everybody knew. Original crazy man. Anything for a laugh. Or a buck.

"Goat piss might be okay," someone offered.

"Milk it, barbecue it...fuck it," Weimer joked. "Those goats must start to wonder after awhile."

"I don't think you can eat them after you fuck them," an agent behind Mitch said. "I read that somewhere. Or you can if you...like...purify them first."

And the argument was on.

"How do you fucking purify a goat?"

"Who'd want to eat them in the first place? Or bone them?"

"Can't say no till you've said yes."

"Jesus, you're a sick fuck. You know that?"

"What site you read that on?"

"I read about a guy in the States who got caught fucking chickens once. Rich guy, too."

"What about those morons in Seattle who fuck horses?"

"No, man, worse. The horses fuck them!"

"Get away from me!"

"True story, swear to God. One of them died from a blown asshole." Hysterical laughter greeted this news.

"No shit. His bum-buddies dumped him out at the hospital. Him and his ass were all over the steps." Guys falling over at the image. Party mood now. You never knew where the talk might go.

"Only one? Not enough."

"Not that it matters but...we're not talking like...those Budweiser horses, right?"

"Think they got bigger dicks than donkeys? I saw a flick once where..."

"After a certain point, I don't think it matters. Why not just ram a baseball bat up your butt and be done with it."

"Percherons are fucking huge, man. You need to be big to pull a beer wagon."

"Those aren't Percherons."

"The hell they aren't."

"I don't know. I'm pretty sure they're the other kind."

"What other kind?"

"You know."

"No. That's why I'm fucking asking you."

"Clydesdales. That the one?"

"Yeah! Clydesdales. Those big mothers with the furry hooves."

"I got fifty of the best says it's not Clydesdales."

"Guys, guys," Gary Epps objected. Freckles scrunched together in disgust. "I'm barbecuing tonight."

"Hope it's not goat."

"No, steaks. I'd rather not listen to this shit, though."

"You're barbecuing in this weather?"

"Yeah, in the garage. Leave the door open. No problem."

"So, Mitch," MacDonald smirked. Switched gears smoothly. "what'd you think of the meeting this morning?"

"Those bitches...must be put down. Hard." Burst of appreciative ho-hoing.

"Glad to see the 'spurts didn't interrupt your snooze." Over the shoulder comment. Ice cube avalanche. Beer hunt underway

"Not at all," Mitch said to more laughter. "Oh, shit. By the way, this is Yaz. He's going to be...partnering me for a while. He's with...was with...the competition."

"Hoo-wheee. Free tickets to the Musical Horseshit." Fraser. No love lost for his old employer.

"Weimar'd be happy. He just wants to try some of that horse piss."

"Long as it's cold and fizzy," Weimar replied.

Brickhouse pulled the thread back. Stared at Yaz. "So you must have come across this group with the Force, eh?"

Yaz cleared his throat. Centre of attention now. Felt like a squirrel among redwoods. Ambush? Catch him up? Hard to know. Assume yes.

"Actually, until today, I'd never even heard them."

"Nothing?" Hogg, skeptical.

"I was mostly in counter-espionage. Interpol. FBI. CSIS. Data-exchange. Chatter monitoring."

"Famous But Incompetent. Canadian Society of Incontinent Suckholes. Nice job." Fraser again. Grudge-nursing master.

"So they've parachuted you in to see how a real security organization runs, have they?" Jenkins slipped in the knife. A few chuckles. All eyes remained fixed on Yaz. The stranger in their midst.

Mitch felt obliged to come to the guy's defense. "The Commissioner said he wants…communication with other agencies. Yaz is the Force's lia…lai… rep."

"The Commissioner likes Mitch," Epps sing-songed. Kissed the back of his hand.

"You have to give head to get ahead," Mitch responded. Rolled his tongue inside his cheek. The tension lifted. Fag mime. Always comical.

"Mitch tells me this is mostly a Toronto issue, the murders. Shouldn't the police handle matters?" Yaz asked.

Hoots and chuckles. Mitch held his hands out, palms up. "C'mon, guys. He's just in from the Wet Coast."

"Yeah, I heard," Hogg rumbled. Dismissive tone. Old line Ontario. Anything north of Barrie might as well have been on the moon. Of no importance.

"Well here's an alert," the man snarled. "Cops in Dumbville are called Doughnut Pro's for a reason. They're hamstrung by the courts. The media, the socialist fuck politicians, they don't care about crime. They like crime. They think it means poor people are stealing bread for their families." Line got laughs.

"So the fucking hippies turned the cops into tax collectors. They're not supposed to catch crims. All they're supposed to do is hand out tickets. Make everything illegal. Everyone's guilty. Pay the fine. Wealth redistribution without representation."

"Cops got the picture." Wills picked up the story. "They're just fucking… shakedown artists. Only they work for the state instead of the Mafia."

"Same difference," somebody said. Mutters of agreement.

"And crims get a free ride. Things are rigged so it's more bother than it's worth to arrest anyone. They're back on the street before you cc your report. Lock up gang bangers? You're a racist. Notify parents their kid's teacher is a fucking diddler? Teachers Union gets vid time. Accuses everyone of being homohaters. YOU get charged. Who needs it?" Epps looked to spit somewhere in disgust.

"So most of them just noodle around in those ecojokes. Hang out at Tim's. Pretend to work by answering the odd call. Write down the victim's name and address. Never go back." Hogg, bitter.

"Put in your thirty. Pension time. See you at the cottage." MacDonald again. Knowing chortles. Bottle clinking from the cottage-owners present.

"Unless he transfers here," ex-cop Shaun Stewart said, hand up. Applause from everyone.

"You'll know things have changed," Hogg continued, "the day you get something stolen returned." Snorts and sarcastic laughing.

"Let's hope that day is coming." Mitch put his oar in.

Yaz listened carefully. Taking the pulse. The front line cynicism was similar at the Force. Everyone felt their hands were tied. It caused some to go rogue. Look for fights. Or round known perps up. Take them out for evening classes in the park. Expedite matters with the systematic use of rabbit punches to the groin.

Knowing this didn't make him feel less the hobbit. Like standing beside foundation blocks. Fortunately, the initial distrust had evaporated. The mood less adversarial. Opinions stated, Yaz had fallen off the interest grid. Suited him fine.

As Yaz celebrated invisibility, Mitch wandered a private memory trail. A grizzled agent held court. Spiny eyebrows working. Listed D.P. benefit programs. Perqs. Pro sports tickets. Stripper outings. Overtime options. Man's long, lived-in face reminded him of a great-uncle. His mother's side. Dead now. Liver gave out. But he had the same bird-of-prey look. Not much got past him, the old man would say. And not for long.

Deadpan storyteller, Mitch recalled. Smallburg good old boy. Like his father. He and his wife visited every five years. The two men would get to yammering over drinks. Solve the world's problems over a crib board. Tell some tall ones. Two tales Mitch never forgot. Odd to think of it. They were cardinal principles of life for him now.

In tiny gas stops all over the West, the Chinese restaurant a farmer's second home. His great-uncle, other farmers would meet there most mornings. After chores. Farmer talk over coffee. Weather. Politics. Hockey. Second breakfast. Maybe a hot hamburg if lunch was closer. Jabbering with whoever came in.

If things got slow, you could count on someone to liven things up. Pull a leg. Take the piss. Nothing too juvenile it wouldn't get a laugh. Loosen the salt cellar top. Switch salt for sugar. Vice versa. Itching powder worked into bumwad. Toss firecrackers over the stall wall. Some days, they'd cement a twonie to the sidewalk. Pull up to the plate glass window. See how many gorbies fell for it. Watch'em scrabble at the coin. Kick at it, toe and heel. Finally give up. Great entertainment. You could only bitch about the commie CWB so often, after all.

And then one August bikers arrived in town. Real excitement. Blew through from the highway spur. Hit the drive-in. Started harassing the kids there. Bullied their way into the kitchen. Scarfed down the burgers being grilled. Ordered up more. Threatened the cooks. Busted shit. Bikers being bikers. Oversized assholes at large.

Mitch's great-uncle and the crew were just about to order lunch. News came over the phone. One of the regulars had a kid working tables there. She'd managed to call it in. Ten minutes later a dozen pickups surrounded the drive-in. More arrived every few minutes. Came from all over. Gunracks emptied as soon as they slammed to a stop.

Great-uncle Henry, two buddies stroll into the drive-in. Loaded shotguns in hand. They have the biker's attention immediately. Quiet reigns. Henry explains the situation. As they're talking, empty cattle-hauler hits the gravel. Back gate touches ground before the dust cleared. Two farmers to a bike. They humped them up the chute. None too gently, to hear the man tell it. Trailer hadn't been cleaned either. Slippy going.

Hauler leaves. Bikers are told their rides would be a mile out of town. Couldn't miss them. Just look for the shiny pile of chrome dumped in a windrowed wheat field. Said the machines and their owners had best not be anywhere in the vicinity come sundown. It's over. Twenty glum bikers troop out the door. Head up the road. Weren't seen again. No cops required. And that little town of wheat and cattle farming rednecks north of Calgary? Never had a problem with bikers again.

"Word must a spread," Henry chuckled. Dug at ear thatch. Gray hair sprang out of his head like ditchweed, Mitch remembered. Saw the man clear as if was in the room. Elbows on the table. Cradling his whiskey in those walnut brown catcher's mitts. Arms like pig iron. Cough any smoker would be proud of. Badlands face. Gullies etched and worn by years of outside hoist and shove. Years spent jouncing on a tractor or combine. Eyes had retreated into his head. A bad sign. But who could believe it then? Man was a rock.

Mitch sat still on his chair. Rarely spoke. Old-time rules. Kids were to be seen. Cuffed or kicked if they spoke out of turn. But his great-uncle Henry was cool. Didn't treat him like he should be elsewhere. Just picked at the ever-present plate of perogies. Glanced down every now and again. Checking to see if he'd gone to bed yet.

Mitch could still see the yellow-over-white check shirt, too. The corny Western necktie. Silvery-gray go-to-church cowboy hat. Weighing down the coatrack. Man even wore cowboy boots. Unique for Mitch. Never seen them in the Kap. Swore they were the most comfortable footwear a man could own. Once they got worked in. Said he had four pair. Seemed rich to Mitch. Still thought they looked like high heels for men. Wisely kept that opinion to himself. Alberta, though. You had to love it. Had that aura. It's own country.

The other story, a curling tale. Mixed bonspiel the man and his wife had entered. Both top curlers. A takeout dispute in the hack. All Mitch could summon from recall was the spirited punchline: "No hundred-and-forty pound woman tells me what to do!" Too true. Always made him laugh to think of it.

Without realizing it, Mitch had embraced those twin philosophies of life. If it's important, figure out how to do it yourself. Or with friends. Looking for outside help is gay. Put on a dress if that's your answer to problems.

Second. Never take shit from a woman. For any reason. They won't respect you for it. Doesn't matter what idiot femmes say. Of course, listening to blather in exchange for fur burger was the exception to the rule. Some things were unavoidable.

"...if it's a real citizen, like the little girl took a bullet before Christmas that one year..." Hogg talking. Mitch in the now. "You turn over every rock. Find the little shit gangbanger. On the other hand, if it's some lowlife bleeding out another lowlife...well...who cares in the end? The wheel always turns."

"And the taxpayer isn't hooked for jail expense," Mankowski noted.

"Amen to that," Mitch said. Turned towards Yaz. "So we're saying... anyone found in the drink or a ditch...like my dead slot...has probably crossed some scum line. Topsoil sandwich. Whoever did the blading will get it back before long. C'est la vie dans la grand ville." Only French Mitch knew. Meant 'shit happens, so crack another can'. Intermissions over. Ref's about to drop the puck.

"Except the corpses are starting to pile up a bit." The elephant in the hot tub. Hogg scratched at his beard. Raised a finger for another beer. Caught it.

"Hey," Mitch said. "What are you doing here?"

The "knight" he'd been prepped by a few days before. Jameson, Mitch thought his name was. Metro detective. A front. CORE analyst and recruiter his real job. Upstairs wheel.

The detective offered a group smile. Wrestled a bottle free from the icepack. Drained half upon opening it.

"Hard night?" someone asked.

"Lake work," the detective replied.

Mitch marveled at the face. He'd seen meth heads looked less nervy.

"Rumours true, then?" someone asked.

Jameson nodded. "Looks like it."

Mitch glanced at Yaz. "Cunt Ovarians! This is what we're up against. Pure whacko's."

"But no one knows why they're attacking...prostitutes?" Yaz said.

"Preliminary update from forensics," Jameson said. Fought down a yawn. "She was holed earlier, then dumped. Like most of the others."

Yaz's earlier question still hung in the air. Someone took a deep breath. Exhaled slowly. Mitch shot a look around. "It really doesn't make any sense, right?"

"NHI's now," Jameson said, "but what happens when they start in on real people? That's when it gets serious. We have to be ready. A shitstorm of some sort is coming."

Yaz caught Mitch's eye. Guessed the reason for the arched eyebrow. "No human involved. Cop shorthand."

"So Metro isn't any more clued in?" Hogg asked.

Jameson snorted. Took another pull of his bottle.

Answer provided. Mitch hitched his pants. "Okay, different question. What kind of an idiot would put out in a boat...at night...in this weather... and deposit a...wormy corpse for us to find?"

"A...fanatic." Jameson said without hesitation. Flicked his empty into the nearby hempsack.

"Beautiful. Like we don't have enough headcases to go around." Mitch felt his com vibrate.

"They know CORE is circling," Jameson reminded everyone. "They're baiting us. Or cleaning house. Nights of the long knives? Weak links disposed of?"

As the agents chewed on that, Jameson made to leave. "Gentlemen, thanks for the beer. I'd like to stick but I'm dead on my feet."

"Because of old," Hogg jibed.

"Sad but true," Jameson agreed. "If I squint any harder, I'm gonna start looking like this guy," he joked, pointing at Yaz.

The oppressive Ovarian weight lifted. Agents shared amused looks. Yaz accepted the gentle jest with a good-natured grin.

Mitch saw Jameson's head nod as he exited. Understood the message. Held up a finger to Yaz. One minute. Joined Jameson outside the lounge.

"What's up?"

Jameson waved Mitch deeper into the corridor. Agents entering saw several seconds of animated conversation. Then Jameson patted Mitch on the arm. Turned and was gone. Mitch returned to a circle of curious agents.

"My ears are burning. You girls talking about me?" Hogg asked.

Mitch maintained the mask. Held a finger to his lips. Looked at Yaz. Whispered softly into his ear, "There's other fingers in the hairpie, it seems." Which had no meaning for Yaz. He stared ahead, baffled.

"Oh, shit," Jasper slurred. "I'm fucking drunk." It was his first and only contribution to the conversation. Five beers in less than an hour. Had already decided to call it a day. The whole Ovarian business depressed him. Plus, getting hammered before noon made him sleepy. His sofa more comfortable than his desk. Far more comfortable. Grabbed one more for the road. Fortunately, CORE had special DUI privileges. Never a worry about getting behind the wheel after having a few.

"So why does the Force have a spy here?" MacDonald asked. Stone face. Spidery veins on his nose visible. MacDonald fond of his Crown.

They knew all along! It was a trap! Yaz hid his horror. Expression never varied. Be the duck, his father advised. Calm and collected on the surface. Paddling furiously under water.

"I swear. This is the first time I've even heard about...Ovarians."

MacDonald exploded in laughter. "Jesus, don't sweat it. Pulling your chain is all. I couldn't care less if you were a spy. I know lots a guys on the Force. They only wish they could work here, believe me. Don't say anything positive. We don't got room for everyone."

Yaz didn't have to fake relief. "I appreciate that...but I'm serious. They... my superiors...told me nothing." Half a lie. "Just...learn how things were done here. Study the culture." Whole lie.

"No culture here," Sims observed. Belched to prove it.

"Thtop it, you brute," Mitch lisped. "And keep thtopping it."

Which triggered lots more gay dialect. Festival of insults followed. When-I-rattle-my-zipper wit. Each more obscene than the last. Mitch steered Yaz away after a few minutes of comic back-and-forth. He'd accomplished what he wanted. Walked Yaz through. Gave everyone a look-see.

"I didn't know anything about this group," Yaz protested. "Until you told me..."

Mitch waved him down. Hard right and into the corridor. "Yeah, yeah, don't worry. That's not what I was meaning." Mitch glanced over his shoulder. No one near. "There's something going on between CORE and the Force."

"What?"

"Unknown. Just that both have ops running. So we might be in the middle of major league corporate clusterfuck. Or we're supposed to be info reconning each other. I don't know. Wheels within wheels." Mitch running the long game Jameson suggested.

Yaz looked at the floor, thinking. The news didn't gibe with his instructions. It was possible. One or both of them being set up. It would explain certain mysteries. Why a vigorously recruited but still low level "digit-shifter," as Mitch described his job, got this assignment? What the purpose might be, he had no idea.

"It could be they…want to avoid…collisions."

Yaz nodded. "Sure."

"Odd you'd show up when you did, though," Mitch said. "Just when there's a push on."

"They told me of the transfer two months ago. Toronto made more sense than Ottawa. I didn't even know why until a week ago."

Mitch patted his pocket. "Look, let's hit my office. Have a smoke. Think this out."

Yaz peered over Mitch's shoulder. No one had followed them out. "I feel guilty and I haven't done anything," he said.

Mitch snorted. Rolled his shoulders. "The best thing for guilt is another beer. The best thing for any problem is another beer. Let's go." They tooled off down the corridor. Never looked back.

BLEACHED WHALES:
THE SAGA OF BELINDA AND MELINDA

---◀ ○ ▶---

P arty in full swing when Mitch arrived. CORE agents packed like rifle
shells around the bar. Everyone bellowing jokes. Laughing. MetroDP
streamers torn from the walls. Trampled underfoot. CORE colours only this
night.

Tobacco smoke cast a welcome haze over the action. From the speakers,
two guitars clashed. "FrankenNazi Gung Ho!" Septic's new high-voltage
webtopper. Uploaded, pumpin' d-bels.

Properly topless waitresses wiggled and wriggled around. Took orders,
got goosed, giggled. Mitch pinched a passing tit. CORE perk. Cherry Bell,
her work password. She turned. Flashed affection. Fiddled with top button
on Mitch's jeans. Slid her free hand down the zipper. Expertly caressed the
cucumber. Mitch leaned forward. Tempted to gnaw her ear to a bloody nub.
Tongued it instead. Ran two fingers through the gap. Silky soft plum punash.
She moaned. Nearly dropped her drink tray. Gave Mitch the naughty boy
finger dance. Slid away.

Mitch watched her sultry rump twitch into the mix. Exhaled slowly.
Looked around. Another blowout bash underway. CORE could throw a
party. And this jump-up looked promising. Some special occasion, he thought.
Everyone looked primed for a good time. Mitch there for business, technically.
But he never turned his nose up at fun.

He made for the bar. Sidestepped a booze puddle on the way. BeerBev
on hands and knees, bartoweling it up. Mitch rubbed her head for luck.
Continued on.

The crush of bodies made progress difficult. As well, Mitch kept running
into friends. Small talk and group turbulance slowed him down. It took ten
minutes before he shouldered his way to the oasis. Two Burlies let Mitch

squeeze an elbow between them. Star treatment. He grinned thanks. If they had names, he couldn't remember them.

The taps were getting hard use. Mitch tried to catch a lackey's eye. No luck. They all moved at lightspeed. CORE blew in thirsty. Mitch waited, uncommon patient. Rapped three times for luck on the bar top. Pride of Billy's Club. Wildly expensive. So the pro's claimed. It could accommodate forty customers, half sitting. Built from Indonesian teak. Illegally imported. Sleek, solid, spectacular. Inlaid mother-of-pearl tracings from berms to bottom. Translucent, carbon-fiber protective glaze. Hand-tooled from a single aged trunk by Zen cabinetmakers. A professional drudge polished it every week.

It had been installed free. Courtesy of a grateful Muskoka cottager. One with deep pockets. Rumours flew. Mick, the manager, had evidently done the subject a serious favour. Exact story a mystery. But Mick was O.C. From when CORE was a loose collection of operatives. Seat-of-the-pants payback operations. Lots of leeway. Fresh grave business.

Whatever the origin, it was a great bar. Damage it, you answer to Mick. Bruise tattoos and a long limp home for offenders.

A gorgeous face suddenly appeared in front of Mitch. Not uncommon. Mitch drew beauty like taxes attract activists.

"Hey, handsome. Need servicing?" Priss eyes, sultry smile, Ukrainian cleavage.

"The powerplant needs a recharge. Can you help?"

"I just might. What does it usually take?"

"Corona, Sharona. Go from there."

"Back with the glass, if you got the cash." Joke. CORE event. Leave the chipclip at home. As she pivoted, a pink tongue snaked out from between porcelain teeth. Slow liquid slide over rose lips. Mitch imagined popping one into his mouth. Gnawing into that savoury, succulent flesh. Made him salivate.

As she walked her udders away, Mitch finally placed her. She was a Churyshyn. Mick's niece. Or sister-in-law. Something like that. He'd seen her a few times before. Weeknights. A few agents had mentioned wanting to tap her keg. She pulled handle with authority. Mitch hadn't given her much thought. Too young. Mitch had mostly done with breaking in fillies. He preferred working on someone who knew how tab 'B' fit into slot 'A'. But the night and light was making him think twice. Now there were two giant wooden bars in the room Pity she was related to Mick.

She returned with his bottle. Set it gently on the coaster. Framed the fence. Looked into his soul.

"How's Western?" Mitch with the casual reference.

She paused. Spun back. "Alright. How did you know I go there?"

"Your uncle told me." Mitch leaned in. Raised his voice. "Third year. Polysci. Says you're going to be a wheel someday."

She flushed at the praise. Gave him an altogether different look. She held up her right index finger. Mitch understood. To be continued. She moved on to deal with the other banshees. Shy smile of pleasure creased the complexion. Mitch was content. Charm. Nine-parts shameless flattery. One part pure oil.

He'd barely finished his first swallow. Felt a jab in his ribs. About to level a reckless glare at the neighbouring Burlie. Heard a chuckle. Craned his neck rearwards. Max Hatchett standing behind. In the flesh. Of which there was plenty. Perma-smirk. Mitch's date. He raised his Corona in recognition. Pasted on a welcome look.

Max had a table. They muscled their way back through the crowd. Found the space. Stage seats, middle in. Room for four in their box. Max's whiskey and ice awaited him. Mitch and the vet dropped. Mirrored sigh of relief.

The old pro put his feet up on the chair opposite. Wheezed from the effort. Mitch pulled out a pack of fresh air. Offered Max one before thinking. Declined. Mitch just then remembered hearing. Man had quit. Getting a lung replaced curbs the urge.

Watched his companion settle into his chair. Sent a lumpy paw through sparse, sandy-coloured hair. Thin, dry. Looked in need of watering. Skin texture a shade of trilight white. Life spent indoors. Near upturned bottles, spouts and spigots. Juicer jowls, jellied eye sacs. Tout squint. From picking lame horses. Wrinkles around the eyes like those Chinese Sham-Wow dogs. Man blinked, a mini-accordion in action.

Mitch followed the gaze. Empty dance floor. Two robotechs whirred away near the stage. Stage lights flashed on and off. The colour spectrum kaleidoscoped down the ceiling. Crossed over a Bev winkling their way. Bathroom bound. Mitch almost reached over. Give her a free rump rove. Held up. Wasn't sure how Max would react. Some guys were uncomfortable treating women as sex objects. Mitch couldn't see it, but why anyone watched soccer was also a mystery.

And other guys liked to play the knight. Buy flowers. Hold a door. Listen for more than a minute. But that writer guy the Sage quoted knew the score. What women and Russians shared? Invincible stupidity. Cater to it. Ignore it. Either way, you still lose. For Mitch, and every intelligent male he knew, women were gym socks that cooked. No more.

Mitch had heard shoptalk about Max, of course. Man was the original fixer. Problem solver. Every organization had one. Which made Mitch wonder what the man wanted with him? Message hint. His rotting trull assignment. Interest sparked in other quarters. Mitch was game for anything. He hadn't made enough headway to worry about things. Any headway. For all he knew, Max wanted to relive him of the chore. That would make his day.

"Open bars," Max toasted Mitch.

"Amen," Mitch responded. They clinked glasses. Another great CORE benefit. General revenues covered the cost. And CORE operations were starting to coin it. Money pouring in. Private donations up, year by year. But CORE was solidly in the black on its own efforts. It had taken time. But a loyal, well-rewarded employee base earned it back. And much more besides. Customer satisfaction—100%.

Best of all? Swilling twelve-year old rye courtesy of a crim. All property or cash discovered through CORE ops reverted to treasury. The crims ended up funding the very people taking them down. Johnny Canuck taxpayer didn't have to. Bureaucrats, old media snakes, other socialist looters. How they'd grind their teeth if they knew. Giving those fuckstick groups grief made everything taste twice as good.

Max clicked on the tab-bot. Punched in a fresh order. Waved at a group gathered around the nearest billiard table. The undercover boys had made it. Mitch guessed from the smell as much as the hair. Not for Mitch. He couldn't wear the mask around shitheads. Catching was fun. But punishing was where his heart lay.

"Hey, congratulations." Max said. Tossed back the delivered drink. Mitch did likewise. Eye contact with the hovering Bev. Antenna alert. Nad's gathered. Mitch shook off the distraction. Looked at Max, puzzled.

"Associate detective. Or that's what the grape vine says."

Mitch smiled. Pulled his nose. "Actually…no title mentioned. Cool though. Not sure it's a promotion or anything."

"You had two knights talking to you," Milt asserted. 'Knights' again. Tongue-in-cheek impertinence. For top echelon dwellers.

Mitch nodded. "Commissioner first. Then…" Loose lips did no one favours.

"Well, man. You're being groomed. Starter's spot, believe me. Good news." Ego massage. Old coaching trick. Jack up the excel incentive.

"Yeah, maybe," Mitch concurred. Sounded unconvinced. "Not sure about the first case they handed me."

"The expired fish mittens?" Max joked. Scanned the tab-bot again. Mitch wondered how hammered the guy was planning to get. Was Mitch expected to join in? He watched the old sack lick the rim of his empty glass. Mitch gripped his own drink. Pulled it closer. Serious juicer loose.

"Hey, you gotta start somewhere." Max said, dialing up another refresher.

"Yeah, but it's not like anyone even cares. I mean…" No need to explain the obvious.

"Better for you," Max remarked, eyebrow arched. Raised his voice. The herd was growing more voluble. Horns up soon, from the sounds of it. "You don't want too much interest. From webmedia or CORE. Then you're dancing to their bagpipes. They gave you this one on purpose. Get your feet wet. You learn about the life. Dregworld. Who to interview? Who to sidestep? How to get information? How to ignore or bury information? That kind of shit."

"I'm not even sure I want to move into investigations," Mitch confessed. He hadn't put it to himself so baldly. There'd been no pressure for results. The last few days hadn't been easy, though. Mitch was accustomed to taking things as they came. No pain, no shame. Looking for trouble? Exciting. Looking for evidence? Following some fucking trail of vague hints? Weighing motive? Tiring. Boring. From what he'd heard, anyway. And at the end of the day? No one gave a rat's ass. Gutter trash got offed. Whoop-de- do. Wheel-of-life litter disposal. Step over it, eyes on the horizon.

Still, his old man couldn't abide quitters. Northern Ontario thing. Bertuzzi-tough country. Difficult times? You see it through, regardless. Or put on your party dress and move to TO. Like the fag you probably are.

Max gave a careless shrug. Belched. Something about the heavy-lidded eyes gave Mitch pause. The man played cartoonish but…Mitch was beginning to sense an act. Clown on the outside. Kidney-punching prick-twister on the inside. Kind of guy in hockey who put could put his blade into the back of your knee so the ref never saw it. And you're on crutches for the next two weeks. Mitch always got caught when he tried it.

Mitch pretended to savour his drink. Let his eyes travel over Max again. Running to heavy. Reflexes would be slow. Booze took more than it gave. But there was an aura of menace he'd overlooked. Something about the set of his shoulders. The boar bristle neck. Any serious scrap, Mitch would take him. Over quick. But he'd want to keep his knees and gonads out of range. And watch for a shiv. Or a chain embedded with broken glass. The guy had dirty combat written everywhere.

Max spoke. Didn't look at Mitch. "You can't say no till you've said yes. That magic forensic shit you see in the vids?"

Mitch nodded.

"It's great. When they use it. Saves us all kinds'a timenenergy." Came out one word. "But mostly we wait for a squealer. Crims always blab. To their bar buddies. Their bitches. Their brothers-in-law. Who phone it in after for points. Get shit erased from their own files. Nine times outta ten, you never have to take your feet off the desk. Who wants to go outside in fuckin' winner anyway?"

"Stay patient," Max continued. "Wait for the break. What the public doesn't know is…most cases solve themselves. Or go away. D.P.'s just step in to steal credit. Always been that way."

Mitch knew Max started out as a siren jockey. Back in the late 70's. When hippies roamed the earth. Possible he knew what he was talking about.

"And if no one talks?"

"Person couldn't have been that important to begin with."

"Like my trull."

"Yep, maybe," Max confirmed. He paused to wave over a Nightingale. (Or "night-in-Gayle," as the boys joked.) Billy's only stocked top lookers. Max took their drinks. Mitch eyed the splendid rack bobbing in front of them. Leered in admiration.

"Hi, Mitch," the stacked Nancy said cheerily. "Remember me?"

"Absolutely," Mitch lied. "Long time. How are you?"

"Lonely. You said you'd call."

"And I will," Mitch lied again. "I've been so busy you wouldn't believe it."

"Too busy for a second helping?" The lanky brunette pretended to wipe the table. Her exposed nips dangled dangerously close to Mitch's mouth. Ordinarily, he'd have clamped onto the bait. Sucked those balloons flat. Felt Max's eyes watching him. Denied her the delicious pleasure. Simply played with her rigid turrets instead. Traced the satiny baltimores with a glad fingernail.

"I'm an uncaring pig," he declared. "Promise to make it up to you soon, okay?" For the life of him he couldn't remember porking her. He'd knocked down so many over the years. Who could keep track? She looked ecstatic, anyway. The Mitch magic.

"So I'll see you at McGoohan's soon?" A persistant rocket pocket, she was.

"Sure," Mitch nodded, already losing interest in her mams. The Bev massaged them for Mitch's benefit. Undeniably firm. Nicely balanced. Heavy but not indolent. Robust but not brassy. A fine set. Mitch and Max dutifully applauded. Eyes shining, the Nightingale pivoted on her stilettos. Melted back into the mob.

Max followed her departure. Looked at Mitch. "What was her name again?"

Mitch shrugged. "Couldn't tell ya'."

"Sweet little quim." Max inhaled, exhaled. Repeated. Oxygen stacking. Professional smoker, too. Mitch knew the signs.

"Easier than in the old days," Mitch acknowledged. "Back then, they say, you had to pretend to treat them like...equals. After the wake-up? Acceptance. A cow is a cow is a cow. Moooooo."

"Except they milk us," Max said. "Fucking divorce laws."

Mitch laughed. "All things in time," the Commissioner told us." Thought of an old buddy doing serious lockup in Kingston. His ex really an ex now.

Permanent cemetery plot renter. Stole money from the husband. Thumbs up from the courts. Bitch's fate sealed. Judges never learn.

Max cocked an eye. "Still a challenge for we old dogs. Pinktown. Businessman special. Rub and tug at the Hot 'N' Taut. CORE discount! You know that?"

Mitch nodded. Heard about it, thanks to Miles Melling. Ironic to hear it again so soon. Wondered if he'd ever go back.

"Still, costs money. Anymore? I stick close to the coffin. Get laced. Alone."

Mitch half-listening. He'd remember the coincidence later. Seeing the Melling rat slink about TechDiv on weekends. That bloated cake-face peering up at him. Body language begged for bullying. At least the lardball tried to curry favour by groveling. "I'm disabling, sir. Disabling. Just like you said. You were right, sir. Simp…li…fy. It's brilliant. I finally understand." Mitch would rub his head. Patronize the sad, sweaty shit.

Bar babble spiked. The dance floor filled. Billiard sticks thunked into place. Nightingales staggered arond, drink trays loaded. The lights flickered. Mitch lit a butt. Figured he might as well smoke his own along with everyone else's. Threw a questioning look at Max.

"Wonder what's going on?"

"Must be showtime," Max said. Glanced at his chrono. An antique. Crevassed. Dents. Band discolouration. Probably only told the time. Worth money now. Something to get idiot Melling on. One-function watches. Shattering proposal. Need a chair for him to fall into when Mitch ran it by him.

"What show?" Mitch asked.

Max shot him a stunned look. "You don't know? Tonight's the big night. Belinda and Melinda are back. Team Beluga!"

Mitch rolled his eyes. Invincible stupidity. Stand aside, Russkie.

"That's tonight?"

"Yeah!" Max regarded Mitch with disbelief. "Working too hard."

A coliseum roar drowned out Mitch's reply. Max out of his seat. Pointed at the stage. Mitch saw nothing but a sea of bobbing blockchops. "Fuck me," he muttered to no one. "Have to stand up."

Clapping, chanting, whistling swamped the room. Darkness now. Mitch waited for his eyes to adjust. A sinewy bass line spilled out from the speakers. The crowd erupted again. Elbows were thrown near the stage. Mitch was intensely curious now. He'd heard about the entertainment. Everyone had. But he had no clear image of what was to come. Ignorance he would regret losing later.

The sightline remained poor. Mitch hopped up on his chair. Balanced himself against a support beam. A large spot hit the stage. A bold, bluesy beat announced the arrival. Half the night's duo waddled into the light. The madding mass bellowed with joy. Mitch felt the energy. Gut punch. Adrenaline kick. Something fun this way comes.

Beluga twin shows were CORE legends. Belinda and Melinda. Not actually twins. A mother/daughter novelty horrorshow out of Windsor. Or so the ads claimed. Mitch didn't think they looked all that much alike. Except for being houseboat huge. Billy's would chopper them in every year for laughs. Mama beluga tipped the scales at 630 lbs. Baby beluga had waved goodbye to 500 lbs some time back.Three years into CORE, Mitch still hadn't caught their act. But he knew they were popular. Soon understood why.

"Dance of the Seven Tents comin' up," Max shouted from a neighbouring chair. Mad Hatter grin. "Isn't she great?"

As if on command, an enormous blue tarp fell to the floor. Wide as a store awning. Mitch squinted through the fog of tobacco smoke.

""Holy Christ," he yelled to Max, "she's ugly!"

"Oh, yeah!" Max bellowed back. "Fuckin' horrible. Jabba the Cunt. Wait'll you see her daughter. Should'a been strangled at birth. It's a…"

Mitch shook his head, laughing. Missed the rest. But it was already shaping up to be a circus. There was big. There was obese. And there was Belinda. The layered sarong made it seem her head was being squeezed from a toothpaste tube. He fought the urge to shield his eyes. The sight was horrifying. Species disgrace.

Belinda began to wallow about the stage.

"Heavy seas," Max screamed in laughter. Loosened his tie.

Hard to argue. Belinda did share similarities with a frieghter in distress. She released another sail despite mock pleas for decorum. Two muscled roadies appeared. Worked in tandem. Managed to pull it and the others offstage.

Belinda lurched unsteadily around the aluminum pole. Another fabric flap fell. Hands reached out. Touched the infamous shroud.

A genuine disco ball spun from the ceiling. More cheese. Mick had rescued it from a lot sale a year earlier. Had his wife patch it back together. Mitch remembered the story.

The music surged. Multic-coloured poker chips slid over acres of flesh. Great cottage cheese bergs collided everywhere. Between beats, Belinda's knees disappeared. Waves of fat rolled over them. Broke, rolled out again. The spectacle's savage awfulness stunned Mitch. It was fascinating, disturbing, tectonic. And funny as hell. He hadn't laughed so hard since watching a CORE surveillance vid of Greek night at Club Patroclus.

Belinda continued to maneuver. In her disjointed way. Often in counterpoint to the beat. The creature was a perfect parody of her sex, Mitch determined. All the same parts. But unrelated on a fundamental level.

And CORE's soldiers wanted more. Agents banged their fists on the stage. Shouted wonderfully crude demands. Their wild enthusiasm spurred Belinda on. Dim awareness flickered across the putty mound holding up her hair. The drugs had lost their strength. Or were just kicking in. Mitch couldn't guess which.

Certainly, the overhead spots did her no favours. Skin tone the colour of rendered horse. Boiled beet nose. Multiple chins. The latter lapped down to the picnic hampers like magma. Gravity's revenge. That anyone had plunked her monkey amazed Mitch. Rape, even at gunpoint, seemed out of the question. Death preferable. Perhaps she'd seduced a lifer on some prison tour. A blind, addled lifer. Not a thought to linger on. Mitch deleted it.

The groundlings took their pleasure. Amplified hoots and howls hurtled about the room. Belinda glistened with beer spray. Her mammoth mammaries slithered above the boiler-sized gut like loose torpedos. Beside him, Max coughed violently. Ran a ragged sleeve across his eyes. The jacket was getting well used. Max would need to wring it out if he kept crying.

Steeling himself, Mitch trained his eyes away from Belinda's upper deck. Let them drift netherward. Down across the barren, lumpy steppes. Down past the fathomless belly button. Down to the far-from-erogenous zone. Just then, Belinda loosed the second-to-last bedsheet. Mitch felt his heart stop.

On an ordinary pole artist, the glory gulch lay hid behind a playing card scrap of glitter. For Belinda's growler shield—the Canadian flag. Olympic-sized. Mock salutes greeted its appearance. Soon sagged badly from suds and saliva. Nor did it any longer obscure Belinda's Siberia-wide ass. Front row viewers got the whole John Ford panorama. Mitch saw two men bent double. Their fists hammering into open palms. Staff medics hovered nearby. They'd be needed before the night was out.

The hunter in Mitch surfaced. Wondered how Belinda would cook down. Probably get a half-barrel of fuel oil out of her. Meat would only be fit for dogs, of course.

No one wanted to imagine the mitt beneath the Maple Leaf. Attention reverted to the vast dimpled thighs on offer. The sight, gross and unforgiveable. Posterity demanded a record. Mitch scrambled to find his com. Fixed the camera. Zoomed in. Felt like a space explorer. His mission task: orbit and record forbidding planet. Current sitrep: landscape damaged. Pocked and perilous terrain. Fissures and crevasses, unsightly protusions. Evidence of volcanic activity. A clear case for terra-forming. Or a mercy core implosion.

As Mitch filmed, CORE agents curled to the floor. Cried with laughter. No amount of bad dancing could disguise the brutal immensity of that butt.

With each gyration her cheeks chewed away at the colours. Soon only a thin red sliver remained. Belinda's traitorous ass had eaten the flag.

The howling spiked. Mitch watched Max nearly fall from his perch. His own throat felt scorched. Too much smoke and screaming. Plus, he was dying for a drink. No barbelle would tempt battery or worse to deliver one, though. It was do without, borrow, or risk the gauntlet.

Belinda was nearly finished. Her flag barrier tattered and twisted. A cue given. The stripper shit got scrapped. Eighty eight youthstomp earwhack tore up the surrounds.

"Septic for God!" someone yelled to applause. Multiple coms went strobe function. Ultra-surreal scene. Mitch put his unit away. He'd never be able to explain the vid.

Belinda glanced back at the flea market curtain. Her anti-rhythmic shuffling never slowed. Mitch tried to think of a description. Drunk, demented hippo-human monster mash. RV with a broken axle? Cash-desperate trailer trash? Put money on the latter.

Finally, the curtain ratcheted up and out. Four men moved into position. Faced each other. Armed themselves. Others propped planking against the stage. Movement visible at the rear. A shadow arced across the far wall startling a stagehand. Sarcastic abuse from CORE witnesses. Second part of the act on the rise, Mitch reasoned. Justified in doing so.

"Ar-r-r-r-g-o-o-o-o-o-s!" the cry boomed over the room. Mitch got it. Their front line contained in a single entity. Linebacker wide, it loomed into view. Mountainous head, massive shoulders. Prodded with poles, she clambered up the ramp. Into the white glow of a hot spot. Melinda! The young one. And did she cut a humungous figure. Husked entirely in green. Platinum white hair.

"Walking corn!!" a drunk yelled out. Applause for the apt take.

"Zeppelina!" Another telling observation to reach Mitch's ears. Sounded right, somehow.

The promo material had to be wrong. No way she weighed less than Monstro, her Mom. Together again, though. Live! On the same endangered stage. Half a ton of dancing mammals. Mitch was beside himself. Just when you were sure you'd seen it all…

Somebody bellowed something about a sofa gone rogue. Now it was Mitch's turn to almost lose his balance. Agents everywhere went beserk. Two behemoths bending the boards. Too much! A cascade of cigarettes flew through the air. The famous fire flies ritual. Mitch had heard about it. Several landed in Belinda's frosted fright wig. It refused to catch. Dsappointment. Experience had taught the ladies to think ahead. Flame-retarding perms, clearly.

Undeterred, agents resorted to found objects. A cueball sailed past Melinda's head as she dropped a sheet. Billowed the curtain fringe. Group groan. Another found newly exposed pillows. Vanished into the crease. Violently absorbed into that mass ass. Never seen again. Gasps, nausea.

Then a full beer bounced off Belinda's back. Foam jetted into the air. Riotous cheering. Congratulations to the ace. Belinda appeared not to notice. Mitch wiped away tears. Festival du la Fatbags. Guys weren't exaggerating. This was an event.

What happened next shocked no one. Mitch had noted the beauty of mob telepathy in the past. Pockets, knapsacks, tables scoured for suitable projectiles. Matter rained down. Pens, pencils, key chains, cigarette lazers, loonies, townies flashed overhead. The ladies remained oblivious.

Time for heavier artillery. A black workboot skipped across the stage. No one hurt, sadly. Then a solid glass ashtray grazed Melinda's temple. Mitch winced. Still, no sign of suffering. Disbelief and dejection mingled. The pair led charmed lives.

A red-faced agent standing on a chair across the aisle caught Mitch's eye. Pointed at the stage. "Don't worry," he yelled. "You can't hurt'em. They're made a rubber!"

Like Mitch cared whether you could hurt them. Too funny. Man had a point, though. All that natural insulation made for an effective protective barrier. Figured it must be like living inside a giant inflated raft.

The agent opposite him tried to say something else. Couldn't. Collapsed laughing. Mitch waved thanks anyway. Returned his attention to the fray. Stood by his original theory. Drug the stupid. It worked in general.

Belinda slowed to a near standstill. She threw an arm behind her. Momentum kept her body rotating. The source of her discomfort came into view. Someone had nailed her with a billiards triangle. Lodged it perfectly between her bumpers. The force of impact completed the flag's transformation into a butt thong. Belinda's every attempt to remove it failed. Mitch watched through blurry eyes.

Ever the trooper, Belinda resumed her routine. Most popular comparison, an elephant losing a fight with quicksand. The whole disturbing scene stayed with Mitch his entire life. As would the sight of a giant spitball spinning into Melinda's face moments later. Mitch registered its mid-trajectory glint. Like an avenging comet, it blazed through the atmosphere.

Time slowed for Mitch. The gob rocket lazily drifted towards Melinda. Found its target. Her forehead. Dead centre. She stutter-stepped, shocked. A trailing rope of drool looped around her neck.

Mitch couldn't breath. Reduced to foetal helplessness. Max staggered up. Hugged Mitch's post. Kicked it every now and then.

Melinda came out of her stupor long enough to paw at the spit thread. Her disjointed efforts tore Velcro seams. More leaves fell. A hidden nest of sequins exploded. Drifted to the stage. Crowd delirious now. An even gluier launch nailed a nipple big as an egg yolk. The house rocked. Mitch was in trouble. Stop watching or shit his pants. That was the choice facing him.

More strafing. Great green horkpies found hide. The Belugas were taking ack ack from all over. Lugies clung like leeches. Some mimicked pizzas. Still the show went on. The two hefties dipped and dodged. Airships in a force five gale. Worst bump-and-grind ever. Shared assessment of every exotics expert.

Grape-shot assault now. Glasses, bottles, several pool balls. A busted off chair leg, the hard back right behind it. Even a Bible fluttered in late. Bounced off Belinda's thigh. Everything thrown found flesh. Targets impossible to miss. Red gouge marks visible everywhere.

The sisters abandoned their laboured gyrations. Introduced a new fiasco. Leviathan lesbo. The sight left even hardened agents thunderstruck. Belinda leaned in. Dragged her tongue over her daughter's heaving boobs. Mitch turned away. Heard someone scream, "Memory erase, stat!" Understood. What he'd seen was so demeaning.

Rioting agents fell over one another. Sightless. Tears of unbidden hysteria spilled down flushed cheeks. Mitch no different. His ribs hurt. His throat felt like minced asphalt. He couldn't remember the last time he'd lost it so completely. Pearson captured it during the post-mortem. You'd pay twice the money at Wonderland for half the entertainment.

Max rolled past. Headed due south of the stage. White table napkin clutched to his face. Looked up to find Mitch looking down. Shook his head. "What is it about the degradation of women that's so funny?" he yelled. Coughing jag hit. He bent over. Pounded his knees.

Mitch couldn't answer. No breath. But Max's example triggered an idea. It lead to one of the evening's highlights. Mitch found and emptied a tissue dispenser. Drenched them with dregs from a discarded bottle. Hand-moulded a sopping bomblet.

Bel and Mel continued their contortions. An angry bass line led them to the lip of the stage. Hands above their heads, they shimmied and shook. Fat wedges met. Slid off and submerged like sea ice. Another boot whipped past. Tragic near miss. O-fer night for footwear.

Belinda latched onto her rope belt.

"Heads up!" a shocked watcher warned. Recoiled in horror. "BDP! BDP!"

Fearsome sight anticipated. CORE training kicked in. Burqa Defense Posture initiated. Mental safety measure recently adopted. Mitch peered through his interlaced fingers. Did feel marginally safer. Knew it was important to avoid an unobstructed view of Belinda in the raw.

He felt drained, defenseless. Some agents could endure vulgarity all night long. Never a complaint. Demand more. Mitch was more sensitive. Had a lower gag threshold. Seeing the corpulent warthog's wicker gully? Even from a distance? Didn't know if he possessed sufficient inner fortitude.

Matters turned out stranger than anyone could have guessed. Belinda pulled the ripcord. Flung her flag aside. Let it hang from her ass like a dragon's tail. Immediately after, peeled off her daughter's salad cover. The climax. Two open sewers for the price of one.

A collective intake of breath. Then shouts of disbelief. The final joke. Better for being unexpected. Both women's modesty, if not dignity, had been preserved! A sporran of belly fat perfectly concealed their wookies. Hoots, whistles, even a cowbell echoed throughout Billy's. Placid as bovines, Bel and Mel gazed out over the applauding audience. An anti-triumph for the ages. The descent of man in all it's idiot glory.

The briefest imaginable moment of mocking acclaim. Then an eco-brown, fist-sized spitball slammed into the ravine between Melinda's cylinders. Propelled with major league velocity. It staggered her. Betty Boop wide-eyed wonder. Knowing looks at the athlete Mitch. He was stunned as anyone. Hadn't expected such a perfect throw. Accepted congratulations. No crowing on his part. Knew it was more luck than planning.

Melinda took a startled half-turn. Began to dig at her chest. Agents that thought they were laughed out found different. And the best yet to come. The human gargoyle made history. Too determined to locate the leaking missile. Failed to see the saliva slick. Her left foot went out from under her. Pudding face dimly registered alarm. Just enough time for one futile windmill. She plummeted down, an Airbus into asphalt. The reverberations shook photos from the back wall. Mitch grabbed hold of his pillar. Felt the quake energy travel through it.

Collapsed, legs splayed, Melinda topped the absurd sight. Released a plank-rattling fart. Mitch heard it clearly over the music. Like a boat hull scraping along a cement pier.

No choice for Mitch. Bang head against post. Pray the pain would keep him from screaming.

Melinda jabbed at the air. Once, twice. Her mother stared at her. Someone for whom befuddlement was the norm. Totally overwhelmed now.

"Rhino down, bwana!" an agent yelled.

"Just stand there, you fat, stupid cow," another shouted to Belinda. Threw his drink at her. Then the glass. Celebrated with friends when it rang off her elbow, shattered.

"Yeah, whatever you do, don't help, Elsie!" cried a third onlooker with overjoyed malice.

Melinda managed a sitting position on her own. She looked disturbed. Eyes glazed. Her breasts hung like great sacks of cheese curd. Sections of her still quivered independently from aftershocks. CORE agents pointed, clutched their sides. Mitch could only manage short breaths. Relied on a Zen method he'd been taught for conserving energy. Worried his knees were going to go out.

Belinda looked down at Melinda. Swiveled to stare at the stage wings. Evidently thought the roadies might read the cue. Appear like angels from the sky. False hope. Melinda tried rolling over onto her stomach. Her first three attempts wasted effort. Disastrous change of tactics.

"Stop. Please!" someone begged. "Can't…laugh…anymore!"

The fourth effort cancelled any thoughts the farce had ended. Mel got a rolling start. Used her elbow as a fulcrum. The strain too enormous. It gave way. She fell back hard, head bouncing on the stage floor.

CORE howled as one. The lofty heights of mirth reached. Men stamped the floor, held themesleves, unleashed banzai shrieks.

On-demand holo sales spiked for the next climactic moment. New entertainment territory explored. A glistening yellow jet geysered out from Melinda's great divide. Doused a dozen crowding agents. Mitch concentrated on an overhead ceiling duct. Black. Very black. Pretended he hadn't seen anything. Tried to ignore the swell of gut-busting hilarity.

Ten seconds passed. Mitch felt elbows brush against his leg. Checked it out. Stream of men headed for the pisser. Many with hair by Einstein. Some wobble-walked. Clutched discoloured jeans. Others, Mitch saw, remained on the floor. Like overturned potato bugs. Their legs bicycling in the air. Meanwhile, two tables over and under, Max had gone Muslim. Ass in the air, head bobbing, fists pounding the maple.

Mitch shot a careful eye at the stage. Three roadies at work. They'd finessed a harness under Melinda's ass. Winched her upright. She took two unsteady steps. The aides backpedaled to a safe distance. Hard-earned knowledge, Mitch suspected. Find yourself beneath either dozer? No guessing who the bottle of Heinz is. Signal the squeegee stooge.

Memorable madness complete. Melinda joined her mother, stage rear. Together they were herded out and away. Mitch was exhausted. Felt shooting pains everytime he breathed. Refused to witness anything else. Agreed with those shouting "No mas! No mas!" There were times when too much was enough.

During the weekly meet later, Mitch heard the rest of the story. An agent-bagged nightingale did some pillow talking. Saw it all on a smoke break. How

Bel and Mel were driven to the loading dock. Crew hosed the stink off them. Steam rose from them as if off hot coals. Their vast wet pelts glistening under the overhead crimlight.

Outside, a specially prepped Airstream sat snugged against the jetty. The insides had been gutted. Only the aluminum shell remained. The rear wall replaced. In it's stead, a thick metal walkway.

Hydrolic motors purred. The ramp lowered to the deck. Both heavyweights whinnied in alarm. Several false starts as they milled about. Pawed at the floor. Slatted surfaces made them skittish, the rep explained.

A sharp-thinking line serf, also on smoke break, saved matters. Absented himself after promising help. Returned a minute later with a large plastic mop pail. Full. Garbaged chicken wings spilled over the rim. Their spicy aroma cut through the chill. Heatlamp blasted onion rings huddled on top. A side sack of Dudley Laws garlic toast to sweeten the deal.

Goodies in hand, the minimum-wager bolted into the mobile pen. Wonderful, greasy fumes wafted out. The Beluga Twins raised their snouts. Sniffed the air. Grunted and woofed. Obvious enthusiasm. Getting them inside a snap after. Team Beluga SecBrutes joined in. Vigorous poking with bullbusters and push brooms. Trotters secured, one cautious step followed another. Both briny babes lumbered inside.

Immediate protest from the suspension system. Counter-attack marshalled. High-pitched compressor whine. Hydrolic stablizers growled into action. The vehicle's rear bumper slowly rose back level with the dock. The attending officials reassured everyone. A mostly routine loading procedure. The Airstream was fully tricked out. Pre-stressed titanium reinforcing beams installed. Plus, everyone present had worked dairy farms or zoos at some point in their lives. Large animal transportation second nature.

The happy heifers bedded down. Tossed fresh straw in the air. Snorted and sported. Giddy at their good fortune. The careful cook dropped dinner. Grease smell penetrated beastie nostrils. Enthused, they snuffled their way to the prize. Opportunity granted, the clever line-monkey scrabbled along the wall to the rear. Then legged it outside to safety.

Outside, he shyly acknowledged praise for his efforts. Tried the "Oh, the huge manatee" gag. Promptly ordered back to the fry pit. Stupid English major.

Prior to leaving, the road crew detailed their tour sched. Bel and Mel would gorge until the grub was gone. Briefly argue over who licked the bucket clean. Then chew cud with noisy contentment. Fall asleep before the 401 Windsor turn off.

The dangers of rollover due to sudden cargo shift kept speeds down. Minimum three-and-a-half hours, then, to the stockyards. The pickiest PETA fanatic would have been pleased, however. Textbook animal husbandry. Minus the grooming for tics and fleas.

Day to recover. Reload the fridges. Two nights at a chiropractors' convention in Cuyahoga Falls. Michigan casino circuit after. Back to Sarnia in time for the planters' bar tour. The women were in demand. Times were tough. Solid laughs needed. Same old same.

And then it was time to leave. Smile and a wave from the driver. Eight-cyclinder roar as the Bronto revved up. Clouds of exhaust steam. Gasoline batteries ejecting healthy ozone. The mobile trailer lurched away. Tour promo lights twinkled on the back wall. Everyone had a good chuckle. Clever play on words.

"Olympic gold," was how McKittrick described the worldwide tube response the next day. "Huge bonuses for everyone!" Holo sales had gone galactic. CORE accountants waxed ecstatic. The abattoir angels far surpassed their previous debacles. CORE minting it. Happy faces all around the organization. Third windfall that year. And it was still only March. Morale through the roof. Workouts grew especially intense. Everyone wanted to be part of the next swag score. The men all sensed fine times ahead.

Downside. Four agents on disability. Two needed hospital treatment. Injuries caused by falling. Two more suffered undisclosed mental trauma. FNG's, Mitch had heard. Too innocent. The fleshpots of Swift Current couldn't compare for twisty shit.

A week of CORE rehab would put them straight. R 'n R at Motel Mohammed. Mitch loved the nickname. Virgins and martyrs meet and heal. If by virgins one meant horny little minxes who couldn't get enough. Just like in real heaven. Mitch looked forward to visiting one day. He'd heard nothing but positive things. And the memorial tatts earned you serious cred. Clear you'd taken one for the team.

So…all taken, a night for the files. Billy's emptied out in less than an hour. People were spent. Mitch never even saw Max again. Bust-up time, no question. Zip back to the condo. Kick start the fuck. Pass out. That was the plan.

Mitch sat in the Gringolet. Slow warm. He was still hot from laughing. Felt like he'd boxed ten rounds with an orangutan. Everything hurt.

Checked his com for messages. A group of rooks passed in front. Hunched low to meet the icy wind. Nodded in respect for Mitch. And the car. Mitch had overheard them talking. Cooz prowl. The married ancients had already departed. Off to home, hearth and the horrors within. Mitch begged off when asked. Younger man's game. That night anyway.

Just as well, it turned out. Who knew what the consequences would have been? Too easy to lose the SD someone had slipped into his smoke pack. Solid tradecraft. They'd still taken a risk, whoever'd done it. Mitch wasn't known to leave his lung bungers lying around. Even tax-free reserve butts were expensive.

Said "light." Examined the item once he could see it better. "Fingernails." Samsung. Spacefoil wrap. Blew it away. Slid the chip into his com port. Machine flickered. Window flared bright, then died. Mitch cursed. Stupid. Stupid. Stupid. What was he thinking?

Window re-appeared seconds later. Short-lived sigh of relief. Etch-a-sketching weirdness now. Crazy graphs. Charts that came and went in seconds. Funnelling. Swirling. Speed scroll of names. Official-looking seals. Government symbols. Provincial insignia. Document headings. Nothing recognizable. Lightning fast album exhibit. Faces snapped in and out. One might have been his sad Sally on the slab. Hard to tell.

A full minute of this. Tech death throes? Did someone want to kill his com? Mitch couldn't imagine why. He'd just requisition another. No biggie. Program could be sending all his data elsewhere. Nothing they couldn't get easier, though. Without arousing attention.

One good thing, if deliberate. A pooched com gave him the excuse he needed to cancel Roger's. That alone would be worth the inconvenience of arranging for a new one.

An animated holo image appeared. Promptly vanished. Heavy-duty codeware. It was redlining his com memory. He nearly dropped it a second later. The word 'BEWEAR' bold-flashed in front of his face. Best not to tell the Sage. He'd want retaliation for the idiot spelling error alone.

Another symbol replaced the warning. A familiar one. Wink out. Bleed and go. Mitch racked his mind. Where had he seen it? Recently, too. Came to him. That day's meeting. The last thing he'd seen on the holoscreen. That very symbol.

So the Ovarians had come calling. How thoughtful of them. They'd found out about his mission. Which made him a target? They wanted to say hello. The Commissioner would be interested. Political, of course. Good post-breakfast confab subject.

Mitch swore. Pocketed the com. The time! Cancelled the light. Dropped the Gringolet into first. Clear the mind. Focus. Unless he drove like Michael he'd miss SportsTornado higlights. Did have 'Nucks/Flames game on the machine if he was too late. Wind down with a bit of fast-forward hockey. Pound back a final rye. Punchboard Andrea. Call it a day. It had been that and more.

Mitch flung the quilt off Andrea's body. Smiled as she shivered. Night air chilly. Mitch liked a cold bedroom. Reminded of the Kap. His old man always kept a window open. Even through winter. Didn't matter. Claimed it killed germs. Wasn't sick a day in his life, either. Until his heart gave out. Waiting in the lunch buffet lineup. Brunch Bonanza at the Fairmont. Third time through. Man had an appetite.

Chest clutch. Punched the guy in front of him in disbelief. Fell. Tried one pushup. Pure obstinate right to the end.

Next thing, gurney jockeys jerking him through the lobby. His mother in the ambulance. Likely telling the medics how the old man had ignored her advice for forty years. As if they cared.

After surgery. The moron doctor "comforting" her. Saying for 30,000 Canadians every year, the first sign of heart disease was sudden death. Prick. Mitch got him back for that. Caught up to his son behind the net one game. Put his face through the endglass. And they played on the same team.

Andrea stirred. Drew her legs close. Hugged herself. Mitch surveyed her in the half-light. He liked to look at naked women...especially sleeping. Botticelli complexion. So said the Sage, admiring the hardvid folder he'd uploaded for the guys at work. Mitch didn't know to compare. Hadn't seen that month's issue yet.

Buttery blonde hair cloaked her shoulder. A loose strand tickled her lower lip. Small rose of mouth. Sleek jawline. Graceful neck leading down to the twin towers. Marvellous udders. Inviting as plump wineskins. He was tempted to huff them in. Or slap down the love muscle. Play a fast game of "fireball."

His eyes moved to the rest of her body. The swift drop off below her ribs. Gentle rise up the hip. Her skin, sheet metal shiny. The rock-hard rump. She kept up with the workouts. Mitch insisted. He didn't pump porkers. Not anymore anyway.

Memory flash. Hockey. Junior. His centre, Gary Arnold, celebrating almost two-hundred fucks before his twenty-first birthday. Asked how many were fat? "Almost two hundred," the reply. Owned a truck dealership in Kincardine now. Doing well, last he heard.

From rack to rear, his woman was an impressive little dick basket. Undeniable. You had to give God credit. The old Sod had outdone himself. Sometimes you wanted to put a Glock in his mouth. Squeeze the trigger. Then something like Andrea gets extruded. And all is forgiven. The Big Guy redeems himself.

Andrea Vaclav. Former Olympic-candidate figure skater. The Vaughn Vixen. Limber as a twist tie. Could glide around the ice on one leg. Hold the other up at right angles. Knee inside her ear. Rest a level on her crotch. Perfect 180 degrees. Never failed to creep Mitch out. Some things were just wrong.

In the time they'd been sacking, he'd bent, folded and spindled her on innumerable occasions. She always sprang right back into shape after. Amazing dexterity. Mitch envied her. By comparison, he was flexible as flatiron.

Which didn't stop him from becoming her off-ice dance partner. Got the look while he stood along the boards. He and a few of the boys waiting for the ice. Lobbing fashion critiques at her partner. Mocking his comically homo skating. CORE didn't do innuendo. Called it as they saw it. Fag was fag.

So what choice did Mitch have? She wasn't going to get dick from the gay blade at her waist. That much was certain.

One more reason Mitch was conflicted. There were moments, like now, when he wondered if he almost had feelings for her. In that event, time to get out the axe. Sever relations. They'd been doing the beast for a few months already. Longer than normal. Mitch didn't usually plug the same socket more than a week. After, they got clingy. And needy. And wanty. And boring.

But Andrea had her good qualities. He couldn't deny it. She was keen to keep house. Whenever she stayed over, she polished more than his root. He made sure of it. Word to the wise. Told her the only way he'd ever hit her was if she made him do it. No arguments from then on. She donned gloves. Did dishes. Worked the central. Cleaned the can, of course. Washed his hockey shit. Picked up. Arranged his closets. Tidied the bedroom. Sanded the badly-painted dresser he'd just inherited from a dead aunt somewhere. Did a little grout work around the tub. And fixed the sliding balcony door. He'd nearly ripped the fucking thing off its runners trying to get it to work right. Kept jamming. So that was a definite positive. She was handy.

Also, unlike the old Septic number, a fry pan was not a weapon in her hands. Chops, chicken, steaks. She did them right. Not too much. But easy on the e-coli. She could even throw a homemade 'za together. Put chain shit to shame.

Once, she presented him with an ultra superior chocolate cake. Some special event. Her period had arrived on time, maybe. Moist as could be. Frosting so delicious he'd ended up spackling her boobs and cooz with it later that night. Two minutes for icing the fuck, he'd thought. Mid-way through drilling her into the mattress. Couldn't stop laughing after. But all in all, not a liability near the stove.

Add to that…she knew to keep her mouth shut. When it was important. Inside and outside the bedroom. Mitch hated complainers. And mood swings. Monthly cycles? The number Mitch ran off the road every thirty days. A stress-release technique. Arrogant pricks in their faggo-slick zipper skins. BSE helmet-heads. Seeing their pride and joy wrapped around a phone pole. Nothing pleased him more. The Gringolet almost knew what to do by itself. The lightest touch on the wheel…a Cannondickface rider slammed into an opening car door. Or flew up and over the curb into a meter. Sometimes, for variety, he'd have them rear-end a bus. All the while scanning for tunes. Smiled to picture them shaking their fists after taking the hard fall. Or holding a bloodied limb, face contorted in agony. Served the shitbrains right. Roads were for cars. Yield or die, bikefag.

Finally, and the one telling feature for Mitch—Andrea was born to be fucked. Regular, ruthless, unmerciful, extreme fucking. What she craved. What her body required. Andrea's Olympic code: hard, harder, hardest. She knew it. Mitch knew it.

Mitch had poled a lot of holes in his still young life. No coochie he'd encountered ate sausage with such ravenous savagery. Her holster demanded constant oiling. Luckily for her, when you needed to slap leather, Mitch was the hired gun you called. Don't bring it if you're not going to use it, his philosophy.

In some ways, Mitch felt he served a higher purpose in the daily dinking of Andrea. Plastering her uterus was like doing God's work. Because even God would struggle to satisfy the tireless strumpet.

That last thought ended the internal discussion. Anaconda roused. Mitch stripped. Carefully got up on the bed. Knee-walked close to Andrea's head. Laid the lumber across her forehead. She moaned. Sixth sense? Scrunched up her eyebrows. Natural reaction. Knew the weight had to be oppressive. Like a fallen tree limb.

Mitch open-palmed his forehead. Homer moment. He'd left his com on the kitchen table. Wasted opportunity. Pics like this always got a big laugh at work.

Decided on another sure chuckler. Snugged his apple up against her nostrils. Covered her mouth with his free hand. See how long before she started to suffocate. Four seconds, five, six…eyes popped open in panic.

Andrea wrenched her head about. Struggled for breath. Mitch clamped and pushed harder. Then broke it off. Laughed long and hard. Then tapped the top of her nose with the tip of his dick. Pulled it away. Let it rest on her open lips. Slipped his left hand between her legs. Andrea quivered. Sighed. Fully awake now. Mitch felt the the sugar bowl warm to his touch. Stroked the velvet hatch covers.

"Mmmmm…" Andrea murmured sleepily. "How was Billy's?"

"Okay," "Mitch said. "Usual."

Andrea giggled.

"What?" Mitch asked.

"I know you had strippers there tonight."

"How?"

"Carla told me."

Ryan's girlfriend. Mitch had seen him there. Near the front, too. Wondered if he'd worn any of the golden shower?

"That's why you're horny."

Mitch didn't argue. What did he care what she thought?

"Absolutely. And you know what to do about it." No throat massage for her tonight. He was too tired. Grabbed the comforter. Pulled it over them. Grunted as Andrea launched her groin against him. Fondled her poonts. Animal urges. You had to love them. Time to hide baby's arm in the candy cave.

An entry squeak from Andrea. Then the smile of empty-headed delight. She threw her arms out. Settled in for the ride. And Mitch did kind of like blissing her out. The tortured expressions of joy. The gutteral, wolverine cries. Plus the climactic 'dying replicant' orgasm. Stellar sex. As a depleted rooster jaw once put it, Mitch was the original performance artist. The fuck-king… from Kapusca-sing. All hail.

Of course, there was more to it than owning the biggest brush. Before CORE, Mitch had been one of T.O.'s highest paid male escorts. He'd put it to all manner of pantsuits in executive suites. Done exploratory sword surgery on countless health industry "careworkers." (Or as he liked to think of them, Doctors sans Boyfriends.) He'd taken Phd candidates to night school.

Lonely pols also got a look in. Provided they weren't too ugly. Or socialistic. Mitch had standards. The taxpayer ponied up for it, of course. Hadn't bothered Mitch at the time. It would now.

All his experiences had taught him one irrefutable truth. The great comic philosopher Ford Fairlane was right. Most women had only one more brain cell than a cow. And that was so they wouldn't shit on the floor while they did the dishes. End. Stop.

Put another way, gash were ruled by emotion. Logic was a meaningless five letter word. Know that, you could do whatever you liked with them. 'Cause explaining shit was a total waste of time.

And the better educated they were, the filthier. Finesse, caress, undress. They couldn't wait to grease his jack. Bathtub bondage, faucet fellatio, cuffs and chains, whippings, beatings, stairwell ravishings, scouring, candlework treatments, leatherings—Mitch complied with all fantasy requests. Even learned to pull his punches. Over time. His motto: Give the customer what they wanted, good and hard.

Yeah, a fun job. The money and perks were amazing. It had certainly cured him of panting after town dirties. The kind that got horny walking past surveyor stakes. STD cesspools at twenty. Annual 'Seasons Greeting' cards from area abortionists. Three likely career paths. Often telescoped into one. Wife of violent deadbeat. Motel hooker. Register troll at the nearest Timmy's.

Remembered what fun it was to get the Kap boys together on Saturday nights. Round up the local bologna flapovers. Run'em to the park. Or Thorndike's shag shack. Dump'em downtown, dutch-doored. Listen to them scream for their panties back as Mitch drove away, waving. Good times. But you can't go back. They all got fat. Thanks for the mammories. Move on.

Woolgathering again! Mitch annoyed with himself. Get his head out of the Kap! He should have been thinking about his done-and-ditched trull. Or why the Ovarians were interested in him? Or the next day's agenda. Reliving past glories accomplished nothing.

He threw off the coverlet. Andrea's frozen face gazed up. Asian eyes, forehead furrowed, mouth puckered. Fuck rigor setting in. Christ only knew how many times she'd come while he was rifling the memory vault.

Pleasure tour over. Mitch revved the engine. Put it in fourth. Finished off with a series of mighty thrusts. Andrea orbited Saturn.

With a roar of completion, Mitch painted the hall. Cleaned off with her llama fleece pyjamas. Scrambled over her insensate form. Burrowed under the blanket. Corralled his pillow. Soft pillow. Wonderful pillow. Out in five seconds.

Andrea lay splay-legged and comatose at the foot of the bed. The cold would eventually bring her around. Then she would find the duvet. Snuggle up to Mitch for warmth. Only to be kneed away. And cursed. It was hard but she understood. No cuddling. Ever.

Morning. Mitch drew open the curtains. Stared out. Fucking early. Dawn still smearing the horizon with a bloody finger. Which meant the sun was close behind. The sun? In March? Mitch shook his head. Rubbed his eyes. Impossible. Must be dreaming. Looked out the window again. Sure enough. Evidence everywhere. Blue sky. Sunshine almost inevitable. Anywhere else but Toronto. Too early to call it for certain. But somebody'd misread the script.

Steam vented past the window. Shower action. Andrea! Sly bitch! Got in before him. Mitch breathed in the sharp apartment air. Shivered. Wrapped the down blanket around him. Waited.

Andrea blew into the room. Smiled. Bent down Tongued his nipples good morning. Untoweled. Raced about the room. Emptied drawers. Undergarment pile. Panties, bra, socks and stuff. Getting ready for work. Mitch still groggy with sleep. Her bosses were totally anal about start times. Corporate fuckwads. He'd met enough to know they were like turtles. All hard shell on the outside. Inside, soup ingredients.

Unfortunately, Mitch could never remember what she did? Or which corporate fuckwads she did it for? Something on Bay street? Or Bloor. Insurance? Investments? Not a bank. But money was involved. Not that he cared all that much. As long as he didn't have to attend any functions. He done enough as an escort to last a lifetime. Lost any dread of Hell as a result.

He heard mild cursing. Understood. She had trouble walking. His fault. No disguising that satisfied smile either. Mitch half-listened to her mumbling. Fished in his drawer for gear. Might as well make a day of it. He was up now.

Another matter nagged at him. Something important. He threw his mind back to Billy's. Belinda and Melinda. A rib twinge reminded him. God. He'd laughed himself helpless. Couldn't wait to hear the stories they'd be telling at the shop. Caught the thought as it was sneaking away. The SD. Wasn't sure if he'd left it in his smokes. Check after his shower.

Icy hello from the hardwood floor. Mitch skipped to the hallway. Head still full of cotton batting. Somebody had troweled smear over his eyes. He rubbed them just as Andrea spoke. Missed it.

"You left the holo on," Andrea repeated.

"Oh, yeah?" Mitch said. "How's breakfast coming?"

"I'm late already. Sorry. I don't have time."

"No, no, I'm sorry," Mitch replied. "I must not have heard you right. The usual is okay."

Mitch wasn't being a hardass. Just keeping to the regimen. Andrea knew the rules. You get to stay over? You get to make breakfast. No moving the goalposts.

There was a pause. Footsteps padding across the floor. Then a cupboard door opened. Rattle of crockery. He headed to the john. Glad in a way he hadn't pissed in the sink. Crossed his mind while she was in the shower. But she'd have probably caught whiff. Maybe risked mentioning it. Woman got exercised for some reason. Mitch wasn't sure why. All went the same place.

Fifteen minutes. Drama over. Shit, shower and shave complete. He rolled out to the living room. Threw his towel over the chair back for Andrea to wash later. Was suddenly ravenous. The aroma hit him like a love tap. Instant salivation.

"Poached eggs, three slices of bacon, hash browns, toast, orange juice and coffee. Fine?" Andrea peered out from the kitchen alcove. Cheerful smile. Eyes twinkling.

Mitch forced a smile back. "No grapefruit? I like grapefruit for breakfast."

Andrea closed her eyes. "Sorry, I forgot."

Mitch shrugged. "Don't kill yourself over it. Just have to get my vitamins somewhere else today, I guess."

Slipped into the bedroom. Out again, dressed. Two minutes. Mystery what women did that took so long.

Arrived at the table, tongue out.

"Sleep good?" Obligatory small talk. It hurt. But Mitch understood the ritual counted with women. Went along to get along. Didn't cost much.

Andrea stood beside him as he sat. "Wonderful," she whispered. "Deep. As always."

"Yeah, me too," Mitch grinned. Reaching up. Squeezed a nip. "Alright, pitter patter…"

Grabbed his knife and fork. Noticed there was only one place setting. Arched his eyebrows at Andrea. "Where's yours?" Andrea wore a pained look.

"I wish I could stay. Really." Chewed her lip. Mitch sighed. Could guess what was coming.

"I…I should phone the office. Tell them I'll be late."

Mitch pulled a face. He never liked it when a biz prick held sway. They were so unworthy. Punched back a quick mouthful of egg and toast. Thought for a moment. Held up a finger.

"I can help," he mumbled while swallowing. Got up. Went to the stand near the door. Shuffled through chips he kept in a widowed saucer. Brought one back to the table. Tossed it to Andrea. Resumed eating.

"Say a cop pulled you over," Mitch advised. "Show suitboy that chip. It's Monopoly. Get. Out. Of. Jail. Free." Gave the hash browns a welcome grin. Back to the happy chore.

Andrea examined the chip as she put on her coat. "My boss is a real stickler…" she said. Doubt coloured the statement.

"Fuck'im," Mitch said around another mouthful. "If he gives you any grief, let me know. Little prick. I'll have a chat with him some night. Before he crawls home to his fat-pig ballbuster."

Andrea beamed. "You'd talk to him?"

"Do more than that," Mitch snarled. Slathered raspberry jam on the browned shingle. Pictured putting Mr. Corner Office in The Chair for a session. Wasn't a bad idea on general principles alone. Maybe work a bonus out of it for Andrea. She put in lots of extra hours for the cocksmokers. She deserved it. And Mitch wanted new speakers in the Gringolet. Win-win.

Plus, the karmic ripples thing. Sage talked about it. Shake some asshole senseless in Toronto. Millions die of famine in Africa after. No more war. Ripples. It was a funny old planet.

He sipped his coffee. Perfect temperature. Sighed. Filed the hard edge off. He looked up to signal gratitude. Andrea seemed to like it.

"Not bad," he nodded at the table. "Hitting the spot, no qestion."

Andrea turned. Beamed gratitude. "I'm so glad. Bacon wasn't overdone?"

"Nope," Mitch lied. She did do bacon a touch crispier than he liked it. He'd mention it another time. Keep it noble, knight.

"Well, I'd better go," Andrea announced. Her hand passed over the lock. ID registered, the door hissed open.

"Have a good one," Mitch said.

"You too, honey," Andrea replied.

"Back the usual time?"

Andrea stopped. "What's today? Thursday?" She paused. "I think so. Why?" She turned back to look at Mitch. He spread his arms over the table. Nodded towards the kitchen.

"Don't worry," she laughed. "I'll clean everything up when I come home. Back here," she corrected herself. "Can't wait."

Mitch shot her a thumbs-up. "Beautiful. Sayonara, baby." And she was out the door and gone.

Mitch swabbed up the rest of the drippings. Wiped his mouth. Belched. Did an injury survey. Seemed okay. Got his smokes. Lit one. Swigged more coffee to ease passage. Still winced. That first drag always murder. Like inhaling shredded glass. Throat took a beating the night before. More Joe. Started to plan the day.

The SD message. Have to get working on that. Could be a break in the case. That's how it worked, Max said. The crims kept your interest up. Usually stupid enough to leave around helpful shit. Or they fucked up so badly you couldn't help finally arresting them. Even if it was a bother.

Wondered about the stupid symbol again. Morons. What next? Decoder rings? Hidden signal com jingles? Play revolutionaries. 'Look, look, look at me!' Immature wankers.

Fuck them, Mitch thought. Someone at CORE would know what to do. He'd drop the SD off with Research. Let them decipher it. That was their job. If they found out anything worthwhile, they'd get back to him. Bingo. No worries, mate.

Mitch congratulated himself. That's how you do things. Definite enthusiasm swing. He'd hit the shop. Trade a few tales about Billy's. See what was lined up in the Tank. Find something to keep his new little buddy busy. Get in a workout. And there was a day.

Mitch yawned. Killed the cig. Threw back the last, luke-warm dregs. Never leave caffeine. Pushed his chair back. Stopped. Radar registering something. Political had told him to pay attention to that sense. Develop it. Let his eyes drift around the room. Supposed to help the mind feed him the tickler. Pretend he wasn't paying attention. Find by not looking, the Sage had said.

Back to the SD again. And the warning. What slick fucker had slipped it into his smokes, he wondered anew? Mitch didn't like people touching his property without permission. It rankled. Impudent swine.

And was it possible? Someone at last night's ugly fest was an agent for the other team? No, Mitch shook off the idea. Inconceivable. When, who, why? Questions that needed answering, for certain. Mitch cleared his throat. One last spine-cracking stretch. Then action time.

Minute later, coat, scarf, boots, gloves readied. Final scan. No flames shooting out from anywhere. Wallet in pocket. Scooped toonies from the tray. SecCard, smokes, lazer, spare chips. Holo still off. Mitch clicked the doorguard. Good to go. Lock down. Out and into a frigid hallway. Eco fuckheads. Building an igloo.

THE DOCTOR WILL SEE YOU

⸺◁◇▷⸺

Mitch had slaved away for almost two hours. Yaz come and gone. Bushy sent on a semi-snipe hunt. File-mining, third floor. Meanwhile, Mitch cleaned up most of his uni mail. E-sparks, Nigerian spamscams, etc., erased.

Next. Online conference review, Billy's Beluga Babes show. Great read. Submitted a case update after. Only took a minute. Progress minimal. Slight exaggeration. Progress nil. No mention of the SD slipped into his smokes. Research had wired the bad news. Routine techmonkey fail. Upload successful. Material looked top-drawer on first perusal. TechChief overjoyed. Huge intel find. Folllowed by huge intel dump. Key mis-hit. Immediate blameshift to robovirus. Backup HD's also infected, wiped. Everything etherized. Thanks for the help. Go back to sleep, digitdick.

"Gone, daddy-o, gone. Vacummed up," the TechHead said.

"Hubba, hubba, Bubba," Mitch replied. Not the least surprised. Propellerheads. Famously incompetent. Expected no better. "Shit happens, boyo. Worry not. If it loves us, it'll come back. If not, fuck it."

The chief flashed the seppuku icon. Signed off. No need for dramatics. Mitch was King Forgive when it came to colleagues. Still, he was tempted to return to Billy's that night. Imprint a message onto a stall wall. "Yo! Weasel sneak. Great SD. Need another. Will pay. Regards, Magnet Milligan." Who knew? Might work.

He'd been putting off the next task. No getting around it, though. She'd contacted them first. Had to be done. Especially since it involved his case. Punched up the number. Watched them dance across the holoscreen. And again with the heebie jeebies as he waited. Second time that morning. Invisible fingers tickled hairs on the back of his neck. Nothing behind him but his office window, he knew. Anything gaining on him was forty feet in the air climbing a vertical glass wall.

131

Three cheery burbles. A woman answered. Mitch apologized for the delay in responding. Brief discussion. They arranged to meet at the hospital. Sunningdale, this time. Second floor cafeteria, Corpse Wing. Mitch figured to fly if he wanted to be there in time for lunch. Not that he was panting for hospital tailings.

He made it, just. Into the lobby. Flashed his com at the sensor. Guardbot released the barrier.

"Dr. Talia?" Mitch said. Hand out to meet the tall, brunette advancing on him.

"Robbins," the woman replied. "Sorry." Exposed a dazzling smile. "Please call me Katherine."

Mitch apologized. Silently cursed Goodfellow. He'd already found out her name wasn't Janet Talia. Idiot kept getting the names wrong. And now he had Mitch repeating the mistake.

The doctor spun around. Headed down the dimly lit corridor. "The cafeteria is over here. Please excuse the stench."

"Yeah," Mitch said, wrinkling his nose. "What is that?"

"The cleaning staff," the doctor said over her shoulder. "There isn't any. No money. Visitors are asked to help out while they wait. One more reason to have them linger here for hours at a time."

Mitch looked anxious. The doctor waved a hand. "Police officers are always excused."

"Actually…" Mitch began. The doctor glanced over her shoulder.

"Or CORE men, of course."

Mitch nodded, relieved. For him, hospitals were death zones. He'd sooner gargle toilet water than be inside one. Wondered what ancient simpleton thought gathering horribly diseased people in one place was a clever idea? He'd huffed enough disinfectant spray before coming to eliminate malaria in the third world. Still had no faith it was potent enough to kill whatever invisible shit lurked around him.

"One good point about the policy," the doctor said. Paused in the cafeteria entrance. Let KillBac radibeams flicker over her. Chime trills. Meaning live hits. Mitch grimaced. Walked through the green screen after. No sound. Still clean. For how long was anyone's guess.

"Low visitor count these days." The doctor headed for the most secluded part of the cafeteria. "No one wants to watch imports play stack the gurneys. It's too depressing. With luck, Grandma's off her head with meds anyway. Best to sneak out. Don't think about it. Not to mention avoid contracting something nasty. Easily done, too."

Mitch could feel sweat bloom. The very thing he dreaded. Catching a case of death. Pasted on a smile. The sarcasm he liked.

"Upside?" the doctor continued. "Our caregiving engineers have more time to tap out extensive reports no one reads. They know the score. You bring an elderly person to a hospital these days, it's to kill them. They miss a meal, no big deal."

Mitch joined her at the sloping table. One leg shorter than the others. The doctor only rolled her eyes. Nothing new.

He glanced around. Pasty gray walls. Stick pattern paint. 50's style dinette décor. To make you feel like you were somewhere pleasant. Not inside a factory that pumped out worm bait. Mitch kept his breathing to a minimum. Short in, quick out. Turtled into his jacket. Prayed the germs wouldn't notice he was there.

"So...how's the food?" he asked by way of starting the conversation.

"We're in a hospital," the doctor replied. Eyes never wavered.

Mitch closed his eyes. Smiled. "Right. Sorry."

Split second decision. One born of experience. Did a long take of the uniformed female sitting across from him. Made it more obvious than usual. Mitch the pro. Figured out in grade school. Say whatever they want, women liked being stared at. Slavered over. He'd already admired her ass during the walk. Had even stolen a side glance at the exposed cleavage easing past to his chair. Impressive ta-ta's for a BigPharm shill. Early forties, he guessed. Very well preserved. Upright, athletic posture. Ink black hair summoned into a bun. Lines around the eyes. But not bitch ripples from glaring, he didn't think. Great teeth. Hint of freckles across the bridge of her nose. Not bad. Not bad at all. Way better looking than Mort. He'd have to tell him that.

"I want to thank you for coming," the woman said. Fished in her lab coat. Pulled out a mini-gravestone. Finecut Virginia deadlies.

"Umm, sorry I didn't get back to you sooner," Mitch apologized again. He tried not to look shocked. This was Moronto. PC capital of Canada. Where fun was forbidden. Yet this woman, a doctor no less, was lighting up. "Just, you know, busy and everything."

Pastel-blue box. Menthol. For bleeders. Or that Winston brand for gays. He wasn't sure which. No worse taste imaginable. Mitch couldn't hack them for anything. If menthol's your flavour, quit fucking smoking altogether. How Mitch looked at it. Made no sense he could see.

The doctor nodded. "I understand. Police work. I don't know how you do it. It must be exhausting."

Mitch said nothing. Hard smile. Thousand yard stare. Too easy.

"Excuse me, but..." Mitch nodded at her smoke. "I thought there's no... well, fuck, nowhere, these days."

The doctor laughed. Exhaled a magnificent jet of smoke out the side of her mouth. Aimed it straight at the next table. Nice trick. Hovered over a middle-aged couple, just sat down. Look of all hospital-goers. Grim, haggard-faced, bagged. Beaten down by boredom. Bed attenders. Waiting for God to finally fucking appear. Flaming sword. Scissors into her unseeing eyes. Garotte. Anything. Call the bank. Release the swag.

Flash of Toronto face. Don't-you-know-smoking-is-awful? We-feel-disgust.

The doctor froze them. Proper sneer of contempt. "Problem?"

Eyes down. Eat the retort. Must kowtow to the new priests. Perfect sheep. Mitch recognized the type. NPOT supporters, for certain. Had that slippery, feral look of the grasping and untalented. Probably worked for the city. Who didn't these days?

"I smoke where and when I want," she said. Extra loud. Mitch struggled not to break character. Added, "It kills the stink of this joint. Besides, anyone complains, maybe I do a Demers on a loved one. Nick an intestine. Forget a scalpel inside. Or a glove. Shame, but…ac-ci-dents…hap-pen."

Cute singing voice. Mitch falling in love.

The couple took the hint. Rose to their feet. Left without remark. Mitch half-amazed they didn't think to offer a bribe. Have mother moneybags put out of their misery. Fifty percent chance they'd be on that world cruise in time for Christmas in the Bahamas.

Mitch licked blood from his lip. Stared at her chest to keep from laughing. Thought about sex. Felt her eyes on him now. Examining him over the barrel of her cigarette. Mitch knew the gaze. Measuring him. Was he sensitive? Self-deprecating? Bookish? Did he suck cock, in other words? And that little curl of her lip telling him she'd instantly read the truth. A CBC careerist? Not a chance.

He swallowed the urge to confirm her valid analysis. Admit he was a certified, bone-crushing Neanderthal. Books were props. Sensitive was what ears got after being frost-bitten. Self-deprecating…he didn't actually know the meaning. Heard it said on the holo. Sounded right. Had to do with whacking off, he knew. Something Mitch had almost forgotten how to do.

He managed a wry, devilish crook of his mouth. Distract her from the sound of fabric tearing. He'd just entertained a smoking fantasy. The doctor, naked, greasing his weasel. Jaw slack. Jugs jouncing. Lust-dulled domelamps. Result? His cock had blown through his boxers. Terrible timing. Tried to clear his mind.

New thoughts entered. Now she was hanging from an ironwood crossbeam. Really naked. Yellow rig ropes cruelly cut into her wrists. Her enormous breasts jutted towards him. Dairy cannons in distress. The ripe, nourishing nipples erect as lighthouses. Beacons begging for assistance. He approached, full prong on. She arched her back. Enveloped him. Joyful peals of delicious anguish.

And forward he pushed, pummeling her axe gash with abandon. Freeing her tortured soul courtesy of a relentless pounding fuck that…

Mitch cursed his incredible imagination. Wasting time. With any effort he could be doing it for real. Worse, the seams in his jeans were weakening. He needed to get his head back in the game. Couldn't take another pair in to get fixed. That Korean sewing slut's perma-frown was getting to him. King Hardon must relax. Otherwise, he'd have to order food. Wait for the tide to go out. That prospect, plus the sight of two sickies shuffling past. Steaming goop on their plastic trays. Metal leeched from the shaft. Another three minutes. He'd be able to walk without doing himself a mischief.

"So you don't mind if I have a breath of fresh air myself?" he asked. Stay on topic. No more mentally undressing anyone.

"Please," Dr. Robbins said. The woman was definitely available. Unmistakeable signals. Parted lips. Darting shot of lizard tongue. Nostrils widening. He'd seen it hundreds and hundreds of times. They usd to have a name for it. Maybe still did.

Anyway, she was one. Desperate and lonely. Clock near ticked out. Body hanging in…but just. Soon enough, the unattached-career-woman Euro tour. Egypt. Turkey. Ur. Group excusions to the Andes. Half the passengers, fat and unfuckable. Bitter maidens knowing they'd been cheated. Dividend checks instead of birthday cards from grandchildren. The other half, fat dykos frantically looking for one last chance at beaverdom. Stupid femmes. Got what they said they wanted. Looked good on them.

Mitch's wood entirely vanished. Remember this cure, he told himself. A Norwegian Liner full of hungry Georges. Proufoundly anti-arousing image.

But the doctor seemed nice. Dark strain of humour. Dating life would suffer in her business. Could hear a Dimitri the lover bar conversation.

"So…what do you do?"
"I work in a pest house."
"So long."

Zero sex appeal to her occupation, apart from the money. And from what Mitch had seen, doctors were only randy in the vids. The ones he'd met would have trouble getting sex from bot hogs. Charisma challenged. Not to mention the sickening hospital smell that followed them around like a bad fart. He did his best to avoid them. Except Mort. Who was normal…in that he could work his mouth with the best of them. And hated PC shitheads.

Mitch lit a stick. Drew in a tasty lungful. Matched the direction of her previous funnel cloud.

"You're right," he nodded. Raised his head to sniff the air. "That urinal cake tang. Not so much now."

Mitch made a show of looking for an ashtray. The doctor winked. Pointed at the floor. Mitch flicked. Shot a look her hand. No ring. Dick alert. Locks were opening again. Mitch wondered if he could catch Andrea on break at her office. Finesse her into a closet. Play hide-the-helmet for ten minutes. He couldn't believe he needed to bleed the valve again. If he hurried, maybe....

"Well," he cleared his throat. Waded in. "Should we...?"

The doctor nodded.

"I've got...these appointments. Witnesses to interview. Deductions to make. Detective shit, yeah. You understand?"

"Of course," Katherine smiled. Took a deep breath. Stopped to look at the ceiling. Mitch got shifty also. Except for the neo-zombies, they were almost alone.

"What?" he asked.

"I was told by someone in your office that...you're responsible for a particular case? One where a...body was retrieved from the lakefront?"

"Yeah," Mitch confirmed, "They found this old chunk-a-slut...oops, sorry..."

The doctor rolled her eyes. "Please. You should work here. I know what you mean. No need to walk on eggshells."

Mitch was grateful. Also amused. He'd never heard that bit about eggshells before. Have to remember it. "Okay, so...out on the beach somewhere. Last week. I forget when exactly. My coach...er, my...supervisor asked me to look into it. Apparently, it's not the first. Why?"

The doctor gazed directly at Mitch. He returned it. What he wanted to do right then was tear her asylum jacket off and clamp mouth on her hooters. Taste those tantalizing twizzlers.

"Well, then, it may interest you to know that...that was no woman you found." The doctor worked on her cigarette. Mitch frowned. Eyed the room. Puzzled on the meaning. Nothing.

"Come again?" he finally said.

The doctor inclined her head towards Mitch. Brown eyes twinkled in amusement. "Your 'she' was...in reality...a 'he'."

"What?" Mitch said abruptly. Prairie gophered erect in his chair. "Fuck off!"

"I'm afraid it's true." Delightful giggle. Cigarette extinguished on the formica table top. Casually backhanded onto the floor. "The...'chunk', as you say, was a transsexual...chunk."

"Ewwww...a tranny?!!" Mitch exclaimed. Disgust contorted his face. He stuck out his tongue without thinking. Retracted it in horror. Prayed he hadn't committed a gross error. Said, "Ewwwww…!!" again. Shivered.

Doctor Robbins tittered to watch Mitch digest the news.

"You know for sure? I mean…how…can you…" Mitch did not want to go where his question led.

"I'm a gynecologist."

"Oh, yeah. Well, I guess…" Mitch talked himself out of simply leaving. Quit everything. Get up, walk away. Move back home. The Kap wasn't Sudbury or anything for night life. But you could live there for another century and only ever see normal freaks. Trannies were outta line. Scandalous.

Unfortunately, he'd be letting the Commissioner down. He was there as a representative of CORE. Options limited. He drummed his fingers on the table, thinking. Unclamped his teeth.

"So, let me get this straight. That…thing we dumped at the morgue. It used to be a woman…at one point. Sorry…it used to be a man at one point… but then it…it…turned into a…woman? Have I got that right?"

"Well, with the help of a lot of drugs…and surgery."

"E-w-w-w-w-w-w! Christ, don't say that!" Mitch groaned. Lowered his head to the table. Banged it up and down several times. Hollow moan. "Fuck me. That's why I was given this stupid case. No one else wants to touch it. Literally. F-u-u-u-u-u-uck! Fuck, fuck, fuck!"

Mitch raised his head. Looked at the doctor.

She pressed her lips together in commiseration. "Tough break."

"Shit," he cursed under his breath. "You don't know the half of it." Spit-laughed in spite of the unspeakable nastiness. "Half…of…it," he choked out. "Geddit? Half-man, half-woman…half-human…half-monster."

The doctor patted his hand. "Do you have any leads?" Compassion for Mitch's obvious discomfort. It softened her features even more. Mitch's other problem. Vanished at first mention of the sexling. Fire out. Send the truck home.

"Hmm?" Mitch broke away from despair. Gestured. "Oh, well, you know, sure…a few. We're on top of things. Doing the legwork. Talking to…anyone. People. Finding clues." Then erasing them, Mitch thought bitterly. Digitdorks. "It' s a 24/7 thing, yeah? Constant."

"I'm sure you'll find whomever's responsible," the doctor smiled. Squeezed Mitch's hand. Embers flared below. "You look to be a very…instinctual person. Someone who sees something that needs to be done and just…acts. Like an animal."

Mitch wasn't so distracted by the gut-drilling account that he missed the doctor's subtle flirting. He could multi-task as well as anyone. And when it came to planning sexcapades while ostensibly working? He took a back seat to no one. Not only had he dreamed of mattress-slamming the good doctor. He'd also pondered how he could slide out from under his assignment some way. And not look bad with Ciccarrelli. Mitch wanted to work a sex-changer case like he wanted to meet Andrea's parents.

Yaz. The perfect patsy. Honest, keen, smart. Except he wasn't with CORE. Everyone would know Mitch was doing the slider act. But who else could he slough this shit file onto? Goodfellow? What the hell did he do upstairs? Other than send Mitch dodgy information? Bastard. The rest would smell trouble if it came from him. No, it was Mitch's anchor to bear. He knew it. And he'd go to the bottom with it. Fuck everyone.

"You know, you have a very strong jaw," the doctor observed. "You look like one of those wilderness survival types…or maybe some tar-field roughhand from Alberta."

Mitch thought for a second. Grinned despite his mood. Just then a plate smashed somewhere in the kitchen. The ringing sounds interrupted his reply.

"Caught it," a voice said. Gales of laughter followed. LUB humour.

A new angle suddenly occurred to Mitch. "Did someone from Metro PD contact you? Or was it just CORE?"

"Both. The police were first."

"Why you?"

"I've had some experience in this…field. They asked for my opinion. But this research is rarely authorized for release. That's why I thought someone handling the case personally should know the details."

"I don't know," Mitch mused, eyes narrowing. "I think somebody else has a hand in the game. I wish I knew who…or why? Was there anything else disgusting about the body? Apart from…?"

The doctor concentrated. "Nothing I can think of now," she said, shrugging. "Just that she…he…"

"It," Mitch helped.

"It," the doctor giggled again, "was well-advanced."

"Meaning she'd been marinated for…?"

"No, no, that she was…fully developed. Her organs were…"

"Argh!" Mitch cried. "Stop. Stop! No more!" Clapped his hands over his ears.

The doctor's eyes filled with tears of amusement. Mitch's disgust was so honest, so unaffected. She'd almost forgotten how regular people responded. Her circle of colleagues and acquaintances had long since embraced the new thinking. Equivocating mental defectives to a person. It left her suicidal some nights.

"Forgive me," she apologized. "It is fucking appalling. But we're supposed to pretend it isn't. It's not you. Don't worry."

Mitch thanked her with his eyes. Kept his hands firmly in place.

The doctor continued as if Mitch could hear hear. Which he could. "And I'm...in my role as a gynecologist...well...I see things every day that would make a...kill-line hog-slaughterer toss his lunch."

"Jesus," Mitch said. Shuddered. Some things were best left unsaid. Especially about wanky worm holes.

"Yeah," the doctor said. Shook her head in wry understanding. "There's a real similiarity there. Hospitals are mostly just abbatoirs with paved parking. Except they lose tons of money."

Mitch turtled again. The conversation had turned awful.

"I'm surprised you're chilly," the doctor said. "Most people complain it's too hot. We like to keep the mercury high. It helps the bacteria breed faster."

"You're joking, right?" a wan Mitch said. Gave up trying not to hear anything.

"Not really," Katherine replied. Broad wink at recently occupied table of rubber-neckers. Brushed a strand of hair back into place. "Well, I should get back to work. Wouldn't want to keep my patients waiting."

"Okay, now I know that's a joke," Mitch responded immediately.

The doctor flashed a girlish smirk. Sat erect. A feigned stretch succeeded in fully displaying her bounties. Mitch did her the honour of bald leering. Mission accomplished. No confusion about where each party stood. The doctor deposited her cigarettes and lazer. Mitch did likewise. They headed for the exit. The doctor waved her card at the wand. "My treat."

"Oh, yeah. Thanks," Mitch stuttered. "What? Wait a minute. We didn't have anything." Cocky spaniel. Woman was a shameless tease. He searched for an approach.

"Well," he said, slight edge to his voice, "Appreciate the...run-through. Most of it, anyway. It's been...um...an eye-opener, for sure." Mitch checked out the taut bottom again as she walked around the corner. Forgiveness washed over him. Usually he hated the idiot blue uniforms doctors wore. Not to mention the idiots swanning about inside them. Arrogant, dangerous, cloth-eared fuckwits, most of them. But at that moment the material shaped the product rather well. He wanted nothing more than to latch on. Take those cheeks out for a back-street test drive. Rex at the wheel. Woof woof.

They reached the entrance. Mitch fumbled in his jacket. Handed over a minidriver. "Umm...if anything else unspeakable comes up regarding that... thing, please don't call this number."

The doctor brought a hand to her mouth. Dignified, tinkling laugh that had his heart soaring like a hawk. Mitch sensed woody again. Telegraphed the thought. Armed doorbot or not, Mitch was ready to pull her into surgery. Salve for the weeping wound.

She took his gift. Held his hand an extra two seconds. Total tell. Slid it into her chest pocket. Dropped her head to the side. Extended a fresh lower lip. Did a coquette sultry pout.

"Don't you want to know how she…?"

"It," Mitch corrected.

"It," the doctor bowed her head, "died?"

"Well after what you've told me, I just figured…shame and embarrassment."

The doctor threw her head back and howled with true enjoyment. Mitch's material—gold. In the admit office, several trolls came to. Lifted their graying heads. Shared questioning looks with each other. The doctor stopped in mid-laugh. Wheeled on them.

"Back to sleep, you fat fucking ruminants!" she snapped. A dozen foreheads promptly found unitop.

"Lazy union bastards," the doctor sneered. Looked off over Mitch's head as she composed herself.

"It was an absolute delight meeting you, Mr…?" she paused. Winking apology.

"Mitch…Mitch, please." Put his hand on his heart. Smiled. "I'll be in touch. That be okay?"

"I'm here all the time," the doctor said, sour.

Mitch raised his hand in a farewell salute. Bounced out the door. Handsome woman. Reminded him of his escort days. They went without so long they turned rabid when the opportunity arose. Case might be worth developing an interest in after all. He wondered if she supervised the cutwork on suspicious corpses. If the past was any indication, more trulls would be turning up soon. Give him an excuse to drop by. Fingers crossed. Little did he know.

Mitch hadn't driven a minute from the clinic when he saw Yaz. Far sidewalk. Heading where he'd just come from. He tapped the bleater. Traffic opening appeared. He cut off a taxi. Ignored the horn. Eased the Gringolet near the curb. Passenger window down.

Yaz hit a break. Raced across to where Mitch idled. Seconds later he was inside, blowing on his hands. Quickly explained his presence. Com signal but no answer. GPS had identified Mitch's whereabouts.

"Fuck! I turned it off," Mitch responded in alarm. "I was interviewing this…doctor." He reached into his coat. Found found his com. Unlocked it. Read the message. Swore under his breath. "What time did they call you?"

Yaz told him. Mitch did some hasty calculations. "Maybe...maybe...
maybe."

He touched the alarm. Silent alert to any local D.P.'s turtle. VIP speeding
past. Relax. Sirens off. Stuff in another crueller, Charlie.

Mitch worked his way along Finch. Blew through the lights at Dufferin,
bleater screaming. Felt the anger. Right onto Bathurst. Home stretch. A late
model Guevara appeared in his mirror. Mitch let it get close, then abruptly
pulled ahead. Deftly boxed it off. Panic squeak of brakes. Tinny complaint.
Furious goatee action from the driver. Mitch held up a middle-finger victory
salute.

"Love doing that," he grinned at Yaz. "Government Motors. Wonder a
fucking door didn't fall off."

He pressed a panel. Grinned again at Yaz. "Seen these?"

"What?" Yaz had no idea.

"New," Mitch chortled. "From China. Ass message. Pre-loaded. Flashed
one to my little buddy behind me." Mitch let loose a malevolent snicker. "If I
wasn't in such a rush, I'd have him to stop somewhere. Invite him to beat the
shit out of me." Mitch said. Regretful sigh. "Duty calls, though."

Yaz sensed the urgency. Double-checked his safety harness.

Mitch gave the Gringolet its head. "And I do not want to miss this!"

LACY LEARNS A LESSON

---◄◦►---

Mitch rolled into The Tank. Pumped and ready.

"Don't bring any paper near me!" he bellowed. "I'm hotter than..." Stopped. Focused on the strange fruit hanging from the ceiling. Punchline forgotten. Instead, the universal query.

"What the fuck?"

Political Bob looked up. Pulled back from under The Chair. Grinned. "Hey, boyo. What kept you so long?"

Mitch shivered, sighed. Walked over. "Don't ask. Tell you later." Thumbed at the dangler. "What's with raw and scrawny? And the Hanes?" Mitch referring to the strapped and hanging. With the grimy-looking Y-fronts. Didn't match safety vest.

"Been prepped?"

Mitch nodded. "Uncle Ben's. I know who and why. That's it. Didn't even look at the monitor. Afraid I'd be late."

The figure suddenly began to kick about wildly. A high-pitched warble pierced the air. Mitch checked for Political's reaction. The man shook his head in disgust. Dome glow. Man had got a serious cut. Already sweating. Not like Political.

"You wouldn't believe this fuck," he said to Mitch. "I hated him before. Now I really hate him."

"You can't do this to me, you fascists!" the man screamed. He wrenched his body from side to side. "I'm a lawyer!"

Political snorted. "Listen to this guy." Flipped his crow bar so the teeth were out. Purposefully raked it across the man's shoulder blades. The sweet, sweet sound of howling. No more guttermouth talk. Only judders and whimpering. Much easier to endure. And more natural for the Tank.

Mitch couldn't take his eyes off the works the man was attached to. "How in hell did you rig this thing up," he asked, pointing at the ceiling. Political snorted. Bent low. Reached back under the Chair. Soft snicking whisper. Panel snugged vacuum tight. Winking, Political joined Mitch seconds later.

"How long have you worked in the Tank?" he asked. Eyebrows beetling. The massive forehead glistened. Popeye biceps looked ready to explode. Mitch thought again of the stories. Political in Manhattan. Beat cop in the "quarter and deuce." The bad old days. Progressives busy bankrupting the city. He later claimed working New York was scarier than anything in Iraq or Afghanistan. Hard to believe. The man didn't look to know fear.

Mitch answered. "Over a year…maybe two."

"And used the Chair?"

"Same amount of time, I guess. Why?"

"Read the manual?" Political asked. Smug expression.

"Yeah," Mitch replied. Squared his shoulders. "Well…some of it. Not all of it."

Political gave Mitch the look. "You didn't read the part about the winch, then."

Mitch's eyes widened. "No way."

Political looked at the now quiet sack of beige. "Only reason I'm not riding you harder is…I didn't know myself. Found out by accident. Couple months ago. So who else is stupid? Twenty bucks says no one else knows either. Check instructions? This crew?"

Mitch looked up, frowning. "It's…but…?"

"So we can do the shit you're about to see," Political read his mind. "It's…a little tricky. That's why I wanted to wait till I got good at it." They both stood and gazed at the unit. Mitch had noticed the iron bar before. Ran the length of the room. Holes punctured it a regular intervals. Thought it was some kind of sprinkler thing. Attached to it, at intervals of a metre or so, miniature flywheels. Six inches in diameter. Hidden above, Mitch guessed a nano reactor. Heat baffles around it. Several metal rings grouped in the centre. Looked solid. Like The Chair. And the Tank.

Political had pattern-threaded #9 rig rope through the rings. Fixed them to the hard plastic vest strapped to Mr. Whiny.

"I tell you," Political said, moving towards the table. Slid the crowbar under. "The goddamn genius that designed our Chair? Man knew something, yeah?"

Mitch nodded. Famous story. Some wizard from Hamilton. Mitch remembered pictures of the prototype. Looked like a golf cart fucking a wheelchair. Nothing like the sleek wonder they were using now.

"Everything is so…well thought out." Political stopped to admire it again. He really did love the Chair. Shit, who didn't? Wonder device.

"So…" Mitch prompted.

"So…now we have us a little fun," Political said with authority. Clapped Mitch on the back.

"Not just us," Mitch noted. "Lounge is packed. You should see it out there. Fucking zoo."

"Yeah? Well, they're in for a show today," Political promised. "I've got a special treat for our friend here."

A string of mumbled threats from the hanging man. Facing away from them. Mitch glanced at Political who made a fist. Mouthed, "Irritating fuck!"

Political moved closer. "Richard M…for Meletus…Vermann," he said. Speaking to the man's back. "Dumbest middle name…ever. Dumbest C&D names…ever."

'Lacy' Vermann. Mitch knew some of the backstory. Online slimecrim. Serial sock-puppet. Blog salter. Privacy invader. Drive-by smear artist. IP hacker. Slander man. As odious a piece of webshite as ever loitered in public washrooms. Which was his weekend hobby, according to police. Mitch could only shake his head. The country was going through a deeply weird patch. The man pulling levers behind the curtain was a lefty loon. Not good.

Worse yet, he'd acted on behalf of the Force. Idiots. Huge embarrassment. Canadian security field disgraced. CORE won the toss. Kicked his ass into a hauler. Brought him in for "questioning." Vermann was a score. Mitch was delighted to be invited to the party.

Political hitched his uniform up. "La-a-a-a-c-c-c-cy! You got some 'splainin' to do." Winked at Mitch, who didn't get it. American thing. Like Piggly Wiggly. Or Dr. Pepper. "You know why you're here, right?"

"You're all going to jail!" Vermann gurgled, shrill-anxious. "You're criminals! Who are you? You're not the police." More comical running in place. Feet a half-metre off the ground. "I demand to be released immediately! Do you know who I am? I have friends in the RCMP. I know journalists. You are all in serious trouble. Have you any idea…?"

"Hey!" Mitch barked. "Shut the fuck up! Man's talkin' to ya'" Mitch shot a glance at Political.

"I told you. I'm so gonna enjoy this," Political growled. Shimmied left. Kept the two-way sightlines clean. Stood glaring at Vermann's pasty profile. "Listen up, Vermann, you motormouth fuckwit. You're hanging from my ceiling. In your underwear. Who's in a world a trouble now? Huh?"

Vermann wheezed, tomato-faced from his exertions.

"You, you fucking suckpoppet!" Political said, jabbing his finger.

Mitch turned to look at the wall.

"Suckpocket, I meant to say," Political self-corrected. "Fuck me! Sockpucket!" Stopped to look at Mitch in disbelief. All his partner could do to keep a straight face.

"Let me try," Mitch suggested. Political waved him on.

"Vermann, you lying...blog-diddling...toiletghost bag of pus." Mitch looked at Political, who bowed.

"Better," Political acknowledged. He pointed at the table. "Continue. Back in two."

"How many fucking secret identities you have anyway?" Mitch asked to kill time. No answer.

Political returned. Sported heavy, rubberized work gloves. Casual approach to Vermann. Drilled an overhand into the ratbag's ribcage. A satisfying screech of pain followed.

"Release me!" Vermann yelled when his breath returned. "Release me now!" He squirmed against the ropes, panting heavily.

"Police release me, let me go," Political crooned.

Vermann paused to shout, "You're all Nazi's! Nazi's! I know all about you! You're everywhere! You're trying to take over. Trilateral Commission! Bilderberg! SPP! Nazi's!"

Mitch looked at the better-read Political. "Bill who?"

Political shrugged, hands out.

Vermann ranted on. Mitch couldn't decipher most of it. Sidled closer to Political. Leaned in. "No one told me he was fucking loco."

Political dipped his shoulder in agreement. Raised his voice into Mitch's ear. "Yeah...I, uh...I didn't know he was this far gone, either. To be honest."

"I mean it," Mitch continued. "He's certifiable. There's no chicken in the bucket. Maybe we should send him back. I think he's broken."

"Well, I'm tired a listenin' to this shit. That much is true." Political muttered. He motioned Mitch back two steps to the wall.

Backs to Vermann, Political said, "The file is pretty clear. He thinks this is the beginning of the...Hitler Republic of Canada. Something like that."

Mitch nodded. Read about that. Tinfoil hat type.

"His kind...believe the Nazi's re-located into the States. They run things now. Just waiting for the right moment."

"We should be so lucky. Listen to him," Mitch gestured. "He really does sound fucked up. Don't you think so?"

Deep breath from Political. Wiped his forehead. "Apparently, CORE's been interested for other reasons. He's had his fingers in a lot of pies. And not those kind of pies, either,"Political said, lip curled. "Our boy's all girl... if you catch my drift."

"Yeah...something about him..." Mitch threw a look over his shoulder. Vermann had gone quiet again. His head was pitched towards them. Trying to listen in. Mitch snickered. Gestured to Political. "Check out rabbit ears here."

Political looked over. Vermann twisted away.

Mitch furrowed his brow. "I honestly can't believe the Mounties had this...dipstick on their payroll."

"Another reason we have him now," Political said. "Heads have rolled. New management moved in." He slid back to the table. Pulled out the magic carryall from under. Mitch tagged along.

Vermann launched into a new round of threats at the whisper of CORE. Put a big smile on Mitch's face. "Hey! He's heard of us."

Political continued to burrow and rummage. Mitch cocked an ear to the ongoing tirade. "Who's Helen Wiels?" he asked.

"Some bitch," Political mumbled. "You should know. She's always on the news. Her and Ribit the Horrible. Flapping their lips about something. Never thought I'd say this, but your femcunts are worse'n ours."

Mitch cleared his throat. Felt like a smoke. "Never heard of her," he admitted. "In fact, I never heard of any of those people he's talking about. Eve Pollet? Partlet?"

Negative grunt from Political.

"Evelyn Poorhorse? Alfred Scrufula? Peter Pavid? Nice name. Somebody or other Rosepick?"

"NPOT," Politcal said tersely. Mitch's eyes grew wide. The National Party of Toronto. That was interesting. Political Bob. He'd know if anyone did.

Vermann redoubled his efforts. To hear him talk, he knew everybody with pull. Mitch had tired of it. He left Political to his hunt. Walked over. Kicked Vermann in the upper thigh. Hard. It felt good to shut him up.

"Thank you," Political said over his shoulder when Mitch sauntered back.

Mitch patted him on the back. "Not to get gay here, but...I told my new partner we'd get after this case I'm on. Like today. Right after this. You think you'll be long?"

"Understood," Political responded. "Almost finished." He tossed Mitch a pair of work gloves. "Yeah, I heard you were being shadowed. How's it working out?"

"Good, so far. He's watching us now. Takin' in the pro's from Dover."

Politcal grunted again. Word received. Together they walked up to Vermann. Frantic neck craning. Left, then right. Looking at him, Mitch thought of a shaved dog. Political gestured at The Chair. Mitch stopped, hand on the frame. According to regs, his job clear. Keep a hard eye on Vermann at all times. Not that he was going anywhere. Didn't matter.

"Hmmmm..." Political murmured. He faced the wall opposite the two-way. Panel lights winked.

"Problem?" Mitch asked.

"No," Political said, absorbed. "Just…"

Mitch took the opportunity to goof around for the lounge crowd. Minced about mimicking Vermann's posture. Inside the theatre, agents roared. Mitch the cut-up. Good wholesome fun. Like tethering a fly to the ugly girl's ponytail.

"There," Political expelled held breath. "Always a little grief before the fun begins." Mitch heard a low-pitched hum. Turbine spin. Vermann jerked like a hooked fish. Mitch grinned. Anticipated grand entertainment.

"Watch yourself," Political warned. Pointed at Vermann. To Mitch's surprise, the shithead was slowly revolving in a circle. He took a cautious step back. Then another. Looked up. Rig ropes seemed secure.

Vermann's ravaged face swung past. From impertinence to panic. Eyes round as sewer lids. Rapid attitude adjustment. CORE terrorgators delighted in them. Not that it would likely do Vermann any good. If you were in the Tank, you were already guilty of something.

Political manipulated the remote. The spin increased. Vermann began yelling. Interesting sound variation as he was whipped in ever-flatter circles. Mitch checked Political, who nodded. He knew.

Around and around Verman spun. He was at a 45 degree pitch when Mitch thought of something. Elbowed Political.

"Reminds me…one a those Cirque de something guys?"

Smile from Political. Head bounce.

"Ever seen it?" Mitch wondered.

Political shook his head. "Nah. Kids wanted me to take'em once. Guess I should. Hear it's pretty good. You?"

"No. But the commercials look, you know…interesting. Bit gay."

"Oh, yeah," Political chuckled. "100%." His index finger danced over the remote. Mitch slapped his thighs. Excellent effect.

"Oh, shit," he choked. "Too funny!" Vermann looked like an Olympic backstroker launching himself from the pool wall. Vermann the Merman. Very wavy.

"Like it?" Political asked.

"It's great!" Mitch replied. Raised his voice. "How'd you do it?" Vermann was going soprano. Political shrugged. Held up the remote. Features. Mitch got the message. Sometimes a good thing.

Roar went up. Vermann the human ceiling fan. Lounge awash with hilarity. Agents pounded armrests, each other. Vid wizards mixmashed a sound track. Chipmunks in a canning factory. Overdubbed Swedish metal. Fed it through the speakers. Perfect accompaniment.

Mitch in convulsions. Another idea sparked. Shared it with Political. Negative response.

"Tried it a couple times already," Political yelled back. "No good. They just throw up."

"Too bad," Mitch yelled back.

Just then, Vermann gurgled. An unnerved Political pulled the string.

"Jesus," Mitch exclaimed. "That didn't sound good."

Political punched away. "I think he's had enough."

Mitch signaled galactic puking to the crowd. Nearly triggered it, guys were laughing so hard.

As Vermann's spin decayed, Political re-visited the carryall. Shyster's face something to see. Checkerboard splotchy. Red patches mixed with white. Fear or G-Force blood erosion. Mitch couldn't guess which.

Political reappeared. "Now then, Lacy," he began. "It seems you like trolling blogs. Leaving fake hate messages. Then complaining to your ass-bandit, trough-sucking buddies at fucking Human Rights."

An evil scowl returned to Vermann's face. He kicked out at Political, who laughed. Mitch wanted in. Political shook him off. His eyes lasered on Vermann.

"My friend here," Political nodded towards the impatient Mitch, "has a bone to pick with you. It seems you hacked into his old girlfriend's computer. Then used it to leave racist comments on various netblogs."

Political playing a bit fast and loose with the truth. Vermann had certainly hid behind proxy computers, and idiot monikers. But it wasn't actually Mitch's girlfriend who found out. Mitch had just overheard the story. In a Beerstore lineup, actually. Some guy knew a guy who knew a guy in Ottawa who knew the woman's sister. Didn't matter. Mitch despised sneaks. And Vermann was among the weasliest lurker he'd ever come across.

Vermann's eyes flickered around the Tank. No help to be found, Mitch could have told him. Copper-coloured crypt. Matte-black two-way. The doom twins. Vermann adrift, blood in the water.

"What kind of dipshit pretends to be a Nazi because he hates Nazi's?" Political asked. Answer buried in the question. A Political specialty.

"Someone who wishes he was a Nazi." Mitch answered anyway. Vermann reddened. Political's head bobbed.

"Yeah," he said. "Yeah. Makes me wonder if people who're always… banging on about how much they hate Nazi's…well, maybe they're…closet Nazi's!"

Vermann goggled at the comment.

"Irrefutable logic," Political said, baby face innocent. "They're in denial. The truth is too much to bear. So they cover their dirty little secret by pretending to denounce the very thing they are. Nazi's!"

Mitch had to laugh at Political's emphatic delivery. Slipped behind

Vermann at the same time. Listened to the fiend's strangled cry of indignation. Pulled his glove tight. Punched Vermann in the left kidney. A different screech of agony emitted. Back arched, Vermann heaved on the ropes. No escaping those shooting pains, though.

Approving nod from Political. Waited until Vermann's spasms subsided. He walked up. Grabbed a chunk of soft meat under Fernwell's right arm with his thumb and forefinger. Teeth exposed in a hard smile, he pinched as hard as he could. "Blackfly!" he shouted, snapping the skin back. Skipped away in glee. New high-pitched skirls of rage and anguish from Vermann.

"Hey, Lacy," Political spoke. Wiped his glove over his brow. Walked near. Gave the slick sack a hard sideways shove. "How much money you made off that Chapter 13 shit?" Vermann's eyes remained shut as he swung back and forth. "Tens of fucking thousands a dollars, I heard."

Mitch coughed. Massaged his knuckles. Felt the bile rise. Social Activist. Was there a lower form of hustler?

Political turned to Mitch. "Think this doofus knows anything about the Ovarians?"

Vermann stiffened. Mitch's eyes saucered. Looked hard at Political. Mitch hadn't given it a moment's thought. Index finger waggle from Political. Follow his lead.

"Oooh, hit a nerve," Mitch jumped in. Winging it.

Political brandished a pair of snub-nosed pliers. Mitch clapped his hands in excitement. "More to come," he joked. The tank was soundproofed. Neither Mitch nor Political heard the lounge erupt in cheers.

Political crept up behind Vermann. Picked his spot. The tender roll of fat unhealthy people cultivated above their waist. Snared a handful. Allowed Vermann's frantic kicking to dwindle. Fed the fat between the plier's teeth. Winked at Mitch, tongue out.

"Horsebite!" he bellowed. Squeezed the handles hard as he could. Vermann unleashed a maniac, throat-ripping cry. Mitch jigged for joy. Vermann looked ready to swallow elephant dick, his mouth was so wide. Great stuff.

Mitch wore an ear to ear grin. "Do it again!" he begged Political. "Do it again!"

The Buffalo Block happily complied. Chose a different zone. Mid-back. Actual horsebite territory. The echoes from Vermann's last savage scream had barely died out when Political pounced again. Touchdown. Vermann climbed the register. Hit notes Mitch didn't know existed.

"Never liked opera," Political laughed even as he winced.

Blood drizzled from the punctures. A sideways all-Canadian tattoo emerged. Boil-red centre on deadwhite field. Flanked by two angry plier tracks.

Something about Vermann's unholy, moldy skin tone. Defined him, Mitch thought. Something sunlight killed. His history revealing. Career as a public nuisance. The kind of shithead who picketed funerals. Showed up at council meetings. Three buddies, two placards and a bullhorn. Vidcam blather monkey.

His peers? Other self-deluded drama queens. Comet tail. Urban dreg. Work dodgers. Parasites. Spikers. Mobile viruses. Mitch had met various elements on his escort rounds. The undead, only not as funny. Not even worth smacking around.

Mitch snugged up his gloves again. The OK from Political. Walked in front of Vermann. Drew his fist back. Threw a perfect strike into Vermann's sternum.

The animal yowling ended. Vermann fought for air. Cheeks and chest worked in tandem. All he needed were gills. Mitch suddenly reminded of fishing. Working the Montreal river. Worthless catch, they'd keep. Throw up on the rocks when they drifted near shore. Watch them gasp, flop and finally fry to death. Perfect ending for Vermann.

Mitch tag-teamed Political on his way by. Unknown to him, Political had suffered an injury. Let his guard down pocketing the pliers. A flailing Vermann leg had accidentally found him. "Groin injury" the sports term. He limped to the table, face screwed up.

Mitch guessed what happened. Banged up balls. "You okay?"

"Yeah," Political whistled. "Fuck me, though. Still hurts like a bitch." Waggled his head at Vermann. "Go get'im."

Mitch grinned at Political. Shot a triumphant glance at the mirror. Line change.

"Lacy, Lacy, Lacy," he murmured, circling Vermann. Examined the target as he moved. The thing looked and smelled off. Funky. Like compost. Vegetarian, Mitch suspected. He'd known a few at Sheridan. Always sick. Not enough meat protein.

"What do you want?" Vermann croaked. Eyes followed Mitch.

"To see you hung from a tree. Soaked in kerosene. A flamer in flames."

Vermann started to breath heavily.

"You and...Nazi's?" Mitch playfully poked Vermann in the ribs. "Seriously. They're like UFO's. Everybody talks about them, but no one's ever seen one. This is Canada."

Vermann's eyes rolled in his head. He avoided looking at Mitch.

"You still got those pliers handy, PB?" Mitch bluffed.

"Roger that," Political said. Misdirection. SOP. Never overuse a technique. That fun was done.

Out of the corner of his eye Mitch saw Political was absorbed. Dug away in the carryall. Mitch briefly speculated on the possible agenda.

"Please...I said it...before," Vermann spoke with exaggerated weariness. "I am a lawyer. I'm with the RCMP. I am a highly respected...investigator. I testify regularly before government commissions and...tribunals. When word reaches the proper ears, you will be charged with kidnapping and assault and...then you will all go to jail. For a long, long time. Unless you release me immediately."

"You stupid fuck," Mitch snorted. "You think the Force doesn't know exactly where you are? You crucified yourself with that stunt you pulled in Ottawa. Pinko moron. You really thought no one would figure out who was trolling sites? Stealing IP addresses? Suing innocent people? You left a sock-puppet trail even a Mountie could follow. And you made the Force look incompetent. They want your fucking idiot head on a platter, buddy!"

Mitch let that sink in. Slid over to see what Political was up to.

"Need any help?"

"Ready...in...now," Political replied, standing. A sound from behind. Mitch turned around to check on Vermann. When he looked back at Political he was stunned.

"Holy Christ!" Mitch blurted out. "Are you serious?"

"Fuck, yeah!" Political grinned. Did his eyebrow thing. From some old American comic Mitch had never heard of. Funny, though. Mitch gave up a chuckle.

"You've never done this?"

"No!" Mitch said. Suddenly astonished he hadn't. It made perfect sense. He shot an over-the-shoulder peek at Vermann. Was he in for a surprise. Mitch could imagine the reaction in the lounge. Guys would go orangutan. Hanging from the roofbeams, beating their chests.

"You don't know what you've missed," Political assured him. Wiggled the machine around. Mid-size. All you'd need, really. Like they said of tits. More than a handful was a waste.

Political continued to regard Mitch in disbelief. "You must a seen plenty of these where you're from?"

"Sure, yeah," Mitch answered. He recognized the maker. Stihl. Top brand. Not made in Canada. What was? He leaned close to Political. "But... in this situation?"

"When better," Political grinned. "Schools out."

Mitch Alphonsed his mentor forward. Political bowed. Sauntered ahead. Grasped the rubber grip. Yanked on the cord. The saw's motor roared into life. Thick blue smoke burst from the exhaust.

"Little heavy on the oil mix?" Mitch yelled over engine howl. Political paused to decipher the shout. Shook his head in agreement. Adjusted the pump. Chatter dampened, revs leveled out. Engine began to purr. Political's eyes shone with child-like delight. Amused Mitch.

Vermann was very aware what the punishing din meant. He twisted about on his ropes. Political stayed out of eyesight range. Wanted to keep it a pretend secret for as long as possible. Goosed the throttle. Couldn't help himself. Air was growing toxic, though. Mitch leapt for the wall panel. Doubled up on the Ridley's. All the fans were working now. The smoke graduated up and out. Mitch loved two-stroke aroma as much as the next person. Still, there could be too much of a good thing.

Political gestured at Mitch. Message understood. Mitch found ear protectors in the carryall. Slung them around his neck. Political preferred to go without. He moved to the middle of the Tank. Raised the saw above his head. Faced the two-way. Roared along with the engine. Mad time! Mitch was ready. Slapped his gloves together. Rejoiced.

Behind Yaz, an eruption. He was stunned by the ferocity of support. Over a hundred very large men bared teeth, bellowed insults, threatened retribution. The fearsome, flesh-ripping intensity. Yaz surprised how it moved him.

To his immediate right, a curly-haired monument shook his fists. Roared violent defiance. The very idea of a Vermann triggered spitting rage. Righteous hate-energy radiated around Yaz like a live electric current.

Inside the Tank, Mitch continued applauding. CORE pride. The man they celebrated in his glory. Rocking to an internal beat. Commie scourge. Che slayer. Inside the ultra-tech Core suit, a soldier's physique. Bridge pylon legs. Upper body, beaten steel. Invulnerable. Meat cladding hardened by the years of training. Political the oldest, meanest gator in the river. And very much intent on delivering a message from CORE to the enemy. You had to like having him as captain.

Political cut the act and the engine at the same time. Placed it on the floor by his feet. Cleared his throat.

"Vermann, Richard M. You are charged with being a sock...fuckhead...a blog poisoner...a moppet groomer...identity thief...false witness...predatory manipulator of the courts...tax leech...and so on. How do you bleed? Plead. Well, both."

Mitch detected a faint, upper register whine.

"CORE requires information," Political continued. Menacing edge. Mitch enjoyed watching the maestro conduct.

Vermann's right leg twitched as Political spun into his view.

Political barked something again. Mitch was busy with his ear guards. Missed it.

"I don't know what you're talking about," Vermann whimpered. Feeble jerk on his ropes. Slumped again.

"You better have something," Political sneered. "'Cause I got something for you if you don't!"

"Please," Verman peeped. "I don't know who...you want?"

"We have your electronic fingerprints, Lacy. We have Force transcripts. We have the blog owners you smeared. They can't wait to testify."

Silence.

"Who put you up to this?" Political all business now.

"You don't understand," Vermann whinied. "They'll...destroy me. Destroy my reputation?"

Mitch looked at Politcal.

"What fucking reputation?" Political stopped to laugh. "As a Net weasel? You're a...a...fucking..." Political trailed off, unable to think of a suitable description.

"Cock-smoking mushball," Mitch finished.

Political had already walked away. "Don't say we didn't give you a chance." He bent over. Hoisted the saw. Yanked the starter cord with purpose.

Smoke churned out from the baffles. Mitch slapped on his headgear. Political nodded at the two-way. They knew what was coming. Mitch bounced on his toes. In his happy zone. Saw exhaust intoxicated him. The smell of adventure. Freedom. Fun.

And he was back in the past. Gravel runs during summer vacation. Flying the F-150 down dusty backroads, Tilbury way. Cousin driving. Mailbox baseball. Intersection doughnuts. Drive-in dirties. Tomato wars. Getting high, high, high. "The Two Terrors" his aunt used to call them. Ironic now, in light of his calling.

In the Kap. Weekends. Head for the lake. Blackflies and beer. Husqavarna, Polaris, Evinrude the magic words. Goofing around in 16-foot pisscutters. Fish a bit, smoke a bit. I've got my hash pipe.

After, batter up some bass. If they'd been lucky. BBQ some salmon steaks if not. Italian sausages. Burgers. Spuds. Puttin' on the foil, coach. More. Beer. Always. Available. Thorogood, Zep and the Hip rattling the podbox. Till the batteries died. Crib and fatties while dinner digested. Zip over to the Flying Chair later. Punish a little loudmouth. Slag people until trouble started. Git into her.

And Winter? Winter. Sometimes better. The sounds of the season. Snow sliding off the roof. Heavy thud outside the window. Crack of tree limbs freezing. Burbling motor. The ol' Cat warmin' up. Snow mobile. Freedom to the horizon. February air cracker crisp. Clean your lungs out. Go. Hard.

Overhead, beautiful blue bowl. Chariots churning up diamond spill. Mid-afternoon, light starts to go. Throttle thumbs frozen stiff. You spot the caribou.

Flank and corral. Herd them over the lake towards that patch of open water. Circling, engines revving. Drive them into the frigid, soupy hole one by one. The does panic first. Jump in. Bambi's are next. They thrash about in the icy gray slop. Helpless and pathetic. Wall-eyed with terror. Failed, scrabbling attempts to climb back onto solid ice. Their tiny hooves carve desperate farewell ruts in the snow. Final exit. Exciting death cries echo off evergreen cliffs. Then silent peace as the last horned head sinks from view. Guys hoot in victory.

Mitch wondered how many times he'd peddled that bullshit? Caribou? In the Kap? Open water in February? Right. For T.O.'s shoe-size I.Q. contingent. An hour north on highway 11? The Barrens. Arctic circle, nezt stop. Simpletons. Mitch had actually made his old girlfriend and her mother cry one night telling that whopper. Still laughed to think of it. City dits. Gull-i-ble.

Fall was the season, though. Hunting with the old man, his uncles. Four-wheelin' with the bushdog boys. No signs, no cops, no rules, no jawing bitches. Drink what you smoke, like what you say. Muzzles are for pets.

Kicking up slopes on wound out machines. Bog-slogging. Log-hopping. See the Shield up close. Too close some days. Remembered his cousin Randy flying over a ridge. Had trouble breathing after. Busted rib. Too drunk to worry about it. Life as it should be. As it used to be before ratbastard, Commie-killjoy, filthy-fuck suck-and-blow peter-puffers like Vermann joined the aristocracy of pull.

Mitch's eyes watered. Nothing sentimental. The saw was pushing out smokestack clouds. Mixture still a bit heavy.

Political mugged some more for the crowd. Mitch moved to the far wall. Better viewing. As he dabbed away tears, Political started in. Showed the saw to Vermann The impact was immediate and gratifying. Vermann redoubled his yelling.

Political eased off the saw's throttle. "Squeal like a pig!" he mouthed to Mitch. Resumed orbiting Vermann.

"She's hungry," he yelled back. Taunted the spazzing dickhead. "What should we feed her first?"

Vermann's back muscles bulged in ropy relief. He whipped his head back and forth, trying to follow Politcal's path. Political pointed the blade at him. Vermann on his bicycle. Away he pedaled, legs up and driving. Mitch on the floor to see it. Vermann looked exactly like a park perp Mitch had worked on once. Guy went epileptic. Right out of the blue. No warning. Ten minutes of thrash and drool. The terrorgation fell apart. Too comical. Mitch couldn't keep a straight face after. They ended up just breaking his arms as a lesson. Medics bound him up. They took him back. Threw him into a bush. Told him how lucky he was to still be alive.

Fortunately, Political was made of stern stuff. Stayed in character. He gravitated around to Vermann's left side, opposite the two-way. Waved the saw near the wretch's ear. Vermann wailed.

Mitch afraid he might piss himself laughing. Walked over. Held up the wall for a minute. Caught his breath. Even Political drifted out of Vermann's line of sight. Gave in to a chuckle.

Vermann's convulsions finally ended. Political let the saw gurgle contentedly.

"You fucking baby!" Mitch yelled.

"Yo! Lacy!" Political bellowed. "Got anything to say now?"

Vermann nodded. Opened his mouth to speak.

Political gunned the saw again. He cupped a hand to his ear. "What?" he screamed. "I can't hear you."

Vermann's eyebrows met at the peak. His mouth opened and closed. Frantic now. Pleading. Nothing reached their ears. Political raced the motor, laughing all the while. Tear streaks on shirtsleeves. Agents leaking badly. Vermann wasn't the only one choking and gasping for breath. Political was building a keeper vid. Something for the archives. Maybe even another bestseller.

Vermann something from a Chinese butcher's window. Sweat ran off his nose. Puddled on the tile. Arrogance evaporated. Political leaned in. Took a knee and spun him. Around he floated. Magnetic motion.

An old Tower of Power number banged out of the speakers during the break. Seconds later, agents were up. Dancing with the beer Bev's. Party atmosphere. Booze flowed freely. Good times.

Yaz turned down a double Crown. Sights like this were not a feature of the Force. He wasn't sure if it would submit a report after all. Imagined the envy if word leaked. No one at the Force enjoyed work this much.

Back in the mix. Political chanted the CORE anthem over engine drone. Drove the audience into an echo frenzy. Glided behind Vermann. Made sure to remain in sight of the two-way. Opened the saw's throttle. Drew nearer. Brought the blade up. Touched Vermann's nutsack.

Again, Mitch had to turn away or collapse. Over the din of the saw he could hear Vermann shrieking. He looked back over his shoulder. Just in time. Terror had given him new strength. Scissor-kicking like mad, Vermann tried to hook his heels into the apparatus above him. Even Political paused to admire the attempt. Mitch caught a glimpse of Vermann's expression. Pervert panic. Priceless. Sweat-coated face, fever flushed. Bulging eyes. Twin rivers of snot that trailed down to an arrowhead chin. A pretty sight? No. Hilarious? Without question.

The lounge was a madhouse. Agents jumped and hollered. Hurled abuse at the screen. Others kicked rigid seat backs. Lofted middle digits.

Two Trogs and a half-squad of Burlies stood standby. A year earlier there'd been an unsanctioned lynching. An enraged CORE audience indulged. A serial diddler served up. Suffered the consequences of evil deeds. No one was ever the wiser, of course. Or would have cared had they learned. All the same, brass wished to avoid a similar incident. Vigilantism had its time and place. Certainly provided the men a chance to blow off steam. But CORE now preferred calculated retribution. Going Black Donnelly, though emotionally satisfying, wasn't professional.

Exhaustion finally overtook Vermann. He ceased the aimless cycling. Sank further into himself. Took great shuddering breaths. Political gave him a three-count. Glanced at the two-way, Cheshire grin. Gunned the chainsaw. Goosed Vermann again. Another harrowing howl. Spasmodic leaping about. And then…the soiling. A rectal Rorschach. Meaty discharge. Undies discoloured. Dignity breach. It was, as the Maginot line went, "le perfect coup d'humilier!"

Mitch saluted Political. Figured he'd dropped a half-kilo from laughing. Political's terrorgations. Top-flight aerobic workout. Bottle it. Make a fortune.

Vermann's stink held its own with the exhaust fumes. Political hadn't yet noticed. He was still doing his Zulu dance, saw aloft. A well-deserved victory celebration. He stopped before the screen. Guessed rightly everyone was up and cheering. The routine standing 'O'.

True satisfaction lay in knowing "Lacy" Vermann—hacker-sneak, "victim of offense" swindler, HRC fake-Nazi troll and worthless POS—had been properly fucked over. And not a moment too soon. As expected, the vid went gold overnight. More than just his victim's were keen on revenge.

Rag doll limp now. The ass-grabber's shoulders shook as he blubbered. No agent watching failed to be moved by the glorious sight. Real Canadians getting some back. And to a man they loved it. Yaz turned around in his seat. Marveled at what he saw. A sea of hard Aryan faces shining bright with resolve. He shivered to think of anything standing in its way. The machine had been primed. It looked ready to roll.

Vermann was a rat. Yaz understood that. A sewer-dwelling, shit-snacking rodent. But he was only a symptom of a larger illness plaguing Canada. Or so it had been explained to Yaz. The creature was a carrier, infected and contagious. But he wasn't the disease itself. Destroying him gave everyone hope. Lifted spirits. Wounded the enemy. But it was only a small victory in a smaller skirmish. Yaz appreciated the concern expressed by agents in the meeting. Theirs was a slippery and elusive opponent. Would beating on them without mercy be enough?

Applause. Whistling. Vermann crying hard. Girl crying. Mitch knew the sound. He'd clocked a few deserving gash in his day. Never with a closed fist, of course. Some things a gentleman just didn't do. None had abandoned their innate sense of self so completely, though. Mitch regarded the putrid, tear-streaked cornholing little predator with contempt. Human filth. Beneath Vermann, a urine-shit slurry accumulated. Mitch wrinkled his nose in loathing. He felt tainted being in the same room.

The i-photo uploads did global business. The ferret's degradation greatly enjoyed. Major product shift. Brazil to Belgium, triptych stills and holoposters sold like hotcakes. Teens around the world loved the 'Norwegian Brown' and 'Vermann's End' pics. CORE couldn't keep them in stock. The terrorgation a major success, from both security and commercial angles.

Mitch dumped his ear protectors back in the carryall. Chucked Political on the arm. Job well done. Again. Wry grin from the master. Wiped down the saw. It was only then Mitch made the connection.

""Jesus!" he exclaimed. "There's no fucking chain on that thing!"

Political straightened. Held a finger to his lips. "Put a chain on this puppy? Rat pate in ten seconds." Mock indignation. "What? I look like some kinda sadist to you?"

"No." Mitch denied the charge. "No, no…well…" Ducked away from the unserious poke at his nose. "Just surprised is all. It sounded completely…real. Never thought to look, I guess."

Political nodded. Patted the saw with fondness. "The Tonawanda Tickler." Knowing smile. "Word to the wise. Nothing better when you wanna make a point."

Mitch dropped his head. Lesson learned, remembered. Pulled a face.

"Yeah," Political said. "It's getting a little rank in here. Time to raise anchor." He locked the saw case. Tucked it under a beefy wing.

"I'm there," Mitch said.

One last look at their handiwork. Vermann's shattered face in full display. Expression blank. Coma eyes. A rope of drool hung from his bottom lip. Mitch marked again the lousy skin condition. The way it seemed to pull over his ribs like plastic wrap. Angry-looking welts and sores visible. And not just from Political playing "At the Paddock." Something was wrong with him. Not that he cared in the least. Like the priest said about the choirboy. "Fuck'im."

"Master class, sensei," Mitch saluted the departing figure. Political raised a fist in triumph. Gone.

Weariness washed over Mitch. Well-earned. Honest afternoon's work completed. Remembered Yaz was waiting. Vaulted for the hatch.

Two Trogs promptly entered. Drudge brigade on their heels. They came loaded. Priority 5. Heavy contamination. Likelihood of communicable diseases. Or worse. Full HAZMATS. All Halloween orange and chimney red. Steam vacs. Anti-bacterial foam. Bleach scrubbers. Sulpheric acid for the unknown. Be prepared and you're never scared.

The Drudges got busy. The Trogs concentrated on Vermann. Both looked perplexed by the task. No concern of Mitch's now. He'd had his shots. Still, he thought a warning might be in order. Ambled up to the leader. The giant was gazing at the complex of ropes holding Vermann in place. Around him, machines beavered away. Hosing down matter, steaming tile pristine. CORE preferred a germ-free work environment.

Mitch tapped the man on the shoulder. Motioned him closer. Whispered into the earvent. The man nodded quietly. Then stiffened as if touched with a hot poker.

"Are you sure?" his Vader vox hissed.

Mitch put his hands up. "Fuck, who knows? Guessing. But...check out those...marks and shit on his neck. Christ, everywhere. Some are legitimate. A lot ain't. Know what I mean?"

"Suit seal! Now! Dead stock alert!" came the command. The Trog bowed thanks Mitch slashed it away. Least you could do. Pinched his nose, Political fashion. Pointed towards the exit. A wave from the grateful Trogs.

Inside Debrief. Quick glance at the lounge monitor. Still a full crowd. Political surrounded by delighted wellwishers. Yaz, nowhere in sight. Mitch turned. Glared several indolent Technits back to work.

Thinking. Political was occupied. Not for Mitch to rain on his parade. Or soak up unwarranted adulation. It was the work of a moment for him to slide out the back exit. Catch up with Yaz later. Right then, a beer and a backrub seemed like the perfect conclusion. Juked off his suit. Made sure a Minion noticed it on the floor. Put on his jeans and polo shirt. Found the extra bar of pitlime. Applied liberally. Evergreeny mint. He smelled great. Royal nod to all. Out and free.

Hadn't taken two steps down the corridor when he thought of it. They never did finish up with fuckhead Vermann about the Ovarians. Or his dead trulls. Something had sidetracked them. Mitch couldn't remember what. Oh, well. Maybe later. Right now, Mitch's muscles needed massaging. Humming "Silky Sue, my balls are blue," he loped to the rec wing. Where relief waited with firm but nimble fingers.

IN THIRTY MINUTES OR IT'S ME

⦉◯⦊

The doorbell bing-ed. Mitch half-buried in his refrigerator. Occupied. Could not locate the last bottle of Corona. Which he knew was in there. Hiding. Looking while lost in thought, Mitch was. Two minutes, carbon penalty! No joke with the fucking socialists in power.

Back in the Tank. Pictured fruit of the loom Vermann. Dangling from the roof. Destroyed. Days didn't come any more memorable. After a great rubdown, he'd linked up with Yaz for a post-mortem. The man still awed by the experience. Mitch could tell. A P.B. & J had that effect on people.

The jelly would spend a night in isolation. Next day, be told to keep his head down. For the rest of his life. Or lose it. Quick load into an empty Bundler. Driven to Etobicoke. Kicked out into traffic. What Mitch hoped, anyway.

Yaz admired the efficient disposal system. Said so. Still confused about a few matters. Mitch cleared them up. Had a chuckle on the last item. Explained that the lounge wenches were all nicknamed 'Bev'. Shorthand for 'Beverage'. So "Yo, Bev!" or "Hey, bev me!" was a normal greeting. They'd gotten a little shirty about hearing "Over here, beer butt" all the time.

So, shadow sent off to do more research. Mitch dashed off a three word summary of the terrorgation. Sent himself a uni alarm. (Easter coming. Phone Mom.) Read some spark alerts. Skipped over the one about another ass-peddler turning up in a mop bucket on Front St. Wanted to stay on a high from the Vermann showdown.

Uni chime. Message from Goodfellow. Always "helping," the prick. New leads. A "FOC" or two. He scanned the attachment. Cross icon. Double flagged it. Auto upload to the Friends of Core folder.

Mitch recognized the name from his escort days. No friend, so he could tell. Father Massey. He'd attended a benefit once with…some desperately horny pantsuit. CFO of …some charity. Massey ran a douche queen shelter downtown. Cover for his real purpose—moppet fondling. Plus, he consumed and distributed kiddie porn. Making him the perfect priest for the Thomson Hall set. Smooth, slippery, sexually suspect.

It was possible the guy had known one of Mitch's trulls. Could be worth a look in. Though not right then. Mitch smiled. The punchline of a joke came back to him. A Bishop fell into St. John's harbour. Police found him three hours later, clinging to a buoy.

Next…Grant Munny. Peace Park performance poofter. Not a fucking chance. Like every other man alive, Mitch hated mimes.

Jack Daugh's bio had him as a downtown 'community activist'. Public parasite in other words. Holocamera slut. No.

A.Caitiff. Trud crud peddler. Mitch got his news needs online. Weakass Red opinionators only made him laugh. Might call him if totally bankrupt for a lead. But for now, no again. Fucking Goodfellow. Man had lost it. Wasting Mitch's time with lepers. Have to get under the trull thing another time. Other things held more interest. Like catching the highlights of last night's game again. Clicked on the sports site. Lit up. Sat back to enjoy.

The door gong sounded again. Broke into his reverie. Wondered who the fuck would be visiting? Remembered as he moved to the door. Disabled the lasers. Dropped his eyes to the sawed off, sand-filled, corked Easton propped in the corner. Never needed it. Couldn't wait to try it out someday, though. Excellent heft. Definite jaw-smasher.

Vid screen image. Smiling angel with gift.

"Wow!" Mitch declared to the door. Let her in. "That was super fast!"

Enamel blaze. "We pay if we're late."

Mitch took in the heavenly messenger. Medium height. Wavy blond hair falling out from under a properly frayed Leaf's ballcap. Cheeks brushed red from the cold. Hollywood smile.

"Smells great," Mitch said. Angled away from the door. Debit chip search. "Sorry. Not prepped. Wasn't expecting…you…so soon."

"No problem," came the reply. "Happy to be in the warm."

"True-er words…" Mitch said. Located item. Waved her forward. Exchanged small square for big square. Unvelcro-ed the portosal. Wrenched out the box. Opened the lid. Quick inhale. El Meat-O Supreme-O. Slaughterhouse Special. Korean Pizzeria. Every kind of flesh but dog. Mitch always x-ed that one out. Gave him gas.

Double cheese, onions, green peppers, hot banana peppers, pinapple, Jalapeno sauce, tonbanjan. Mitch liked a pizza with punch. Plopped it onto the table.

"Sorry if it's not so hot," the young cooz apologized. "Ten minutes in the oven. Don't worry about the box. New. Safe. Transfers heat to the food."

Mitch waved her off. "I usually do that anyway." Watched her slip the chip into the groove. Returned it. Extra pressure for luck. Removed her cap. Ran her fingers through the groomed shock. Squared up again.

Mitch took the cue. "Leaf's forever."

Disney slut smile. Mitch heard birds. Prettiest delivery trollop he'd seen all night. Cold gave her a glowing complexion. Barest dusting of makeup. Sculpted button nose. Firm, chewable lips. Hard to tell about the body. The windproof shellsuit didn't reveal much. Looked to match the face, though. Mitch felt plank develop.

"You worked this neighbourhood long?" Mitch asked. "I think I'd remember you."

"Only for the last few weeks," came the reply. "I'm substituting. It's fun. Money's not so bad. I might need some extra when I graduate. Pay off my debt"

"University?" Mitch asked, startled.

She giggled. "Not yet. I start next year…if I get accepted."

"Oh, you will," Mitch said. Charm opening. Seen and exploited. Fresh girl! Poon readings off the scale.

"They'd be crazy not to let in someone so sexy. Get a little older, some guy with a Benz and no class will pour money over you. Just so you'll let him grope your bouncers." Mitch kiddin' around. Also planting the thought. Rough hands squeezing, massaging, rubbing the goods. Mitch moved in another direction.

"Sweet Jesus! I just noticed. Your eyes are…green!" Mitch peered closer. "Ah, no. Sorry. Regular blue." Pictured the head-shakes if the guys overheard him. Douchebag 040. Mitch enjoyed slumming.

"You like green eyes?" the teen asked. Tried to hide her disappointment.

"Absolutely," Mitch replied with genuine enthusiasm. "Killer." Always play to their low self-esteem. Classic maneuvering. Mitch knew the drill by heart.

"I could wear 'tacts the next time."

"Don't even think about it," Mitch dismissed the thought. "Blue is okay. Second best colour."

Ear-to-ear smile of relief in return. "The receipt should arrive shortly." Mitch never moved. She stared right back at him. Contract signed. Receipt unnecessary.

"What's your honeypot?" Mitch asked. Made his eyes dance. "Sorry. I mean what's your name? Honeypot?" Wicked chortle.

"Glenda. Glenda Billington." Shy attempt to avoid Mitch's leer. Room peruse.

"Billington, eh?" he said. "I used to know someone with the same last name. While ago now. Jean, I think. Or Jane. She worked for some…firm downtown. Securities, maybe. I forget."

The girl shook her hair. Bit her lip. Practiced but fetching act. "I know," she giggled. "That's my mom."

Mitch was momentarily confused. "Shit, that's a weird coincidence."

"Maybe," Glenda said. Cocked her head in a way to suggest the opposite. Mitch's mind circled around looking for danger. Nothing he could see.

"Look," he recovered, "if you're not doing anything when you get done work…"

"I'm done now," Glenda replied. Unsnapped her jacket. Removed her cherished cap. Tossed the sexy tresses. "This was my last delivery. That's why you got it so quick."

"Well…feel free to take off your…oh, okay," Mitch took the jacket. Went to point at her boots. Wondered how she'd removed them without his noticing.

"Sorry. I was kidnapped by gypsies. Never learned any manners," he joked. "Mitch. Mitch Milligan."

Glenda giggled again. Large round things under her jersey jumped up and down in rhythm. A good sign. A closer look at the Neopolitan hairwork said money. Mitch knew to spot that now. Also remembered Momsy had the folding stuff. Revealed how she'd gutted her husband in the divorce. Mitch on the alert. Vicious vipers everywhere.

He grabbed the pizza. Walked it into the kitchen. Said, "I'm a pretty regular customer of Park's. How is he anyway? Haven't talked to him in ages."

"I don't know," Glenda answered. Curled a strand of hair around her finger. "I haven't even met him. Just the manager. This is, like, only my fourth delivery."

"Really," Mitch said, not listening. He'd done something with the oven tray. "Tell you what. There's a beer in the fridge somewhere. You find it? It's yours. I'm going down to the basement. Hunt around. See if I can't scour up a few more. I think Andr…I've put them them somewhere they don't usually go."

"You hide beer?" Glenda laughed. "Hey, wait a minute. This is a condo. You don't have a basement."

"Joke," Mitch said over his shoulder. "Secret place. My buddies are beer bandits. Swine would clean me out if they could. Try the kitchen." Thumbed her into the room. Disappeared down the hall. When he returned, he was carrying a six of Coors Light. Plus two German pilsner's he'd been gifted a while back. Black shit. Emergency brew only. He nearly dropped them when he saw Glenda on the sofa. She'd found his Corona. And lost all her clothes. Perfect swap.

"I hope you don't mind?" the toothsome tramp tittered. "I hate wearing uniforms."

"Not at all," Mitch said. Hustled into the kitchen. Almost dropped the bottles again. Quick bit of juggling rescued them. Tried to open the fridge door, deposit beers, and remove his pants at the same time. Unwise. One of the Pilsners nearly went to its reward. Last thing he needed. Hitler's piss all over the floor. And no Andrea to clean it up. Mitch closed his eyes. Andrea. Shit. He'd promised to meet her after work. He glanced at the wall clock. Twenty minutes ago. Some celebration. Four month's anniversary? Her birthday? Promotion? Cancer? Fuck if he could remember.

He leaned against the kitchen archway. Tripod no longer. Clinked his beer against the wooden pillar. Glenda looked over. The cushions were artfully arranged. Her tits rested on top of each one like massed artillery.

Mitch held up his bottle. Said, "I'll be back in a minute. Don't go anywhere. Don't get dressed. Start into my beer if you like. I'll...be...right..."

"Okay," Glenda cheeped to a vanishing shirt.

And he was. In seconds. Easier than he'd expected. No answer on her com. Left a message instead. "Can't see ya'. Diarrhea." The classic bail line.

"Sorry," he apologized. Collapsed into his recliner. "Had to cancel something."

"Important?"

"Nah." Mitch raised his glass to Glenda. "Here's looking at you, kitten." Drained half the bottle. Admired the candied cushions. The brute grew large. He scrinched about in his seat. Growth room required. Thankful he'd doffed the denim. No meeting the evil-eyed Korean hag.

"You sure you're nineteen?" Mitch asked. "If the other cops knew what I was thinking now...they'd want to join in."

Glenda batted her eyes in mock alarm. "You're a policeman?" She lifted one cushion to plump it. Exposed just the right amount of hump puppy. Mitch gave her the convict pant. Femnots could deny it all they wanted. Mitch and every other man knew different. Authority revved genitals. He didn't know the psychology. Didn't care. Just nature at work. The king's guards get pussy. So suck on it, dykos.

"Kind of," Mitch answered. Bit cryptic, he realized. "More like...a consultant. I'm with CORE. Ever heard of 'em?"

"Have I?" Glenda answered with enthusiasm. "You're like a...trained assassin or something. And here I am, naked and helpless. Have you ever killed anyone?"

"Not yet," Mitch grimaced. "Someday, maybe!"

Glenda giggled to hear Mitch sound so keen. Ran her tongue around cherry lips. The cushion slipped again. Mitch salivated. Magnificent mams. The soft, pliable kind. As seen on holovids. The chill air plumped her nips nicely. Baltimores styled out in edible icing. The newest fashion. Mitch approved. Sweet to see the girls highlight their valuables that way. Charming, feminine.

Glenda gave over being coy. Tossed the pillows aside. Lay back. Let the marmot breath. Mitch finished his beer. Fitted it into the chair's empty magazine rack. Jumped up. Pulled off his shirt.

"I love your pictures," Glenda said. Glanced at the tent with hunger. Then pointed up at the wall. Across from the holovid. "That goalie? He's got, like, a serial killer's mask on."

"Christmas present."

"I like the one next to it. Is that you? With the white pajamas?"

"It is so," Mitch said. Eased the boxers over his exploding package.

"Were you some kind of kung-fu champion?"

Mitch laughed. "Nah. That was taken at my old club. But I've studied a few things. Tae kwan do. A little karate. Some boxing. Other stuff. Not K-1 or anything."

"I'll try not to pick a fight," Glenda winked.

"That's smart," Mitch winked back. "I've beat up women before."

"Really?" Glenda's jaw dropped.

"N-o-o-o-o," Mitch chuckled. Kicked away the trunks. "Not women, really. Dykos. But that's more for training." Grinned to see Glenda's expression.

And like that, flashdrive memory. Happened just a few days earlier. Routine terrorgation. Anderson running things. 'Spect some toothless slattern. Street creature rolled up for impersonating a human. Uptick of interest at a dropped name. A few headshots later, she was even more forthcoming. Slobbered up several notorious dyko bars. One, it was learned, popular with Mitch's dead one. Alerted in time to catch the last period of Anderson's game. Decided to maybe act on it. He wasn't that busy.

Intel confirmed it later. All the establishments were likely trull havens. Many turned dyko after hours. True. "Minge Meadow" got mentioned. "The Watering Hole" and "Beeves" also. Mitch chose "Beldam's" for a first visit. He knew the strip mall out on Danforth where it was hidden. Corralled "Chick" Esposito for shotgun. Yaz volunteered. Seemed like a good chance to get his feet wet on an op. Mitch said sure. Been thinking the exact same thing.

Things went south fast soon after they arrived. He and Espo flashed I.D. Blew past the beefy bouncerettes. Yaz stayed in their wake. Hard looks from the hard-to-look-at. Mitch and Chick did the King Cock strut to the bar. A clutch of beady-eyed Sisters clucked disapproval. Mitch egged them on with a tongue dance.

Elbows down, both agents immediately started goofing. Espo Gillespied his cheeks. Broad wink. Reached over the counter. Helped himself to the nearest bottle. Vodka. No brand he recognized. Asked what kind of sand... witches the place served? Sneer answer. Hearty laugh from Espo. No hard feelings. Just taking the piss.

Mitch made a big show of wiping the bottle top with his shirt. Then the glasses. Poured three shots. Tossed his and Yaz's back. Espo right there with him. Counted to three. Brushed the empty shot glasses onto the floor. Only one smashed. Mitch had to step on the other two. No shortage of snarly butch attention now.

Mitch started firing questions to the insolent brillo munchers. Espo slapped his arm. Thumbed to their left. A mountainous thyroid condition in coveralls had stumped up. Mitch pointed at her. Joined Espo in window-rattling guffaws. Stopped to moo in unison. More thigh-slapping.

The creature's veiny bulb twitched. Heavy-lidded perusal of each man. Offense taken, which delighted Mitch. A flurry of insults launched. Both agents concentrating on her resemblance to the larger African mammals. Cape buffaloes, hippos, wildebeest. Chick got away with suggesting Mitch go paddle the Gnu. Mitch busy mocking the mutant.

"Kiss my dick, Herm," he kept repeating. "Kiss my big and angry."

And she might have a been a half-and-half. Mitch wouldn't have bet on it either way, she was that ugly.

Espo ended the fencing in classic fashion. Grabbed his unit with both hands. Thrust it at "Herm" several times. Gave the gesture for cross-wired. Iced it by jabbing his middle finger in the haystack's face. Mouthing other nicknames for her serial sins.

Mitch slapped the bar, roaring. Yaz kept the bronze railing to his back. Reviewed the crowd with concern. They weren't taking the abuse well.

The big beastie telegraphed battle. Snuffed the air. Pawed the sawdust. Hitched up the denim tent. Mitch did a quick appraisal. Figured it carried 50 kilos more than he did. Stood maybe an inch taller too. Banker square hair, dyed black. Laser part. He and and Espo joked about it later. A little grout work to fill the acne canyons. Clip the 'stache. Push the potato eyes a bit further apart. Voila! A six-car pileup. Or a rockslide.

The slab-sided sasquatch balled it's fists. Curled a heavy lip. Shot daggers at the three of them. Mitch had faced off against slit-lickers in the past. None had been any more formidable. He prepped himself. Deep breaths for energy. Shook the triceps. Opened his mind to the entire scene. Sensed the bar bitch behind him weighing up her options. Organized his plan of attack. Roughly fourteen steps to the exit. Maybe thirty carpet chewers to clear before leaving. Tough, probably. Not biker hard or anything. Backup shouldn't be necessary. Espo benched 400 lbs. Prone to going beserk when angry. Mitch had been in more brawls than he could count. Between them, he didn't think they were overmatched.

A group chant sounded. "Totoro! Totoro! Totoro!" Mitch had no idea what it meant. Diesel code. They were goading her into it. Mitch memorized the faces closest to he and Espo. Five would get you ten Metro had most of the beauties in their crimfiles. Visit a little discipline on them for encouraging illegal behaviour.

"I wouldn't," Mitch warned the hyperventilating freak. "I break your leg, no more ballet." Espo gagged. Explained after how he'd suddenly pictured the Raptor in tights and tutu. Not good. Worse than plaid.

Her grumbling. Muttered threats, muted lowing. Mitch did a final sitrep. Let peripheral vision inform him. Suddenly, Yaz sidled past. Espo looked at him in alarm. Took a step as if to catch him. Mitch grabbed his arm. Spontaneous reaction. Might have wondered what the little guy had in mind. More likely for cheap laughs. Rittle Wietnamese versus Kathy the Kelvinator. Can't let an opportunity like that go by.

What came next Mitch wouldn't have predicted in a thousand years. Yaz had started in with soothing shit. Cop talk. We can work this out. No need for violence, ill will. Pure rubbish. Ms Abominable listened for ten seconds. Then aimed a kick at Yaz's groin. Mitch and Espo instinctively tensed, ready to jump in. The blow never connected. Yaz had vanished. Seconds later, she was wearing him like a backpack. A deafening roar filled the room. Yaz had buried his teeth in her neck. Mitch and Espo were paralyzed. Hunters both, they recognized the satisfying scream of a wounded herbivore.

The following three minutes, a revelation. And a lesson in modern martial arts. Mitch had never seen anything like it. Yaz called it "gymno." Self-developed, he explained. Like Bruce Lee's shit. Mitch would have laughed or scoffed to hear it described. Seeing it in operation was a different matter.

Espo witnessed it from beginning to end. Still didn't believe his eyes. Ran sausage fingers over his fresh prison chop. Picked his jaw up from his boots. Declared, "Shit! We're dinosaurs."

It was over before it began. The Sarge never laid a hand on him. Lightning fast moves. Mitch had trouble keeping track of him. Front flips, back flips, that old movie guy's akido stuff. Use your opponent against himself. Herself. Itself. Whatever.

As it was, Yaz took her apart like a Jenga tower. A thing of beauty to watch. He used everything—tables, chairs, posts, ceiling. He was a combination pinball, jack-in-the-box and spider. Cartoon character dexterity. Punched, slapped, elbow-chopped, kneed, kicked and punted the fat sack senseless. She swung on empy space. Grabbed at vapour. Responded late, anticipated nothing.

Dazed and bleeding, she felt for the chewed-out hole in her shoulder. As she did so, Yaz materialized from behind her. Both Mitch and Espo started at the sight. He dropped to a squat. Right leg shot out like a rail gun. Pistol crack. Ligaments blown out. Mitch winced. That kind of injury hit close to home.

Cathy colossus toppled forward. The vibration rattled bottles and glasses. Shadows danced on the walls. Mitch braced himself in time. Rode it out. From the corner of his eye. Saw a spectator about to interfere. Espo a step ahead. Reached behind him. Found an unopened longneck. Threw it in one smooth overhand. Pinpoint accuracy. Excellent thud impact. The solid bottom caught the evil Samaritan square. Forehead blow. Pole-axed. Heifer legs exploded out. Comical drop.

Had them in stitches in the shop the next day. "Went down like the Titanic," Espo laughed. Mimed it. Great act.

Mitch whooped. Jack-knife fist pump. Shoulder slam congrats for Espo. Perfect toss. Bottle never even broke. Mitch made a mental note. Trophy hunt. Save that brave longneck.

Yaz hadn't slowed or noticed. Espo gaped at his next move.

"Holy shit," the agent said. Stared at Mitch. "Did I see what I think I saw?"

Mitch was also open-mouthed. Even replaying it in his mind's eye, he wasn't sure.

"I think your man just landed a…a quad, if that's what they're called. On her face."

Mitch spit-laughed. Wiped his mouth. "I don't know. Too technical for me."

Espo pursed his lips in contemplation. Kept a watch on the surly cud-chewers. Yaz, meanwhile, remained focused on the job at hand. He hooked knees on either side of Ms. Godzilla's udders. Set in position, he proceeded to batter her face to pulp. Cuspids flew from her mouth like breath mints. Burst blood vessels spray-patterned the floor. Yaz not even breathing heavily. In shape, both agents realized. Good sign.

Mitch spun. Grabbed the bartender's knife hand. A second's cold smile of triumph. Then he drilled the treacherous bitch. The overhand right nearly split her face. Instantly out. He gave her falling body a half-twist. Might be enough so she landed on the knife. Gutted herself.

Mitch's quick reaction quelled a growing restlessness among the grumblers.

Espo ground a hamfist into his palm. Daring anyone to come at him. Mitch was also ready for a friendly punch-up. Happy to greet all comers. Keep the grail grazers away from Yaz. Man preoccupied with unlicensed dental surgery. The floor crunchy with broken porcelain.

They let Yaz work a little longer. Mitch admired the man's calculation. It was instructive. But muff maven indignation on the rise. The herd unsettled, upset by the relentless beating.

Mitch launched himself at the nearest table. Grabbed two chunkies by their lumberjacks. Smashed their heads together. Espo followed suit. They'd barely got a sweat on before the competition surrendered. Mass rush to the far wall. Mitch wiped gunk from his boot onto the ass of his last kill. Spit on her. Triumphant gorilla chest bongo. Returned to the bar. Thirsty now. Wondered if they had time for a quick one.

Espo had easily dispatched his challengers. Tossed them against the toilet door, crumpled and bleeding. Now cooling Yaz off. Total victory well and good. But atrocities attracted media attention. Sometimes it was enough to win big. Grinding their faces off, while fun, wasn't necessary.

Mitch joined them. Let Yaz know he was impressed. Controlled Gestapo. Liked to see it. Yaz an obvious force. Retrieved the man's coat. Tap on the shoulder. Job well done. Looked up. Crowding movement again. He glared down an approaching duo of dykos. Patted his jacket. Gun. Big gun. Big fake out.

Espo whistled.

"Yep," Mitch gave a dry chuckle. "I think she's had enough." They all looked at the lifeless, one-eared figure. Mitch could barely make out a face. No piling on today, tempting though it was. Blame that old Canadian sense of fair play. Plus, didn't look like much left. He satisfied himself crushing several fingers while walking Yaz away. Not a sound out of her. Yaz had done an exquisite work.

Espo confirmed Yaz unhurt. They swaggered to the bar. Espo loaded up with their rewards. Fit a 26-er in each pocket. Smile of thanks to the still unconscious Betty on the floor. No blood pool. Mitch's gambit a fail. So it went.

Mitch stared a threatening meatstack back two steps. Bent down. Retrieved Espo's magic bottle. Remarkable. Undamaged.

Espo kicked over a couple tables on the way out. Mitch grabbed a free chair. Hurled it against the wall of bottles behind the bar. Smashed a half-dozen of them. Gloating chuckle as they hit the door.

The bouncerettes withdrew. Showed teeth. Growled. Flexed heavily muscled arms. Nothing worse apart from bad breath. The three heroes pushed out into the cold, refreshing night. Success felt great.

Something broke against the door after it closed behind them.

"Too late, ya' twisted cunts!" Espo yelled. Ran back. Booted the door hard. Two bystanders retreated. Nervous fear in their eyes.

"Dyko dive!" Espo announced. Jerked a thumb behind him. "Don't go in there. You'll regret it."

Mitch laughed long and loud for the benefit of anyone listening. Pressed the Prowler's starter chip. Motor woke. Roared alive. They hopped in. Mitch quickly gunned it. Hope the sound carried into the broken bar. Surfed the pleasure he felt. Chucked Yaz on the arm again.

"Fucking amazing," Espo said.

Mitch, doing a music search, nodded his head. "What is?"

"Guy's hands. Look."

Mitch turned to see.

"They're unmarked," Espo pointed out.

"Oh, yeah," Mitch nodded. "Shit."

Espo couldn't stop telling the story next day. Word spread quickly. Everyone wanted to hear about the 'gymno' demo. Yaz had gone from shadow to celebrity overnight.

"No autographs. Sorry," Mitch took to saying whenever people approached them. He was openly pleased about Yaz's newfound notoriety, though. It meant he was less likely to hear any more Jet Li cracks. Plus, the guy had proved himself. He'd made his bones. And in the event Mitch needed his back covered? He felt a lot more confident Yaz could hold his own. At least if dykos attacked.

It wasn't until they were blurring out the exit that Mitch remembered. Pounded the wheel. Cursed. Espo roared at the explanation. Drive all the way over to Muff Alley. Get caught up in a tongue tribe drama. Fuck their shit up. Then forget to grill anyone about Mitch's old, cold tranny. Took their eyes off the ball. You had to laugh.

"We could always come back tomorrow night," Espo suggested. Flexed his forearms. "My turn."

Mitch wasn't so enthusiastic. "Not sure about the hospitality. Better leave killer here if we do go." Grinned at Yaz in the rear view. "Or we can ignore all this nasty tranny shit. Let's go drinking, boys! Celebrate. What do you say? There's a new strip club I know. Sweet spot. Get our sticks polished, play our cards right." Which is exactly what happened.

Glenda's shaky pudding. Mitch back in the present. Standing before her, rod-ready and able. Glenda's mouth went slack.

"Hungry?" he smiled.

"Not for pizza," Glenda replied. She slid two fingers deep into her mouth.

Prepping. Mitch approached. Watched her eyes linger on the throbbing banquet.

"Sorry," Mitch apologized. "I'm afraid I'm going to have to fuck you blind before I feed you."

"Bring it!" Glenda shouted. Hands raised in touchdown triumph. "Mom was right. You're a knight and his stallion all rolled into one."

The first hour went as normal. Mitch congratulated himself again. A soundproofed bedroom. Twice the money? Still worth it. Now whoever he bulled to Valhalla could glory in it at full volume. And didn't they just, though. Mitch was a one-man force multiplier. Shock and awe, his stock in trade. Once the ladies got a look at his weapon, well…sound the klaxons, blow the hatches, lube the tubes. Full steamy ahead.

Ship boarded, Mitch stayed with the game plan. No fancy variables, no tricky decoys. He began his assault with the tried and true. "Candy Cane." Followed up with "Flames in Five," "Switchback," "Nobody's Business." And a spirited "Octoberfest" brought them to the break.

Glenda gasped her gratitude. Mitch took it in stride. He was the mattress master. Undisputed. Nobody knew bed wrestling better. Nor was it a surprise to come back from a piss break/beer snag. Find Glenda gnawing on a bedpost. He'd seen it before. Mouth-foaming, over-fucked females. Weeping, laughing hysterically, deranged. Once had to belt-lash a maddened flesh thresher. Caught her clawing up his drapes. 911 nightmare. Sirens. Ladder truck. Morgasmic insanity. A wonder there hadn't been research into. Not gay. So no money, probable explanation.

He cracked his beer. Drank half off. Barley recharge. Hopped on the bed. Throat slashed at Glenda.

"Yo! You're marking up the mahogany!"

"Sorry," Glenda apologized. Scampered down the headboard. Springboarded off the mattress. Caught air. Ass landing. Elbowed forward. Deftly impaled her snatch on Mitch's standard. "Can't understand what's got into me."

Mitch snorted a "ho, ho." Two-hopped his beer to the night table. "It's called a tube steak, darlin'. A few more thrashing O's…call it a night, yeah? Put Secretariat back in his stall. I make sure you get home safe. Sound good?"

"Mmmm…" Glenda replied. Arched her back. Fondled her breasts. "One more…trip around the universe. God, I feel like I've been fucked into another dimension. Mom wasn't exaggerating. You're a king hell prod."

"I know it," Mitch agreed. "But I'm due for some food. And the long snooze. Know what I mean?"

So saying he grabbed two handfuls of mattress. Braced his feet against the endboard rigging. Poled for home. Aim…thrust…reload. Aim…thrust… reload. Mitch Milligan, metronome. Or the "Oil Donkey" as that Calgary tart exec used to call him when she came to town. Wondered if she ever got that promotion? Supposed to be a trip in it for him. Must have hit her head on the ceiling. Never heard back.

Glenda writhed beneath him now. Whipped tongue spray bathed Mitch. Subhuman sounds. Gurgling, gargling, gagging. Mitch ground away. Hoped she wasn't swallowing her tongue. Always a little awkward esplaining that to the medics.

He stifled a scream. Glenda's fingernails buried in his butt. Doing neck bridges. Her jugular a pulsing sausage. Slow-building convulsions. Whiff of charred thatch. Glenda's wild churning threatening to chuck them off the bed.

Mitch righted them. Greenlight time. He was good to go. And then the glorious release. A bucking, thrashing masterpiece. A heaving, tectonic display of virtuosity. The pleasure of draining the nads into rippling uterus just never got old. South mouth meets its match. Mitch Milligan. When you want it done right.

"So that's what it means to be ultra-fucked." A somber, zombie-faced Glenda gave out an exhausted sigh. Gingerly crabwalked off the still rigid stick. Collapsed on his pillow, a picture of perfect contentment. Voracious teen lust sated. For the time being.

"Oy!" Mitch snapped, wind returned. "Don't get comfortable! I need you dressed and on your way. Fifteen minutes." Stopped to yawn. "The Mitch needs some 'za and some zee's"

"She still talks about you, my mother," Glenda purred. "With her friends. You made quite an impression."

"That's nice," Mitch replied. Slapped haunch. "C'mon. Off the bed. Pitter patter…before you get fatter."

Glenda righted herself. "Hey! I'm not fat!" Ran her hands across a pan-flat stomach. Let them drift too near the wookie. A delayed spasm flung her down on the bed, groaning in joy. Mitch watched, amused. The shameless sexpot shimmied and shook. Her fried eggs sizzled. Wiggled and wobbled like giggling pigs. He'd tazered people who didn't flail about so much.

Glenda's flash return to Nirvana ended. She gave a "whew!" Happy relief. Mitch humped over to the side of the bed. Glenda looked up in alarm. Scrunched closer. Ran her hand down Mitch's slackened drill. Pouted. "Mom says she wishes she could have made a plastic cast of this. She'd have made a fortune selling portable pothole pleasers."

Mitch grimaced at the comment. Paused before answering. Then said, "I think she meant plaster cast. And she can have it whenever she wants. You too. Google 'Superdick.com'. Thirty bucks, you get a top-seller. Absolutely true to life or your money back. Energy bar not included."

"Really?"

"Blood honour. In fact, you can get the same thing at 'ninthwonders', 'itsaickworld', 'Nomanforme', 'Willywhacker…two or three other places as well."

"Wow," Glenda said admiringly. "You must be rich."

"Yeah, talk to my accountant. If you can find the thieving little Bernie." Bitter episode. "Sold the rights to anyone who asked. I never saw a penny. Circumcised cocksmoker. Probably porking ten-year old boys in Thailand as I speak."

Mitch figured to run across the balding motormouth one day. Bit of Hun reckoning to follow. International pastime, every half-century. Roust the sharpers. Get your money back.

Later, in the tub. Mitch playing "Up Periscope." Glenda laughing with delight.

"Ummm…Mitch?"

Mitch started. "Ah, sorry. Off in space. What?"

Glenda offered the worshipful gaze. Doll eyes round and imploring. Her earlier wheedling had succeeded. Mitch checked his com. Then changed his mind. No kicking her to the parking lot. Instead, let her deliver the thirty minute bj she begged for. A proxy thank you from her mother. Very progressive, Mitch thought. Very Toronto. Kept smiling, despite the contempt he felt for that kind of PC bullethead. Someone who'd sell that shit philosophy to her daughter as something socially advanced. Slut power. Good luck with that. Still, no quarrel with the oral. Kid was a pro. Mom had trained her well.

Mitch still occupied with the trull business. Becoming a mood anchor. No Tank missions were on the next day's sched. So he'd no excuse for avoiding the file. But mysteries were more annoying than he'd realized. He'd kind of hoped Max was right. Somebody would phone in the crim's name. Mitch and whomever would roll up to his shack. Public arrest. Camera's rolling. Viral vid. Thankful Commissioner. Take the bonus money. Get hammered at Billy's. Or meet up with the crew in Cuba. Shake his wang at Castro's bro. If he was still alive. Capital dining, commie boy.

So far, though, nothing like that. It had been a slog just thinking about it. Good thing he had Yaz on top of things. Otherwise, he'd have trouble listing any news. And more stupid trannies in the roll call of dead dolls. Not just his. It was an avalanche. People were really noticing.

Glenda slapped water. "You're not listening!"

Mitch focused on her again. Returned Glenda's syrupy smile. Happy as a harp seal in June. Her splendid boobs bobbed on the surface. Float plane pontoons. Mitch nudged the left one with his submarine. Glenda gave it the hungry leer.

"What?" Mitch asked again.

"Oh...just...I know you have a girlfriend..."

"Yeah..." Mitch nodded.

"...but my Mom was wondering if...?"

"Yeah?" Mitch said, antenna up.

Coy was never packaged better. "...Just...you think you'd be interested in a twosome maybe...some day?"

Mitch slid down into the steaming soup. Did an idling motorboat. Sat back up. Fake mulling. No brainer from first mention.

"Yeah, shit, why not?" Mindless animal sex. With two randy stoats. What could be better?

Glenda's face lit up. She clapped her hands together. "Mother will be so happy. She's always said that..."

Mitch's eyes narrowed. "Go on..."

"Oh, just that...she's...she's never felt more alive, more of a woman than when...you were pounding her peach."

Mitch smiled. "So...just you two? No horny aunts? Sisters? Where's granny these days? Bet she's not getting it like she used to, the old slut."

"Oh, you," Glenda said. Playfully throttled his undersea cable. "I think we'll be more than enough for you."

"Talk is cheap," Mitch responded. Tried to put a face to Glenda's mother. Kept confusing her with all the other Bay street whisker biscuits he'd known and tapped. Fuck it. Two tits and a snatch. The holy trinity. Put twenty years on Glenda. Problem solved.

Mitch felt his eyes drop. Half a pizza. Three beers, bj and a hot bath. Barely hanging on now. Half aware of Glenda toweling him dry. She couldn't help lingering on his joint. Fortunately, the big unit was as tuckered out as he was. Lead to bed. Coverlet in place. Forehead peck. Soap-scrubbed skin smell. Pleasant. So what if she was an amoral bimbo. He wasn't going to marry her.

"I'll let myself out."

"Dishes..." Mitch murmured.

"Don't worry. I'll do a hurricane clean before I go."

"You better...," Mitch mumbled. "Owe me..." Couldn't finish. Entered dreamland.

"You're so right, sweet prince," Glenda cooed. "I'll send a spark. Don't forget your promise."

A light snore greeted her. And man musk. Every real woman's favourite scent. What fun she and her mother were going to have. She pushed a lock of damp hair back. Ran a finger down the Navarone brow. Traced the bunker fringe. Felt the snaky scar trail buried over his right eye. Caressed the armored cheekbones. Field of stubble to the cleft chin. A modern Adonis, she thought. Wished she was older. His girlfriend. Pictured the daily rogering. His willing sex slave. No demand too outrageous. No desire too sick. No act too demeaning. Indeed, did there exist the sexual request or position she couldn't satisfy? Hadn't already explored in junior high school? Glenda was skeptical. But more than willing to find out.

Mitch awoke briefly. Placed the sound. Laser click. Door secured. Sanctuary restored. Slept on without stirring.

HARVEY'S MAKES IT YOUR WAY.
EVERY DAY. HURRAH!

-◄◇►-

Mitch made it into the office by 11:30. Responded to the impertinent joshing with customary good grace. An upraised middle finger for one and all. Just finished up a series of phone calls when Yaz buzzed. Mitch vanished the door.

A fresh-permed head appeared. "Busy?"

Negative response. "Closing it up for lunch. Fucking Goodfellow. Those slut leads he provides. Worse than useless. Been chasing phantoms for the last thirty minutes. Nobody at the National Party of Toronto has heard of a spokeswoman called Lotta Scheisse. Downtown D.P.'s are supposed to have interviewed this guy." Mitch pointed at his holo. "A former client of my creepy. Pre-tranny era," Mitch amended. "I contacted his job in North York. Secretary says the dealership has no record of a Stew DuBaekker on staff."

Mitch paused. Pointed. "Some Christian happy clapper does an outreach thing for skids. Supposed to have a storefront place near the strip. I call the number. Receptionist says she's never heard of Evan Jellicle."

Famous Milligan snort. Names and businesses materialized. Waved the holovision in Yaz's direction. "Look at them all. The stars are where I've checked. Unbelievable."

Yaz scanned the list.

"Like Goodfellow thinks I'm going to find Austin Tayshis at a gay nightclub. Not this cowboy. Tell you that now."

Yaz frowned.

Mitch curled a lip. "Apparently some kind of cross-dresser entertainer. They like that."

Mitch gestured down near the bottom. "See this? A carny retirement home. Your tax dollars at work. So astrologers have somewhere to die. Anyway, I'm to contact some crystal ball fondler. Claims she had a dream about my trull. Get on the com. Lady answers. I ask to speak to Claire Voyent. She hangs up. I phone back. Same thing happens. Third time, this fucking Alzeimers bitch starts yelling at me. Fucking scandalous! If I wasn't so busy I go over there and kick some gerry butt."

Mitch shook his head again. Set the uni on idle.

"You know," he said. Fixed Yaz with a serious look. "For half the price those pachouli cunts charge, I'll map out any hooker's destiny a year in advance. Like, for example, Monday the 10th, 2025. You're gonna suck off a big, fat postie. Then lay more track. Next day? Same again. Ha ha. Now pay up." Mitch roared. "And if you're real lucky, you can pick up some extra cash getting cornholed as a porn extra."

Yaz stared at the glimmering graph. Made a mental note. Have the Force run the name Goodfellow through its computers. Seemed a roguish sort. The Force frowned on frivolity. They wouldn't like this character.

Mitch yawned. Jaw muscles cracked loud. Belched once. Scratched his back. Then his butt. Patted his stomach.

"Long night?" Yaz asked politely.

Mitch shook his head. "Not really. Slept great. Almost too deep, you know? Been yawning all morning. Need some fuel, maybe." Fought against yawning again.

"So what brings you by this fine spring morning anyway?" Bitter sarcasm. An icy rain beat against the window. "We didn't have a meeting or anything, right?"

"No." Yaz held up his hand. "I'm finished the circuit review. And the research department is running a kill scenario. Won't be finished until this afternoon. Just wondered…if you're hungry, maybe we could go somewhere for lunch? I'll buy."

"Beautiful," Mitch said. "Perfect timing. Thunderbirds are very go on that idea." Mitch grabbed his smokes. Pushed his chair in. "Where to?"

"No car. I thought you might know of…a place nearby."

Mitch took a deep breath. "Yeah, it'll have to be nearby." He reached into his pocket. Handed Yaz a bizchip.

"Goodfellow again. Guy can't do enough for me. Don't know why. Press the middle. Guy will pick you up anytime, day or night. Good luck. I've tried twice. Never saw nothing."

"Rick Shaw Car Service," Yaz read aloud. Nodded to himself. Peculiar coincidence. Pocketed the item. "We might need umbrella's. It's supposed to be raining."

"We're not in Vantown," Mitch sneered. "Umbrellas are for Nancy boys. This is CORE. Suck it up. Five minute walk. I know where. The Bloor one is closest."

Down the stairs. Outside. Immediate policy review. East wind. Sheet rain. Mixed with ice pellets. Mitch grunted in disbelief. Put a hand out. "Fuck, man. Look at this shit. We need umbrellas."

Back under the overhang. Com link to the garage. Minute later an ink black Torpedo tore up the ramp. Braked in front of the entrance. The lot lad hopped out. Saluted. Scurried back to safety. Mitch waved Yaz forward. Took the wheel. Bulled his way into traffic. Made for his favourite hamburger haven.

Parked. Dash to the doors. Inside. Mitch wrinkled his nose. Shook like a wolfhound. Moist greasy warmth. Welcome to Harvey's.

Mitch kicked out. Irritating absorbobot the object. Nodded sorry to the teen who's ankle took the blow. Initial scowl wiped off. Proper bow and scuttle followed Mitch's glare.

"Mmm...mmmm..." Mitch licked his lips. Grinned at Yaz. "You got Harvey's back home, right?"

Yaz knitted the brow. A mole moved. Back jaw. Mitch hadn't noticed it before. Cancer marker, he'd heard. When they turn green, order an urn. It's over.

"I've heard of it."

"What?" Mitch said, stunned. "That's it? N-o-o-o-o-o! Harvey's! Make your own burgers! Harvey's onion rings! Baconettes! It's a beautiful thing! C'mon!"

Yaz looked perplexed.

"Oh, man. Time to pop your cherry, Barry." Mitch strode past the lineup. Man on a mission of mercy. Returned seconds later. "Everything's taken care of." Waved Yaz to follow him. Empty back booth. They sat down.

"Reserved for VIP's," Mitch said.

"We're...VIP's?" Yaz asked. Pronounced it as Mitch had. A single word. He'd noticed the barrier beam engaged once they passed by. "You must come here often?"

"Can't." Mitch said. Slapped the grill under his shirt. "But when Mitch has a grease need, there's no better place."

"Salad bar?" Yaz asked. He was facing a wall.

"Wouldn't know...fag," Mitch needled. Mock sneer.

Yaz caught the cigarette Mitch tossed him. Looked behind. Mitch left the pack on the table. Lit up.

"They let us smoke in here?"

Mitch smirked. "I smoke in here. Owner's a...supporter. We did him a favour a while back. He lets some of us sit back here. Smoke if it's not too busy. Usually, no one complains. As long as we keep it...not too obvious." Mitch blew a plume ceilingward. Smirked again. Flicked his ash on the floor.

Yaz dropped his shoulder. Quick scan.

"Let me know if you spot any potential squealers?" Mitch said. "Women are the fucking worst. 'Excuse me, excuse me'. 'You're not allowed to smoke in here'," Mitch mimic whined. "Shut up, bitch."

Yaz blew smoke sideways and down. "It feels strange," he admitted. "Now."

"Yeah, it's fucked up. This city. Ass-head magnet of the world."

Mitch laughed to see Yaz pocket his cigarettes.

"Jesus," he chided, "you are well trained. Stop looking so guilty. We're cops, for Christ's sake! Well, kind of. You are, anyway!"

Mitch spotted Yaz's lazer. Examined it. Touch expensive. Didn't know the maker. Happened to notice the owner's picture on the wall. Between the barred windows. Directed Yaz's attention to it. Yaz took it in. Looked back at Mitch, eyebrows questioning.

"Owner. Lebanese. Or Ismaili. Something like that. I forget. Rich as God. Owns a bunch of properties. Kind of a slumlord. But a hell of a good shit."

"How did you…?" Yaz began. Ready to memorize the information.

Mitch held up his finger. Touched his nose. "Can't say. But he's been very generous with CORE every since. So order whatever you like. It's on the house. Lucky you. And here she comes now." Mitch flashed his widest smile.

"Sorry, Mr. Milligan. I didn't see you sitting here. I was on a break." The speaker smoothed a stray curl under her hairhat. Pixie eyes. Pixie-cute sloped nose. Peppering of freckles. Cocktease smile. Juicy-looking baby silencers. Teen-tight tush. Mitch never saw her, he didn't want to tuck her under his arm. Bundle her home. Toss in shower. Suds up. Hose down. The Hungry Man Special. Serves one. All night long.

"Not a problem, honeybuns," Mitch said. Radiated lust. Thumbed at her. Said to Yaz, "Picture this hot moppet wrapped around your Johnson."

Yaz maintained. Straight face. Looked between the high-schooler and Mitch.

"Just say the word, handsome," came the swift retort. "I'm of age."

"What a heartbreaker!" Mitch cried. Spanked the fake formica. Leered at her hovering hooters. "Why can't I be eighteen again?"

"I'd have trouble walking straight to school every day. I know," Adelaide winked. "Your regular order is being prepared, sir."

She placed her hands on the table. Leaned in. Twenty seconds hang time. Canteen quake sway. Mitch gulped. Pretended to fan himself with a tissue.

"What would your friend like?" the tartlette asked. Beamed a gracious smile at Yaz, who nearly blushed.

"Rabbit food," Mitch interjected. "What's back there today?"

Adelaide plumped her tits as she thought.

Mitch groaned. Covered his eyes. "Stop it, you terrible tramp! You're givin' us wood! Unfreeze a quiche or…whatever you got. Now get!"

Throaty chuckle from Adelaide. She scampered off, propelled by a complimentary Mitch ass whack. His fresh-brewed coffee demand echoed off the walls.

"…used to work part-time at Kentucky Duck during school," Mitch was explaining when their food arrived. Adelaide set their trays before them. Extra napkins. Ketchup containers. A Corona for Mitch.

"I'll be right back with your drink," Adelaide sparkled to Yaz.

"So those little turd balls in the bottom of the bucket?" Mitch finished. "Avoid. Unless you got kids. It's no urban myth. Deep-fried flies. Other shit. Believe it."

He popped a fresh ring into his mouth. Pounded the table. Inhaled and exhaled rapidly. "Hot, hot," he winced. Took a hard pull from the Corona. Sighed with pleasure.

"This is quite good," Yaz said around a mouthful of salad.

"What is it?"

"Ham, carrots, broccoli, celery, snowpeas, okra, babyleaf and…feta."

"No shit." Mitch unwrapped his cheeseburger. "Sounds…healthy." Pushed a wedge in. Grunted happily. They munched away in silence. Delicious. Mitch hadn't done fast food recently. Forgot the joy.

"Like I always say," Mitch added to Yaz's service praise. "All I've ever asked for is special treatment."

And because they were with CORE, Ahmed dipped into the premium burger reserve. Choice, top-grade Ontario ground beef. Multiple seasonings. Thawed, with warning. Carefully nuked otherwise. Then grilled to a crusty T. Farm cheddar, bubble melted. Toasted bakery bun. Soft and chewy. Real sesame seeds sprinkled on top. Ambrosia.

Add in rings that weren't greasy. Fries that were crunchy outside, soft and tender inside. Even the Coke had that old-time bite. Poor man's Calvados. The Sage being sarcastic, Mitch knew. Didn't know what it meant. German humour.

"So, not much further ahead on the case," Yaz observed. Wiped his mouth clean with the warmed, scented towels Adelaide brought them.

Mitch nodded. "Yeah, it's crap. Not as much fun as I thought, to be honest. Shit, I was half promised we wouldn't even have to leave the office. Some skeeze would roll over. We bring the clown in. Turn him inside out. Then leave him for the D.P.'s. They get the applause. We get the credit. Hasn't worked out that way."

Mitch stared off over Yaz's shoulder. Business increase. Late lunch crowd. More ties. Office trim.

"Actually did get an interesting link before we left the shop." Speaking of Max. Still in the loop. So Mitch promised to look into it. "'Lanny the Tranny' may have come from money. That's why there's sudden interest in this thing. Or at least, that's the guess."

Yaz chewed slow. Reflected on the matter. "You think…they think maybe blackmail?"

Mitch shrugged. Finished off his burger. Crushed the wrapper. Wiped his fingers on the countertop edge. "Fuckin' mystery."

"Maybe the murders are…political."

"Maybe," Mitch agreed. Smiled. Found a last ring hiding in the paper hamper. Popped it in his mouth. Still a tasty wonder.

"Or could it be evidence of a gangwar? Many of the victims would belong to the stable of one criminal organization or another."

"Makes sense," Mitch nodded. Dug for ketchup with the last fry. Waste not, want not. Somebody used to say that. A relative? Voice but no face.

"Why choose prostitutes?" Yaz mused.

"Easy practice," Mitch said. Matter-of-fact tone. "Trulls are a dime a dozen in this pit. One less, ten less…who the fuck's gonna notice?"

"You mentioned the…flags were raised after this one…victim was discovered. So family connections to…the power structure or police… could impact upon the case?"

"Always do, I'm told," Mitch said. "Pull. Favours done by friends in high places. The new thing is the old thing." Mitch worried a meat thread trapped between two molars. Noticed how bendy his tongue was. Weird.

Eyes drawn to a nearby peasant. Half-assed wipe job on the tables behind them. Twice she'd shot him heavy looks. The uniform trumpeted her charms. Third time peeking! Mitch gave his best smile. Head duck, deer-shy. Quadroon, Mitch figured. Jamaican mix. Good complexion. Sound teeth. Tight nap, glitter highlights. Grade 11 maybe.

She turned around, rag in hand. Faced them square. Displayed the goods, then queened away. Mitch smiled to himself. Adelaide had been talking. The trollop.

And Ahmed. Clever little Levantine. Just the kind of top-heavy merchandise the man stocked. Only hired the best, most edible teen cupcakes. Put them in uniforms two sizes too small. Paid above average wages. Doubled his investment. Drooling hopefuls came from every corner of the city. Punched processed shite into their pimpled blocks. Stared and dreamed. The money poured in.

"And you think that's why you were given the case? " Yaz on point.

"Yeah," Mitch exhaled loudly through his nose. "They might need a scrapegoat."

Yaz frowned slightly.

"I mean, I don't think the Commissioner is in on anything like that. Just…politics, yeah? Someone has an agenda." Suddenly cancelled the idea of a post-lunch butt. Falling into the grease trap always gave him the guilts. He'd committed a self-health crime. Time to slink from the scene. Promised his body an extra hard workout that afternoon.

"Oh, well," Mitch yawned, scratched his left tit. "Fuck it, eh?"

On the way out, Mitch elbowed Yaz. Pointed at a t-shirt. "Look at that. Nice."

Yaz read the message. 'I had an abortion' in block letters. The wearer looked to be in her early twenties. Grimy, matted black hair hung straight down. Stopped below her ears. Dyko-style repellent. Mitch recognized the ski jacket brand. Not cheap. Priorities. Fashion before family. Welcome to the era.

"Too bad your mother didn't have an abortion," Mitch said as they passed by. Yaz didn't hear the reply. Did see Mitch raise his middle finger. Snap his teeth together several times. More angry sputtering. Mitch's goading laugh. Words exchanged. Recognized the phrase "ugly skid cunt." A Mitch favourite.

And then they were out the door. Sound of crying cut off. Yaz wondered if he'd ever met someone who looked for and found trouble so readily.

Back in the car. Weather mixup, Mitch proclaimed. Nasty-looking clouds still lingered. But the sun had beaten them off for a bit. The Torpedo perfectly positioned to catch rays. Interior almost comfortable. Mitch and Yaz sparked cigs. Mitch hummed along to the FD. Faintest touch of distortion. Have to look into that. Shouldn't be.

"You were going to tell me about the Tank before," Yaz said. Covered his mouth. As though covering a yawn. Checked Mitch's expression. Nothing suspicious. Yaz had been tasked to learn more of this wondrous device. Rumours had reached The Force. Interest high.

Mitch glanced at the clock digi. "Yeah, we got time. Interesting story. Some wizard millwright from Hamilton built it. In his spare time. Fucking genius. Worked at Domtar. Military research. Slow days, he'd tinker with it. A portable bunker. Military name…the T.H.E.R.K. Stands for…Thermo… Exo…something, something. I forget. Bullet proof. RPG proof. Cannon proof. Comsat wired. Self-sustaining. Water extraction machines. Heat pumps. Camo exterior. Buckyball carbon fiber skin," Mitch repeated in a monotone. "Whatever the fuck that means. Deflects incoming rounds. Or so they say. Fuck, who knows what else? Probably flies. It was for Afghanistan. Or any place like it. Including the moon."

"Anyway, word got around. Somebody talked to somebody. Next thing, he gets a contract to build another one. And then…more. Now? Let's just say he's moved outta Hamilton. CORE got a special model. He reconfigured it for our purposes. Helped install it. We couldn't be happier."

"The Chair came with it?"

"Yeah," Mitch nodded. Expelled a perfect smoke ring. Watched it drift into the windshield. Spread out. Hit the cleanser fan.

"Saw this program once. Animals at play. Monkeys, lions, even crows. They had cameras in fake sea turtles. Followed these dolphins close to shore. Just goofing around. They'd blow perfect air rings underwater. Then nose them bigger and bigger. Like into a small hoop. And push them around. Fucking incredible."

Mitch erased the heater. Not necessary.

"Actually, no. That's wrong. The Chair was a side order," Mitch corrected himself. Also military. For our Taliban buddies way back. After that fake scandal about d-d-d-detainees. I'll show you the inner workings some time. Usually, if you need something to fail at an important moment, ask for modtech. But this thing was thought through. Intelligent design. Easy-to-use. Well built."

Yaz nodded respectfully. He wondered what Force guidelines were regarding such a tool. Likely forbidden. From what he'd seen of it? The Force could benefit from its use.

"Shit, we're still figuring it out. The guy crammed it full of absolutely deadly stuff. It's just…too much fun to use. All the terrorgators love it. The Tank, the Chair…" Mitch held out his hands. Nothing more you could say.

Mitch held his dying butt near the dash slot. The vacuum tray appeared. Ate it.

"You know, I'd hate to think of not having it now," he said. Dead serious. "Man, if we got some of our Ovarian horrors into one. Well…this thing would be over."

Mitch's com burbled. He found it. Read the message. Dropped the beast into first. Nearly side-swiped the pro-abortion slag as he squealed away. No time to abuse her. Peeled out of the lot and back to base.

Yaz scrambled to attach his harness. Saw Mitch glare out the windshield. Nostrils flared, breathing audible. The big, rawboned hands looked ready to sqeeze the wheel to dust. The knuckles white as tree roots.

"What's up?" he asked. Caution advisable. He'd seen the man transformed. From jovial to displeased to murderous. In a matter of minutes.

Mitch struggled to swallow. "Speak of the fucking devil," was all he could get out. Threw the car up the street, bleater clearing a path.

MITCH MANGLES A MODGE

—◄○►—

Mitch entered the Tank. Still walked a little strange. Deep fried fast food. Worked on him like Drano. It just elbowed everything else out of the way. Felt like someone took a vacuum to his butt. Sucked everything right through. No waiting. Result? His ass gave birth to a spanking four-pounder. Pitied anyone entering the john during the next...hour. Gaggo stinkland.

The yellow carryall hit the floor. Proper thud. He motioned the uni on. Bright rainbow spectrum as the holo powered up.

Mitch kneeled down. Began the formal sift. Ran his fingers over his limited edition Gerry Cheevers. His first CORE Award. No mask today, though. He wanted to be seen.

Stood up. Discomfort. Ass and boxers contesting. Mitch yanked at his suit. And again. Waited. Correction accomplished.

Checked his sitrep pad. Re-read the highlighted material. Stooped again to unload equipment. Two crowbars removed. Rang off the tile. The sawed-off Easton bat got the nod. Good for close-in work. The homemade nunchuks added. More for looks. Mitch sucked with them. Tried a few times. Nearly took himself out. Vowed to learn how someday. Maybe get Yaz to teach him. Heard they got taught that shit from birth in China.

Low rumble from The Chair. Mitch ignored it. Rummaged deeper. "Hang on, princess," he muttered under his breath. Came across a roll of premium grade, low spool memory mono line. Kept it. The brand new Osprey Gaff Hook. Why not? Mitch hesitated over the Milwaukee Deep Cut portable bandsaw. Placed it under the table within easy reach.

More culling. Using The Chair exclusively today. The Klein block and tackle wouldn't be necessary. Also left out—the Hiatt handcuffs and leg irons. Fun but unnecessary. No to the modified acupuncture set. No to the special order Yokohama gardening shears. Although Mitch quite liked them. No to the three-litre jar of pickled swine testicles and hair ribbons. Hitchcock gag, Political explained. He seemed to think it was funny as hell.

Mitch spied three Proctor 'Little Nipper' mousetraps. Nabbed them. Somebody in Weapons had re-jigged them into excellent toecutters. Definite laughs with those.

He pawed through other gear. There was a Jeffers cutting spur with 10-point rowel. No. His eyes lit on the L&H copper alloy branding iron. Burn the CORE brand into her fat, greasy butt. Had appeal. Poetic justice. But it was trouble in other ways. He passed.

Other tools up for consideration. Lodged in the corner, a 100-volt cast bronze dehorner. What you couldn't do with it. One of Wilson's favourite toys. There was the Ryobi 12-volt cordless drill with diamond-head bits. Interesting reactions when it appeared. Under it, the surprisingly decent three-piece Mastercraft offset pliers unit. The velvet case a nice touch.

And then…Mitch's pride and joy. His Ros Arms, Zlatoust forged bush knife. A work of art. 14 1/2" long. Laser-sharp 9" blade. 3/16" at the tang. Wicked sawback. Crim howls of alarm whenever he brought it out. Mitch slid his fingers over the sleek tooled leather scabbard. "Not today, baby," he whispered. "Sorry."

Inventory complete. Mitch toed the box under the table. Turned and stared over at the target. A woman. More or less. More, actually. Lots more. Wearing a stressed orange COREsuit. It gave her the appearance of a shrink-wrapped maggot. Or a carrot topped with a scoop of zit.

"When she slept around the house…" Mitch thought of the old Youtube vid. Lard spills above the armrests. Medallions of plasticized flesh extruded from the ventilation holes. Mitch pictured the Chair collapsing upon itself. Julienned occupant. Nasty image. Hence, the double-strength suit. Hydrolic squishing would only jelly her organs. No comic sausage launch.

Mitch mentally reviewed the order sheet. "Mad" Modge Barstew. CORE code name—"Bibendum." A human forklift. Files said 293 kilos. Which seemed forgiving. 165cm tall. Profession? 'Activist'. Meaning no real job. University stupid. "Cartoon U," the Sage had joked. MA—Wymmyn's Studys. You couldn't pay more and get less.

HumIntel painted a recognizable story. Textbook shit disturber. Product of privilege. Typical comsymp tale, according to Political. Told Mitch all he needed to know. Another head-fucked fembot. Member of ultra-bitch collectives. Panic-peddler. Anti-Yank. Anti-biz. Anti-free speech, free thought. Waterwitch. Loved abortions. Loved terrorists. Loved BigGov. XXX trouble, whichever way you looked at it.

Mitch strolled nearer. Hooked his thumbs into the chest pocket ventricals.

Cletus come to chat. Sucked on his teeth. Said in his best Bubba, "Modge Barstew. Well, well…you're quite the, uh…the hefty thing, ain'tcha?"

A cold, malignant glare fell on him. Tapioca eyes. Nose an electrical socket turned sideways. And again with the pasty skin tone. Didn't these people ever go outside, Mitch wondered? Or they just sit inside and nurse grudges all day?"

"293 kilo's?" Mitch gave her a prolonged once over. "In your fucking dreams, Tantor." Mitch didn't have to fake disgust. "What'd they do? Run you over to the 401 transport weigh station? We don't got the Big Bertha scales here." Mitch ambled back and forth. No hurry. Take the measure of her. Gauge reactions. Probe for weakness, chinks in the blubber.

"I understand you need work. I can think of an outfit in Windsor. Might give you a try. Ever do any exotic dancing?"

Mitch nodded. "Nah, I can't see it either. Comedy. Horror. Fine line sometimes."

The woman seemed not to be listening.

"Modge! Modge, Modge, Modge!!" Mitch exclaimed. "You've been a…a b-b-busy c-c-cunt, haven't ya'?" Founder of some political branch of the NPOT. Front groups for front groups. NGO's on the government teat. Legal theft. The Sage setting the stage. Telling Mitch of secret crimes he had trouble comprehending. And to top it off, a high priestess of The Wickers. Dykos weaving veranda furniture. What next?

Malice contorted Modge's face. Mitch braced himself. Waited for a snake tongue to slither out. Modge looked the type to have one. But nothing happened. Just as well. The fact remained. Inconvenient truth. He was staring at a strong argument for abortion. Whatever the angle. Woman was baboon butt ugly.

Mitch took a deep breath. Thought back to the briefing. The decision to act only days in the making. CORE now believed the Ovarians were laying out bait. Dead trulls were turning up right and left for a reason. More even than Mitch knew about. People couldn't leave their houses in the morning without stepping over one. Storm sewers backed up. Another garbage disaster Toronto didn't need. Pols forced to act. CORE quietly asked to gird up. Why the Ovarians chose to harvest hookers no one knew. Mitch's job? Find out, if possible. But more important, terrorgate the parade float. Terrorgate her with extreme persistence.

The task dovetailed perfectly with CORE's ultimate agenda. They put the word out. Top floor approval for bitch lassoing. Known agitators spirited in. "Detained for questioning." One of them coughed up Barstew's name along with lung blood. Rendition from her Ottawa lair followed. CORE wanted her broke. According to crim complaints, Mitch was among the most wisely violent of all their Tank operators. High praise. Plus, he was off the books. A cipher. He wanted a mission. And for his sins, they gave him one.

Mitch continued his examination. Modge owned a large, large head. It sat on her neck like a concrete block. Square, imposing. Hydro hair. Warped, bent bristles shot out of her skull. Bride of Frankenstein bolts of gray. The entire broomhead bound into a bun. CORE regs.

Mitch moved to the wall. Felt for the depression. Deftly palmed the ejected remote. A gentle hum filled the immediate space. Chair activated. Five count pause. Tried the swivel toggle. The Chair silently spun left 30 degrees. Then right. Settled into default position. Slick-as-grease action. Always a pleasure to see it work.

Mitch tested several other options. No problems. Replaced the handheld. Dug at his butt again. Must be using tasty laundry soap. Sudden case of hungry ass.

"I guess this is my brush with greatness," Mitch said. Modge held his gaze. Dead stare.

"No mic for you. Sorry," Mitch apologized with perfect insincerity. "No bullhorn. No cameras. No suckup media." Her fucking hair. He couldn't not look at it. Crimp on crimp. Like God had run a hundred-thousand volts through it at birth. Trying to kill her maybe. He knew what was coming.

Archive shot bubbled up for his mind's eye. Taken from below. Background a prairie sky. Modge looming large as a grain elevator. Some whackjob CUPE rally. Or an address to escaped asylum residents. Hard to tell the difference. Deranged moonbats sporting papier-mache costumes. Skincrawl crowd. Bring the chains, Ma. Loons are loose again

Mitch pursed his lips. Shifted his feet. Looked hard at her. Focused on the Commissioner's words. The man's hatred for the woman ran deep and true. He was a righteous man. A religious man. A Canadian patriot. Her very existence offended him on several levels. That she had political influence? Beyond his understanding. Seeing her screech and blather on the holovid… it tore the man up inside. You could see it.

Mitch idly scratched his chin. Mused on the matter. Yawned. Dug out a cigarette from a side pocket. Fired it up. Stood over her. Jetted a thick stream into that wild pig face. Excellent response. Better than Mitch hoped for. Creature went batshit hysterical. Way, way over the top. Held her breath. Launched herself against the restraints. The head lashed from side-to-side. Eyes cannon mouth round. Milky white with rage.

Antic madness ended. Mitch blew smoke in her face again. Second time, same fun. High drama lunging and snuffling. But enough theatrics. Mitch stepped forward. Ground the cigarette out on her bound wrist. Sweet muffled howl. Her enormous bulk strained against the bindings. The ballgag ran with saliva. Popeye cheeks, plum-coloured from strain.

Mitch broke character. Laughed hard. Didn't yet know the full story. Might have held off otherwise. CORE researchers only learned the truth later. "Bibendum" Barstew. Batty. Clinically nutso. Bedlam ready. Tranks and wire-pajamas time.

Modge, it turned out, believed herself the avatar of an ancient Greek goddess. Ammonia. The deity charged with keeping Olympus tidy. Barstew was convinced Ammonia had returned. Possessed Modge. Her purpose? To reverse the common order of things. To destroy normalcy. Modge formed The Ovarians to realize her twisted aims. It was the public face, investigators discovered, of a far older, more sinister movement—Witchery.

The demonic pursuit of Witchery was first pursued a millenium earlier. It began in England. Then spread throughout Europe. Pagan circles. Known as The Harridans. Obnoxious, brassy, bothersome. These shrikes were feared and reviled. Finally outlawed. Stalwart Saxons banded together. Hunted them down. Drowned some in great barrels. Or bound them and their cats in stiff mill bags. Launched some from high cliffs into the roaring surf. Burned others at the stake. Buried a bunch alive. Hung them. Ran them through with sword and spear. Stoned them to death. Locked them in thatch huts. Set same aflame. Used them as bear bait. Impaled the viragos on sharp spikes. Tied them betwixt two horses pulling in opposite directions. Yet like dragon's teeth did these fiends multiply.

Nor did they think. Wandering from village to village, they launched lunatic demands. Denounced the natural ways of life. Celebrated vile, immoral perversions. Worked to set man at man, woman at woman. With their green warty noses and hate-twisted faces, it was rightly assumed they bred with demons. Merciless eradication the only option.

So with holy resolve brave Christians drove the broom-riders from their midst. Exorcised their communities. Knew happiness again.

Some of the worst creatures escaped, however. These Furies fled into plashy fens. Found sanctuary far from human habitation. Foraged as did their neighbours, the fox and hedghog. Grew cunning. Nature became both fridge and pharmacy. They learned of a herb's dark powers. Unleashed weeds. Transformed timid tubers. With mortar and pestle they wrestled. Mingled things inside vast vats. Evil draughts crafted, consumed with much cackling. Ever strove on behalf of wrong ends.

Or so the story went. Mitch knew shit about witches. Cared less. They wore pointy black hats. Flew around on Halloween. Lived alone in candy houses. Baked kids for lunch. That was it. He was a little surprised to learn they still existed. Thought they'd been exterminated years earlier. In the war.

He also knew nothing about their rites and rituals. Few did. Or that a storehouse of secret knowledge had been passed down over the generations. Spells, curses, charms and incantations. Each employed with wicked intent.

For more advanced trainees, demonology beckoned. Conjuring the dead a Sabbath routine. Blasphemy commonplace. As far as Mitch could see, deranged didn't do them justice. Weird sisters running the world? Not while Mitch held the whip.

Extensive research revealed Barstew's introduction into Witchery. A campus recruiter spotted her as an undergraduate. Personal grooming followed. She was a natural. Given to wild emotional swings. Disordered personality. Exceedingly modest intellect. Subject to unsound reasoning. Narcissistic. Best of all, a fanatic lesbo. For movement leaders, the Missiah had arrived.

Modge quickly mastered "Witchfare." Third year at Carlton, conducted blood ceremonies. Oversaw coven conclaves. Graduates soon seeped into humanities faculties. Infected other departments. Their soul-poisoning influence spread ike an oil stain. The civil bureaucracy, media, arts—all afflicted. The purpose? As old as the profession they were winnowing. Divide and conquer. Or something else entirely. They were women. Logic didn't enter into it.

"Hey!" Mitch snapped his fingers in Modge's face. "Earth to barge."

The cherry ballgag gave Modge the look of a hostage clown. Mitch would have laughed again except he was working. And she wasn't cooperating. He circled behind her. Tapped his fingers on The Chair in admiration. Top-drawer craftsmanship. Bulkhead riveting. Slickly hidden works. No-slip rubber grips. Hooks, latches, fasteners. Nothing had been overlooked. The Tank was not your daddy's terrorgation chamber. Likewise, The Chair was not some folding piece of crap dragged from the closet when guests threatened. It looked exactly like what it was—a weapon from the future. With a sack of fat lashed to it. He rubbed his hands together. Mood swing! Suddenly in excellent spirits.

"Modge-y!" Mitch bellowed in her ear. Nasal blast of surprise. Her restraints held. Perspiration found the gullys. Dripped onto her suit. Ran down onto the accordion folds of her lap.

Mitch pinched her nostrils shut. Modge's eyes ballooned out, white and waxy. Chuckling, he wiped his hand on the hanging sweat towel. Sound of wind whistling in. Mitch tracked back out of her field of vision. Chuckled low. Doing his ominous and lurking thing. And getting paid for it. The best part.

"'Red Menace'," Mitch mocked when quiet resumed. "'Hellion on Wheels', 'Gargantua'. What else did the boys call you?" He gravitated around. Smiled. Still the unforgiving gaze. Spooky yellow spears radiated from the centre of her irises. Mitch thought to share that with Ivan. Might mean something.

Lightning fast, he swung his boot tip. The Milligan Special. Done right, it neatly separated the kneecap from the knee. He knew the crowd would be up on its feet. He wanted a memorably heroic intro. Break through her mental defenses. Wall breached, he could wade in. Muck about a bit.

Modge's head slammed hard against the back of the chair. Agony crumpled her face. She balled and unballed her fists. Mitch strolled over to the table. Break time. Lit a smoke. Didn't register at the time. She'd made very little sound despite the pain. Which should have been considerable.

He inhaled the nail in under a minute. Lazered it to oblivion.

Modge had already recovered when he returned. Surprising. Gave no evidence of being in discomfort. She even launched herself against the bindings at his appearance. Mitch gazed at her forearms. Hadn't noticed how monstrously large they were. And the burn crater where he'd snuffed out his smoke. Barely visible. Saw a doc once about fast metabolism animals. Must be she was some kind of mutant.

Great veins pulsed on her neck and forehead. The temples throbbed. Jaw muscles twitched and jumped. Mitch hoped she wasn't having a heart attack. That would have spoiled his afternoon. But considering the tonnage her ticker torqued blood through. Can't say he'd have blamed it for throwing in the towel. You can only ask so much of anything.

Mitch couldn't resist looking at the two-way. Viewers read his mind. The jubilant mood had been queered. Was she going to rob them of victory by dying too soon?

Modge rocked in her seat. Futile. Surely obvious, Mitch thought. Still, she poured energy into the attempt. Back and forth. Sideways. Up and down. She rolled her massive shoulders. Bent against the restraints with serious effort.

Mitch was content to let her run herself down. Until he heard something. A bad sound. Unmistakeable yet unbelievable. Again, the same disturbing crack. Metal fatigue? He'd have laughed in the face of anyone who suggested the possibility. Nothing short of a direct nuclear strike looked capable of damaging their favourite piece of furniture.

Silence, too, in the lounge. Excited shouts demanded explanations. Holo replays. Even though everyone knew. Incredibly, Modge had…done something. Icy fingers of doubt ran down spines.

Mitch was off his uni perch and in her face seconds later. A clenched right fist cocked above his shoulder. "Oi!" he snapped. "Enough of that!"

Modge ignored him. Wild grunts accompanied buffalo heaving. Her entire face bloated out. A Niagara of sweat spilled off her. Mitch was quietly incensed. No terrorgator abided insolence. It broke the rules. Double-pumped. Waited for it. Then delivered a solid jab to her left eye. The skin instantly parted. Pink flesh quivered beneath puddling blood.

Reason returned to its throne. Modge stopped moving. Thirty seconds later, it was as if nothing had happened. Modge breathed through her nose. Normal manner. The face resumed its natural shade of old tofu. Even the mouse under her eye had grown no larger. Med wing analysts never did explain it to anyone's satisfaction. But it was the first indication of something amiss. A sign Modge was more than an obese, blustering bullock.

"Okay," Mitch said, game face on. "Let's get something straight here. You're not going anywhere. Those are rig ropes. They're used to strap down… heavy equipment, like dozers, backhoes, terraformers and shit…on transport trailers. And this is a state-of-the-art terrorgation Chair. Meaning…you're here until I say otherwise. But if you ever do something to it so it doesn't work right…" Mitch paused. "Well, I'll be…pretty disappointed."

High road it. Amiable smile. Keep the feeling light.

Modge lay her head to one side. Somehow, despite the ballgag, Mitch sensed a smirk. Meaning clear. She hadn't grasped the situation. Mitch thought of his training. How regular interrogations were about persuasion, not coercion. Terrorgations were the exact opposite. Persuasion not an issue. The point was to scare the shit out of some misbehaving fuckwit. Have them change errant thought patterns. Some immediately took the lessons to heart. Others were lost causes. He had a feeling Modge fell into the latter category. Reversed course. Decided to go large on her.

"Boat-butt!" he screamed. Snapped his teeth at her. "Yeah, I mean you, you fucking horrorshow. Ovarians. You're the Queen whackjob. How many we looking at anyway? Is this some sort of coast-to-coast clusterfuck or what?"

Modge sniffed. Her mammoth head telescoped down and in, like an incurious turtle. This also creeped Mitch out. Coughed to disguise his revulsion.

"What does your group have against curb cunts anyway?" he pressed on. "I thought you people were all in favour of…the sex trade. MTF's. LTG.. BD's…DF's…whatever the fuck they are?"

Blank expression on Modge. A snicker? Did Mitch actually hear that? Was it possible? It left him speechless. He stood up. Stepped back one pace. Nodded. "Alright," was all he said.

With a honed showman's touch, Mitch unzipped his suit. Buzz of anticipation raced through the lounge. Mitch doing his Chopper Read impression. Bound to be hysterically funny. Even the brass had trouble keeping straight faces. Whiskey glasses clinked. Old-time comedy.

"Fatbag Barstew...I'd like you to meet...the King Snake!" Mitch reached inside. Dragged out the pride of Kapuscasing, Ontario. Steinberg moment. The glory of his unit did fill the room. Roars and fist pumps erupted among delirious viewers. Two accountants huddled near the back wall. Calculated holovid sales. Happy Mammon moment.

Mitch swaggered in front of The Chair. Twirled the licorice. Modge sat transfixed. She was staring at a live armadillo. Agents pounded their armrests, each other.

"Fifteen-inch! Fifteen-inch! Fifteen-inch Mitch!" came the chant. The Commissioner nodded to his aides. Everything was playing out exactly as he'd hoped.

Paralyzed and appalled, Modge couldn't help looking. Her tormentor's penis was enormous, unearthly, obscene. It couldn't be real. It couldn't be bobbing merrily before her very eyes. And yet it was. She shrank before it's magnificence. Adding to her horror, it continued growing larger. Despair flood. Nothing in the Witchery training prepared her for this nightmare. She shied in fear from the phenomenon. Even the stoutest bull lesbo would quail under such an assault. Modge prayed to Ammonia for strength in her hour of dread.

Mitch relished Modge's reaction. Stage fright was never an issue for Mitch's trouser lance. It loved the limelight. Being exhibited before an open-mouthed audience. Routine. Hockey helped. Mitch a star sniper in tier two Junior. On and off the ice. He'd bulged twine throughout the North. From Cochrane to Kenora. The rink Ruby's revered him.

Turned a different kind of professional after the knee injury aborted his NHL hopes. Joined the escort industry. Moved to the Big Stink. Serviced hundreds upon hundreds of lovelorn corporate cookies. Could remove a pantsuit and be inside the temple of poon before sensors fogged the glass wall. Satisfied all. He'd put his wang up against any the competition had to offer. Whatever the game, Mitch could play.

It was no idle boast. The man they called Magnet brought the goods. He'd won any number of ill-advised bets over the years. He'd plunked the python down on bartops and barhops. On hope chests, tool chests, chesterfields, chests of drawers, and of course big, plumpy chests. He'd laid it over coffee tables, picnic tables, end tables and night tables. Drunkenly unfurled it from a flag pole once. Draped it over a balcony railing. Whatever laughs or screams of terror you could get exposing your dick, he'd had them. Being bounced off someone's brow wasn't even that exotic.

Modge was enraged, though. The big apple loomed large as life. Mitch drove it from hairline to chin. Back again. Surfing the lumber was a hoot. He blocked Modge's nostrils. Watched her snuffle for air. Slow-dragged it across her eyebrows. Patted it on her whitened lips. Poked her about the cheek. Chortled as her eyes rolled back into her head. In-your-face indignity. Excellent fun. His CORE brothers were in stitches. Provided she didn't go catatonic, prospects for more yuks looked good.

Mitch chose to finish the program. Rammed his pole into the waxy shell. Gave it a quarter turn. Locked and loaded.

"Just like Iggy," Mitch crowed. "Now you can tell people you've had it in the ear before." Held up his free arm in triumph. Hoped the cameras could catch the money shot. They did. Ivan had made it very clear for the techmonkeys. No excuses. Castration the reward for failure.

Viewing agents, detectives, brass and guests screamed with pleasure. Bikinied Bev's bustled about. Refreshed drinks. Lit cigars and cigarettes. Enjoyed group gropes and gooses. Savoured their privileged position as company sexpots.

"Prick up your ears," Orton the towel boy lisped. More peals of laughter. High spirits everywhere.

Mitch disengaged. Burrowed the purple into Modge's neck folds. Spin dry. Shot Modge a gloat and a wink. Held up the tormentor. Gave Modge a final view.

"Amazing, isn't it?" he said. Briefly regretted she was restrained. It left her unable to run a hand the length of his turgid beam. Forever cement its immensity into her memory circuits.

"Sure you're not hungry?" Mitch joked. Reeled it back. Put it into the stall. Wasn't remotely serious. Did enjoy the flicker of fear on her face. She still couldn't stop gazing at it. Fun as it might be to give her a good face fuck, he'd never endanger the big fella near Modge's choppers.

Her jaw muscles flexed. Lizard eyes narrowed. Modge looked bitter and unhappy. Things were going swimmingly.

"Well," he said. "Nobody enjoys a good gag more than I do. However, maybe it's time we removed yours. I have a feeling you've got something to tell me."

Mitch hadn't been in the crime management game long. But he knew good agents developed an instinct about crims. Mitch was under no illusions. Modge wasn't ready. She knew about the recent tsunami of slaughtered sluts. But she telegraphed resistance. Which played right into his hand. An unmoveable Modge about to meet an irresistible Mitch. The download revenue would surpass even the most hopeful projections.

Mitch gave the sign. The hatch sprang open. Intern First Class Catalonotto stuck his head in.

"Sir?"

"Bring me my gloves, please," Mitch said.

"Yes, sir," the lieutenant replied. "Commissioner's question. Anything you need?"

"I'm good," Mitch said. "No, wait." He held up his hand. Walked to the uni. Pulled up a file. Read it. Stared into space. The intern waited. Beefeater rigid.

"Changed my mind." Mitch waved the holoscreen down. "I want you to clear all this shit away. When you're finished, I've got one more favour to ask. Okay?"

Yes, sir." The lieutenant bowed. Pointed at the box. Mitch nodded. Catalonotto gathered up the tools Mitch had prepared. Disappeared.

Mitch adjusted the room temperature. Boosted the Ridley. Began breathing exercises. Did his warm-up stretching. Saw Modge from the corner of his eye. Her lamps were on full. Glaring at him. Without warning she re-launched herself against the metal barriers. Strained the rigropes. Mitch turned to her. Pulled his suit pants leg tight. Outline of a still thick prick appeared. Modge averted her eyes. Ceased being annoying.

"Liar," Mitch snorted. "You love it. All real women do."

Pneumatic hiss. Catalonotto re-entered. Held up Mitch's gloves.

"Thanks, guy." Mitch waved him forward.

The lieutenant passed over the gauntlets. Logging gloves. Worn, heavy. Almost old as he was. Greasy black from years of absorbed oil, grease, sweat. Mitch's old man had bought them years earlier. Hand me downs. Mitch pulled them on. Flexed away the stiffness. Grinned at the awed intern.

"Beautiful, ain't they?" Showed them to Catalonotto. "Can't buy anything like this today. Cowhide. Double-stitched, double palm. Fucking indestructible." Keepsakes from his summer job days. Used them a lot more than he'd ever expected to.

Catalonotto stood at ease. Sneered at Modge while Mitch worked the gloves loose. Noticed the thermos Catalonotto held.

"Water?" the intern asked.

"Perfect." Mitch opened it. Drank thirstily. "Thanks. That hit the spot."

"Sure I can't get you anything else?" Catalonotto looked concerned. Mitch held off a smile. A room full of men aching to rip the hide off Modge. And this young Turk was worried. Still, he was nearly as tall as Mitch. Linebacker's physique. Ropey veins everywhere. Gym rat. He could do worse than have this eager wolf cover his back. Too bad about the man's face, though. Cherub cute. Looked a bit like that guy from that vid show. Mother must have been a model, Mitch figured. No other explanation.

Mitch waved the offer away.

"The regs say…"

"Never quote regs at CORE," Mitch's said. Regretted the tone. "They're more like guidelines, is all. We're not bots. Or suits."

Catalonotto nodded. Turned to stare again at Modge.

"Actually," Mitch remembered, "there is one thing you can help with. No other duties at the moment?"

The intern bounced on his toes. Eager to play. "Whatever you need, sir. I'm not even on the clock now."

"Okay," Mitch continued. "You're going to be my 'second' in case things… go south. Know what I mean?"

The intern's eyes widened at the honour. Expression grave. "I understand. I'll be ready."

Mitch gestured at the two-way. "How's the audience?"

"Full house," the lieutenant replied. Big smile. "Place is jumping. No one wanted to miss this. Top floor, too. Very hot ticket."

Mitch pursed his lips. Game face on. Squared his shoulders. Nazi boot salute. Good for a giggle. Mitch knew how to play to the crowd. Pulled his nose for luck. Welcome tang of motor oil. Wink at Catalonotto. "Drama time," he whispered. Waved him to follow.

The two men moved towards Modge. Mitch heard the intern's rapid breathing. For the kid, an exciting moment. In the presence of evil. But safe. Something to share with the other rooks later.

Mitch stood near The Chair. Kicked Modge's leg to make way for his own. Placed it on the footrest. Set his hand on his knee. Scrunched up his nose.

"Whoa," he complained, "you're smelling a little salmon-y, Modge."

She avoided his look. The ballgag glistened with sweat and snot. Mitch stepped off. Kodiak-ed The Chair again. Got her attention.

"We know you're a famous twat, yeah? Always on the holo. Always running your fat mouth. Piss and moan. More funding. Piss and moan. More funding."

Ebony eyes betrayed nothing. Sat in suet pillows. An offensive odour did cling to her. Mitch looked at Catalonotto for confirmation. Heard a warning growl. Doberman effect.

"Easy, boy," Mitch said to settle him. "Easy."

Grabbed iron. Pulled him away. Pointed at Modge. Said, "I need you focused. I'm gonna cut her loose."

The intern's eyes went manhole. "What? Are you sure?"

"Go ahead," Mitch encouraged him. "Start low, go slow. Watch her teeth."

The intern approached The Chair. Caution the word. Modge a motionless lump. Eyes alive with animosity. They followed Catalonotto as though roped to him.

The intern worked swiftly. Springs, bars and bindings slicked into position. Straps retracted. Mitch liked how the overhead lights shifted across The Chair's glossy surface. Beauty framing the beast.

Mitch followed his man's progress. Up over baguette calves. Press on to silo thighs. Hiss, click, snap, thunk. Restraints snicked away. Nothing hourglass about the figure. More like piled shit.

Catalonotto stood up. Quick glance at Mitch. Approving nod. He unhooked the clamp. Shot a warning look at Modge. Wrenched hard. The ball sprang loose. Bounced once. Glued itself to the wall.

Modge snapped her teeth. The intern leapt back. Gutteral amusement. Mitch silently applauded her intransigence. A brute worth breaking.

Modge took three deep, shuddering breaths. Turned to Mitch. Icy skeleton smile. Said, "I'm going to see you and everyone in this fascist menagerie imprisoned!"

Mitch applauded again, hands together this time. No choice. "Listen to her," he advised Catalonotto. "Isn't she great? Huh? I love her. Can't understand her, but I love her."

The babyfaced intern beheld Modge. Given the green light, he'd have torn into her. Mitch could tell. The man was on the balls of his feet. One whistle. Sic'em, boy. Modge the blodge would eat her teeth.

Barstew rotated her head to glare at Mitch. A tank turret swiveling. "If you have any standing with the authorities, I'll tell you this once. Release me immediately. I can guarentee you…proper legal representation…during the court proceedings. Otherwise…"

"This old gasbag," Mitch chuckled. "I mean, what can you say?"

"You'll do exactly what I say," Modge snarled, "or you'll spend the rest of your life behind bars. You seem not to know who I am. You are in serious trouble. I suggest you consider your options carefully. You can't pull this Guantanamo Bay nonsense with me and get away with it. This is Canada."

Mitch folded his arms. Catalonotto finished releasing the last arm hold. His eyes never left Modge. Backpedaled away as directed. Rejoined Mitch.

Modge placed her hands on her lap. Razor mouth set.

Mitch took a quick gander at Catalonotto. Not the least intimidated. Only cold fury. Mitch promised himself to tell Political. Possible terrorgator trainee in their midst. Still have to do something about those model features. How could you play hockey that many years and not have train tracks? Mitch had a couple of dozen. Most hidden, it was true. Hairline, chin, eyebrow, knees.

He thumbed the youngster to the hatch. Let his eyes swing to the lard-

assed larvae. "Well, Buffalo Gal, I'll tell ya'. I don't know much about...
Guano Toe Bay...or...can't even pronounce it," Mitch laughed, "but I do
know you're not going anywhere until I give the word."

"You have absolutely no right to...kidnap me," the bitch spit out. "Where
is this...fascist bunker? You are breaking the law! I fully intend to see you and
everyone here severely punished. Do you understand that, you..." Modge was
unable to finish the sentence. She made to rise. Mitch took a step forward. Shook
his head. Blaze of feral hatred from Modge. She sank back into her seat.

Mitch gazed up at the domed ceiling. Followed the walls down. Took quick
note of the energy ports, the satlinks, the gas taps. He liked the warm caramel
colour. So...homey. Terrorgation chambers didn't come any more comforting.
Throw in a sofa, a holo and a beer fridge. Mitch suspected he could live in one.
Except for it being in Toronto. Make a nice fishing lodge, though.

"Technically..." he said, switching gears, "I'm not a...made member
of the...uh...Nazi crew here. I like to think of myself more as a...Nazi
consultant."

"An assassin," Modge sneered.

"Yes!" Mitch hooted in delight. "Yes! That's it!" Slapped his thigh. Pointed
at the two-way, then at himself. Sure to have laughs with that line later. An
assassin. Mitch Milligan 3.0. Licensed to kill you. Again and again.

Modge was not amused. Her beams became glittering pinpricks.

"Yep. I'm a paid killer," Mitch said in celebration. "And you're a dirty
commie bullethead."

A moment's silence. Modge absorbed Mitch's comment in disbelief. Her
face coloured.

"Every minute I remain here," she recovered, "adds to your sentence.
I'll see to it. You have no idea how important I am. When they learn of this
atrocity, the people of Canada will rise up. They will destroy you."

Mitch rolled his eyes. Dropped the friendly act. "You're fuckin' deluded
if you think that, lady." He snorted. Looked at the two-way. No accounting
for stupid.

Barstew went livid. With witchfare, the Old Harpies survived centuries
of righteous persecution. Modge taught to channel those self-preservation
skills. Transform it to chemical venom. Direct the surge outward. Magic
cobra power.

Modge opened herself to Ammonia. To the immortal universal current.
Became the Primeval Sorceress only a few ranking Ovarians had witnessed.
Blood flooded her extremities. Her body vibrated. Above her head, static
charges snapped. Locomotive huffs sent vortices of stench Mitch's way. The
same dark energy spinning heavenly spheres, hurling asteroids at earth, hiding
itself from telescopes, exploded inside Modge.

Modge pushed herself from The Chair's unwelcome embrace. Ancient hormonal elixir sloshed about in her veins. The demonic curse that took women every month. It now consumed her. She quivered with cosmic anger. Slavered, insane. Slaughter keen.

Mitch was properly repulsed. Took a questioning look at the two-way. Behaviour veering slightly from the norm here. Doubt flared. Only for an instant. But he admitted it later, to his credit.

Modge launched herself towards Mitch. "I'll be leaving now." Regal arrogance. "Make way."

The lounge was in anarchy. Modge's fogged attitude escaped no one. But the techmed readings were stable. No aura alarm. Confidence on their end remained high. Mitch was their man. The King of Kapuscasing. Agents kicked at shadows. Others attacked the Bev's in lieu of Modge. Trogs tackled them. Told them to behave.

Somebody yelled "Cut ya' some witch, Mitch!"

"Get some! Get some" another offered.

"Spring her to the yard!" growled a third. Knowing laughter followed.

"G-o-o-o-o Leafs!" Brought the crowd to its feet as one. Everyone took up the chant. The old Garden rafters would have trembled.

"Anytime, airship," Mitch goaded her on. Skipped lightly from foot to foot. Paused to adjust his package. The crowd howled approval.

Mitch expected more grunting. The behemoth was moving a lot of meat. Yet she advanced on his position at speed. Floating almost. Mitch had seen super heavies show ankle at country dances before. Same ability. Light on their feet, despite the tonnage. As she closed, he noticed a sparkling shimmer of light. Surrounded her skull. Had no idea what to make of it.

And then she was on him. Her talons slashed at his eyes. The quickness was wrong. Far too fast for a bulkbin. It startled him. Forearms locked, he blocked the assault. Slid away. Her momentum carried her past. She hissed in exasperation. Spun. Charged again.

Rhino's were surprisingly nimble, despite their size. Mitch had seen a nature doc on them once. Modge reminded him of one. Same rough dimensions. Each heavily armored. One with muscle, the other hard margarine. Not to mention the average rhino looked friendlier. Mitch didn't like where his thoughts were leading.

The tank became an arena, a pocket stadium. Mitch the matador. Modge his snorting Iberian. And like a professional bull-baiter, he knew how to give a target. Then take it away at the last second.

He ducked a clawing. Accepted a hip clip on the way past. Quickly regained his balance. Onto the bicycle while Modge orbited around The Chair. Gravity sling. Velocity boost. She headed back at him, teeth snapping.

Mitch glided away. Felt the telltale sensation. Liquid trickle. His arm. Should have been impossible. The COREsuit impervious. Yet Modge had somehow drawn first blood. She wore a look Mitch vowed to wipe away. In the Tank, only Mitch did smug.

The pain invigorated him. Adrenaline jets on full. His eyes dilated, focus narrowed. Centre ice fight effect. Time slowed down. Yet his reactions were quicksilver fast. This wasn't some fun tilt with the other team's enforcer. Something was different. Mitch couldn't put his finger on it. Sensed it all the same.

Mitch gauged her next charge. Sidestepped it. Modge's swing found only air. Wideload she was, but agile. With a sneaky-slick bounceback. Mitch juked and weaved. Relied on his gloves to parry the nail slash. Marked her footwork and balance as she moved.

Suddenly, Modge stumbled. A feint. Mitch suspected as much, even as he reacted with a left jab. Modge was ready. Took it on her shoulder. Return swipe at his neck. Lightning reflexes saved Mitch. Threw his head to the side. Just in time. Had he not, she'd have opened his jugular. Game, set, death.

As it was, her thrust broke the skin on his cheek. Three faint grooves appeared. Mitch gloved the spot. A weak smear of blood showed. Modge had scored on him a second time.

Mitch was more embarrassed than hurt. In fact, he wasn't hurt at all. Could barely feel anything. Resisted the urge to check the wound in the two-way. No telling how the superhero herd would take it. Time enough for that later.

He deked left. Modge closed again. Persistant freight car. He eluded several lunges. Rope-a-doped against the two-way. Threw a grin over his shoulder. Behind on points maybe, but far from out of it. Just letting the judges know. Relax the bell hand. His confidence had returned. He'd sussed out her style.

Modge's early success had certainly taken the crowd out of the game. Cigarettes hung unlit. Beers got warm. Or were sprayed at Bev's in dismay. Muted conversation. Feelings mixed. Half the men wanted to stomp Modge to death. Other half wanted to bury baling hooks in her back. Take organ inventory.

Mitch shot a diversionary kick at Modge's left post. Reversed course. Wound up near the Chair. Modge followed. Face a fright mask. Lips a purple slash across pancake batter. She held her hands up. Dagger fingers. Eye level. Mitch recognized the stance. Khazak-attack coming.

Out of the blue, a great business idea. Dyko-sumo. Mitch wondered if there was a market. Modge certainly shared a physical resemblance to those massive Jap wrestlers. More mobile maybe. Or Modge versus the Beluga Sisters! Modge versus mixed martial artists. Shit, Modge and a bear. Staple a cub to her neck. Watch the fun. Tickets would sell themselves. Definite suggestion file item. Bit unusual, but CORE was always on the lookout for moneymaking enterprises.

Back to the work at hand. Mitch kept the Chair between Modge and himself. She continued her stalk. No sign she suspected a trap. Dragon feet slapped the floor. Mitch faked fear. Thought he saw her tongue flick from her mouth. Test the air. Like he suspected. Lizard in disguise.

Modge windmilled her arms. Mitch glanced at the mirror. Looked at the corner cam. Shook his head. No help. He was fine. Ths play was developing as planned. He made as if to catch a hip on the Chair's corner. Staggered, unsure of footing. Modge took the bait, as Mitch had earlier. She humped near, mouth wide. Eyes telegraphed malice.

As with any hurtling mass, inertia rules. Mitch nimbly rolled off the rush. Her haymakers passed harmlessly overhead. He was on her as she reversed screws. Unloaded a staccato flurry of punches. Ribs, upper arms, back. She threw an elbow. Missed wide. He was already gone.

Counterpunching was an art. Mitch had mastered it through many a brawl. Very few friendly rinks for a power forward/sniper/thug like Mitch. What happened on the ice often got carried over to the parking lot. Fact of life. And practice did, sometimes, make perfect. People dropped their guard once they threw fist. Mitch learned to reward that carelessness.

They joined again, opposite direction. Mitch continued to draw her out. Bobbing, slide-stutter steps. Goofing around, a bit. Had his Navaho back. Landed a few light blows. Nothing serious. But something was still wrong. He'd tackled dykos before, of course. Some were upright bathtubs like Modge. He remembered how Yaz had dismantled that one ball-less Goliath in particular. None posed the sneaky danger of Modge.

So Mitch waited, observed. Took a shot on his shoulder. Numbed it. Turned on another that landed near his spine. That one hurt, too. The rest he blocked, avoided. Still, Modge kept swinging. Advance, swing, advance, swing. Not much in the way of a boxing clinic. Mitch noticed her breathing had grown more ragged. Go opposum? Lull her into an error?

On her next pass, Mitch ducked a wheelhouse swing. Hammered Modge's kidney. She cruised through it, unharmed. Mitch took note. It was becoming obvious. Whaling on Modge was wasted. Like blouncing sledge off a tractor trailer tire. Ivan had actually warned him about this. Among professionals it was known as the "Dworkin Effect." Beating blubber garnered bupkus.

While Mitch weighed options, Modge underwent a striking change. The eyes turned mustard yellow. Swollen capillaries webbed her cheeks. Her teeth looked longer. Pointier. There was more drooling. And tongue-flicking. Which Mitch didn't much like. A little chilling.

Modge's breath, never good, was now rancid. Her skin colour screamed expired. The cunt had gone off as far as Mitch was concerned.

"Should have brought a stake," Mitch, said over his shoulder. Back to the screen."Or holy water."

Modge growled at the comment. Crocodile irises clicked open. Closed again.

Mitch danced and shuffled. Even mildly stressed, he still enjoyed hamming it up with his own boxing act. Jab, move, jab, move. Look, ma! Heavyweight champ of the world, ma!

Wounds ignored. Fixed his attention on Modge. Time she tasted some of her own. He tagged her one on the ear. Clipped her jaw with a left immediately after. She missed her own shot. Several more jabs, still backpedaling. Modge was determined. It was like being pursued by a Orange Julius stand.

Mitch's footing failed for a second. Quick recovery. Filed it away. A slip on drool? Fatal. All Modge needed to do was fall on him. Contest over. Send for the squeegee squad.

Modge wheezed forward. An unimaginable reek reached Mitch. Crabber ship capsized. Mitch breathed through his mouth. Let the trawler wallow his way. Which it did.

Ham-sized fists bounced harmlessly off his meaty shoulders. He absorbed or slid away from her best stuff. Finally his moment came. Weary, she let her arms sag. Mitch's heart soared like a hawk. He drifted in a straight overhand right. She turned too late. His fist exploded on her left temple. Rocked her. Gator eyes went greasy. The pistons wobbled.

Now it was Mitch's advantage. Modge drifted away. Cottage cheese complexion. Mitch feinted Modge onto open floor. Middle of the Tank. She took a series of pinpoint punches to her face. Blood flowed freely. Her right eyebrow disappeared. Spattering all over her suit.

Mitch faked a headshot. Modge instinctively raised her arms. Her first major blunder. Mitch gathered himself. With an explosive cry, he drilled a magnificent kick at her sternum. Modge doubled over, gasped, scratched the air. Her legs went out. She looked up in disbelief. Fell heavily against the rear wall.

CORE agents exhaled. Worry evaporated. Mitch had the stick again. All was right with the world.

Yaz was struck by the unforced comraderie. Everyone pulled for Mitch. No jealousy, no resentment. One for all, all for Mitch.

Their man stepped over splatter. Approached the two-way. Kill moment. A groggy Modge scrabbled upright. Dulled but still feral eyes followed him. Mitch leapt, fists a blur. Lefts, rights, uppercuts, overhands…all found their marks. Blood geysered from opened cuts. Welts rose under both Modge's eyes. Her lower lip ballooned. Her skin tone changed again, from shock white to moldy grey. Bruise plums appeared everywhere.

Having watched Modge go weird, Mitch turned pro. He hammerjacked punches into her upper arms. Paralyze the main bundle of nerves. Simple neurophysics. Mitch disabled her defense systems. Modge couldn't raise her hands.

An exact elbow smash reduced Modge's nose to jelly. A sudden sidekick blew out her right knee. Sneering, Mitch drew back. Drove his fist into a useless tit. It disappeared. Momentary alarm. He pulled it out. Examined it. No alien tentacles attached. Surge of relief.

Modge rallied. Pushed herself off the wall. Mitch kicked her in the stomach. Twice more. She swung blindly in retaliation, fighting for air. Mitch chuckled aloud. For the obese butthole's benefit. Payback. Twisting the knife. Homage to the great 'Tin Eye' Stevens. The Sage often referred to the wartime Brit as a master 'spect griller. Dissimilar tecnique. No high-spirited violence like Mitch. He preferred to torture psyches. Those spies captured that he could use, he kept. The rest—executed. Things were simpler in the old days. And often better. Or so it sometimes seemed to Mitch.

Mitch thought of the anguish his buddies watching had probably heard about. Friends and neighbours sacrificed on the alter of a sick, twisted philosophy. Raped and ruined by corrupt divorce courts. It was so wrong.

And what of the innocent quim too soon removed from the pool? Young women despoiled by deranged dykos. Forever lost to the normal pleasures of life. Reduced to growler grazing. Tragic.

Mitch set his mouth. Time to earn his salary. Faked a groin kick. Landed what he later claimed was the most satisfying punch of the afternoon. He swung for the fences. Connected. Sweet spot. Perfect transference of energy. Almost didn't feel the blow land. Modge's cheekbone melted on contact. Creamed cartilege. Like ironing butter.

The echoes from Modge's scream hadn't died when Mitch drilled her again. Reminded himself of her impertinence. Her idiot defiance. Destruction rained down. The rubbling of Modge. Live. Visited carnage upon every inch of her corpulent carcass. The lounge loved it.

CORE top floor. The Sage pounded his uni top with satisfaction. "Gotterdammerung, my boy!" he whispered with joy. "Vorher hat sie nicht die Welt zu verstehen. Heute ist das Tier hat etwas gelernt!"* ("Before, she didn't understand. Now she does.") Pleasure animated the careworn face. Softened the wrinkled mask. Merry eyes under the Junker brow. The straight, hard jawline clenched as the victory orgasm neared.

CORE's revered intellect insisted on watching the contest in private. Much rode on Mitch's performance. While enthusiastic, he was still young. And the Sage had inklings of Barstew's secret strengths. He feared letting others see his concern. Now he knew a great and abiding happiness. His hunch had paid off handsomely.

A slow start. Ever the Canadian way in important battles. But now Mitch seemed to have matters in hand. The terrorgation had been an absolute delight for the Sage. To then witness such a glorious finish? Beyond imagining. Especially for an agent who's spelling was so atrocious. How many times had the Sage returned red-slashed attachments? How many times had he described the difference between "loose" and "lose?" Or that there were two 'f''s in faggot?

In time, and with more success, another positive change on the social agenda. Eliminate the idiot indoctination industry. Re-education camps for the teachers. Somewhere far away from impressionable children. Start over. Back to absolutes. Self-esteem attends achievement. Mindless happy talk verboten.

But that was a dream for the future. For now it was enough to watch the young stud revenge them all. And he was doing them proud. The Sage ordered a $500.00 gift chip from The Swillery. A bottle of their best for the meister drachentoter.

Likewise, agents witnessing the rout punched the air with joy. Some wiped away tears without embarrassment. Officers shook each other's hands. Wore serene smiles of triumph. Wagers were settled. New ones placed. Several of the Bev's threw away their g-strings. Puss-in-boots party mode. All premature.

Mitch continued on. Unaware of viewer ecstasy. Blow after superb blow hooked into the target. A techwit sampled a loop from Beethoven's fifth. Blitzkrieg beat. The music's power, combined with the bombs Mitch unleashed, propelled the crowd to new heights.

Yaz was drawn into the happy tumult. He, too, felt elevated by the mood of triumph. It was a masterful demonstration. Dragon slaying done stylish.

Modge's eyes flickered. She appeared to slide in and out of consciousness. Only Mitch's trunk shots kept her upright. The strain told on him, however. Sweat had pooled in his boots. His efforts flagged. Pausing, he cleaned gore from his gloves. Massaged his knuckles. Gave a small fist pump for the crowd. Knew they were likely enthused.

Modge revived. It took no divine assistence to warn her of peril. She had sandbags on her eyes. It felt like someone had used an axe handle on her. Pain lived everywhere. Before her, a figure shimmered. Waving his hand. Inviting her to reengage hostilities. Mocking her with his Einsatzgruppen arrogance. She expected no less.

Her training summoned. Every particle of remaining strength gathered. Casually Modge stiffened her spine. Her persecutor's attention had clearly wandered. The show pony seeking applause. She propped her good leg against the base of the wall. With a screech of rage, she pounced. Desperate, possibly doomed.

Mitch caught watching. He threw himself backwards at the last second. The boxcar blew by. Pure hate animate. Fingers extended. Flashpic of face. Dripping flesh, raw, unrecognizable. Human sushi. Pass the radish.

Modge's leg gave way. As she fell forward, a final swipe. Nicked Mitch on the way to the floor. Gasps reverberated throughout the lounge. Then outrage. The fat, horrible shrike refused to submit. Heads turned toward the Commissioner. A word, a gesture, all that was needed. The Tank would fill with ass-drilling agents.

Mitch understood the gravity of the situation. Promptly waved at the two-way. All-clear signal. Pointed his finger at his chest. His error, his responsibility. He dabbed at the injury. Checked the mirror. A tiny spot of blood. Terrorgators were reminded time and again. Never let your guard down. Crims were cunning. Always on the alert for an opening. He'd get docked for being derelict. Deserved it.

Mitch mock-saluted Modge. Booted her in the head. Minor response. She lay face down, morose. The counter-attack had fallen short. Abandoned by Ammonia. She had failed her goddess. The future black.

Nearly blind, she could just make out the contours of The Chair. She threw an arm forward. Wrenched her body. A sea elephant humping for the surf, wits later observed. No clear idea of her next move. She hoped only to reach shelter. Retrench. Meet with her staff. Review the mission plan. Set achievable targets. Issue talking points to the media. Count the money.

Mitch never hesitated. Retribution roar. Launched himself onto Modge's backside. Agents exploded from their seats again. Shouts, questions, bellows of alarm. "The Mired Rhino" takedown forbidden after the Patterson tragedy. Even mortally wounded, the grotesquely overweight could be dangerous. Half a dozen men bounded down the steps. Headed for the Tank hatch. Brought up short by a sharp whistle. The Commissioner stood. Held up his hand.

"Hold off, boys, if you don't mind," he said calmly. "Let him finish what he's started. It's against regs, I know. But if you rush in now...well, you rob him of the glory he's earned. Understand?"

"But what if...?" a voice queried, then stopped.

The Commissioner cleared his throat. Wire brush on a barbecue grill. "He'll be okay. Trust me."

The debate had no impact on Mitch. He concentrated exclusively on the task at hand. Handholds secured, he clung to Modge like a dock spider. Playground rules. Braced his head against the back of Modge's block skull. Head butt threat erased.

The stench was inhuman. The intimate contact revolting. Fortunately, Mitch hailed from hardy stock. His ancestors survived the prick Stalin. Riding a plastic bag of liquid shit was nothing.

He held his breath. Burrowed his arms down. Brought them back up. Stitched them together behind her head. Modge ensnared in a full-Milligan. Endgame.

"How many fucked-up gash in The Ovarian's?" Mitch snarled into the hole where an earflap dangled. Muffled reply.

"Shut up!" Mitch screamed. Slammed her forehead down. "Eat tile, bitch! Now talk to me! Describe your organizational chart."

Modge's lips moved. The sight infuriated Mitch.

"Shut up!" he bellowed again. "Shut your fat, filthy hole, you fat, fucking disgusting bag of fucking whale fat!"

Mitch released his hold. Scrambled to a better position. V-kneed on her gargantuan butt. Fists locked. Hammered Modge's spine.

"You'll talk or I'll know the reason why," he vowed between blows. "Where is Ovarian headquarters?"

A faint whistle, as of air escaping from a raft. Mitch went wild. "You gross bag of puke! You stinking sack of...shut up!!" He drilled into her shoulder blades with the points of his elbow. Tried to think of a useful question. Nothing. Mind in full destroy mode.

Hunching forward, Mitch cocked an ear. A puling squeak, soft as a fairy fart. Was it possible? The monster crying? Mitch sat up, open-mouthed.

"You cheap, big-talking...fungus cunt!" he laughed. Punched her hard in the back. And again. "What've I been telling you? You are the walrus!" Mitch roared. "Shut...the...fuck...up. You are garbage! You are unfit to live! You should be...exterminated. You fucking...feminist fuckhead!"

Yaz took a knee in the back of his head. The agent sitting behind him apologized. Doubled over, laughing. Yaz could barely hear him over the singing. Mitch had run down some of the CORE favourites. With voices raised they gave lung to Septic standards. Spirits through the roof. Incredibly, more and better to come.

Mitch wiped sweat from his brow. Winked up at the camera. "One last chance, you humungous cow," he exulted, rolling off her. "Get the fuck up. Now!"

Modge lay motionless. No response. Mitch punted from twenty yards out. Ass quake. The ripples spread up and down. He kicked again from the thirty. Low moan from the lump. Game on the line. Crowd on its feet. Seconds ticking down. Mitch got a running start. Put his boot in hard. Split the uprights. Subterranean groan. Her head moved. A great paw reached for the Chair. Mitch smiled. Like a tug with an ocean liner. He forcefully toed Modge forward. Her fingers touched strut. Wrapped around the post. Progress over.

Mitch sighed. At this rate, they'd be another year. He reached down. Grabbed a handful of thatch. "Christ, but you're fucking useless," he groused.

With a grunt, he pulled Modge to her knees. Grabbed an arm and threw it over the Chair back. Took a deep breath. Stood her up. Spun her around. What he had planned, everyone would want to see.

The lounge electrified. Modge's face a scalloped roadbed. Or a garden salad. Vegetable reds, greens and yellows abundant. The stumps of two teeth peeked out from where they'd been driven through her bottom lip. The pulverized nose was a rainbow riot. Wild cheering greeted the sight.

"What did you call me before?" Mitch whispered. "A Nazi, wasn't it? A fucking Commie twat calls me a Nazi. That's rich." He tightened his grip. Set expression. With an explosive cry, he frog-walked Modge up to the two-way.

The audience quieted. Impressive to see superhuman strength. Mitch would have credited it to his first after-school part-time job. Wrangling stoves and frigs for Mayflower. Learned lifting techniques he'd never forgotten. Useful in hockey. Got so he could deftly deposit an opponent into the penalty box barrier. Or his own bench. Simple hip-flip and twist. Became one of his signature moves. Angry fans in North Bay once torched his team's bus. Pissed about losing their star to a concussion. Needed a police escort out of the arena. Great days.

A satisfying smack resounded around the Tank. Modge's face meeting glass. Men leapt to their feet. Applauded with vigour. Middle-finger salutes followed. Several agents vaulted over the front railing. They gathered in front of the shimmering picture. Went Muslim, kicking Modge's image. A detachment of Burlies worked their way forward. Intervened between men and screen. The state-of-the-art holomachine an expensive device. Bonuses affected in the event of repairs.

Mitch had no idea of the stir he was creating. He was merely administering justice. Used her arm for leverage. Manhandled Modge the entire length of the two-way. Every ten feet he stopped. Bashed her bleeding fright mask into the black. On the other side of the wall, pigcalls and applause. The Commissioner wiped away tears of laughter.

End of the mirror, Mitch paused. Modge refused to stay conscious. He didn't want her to miss anything. With his free hand, he elbowed her twice in the head. That brought her around again. Mitch glanced at her reflection. Blood, sweat and snot. Smeared all down the mirror, too. The Drudges wouldn't be thrilled. He'd have to beer them. That always smoothed the waters.

Mitch ran Modge back and forth several more times. As before, each seam reached, she got a glassing. The tuck shop staff, gathered around the live feed, hooted, high-fived each other. Mitch was bringing what everyone wanted—a smashing success story. Would he satisfy the deepest cell memory? Tear off an arm? Nail it to the wall for all to see? A timeless trophy of triumph. It seemed possible.

He couldn't. In truth, Mitch was whipped. And winded. Working Modge over had taken it out of him. But the vomit sack was clearly done. Mitch let her drop. Jumped onto the gridiron sprawl of her buttocks. Herc pose. Archer pose. Raising the Stanley Cup aloft pose. The usual comedy bits. Curtain call complete, Mitch called it a day. Doffed the gauntlets. Tucked them under his arm. They'd need fumigating. No way he wanted to catch anything.

The hatch whisked open. Two medics raced in. Protocol. Unthreaded Mitch's suit sleeves. Examined his arm wound. Clucked in concern. Meaningful glances. Tetanus shots. Mitch figured as much. The risks you took in his business. He'd be taking his regular shift later on. No doubt.

Several Trogs trundled in. 'Spect detail. Mitch watched while the doctors wrapped his wing.

The Trogs gathered about the prostrate form. Conferred. The sheer enormity of her bulk posed logistical problems. Lead Trog talking into his com. The regular gurney wheeled back out. A reinforced, all-purpose minge barrow appeared a few minutes later. The driver hopped off, eyes wide. Another conference. Unanimous agreement. The forks rammed under an unmoving Modge. The hoist motor promptly stalled. Re-started. Three Trogs jumped on the barrow's rear ledge to balance it. With furious effort the machine managed to raise the deadweight Ovarian several centimtres off the floor.

The lead medic clapped Mitch on the shoulder. "You think you're okay to walk?"

Mitch half-cuffed him back. "You actually get paid for this?" he joked. "See if we can't get you a government job so you can rest more."

They beat the salvage crew to the exit. The skid wall wrinkled away like an accordion. Wide-load Modge. No getting her out otherwise. Waiting until she mummified to dust was not on.

Mitch entered debrief to a standing 'O'. Responded with a low bow. Winced. The antiseptic spray bit into the cut.

Ivan and his assistant tekheads put their hands together. Ninth floor Minions and Toadies had assembled for the tribute. The sound grew thunderous. Mitch tried to wave it off. No go. For some, it was their first live terrorgation. Mitch's performance left them awed.

Catalanotto boomed in from the back, goggle-eyed. He liberated a sweat towel from the stack. Handed it to Mitch. Nod of thanks. Mitch suddenly pillowed by weariness. Both Catalonotto and Chamberlain helped Mitch exit the suit top. Placed it in the incineration sack. Pants to follow later. No chances to be taken with stray Modge matter.

"I've never seen anything like it," Catalonotto declared. "You were... unbelievable!"

Mills from R&D Weapons Unit also gazed on in frank wonder.

Ivan entered the inner circle. "Anyting about de sluz?" the grizzled vet asked. The debrief chief sported his usual two-day growth. Made him look like a pot scrubber.

"Ahhh," Mitch rolled his eyes. "Shit. Started in there about the Ovarians but she was being a real hardcase. Extreme non-cooperation."

Caterpillar eyebrows shot up at the statement. "No apologize!" Ivan said with passion. "You do great. We love!"

A new wave of applause. Mitch reddened. Lengthy salutes embarrassed him. Hockey 'O's were different. Being celebrated by co-workers? Meant more.

Chimes sounded. A Tekmonkey temp monitored the alert.

"Trogsalvo," he announced excitedly. "Also, in person...five, four, three, two, one..."

The lounge hatch hissed wide. Goosen, ward chief, stuck his skull in. "Everybody heard?" he asked. Ear-to-ear grin. The room fell quiet.

"Fat fuckin' Bibendum. Croaked on the way to the infirmary," Goosen laughed. Fist pump. "Hey, ho! The wicked bitch is dead!"

Hoots and howls bounced off the walls. CORE intranews flashing word of Modge's demise. The whole building would soon know.

The lounge party got jazzed to a new level. Everyone immediately crowded around Mitch. Handshakes and backslaps. Yet even at the moment of his greatest acclaim, Mitch's thoughts were elsewhere. He pictured the bloated slab of whale scat's legacy. A generation of bright, innocent women corrupted into hateful dykos. A political process irrevocably poisoned. Natural law upended. Perversion glorified. The fixed geometry of life adulterated. The lingering damage to decency, normalcy, truth and honour. Sure, he'd potted the game winner. But the series was a long way from over.

A chorus of hip-hip-hooray's filled the room. The Commissioner appeared. A ghostly Knight Templar. Waited patiently at Mitch's elbow. A hush fell.

Mitch was as startled as the rest when he turned. Stuttered, "S-Sir?"

The Commissioner didn't speak. Tried once. Overcome. Eyes shining, he clasped Mitch's hand. Took notice of Mitch's bandages. Squeezed harder. After a strangled, "Well done, son, well done," he waved to all and departed.

Mitch nodded. He'd never seen the old man look so happy. Or at peace.

The next day a procession of CORE wheels would visit Mitch. Each stayed but a few seconds. The solid handclasp. Quick word of praise. An envelope left behind. By lunchtime, Mitch had a towering stack of old-style cash. Off the books. No tax. Seeing it left Yaz open-mouthed.

"It's not Libola," Mitch noted, noting Yaz's expression. "I earned it. You saw me."

Yaz nodded.

"Best part is, government never sees a dime."

Yaz smiled. Screwing over Revenue Canada's organized crime syndicate a cherished CORE activity.

Mitch hopped off the massage bench. His third wind had arrived. Lifting a little iron suddenly had merit. Do a workout. Bolt for home early. Who deserved it more?

"Guys?" Mitch said. Held up his hands. "Appreciate the support. Really. Right now, though…I need a blowjob in the worst way." The room exploded in laughter. Mitch waved everyone quiet.

"Which is the only way I get it from most of your girlfriends. Seriously, though…" Ribald backtalk drowned him out. Squawk kissing sounds. Ancestor smears. A smiling Mitch flipped everyone the classy Salmon Arm salute. More good-natured heckling.

He leaned over. Thanked the medics. Whispered a message to Ivan. A fist pump for the cheering celebrants. Beat it out the rear exit.

Word reached the lounge crowd that Mitch had vanished. Disappointment. Drinks had already been ordered. Eventually, people dispersed. Discussed highlight moments on the way out. Some returned to uni stations. Others passed out in the library. Bev's dressed. Began cleanup. Felt the glow of shared success. Hope of sex. With Mitch. The common, oft-realized dream.

And while Mitch's case may have experienced a miss, Barstew's successful terrorgation paid other dividends. CSIS, the Force, DND and various security organizations world-wide learned of resulting turmoil among the femme rabble. The Ovarian command structure had suffered a serious hit with her loss. Barstew was the brains. Which said volumes about the movement, Mitch thought.

Sigint traffic redlined. Panic and paranoia in the COTU. Everyone suspected CORE involvement. Femmoles salted about the bureaucracy sent out distress messages. Betrayal's rank stink penetrated government offices everywhere. Necks prickled. The axeman cometh. But for whom? Which bulldykes wore bullseyes?

CORE ran comic WebAds promising more. Fears of rape or public flaying soon flew. Comsymp columnists, media weasels eeled back into their crannies. Swore off faggo cheerleading. Life was sweet. For a week.

Things returned to normal in Debrief. Ivan pored over his graphs and charts. Tekheads re-wrote bad code. Disabled idiot features. Streamlined systems for sale in the marketplace.

Toadies and Minions got kicked back upstairs by two half-cut Trogs. The Drudges stayed hard at it, sterilizing the Tank. Their cheerful humming heard through HAZMAT mics. Mitch's drink prize invigorated them. Merrily they steam-erased all evidence of Modge's presence. Made the Tank beautiful again.

MITCH MEETS JILL,
CLIMBS UP HER HILL

---⊲◇⊳---

Mitch exited the wing washroom near his office. Shook his head at an approaching Yaz.

"I wouldn't."

"Again?" Yaz asked in disbelief.

Mitch rolled his head on his shoulders. Shrug and grin. "I don't know what it is. Must be a little burrito blowback?"

"That was days ago!"

"Yeah, yeah, you're right," Mitch said, doing the math. "Well, something is scouring the works. I've dropped five kilos of rot the last day or so. If I knew what it was, I'd sell it. Retire."

He motioned towards the library. "The one in there's pretty good. The door vids all work. Try it out."

Yaz nodded. Trust had grown between them. Yaz had already encountered some of Mitch's 'bombs'. Hard to believe anyone healthy could generate that kind of industrial stench. He turned towards the library. Mitch lay on the beefy limb.

"Say," he said, "seeing as you're going to be in the library anyway..." Dropped a rainbow-coloured FD into Yaz's pocket. "Goodfellow, the helpful prick. Laid a few more names on me. Something's come up, though. I'm strapped for time." Laughed to see Yaz's expression.

"No shit. Help me out with this, I promise we'll go out and...I don't know...roust some of these fuckers. Soon. See if they're just after the reward money or actually know something that will...solve the case for us." Mitch's roar of mirth filled the hall. Several analysts turned to look. Smiles of recognition. Youthful exuberance. Always a pleasure to witness.

"Anyway," Mitch continued. Patted Yaz's shirt pocket. The FD vault.

"I took a quick look. The marketing exec seemed ripe. Suffers trull lust, according to Goodfellow. Rich kid. Family owns the company. Bord and Associates. Call the number. Ask for Bill."

Research library glass whisked open. Mitch stopped. Breathed in. Said, "I've always liked this."

Yaz did likewise. "Candle wax…sandalwood…cedar…lemon…coffee…"

"Holy shit. You can smell all that?"

"I believe that's accurate," Yaz answered.

"Wow….Okay, quick. Couple other hopefuls. The Way brothers in Chinatown. Own a diner. Street creatures known to congregate there, apparently. Take my pad. I've uploaded the morgue shots. They might remember faces. 'Li' or 'Phree' will be running the chip wagon. Speak slow and clear. They can all understand English perfectly when you do that."

Mitch paused in mid-handover. Punched in a request. "Oh, yeah. This thing operates in the area. You'll know him by the dresses he wears. Performs 'services' for civil servants on lunch break. Known to police. Wink, wink. YugoSerbo or something. Goes by the name Anne Drojinus. Probably associated with our ninja boot. With luck, you don't see her."

"You're not coming?"

"Sor-ry." Shifty-grin-Mitch.

No matter. Yaz also being sly. He was more than happy to have access to CORE's supercooled Magneto ethercloud. Unlimited memory. Unmatched data recall. Questions answered before fully uttered. One of only five in the world. Hacking into it would have been time-consuming.

"Couple others may be witnesses too, according to Goodfellow," Mitch said as he was about to leave. Closed his eyes to think. Snapped his fingers. "Mack Remay. Sells hobby shit on Yonge. And some night security droog. Gus Tappo. Company listed there."

Yaz was impatient to begin. Said, "I'll get started now."

"Pay you back soon. I promise," Mitch joked. The loadie pledge. Always made him laugh. Ghost of a smile from Yaz.

Mitch moonjived back to the entrance. "Research cavities are left and back. Use my password. 'Mags'. Goose the librarians if you get a chance. They love that."

Mission accomplished. Mitch headed for his locker. Then the basement exit. The Barstew shellacking was still fresh at CORE HQ. Meaning Mitch had carte blanche for the next week. He intended to exploit it.

Outside, a gay, gauzy sun. The sidewalk a wind tunnel. Hard off the lake. Welcome as a prostate probe. However that worked. The old guys would talk about it. Made his flesh crawl. Mitch pictured some thick metal broom handle. Being put somewhere no one armed should go.

A McMoney's hamburger wrapper plastered itself on his ankles. Tore away again, the empty bag in hot pursuit. He walked beside along a row of year-old saplings. They looked bitter and depressed. Branches scratched at empty air. Mitch was bone-weary of March. Thirty-eight days of crap. Time to lodge a complaint. Demand better. Mitch went for his gloves. Fuck! Forgot'em.

He skirted the corner. Cut through some naked, knee-high bushes. Hit sidewalk going right. The wind magically increased in strength. So concerned with keeping his balance he nearly ran over her. Jill Baxter. His planned rendezvous.

"Sorry. Didn't see you," he apologized immediately. Gave her the delighted eye.

"Mitch Milligan. It's been too long" The woman took his hand. Clasped it like treasure.

Mitch zeroed in on those classic eyes. Green as jade. Same colour as the curly leaf thing in marbles. When she crinkled them, your heart stopped.

Miss Rosedale. Mitch had forgotten. Hazelton Lanes, baby. Creamy clean. Dressed to draw DB's. Cows volunteered to take the hammer, she looked so good in leather.

"You on your way to the AGO or something?" Mitch gibed. Moved in close. Used her beef shield as a blocker.

"Better," she said. Leered at Mitch. "I'm meeting an old friend."

Mitch bear-growled. Shared joke. Said, "Look, let's get outta this goddamn…gale. Grab a coffee or something."

"You should wear a hat on days like these," Jill admonished him.

"Fucking tell me about it," Mitch hurled back. Balanced himself against a mailbox. A vicious gust nearly took his feet out. Then grit in his eyes.

Taxi search. A late model Fiat Accompli quivered near. Behind it, a Rio Motors Chihuahua. Otto Pilot the driver. Put it in neutral, Mitch thought. Fucking wind'll do the rest.

A clutch of ecojokes chattered past. Panda Pandas. Fauxhydro buggies from China. Light as kites. Easier to fly. Owners had to tie them down at night. On the positive side, least-stolen vehicle ever manufactured. And Mitch's favourite. Subsidized all the way from Cuba. The notorious Guevara. Built from crushed cane. Held together by paint and hope. Safe as a Bolivian bus crossing the Andes. Great smell, though. He had to admit it. Like a doughnut store slowly collapsing beside you.

The next one he'd only heard about. The Juju from Joburg. Hanging from a tow-stud hook. Obvious accident victim. Front end mating with the rear end. Another collision with a tricycle. No survivors apart from the three-year old.

The gods finally responded to his plea. A pedestrian carrier hove into view. Veered to the curb. Rear door swung wide. Inside, blast of a nastier variety. Mitch's eyes watered. Grimacing, he turned to Jill. "Motherfucker. That's horrible."

Jill could only nod. Breath through her mouth. On her face, curled lip disdain. Like meeting a leper.

Mitch banged on the metal slats separating the seats. "Yo! Gupta!" he bellowed. "Crack a window, buddy. We're lookin' at a five-alarm curry alert back here!"

Jill laughed. Glistening array of pearls exposed. "I have to say, I'd forgotten your fizzy wit."

"You always liked it rough," Mitch joshed. Seductive tongue waggle. Struck anew by her beauty. Some natural. The rest purchased. Not cheap. Cross-hatched eyebrows. The fashion. That bill over five. Face by Raped Angels. Mitch recognized their signature cheek stylings. Empty the other pocket for that shit. Hair by…HAIR!!. Bobbed. Gold threads woven into it. That needed at least two visits to The Barricks. Little Miss Trust Fund. Smelled great. Smiled great. Fucked great. Plus rich. What more could you want? Why had he dumped her in the first place? Some reason.

They jounced about together. Budget time. Road crews busy tearing up perfectly good highway. Exhaust the money. Profile glimpse with each vehicle lurch. The Sherwood Forest hood getting him hot. Mitch nearly pawed a hole in the floorboards. Christmas morning. He wanted to open his present. Fucking now!

"How…how have you been." Voice caught. She smiled in apology. The Mitch effect. Hormone bath from both quarters.

"No complaints," Mitch answered.

"Are you still with the…agency?"

Mitch had been a little vague during her call. The first rule of CORE was…change the subject.

"Moved on," he said. Held her gaze. "Kind of like…law enforcement now. In a way."

Jill brightened. "Oh, that's…wonderful." That nose twitch Mitch loved.

"Yeah," he concurred. "I like it. It's challenging. But fun, too. I work with a great bunch of guys. We, you know…do good. Help the public. Shit like that."

"That's just…" Jill gushed. Ran her fingers over Mitch's hand as it burrowed under her skirt. Sweetmeat raid. Two pair of cherry lips parted. Mitch saw porcelain neck. Pushed aside the braided ropes. Nuzzled.

The cab herky-jerked its way through the mid-morning traffic. Mitch paused from noshing. Radar up. Glanced at the sideview mirror. Then out the back window. A courier was hard at it. Closing on them. Head down over the handlebars. Their Bengali jockey spotted him in time. Turned the wheel hard right. Mitch heard the furious scream of surprise and shock. Saw the clenched fist as the rider went down. Not under the wheels of a braking GO bus, Mitch was disappointed to see. Still, entertaining. Full credit to the driver. Alert response.

"Yo, Ahmed!" Mitch yelled at the NC. Tapped the opticbox. Gave his best playing card grin. "Goose this wagon! I got business elsewhere." Leered at Jill.

So advised, the wily old gentleman raced towards Harbourfront. Arrived without incident. Jill placed her bank chip in the reader. Mitch covered the tip. Ever the prankster, pushed his fingers through the slats. Trapped a twonie in the back of the man's towelhat. Great sport. Giggling, the two passengers stepped out into the harsh and foul. The driver waved thanks. Sped off.

Mitch and Jill in tres haste. The condo guard bowed low. Buzzed them in. Mitch never broke stride. Time permitted a brief elevator grope. Then they were on his floor, running down the corridor. It wasn't until he was at the door that Mitch remembered. Andrea might still be around. It was her day off. He'd told her to scrub the balcony before she left for home. The wind had uplifted a planter. Dirt everywhere. He checked his com. No idiot blinking icons. Could mean she was on the premises. Awkward.

He gave the 'shush' sign to Jill. Swiped the sensor. Thinking what to say when the locks released. Andrea stood in the entrance. Of course. Broad smile of greeting.

Mitch strode in. Jill behind.

"Hey, ho, how are ya'?" Mitch said. Relaxed, expansive. Jerked a thumb at Jill. "This is my…uh…lawyer. Jill…Berg…levystein…berg. We have some… uh…lawyer crap to do now. For work. You finished?"

"Hi. How do you do?" Andrea beamed welcome. Shifted the dishtowel. Shook hands. "You must be cold. Would you like a coffee?"

"Thanks, no time," Mitch said. Shed his coat. Handed it and Jill's to Andrea. Head gestured towards the closet.

"You get to the balcony by any chance?" Mitch said. Covert looks at Jill. Patience.

"All done," Andrea declared. "Boy, that's a chilly day, though. My hands are raw. Did you kick the planter on purpose? There was dirt all over."

"Yeah," Mitch snorted. "Came home a little juiced last Saturday night. Thought I'd kick frozen soil all over my balcony." Winked at Jill. "I do that all the time for laughs."

Found Andrea's black jacket lying over his Commander's chair. Grabbed it. "Anything else left?"

"Just doing the dishes when you came in."

"Okay, good. Tell you what. Come by later. Say…" Glanced at Jill. "…
around five or so. You can do the rest up then, okay?"

"You're sure?" Andrea looked alarmed.

"Yeah, yeah," Mitch said. "No worries."

"I can stay. Whip up a snack."

Mitch smiled at Jill. "Isn't she something?" Led Andrea to the door.
Pointed at her calfskins. "Do me a favour?"

"What?" Andrea looked up as she strapped on.

"Slide by the SinShop on your way back tonight. Pick me up a case. I'm
gettin' low."

"Okay," Andrea said brightly. "Anything else?"

"Nah, I think that's okay for now." Mitch thought. "Ah, wait. Maybe a
couple packs of smokes too. My reserve buddy hasn't been back to work yet.
Haven't got this month's supply."

"DuMaurier's?"

"Of course. My brand. Are you stupid?" Mitch shot an embarrassed look
at Jill.

"Okay, you're almost ready. Bootsies on. Here's your mittens." Graciously
allowed Andrea's cheek peck. Firmly shoved her out into the corridor.
Reminded her again about the beer. Obligatory wave. Lock, spin, grin.

"Fuck. Forgot all about her till the last minute."

"Please…" Jill said. Shrugged out of her vintage Diesels. "She looks
delightful."

Mitch couldn't help a discreet fist clench. Those perfect Barbie legs.
Glowsheen. No panties. Exquiste.

"Bedroom's still the same place?" Jill asked.

"Was this morning," Mitch rejoined. "Drink?"

"Love one."

"Finish unwrapping. Back in a shake."

Jill scampered off. Mitch salivated to see her cinnamon buns. Felt a bit
woozy. Always happened when the unit began to tank up blood.

Decided on whiskey. Quick lift. A double shot of Algonquin Pure. Rocks.
Canned Caesar for Jill. Poured out the cocktail. Took a sip. Jacked it up with
a blast of Tobasco. Much better.

He took both glasses into the bedroom. Jill under the coverlet. Mitch
heard purring. Left her drink on the table. Took a taste of his. Candy for
Daddy. Beautiful. Just the right bite. Let it burn the vertical. Elephant
trumpet. Landed it.

Jill crawled out. Sneaked a swallow of Caesar. First gulp generated
gagging. Then a prolonged wheeze. "Did you…?" she croaked. Another
coughing jag.

"Yeah," Mitch said. "Bit strong?" Sipped. Pronounced it perfect. Placed it on the nightstand. Stripped. Slid under.

"Always thought you private school princesses were liquor soaks," he said. "Least that's what I heard. You need more bottom."

"I've got bottom," a protesting Jill choked out. "Feel this." She placed his hand on the firm, silky smooth crescent moon. Fresh from the oven. Mogul free.

"Dr. Mitch requires a more thorough examination," he said.

"I didn't even have a chance to finish my drink," she whimpered.

"Thirsty?" Mitch said. Wicked look. By way of an answer, Jill grappled with his tackle. Paused. Rubbed a nubby ridge on his shoulder. Old fascination of Jill's.

"Oh, not another one."

Mitch tried to remember. "What colour is it?"

Jill jigged herself up closer. "Purple...ish."

"Yeah, pretty new."

"How did you get it?"

Mitch coughed, yawned. "Not the usual heroic shit. Did it to myself. Kind of. Back in...January. Early. Argument with a dickhead. Went outside to settle it. Got rolled into a fence. Some twist tie thingy on the post gouged me. I didn't even notice it. One of the waitresses saw me bleeding. New shirt, too. That really hurt." He shrugged. "What're gonna do?"

"My poor warrior," Jill cooed. "You shouldn't fight. It's not safe. You could get badly injured."

"Yeah, but it's fun," Mitch countered. "Besides, it's good practice for..." Caught himself. Loose lips.

"Practice for what?" Jill said.

Mitch casually mentioned his new job. And how he was in charge of an investigation into disappearing trulls. Jill clapped a hand to her mouth.

"My God. My mother's friend found one in her garden the other day."

"How'd she know it was a...?"

"The police said. It was covered in...tattoos. She even had one on her forehead. And her face was pierced everywhere."

"Ah," Mitch nodded. It distinguished them from suburban posers. Mitch prided himself on not getting ink. Unless you were military, bikers or genuine jail trash. Otherwise, the mark of wannabes.

Jill pulled him closer. "Let's think of happy things."

"Such as?" Mitch asked. Ground bone against beetle hood.

"Do you remember? We used to play that business game? 'Pink Funnel Unlimited Merges with Clam Industries'?"

Mitch remembered. Decided on a different activity. Whispered it. Jill moaned at the mention. Reached down. Stroked his stallion.

He flipped her. Entered the paddock. Saddled her up. And the sport of Kings was on.

Jill was practiced at being ridden. Fast out of the gate. Headed for the rail. Moving good. Hit her stride by the first pole. Settled into a an extended lope. Mitch right with her. Perfect rhythm.

Come the turn, her first burst of fireworks. Mitch endured the savage, vice-like claspings. Never slowed. Rode her through it. Second pole, gave Jill her head. She whinnied with eager delight. Full gallop now. Mitch lengthening his stride. Smooth gait. Field left behind. Surroundings a blur.

Three-quarters pole. No more spur required.

Final turn. Digging for home now. Mitch found his belt. Whipped her flanks. Down the stretch they charged. Jill pie-eyed, blowing hard, muzzle froth flying. Full extension. Roar of blood in their ears.

And then the photo finish climax. Jill, arm raised in victory, edging out Mitch by a nose. Backfield warm down. Slow, gentle canter. Mitch stroked her withers. Murmured praise in her ear. Playfully wiped sweat from his hands in her mane. Left the stable.

"My God," Jill groaned. Her face found pillow. "I forgot. How is that possible?"

"No men in the set you run with," Mitch said matter of factly. "Gallery goers. Same people you see wearing leather thongs during that Proud-to-suck-cock-Parade. You'd get more action from a eunuch."

A soft sigh of pained regret. "It's true. So true."

Mitch bent low. Whispered in her ear again.

Jill expecting nuzzle, exploded in surprise. "Oh, my God. Really? Are you sure we have time? I thought you said…"

"Fuck it," Mitch said. "I'm gold at the shop. Besides, I've gotten even better since we last screwed. Twenty minutes. Three morgasms. Minimum. Grand mal guarenteed. The last one, you'll wake up unconscious. Uh,…no. The other way around. Screw it. Never mind. Roll over."

Mitch true to his word. Closer to thirty minutes by the time he'd totally ruined her, though. Another five since then. She hadn't come to yet. He slapped her ass, hard. She awoke with a start. Blinked several times. Looked up through a screen of loose hair. Beheld Mitch with loving wonder.

"You're a regular torturerer, you know that?"

Mitch laughed. "Keep that to yourself, okay?"

Jilll burrowed deeper into the bed. Grabbed Mitch's hand. Pulled him close.

"Queen's Plate. I'll never be able to watch without thinking of today," she said, stroking his chin. "I feel…reborn."

"If I had a nickel for every time I've heard that." Mitch joked. "Still. You're right. We were pretty damn fantastic. It's like some people fit together better than others. Backwards, forwards, upside down. Weird."

Jill listened quietly. Twirled his chest hairs.

"I mean," Mitch continued, "you think, like, rabbits or raccoons or... wolverines? You think they notice any difference between one fuck and the next? Keep score?"

"I don't think they analyze it," Jill said after a few seconds. "But who really knows what goes through a...wolverine's head when it's making love?"

"Not me," Mitch admitted.

"What do you think about?" Jill asked, smile playing about her lips.

"Traffic, hockey, dinner," Mitch answered truthfully.

"Really?" Jill's mouth half open.

"No, of course not," Mitch lied. "I think about...two hearts beating as one..."

"You do not."

"Bunnies, bumblebees, rainbows, the poor..."

"Stop it," Jill said. Twisted a nipple. Mitch had to slap her hand away. It returned to wander down his chest. Slid into Mitch's groin. Touched the slumbering beast. Felt it stir ever so slightly.

"Fifteen inches," she said with respect.

"Yepper."

"It's like a..."

Mitch waited for it. Top three comparisons. Gymnast's beam, armadillo, space station.

"...an armadillo," Jill gushed.

Mitch shut his eyes. Let his annoyance ebb. "Have you ever actually seen an armadillo?"

Jill looked over. "Documentaries, I guess. I think they had one at the zoo. Why?"

Mitch shrugged. "I don't know. Just women often say that. That it looks like an armadillo. Or an Anaconda. I get that, too. You know what I mean?"

Jill frowned. No idea.

"I mean, an armadillo. It's this...armour-plated...woodchuck." Mitch tried for wounded. Couldn't sell it.

Amused chuckle from Jill. Flicked hair from her eyes. "Would you like it better if I called it...your mighty oak?"

"Yes. Yes, I would." Mitch said. Squeezed a willing poont.

"I certainly don't think your cock is like...a woodchuck," Jill said with conviction. Moaned suddenly.

"What's wrong?"

Jill's face contorted. Obvious pain. "My hand…when you moved. It's… it's trapped!"

"Good grief," Mitch said. "Don't be such a…just pull it out."

"I…can't," Jill grunted. "God, your penis weighs a ton."

Mitch paused to consider the issue. How much did his dick weigh? "Can't say it's come up in conversation," he admitted. "But it does probably tip the scales. Fully loaded."

"Well, you'll have to help me," Jill pleaded. "I'm starting to lose feeling now. No wait!" They both stopped to watch. "I think it's going to be okay. It's moving on its own."

"That's because you were rooting in there like a dingo hunting bush baby."

"I'm out, I'm out," a relieved Jill cried. She held up the freed hand. Massaged it. "That was close."

"Amputation avoided," Mitch added. Heavy sarcasm.

Jill missed it. Looked at Mitch. "Oh my. Did I do that?"

"Yes!" Mitch replied. Exasperation. Mr. Majestic already throwing shadow. "You realize I can't go back to work like this? I look like a fucking sundial."

"I can help." Jill licked her lips. "I suppose it is kind of my fault."

"Not kind of," Mitch corrected.

"Yes, of course you're right, darling."

""Okay." Mitch lay back. "Just…" He picked up his com. Showed Jill the time.

"I'll hurry, honest," Jill promised. Bounced to her knees. Latched on to the stiffening silo. Partook with genuine gusto.

Mitch vaguely recalled her past efforts. Adept enough. Came from money. They got introduced to the business as early as any ghetto skidlette. He left her to it. Thought of his route to work. The DVP? Bitch fight. Gardiner, too. Expecially in bad weather. He could take Spadina. Up to Bloor. Koreatown could be ugly. Diner crowd heading back to work. It was all grief, no matter the way. He knew that.

Jill slurped away. Happy as a kid with a cone. Mitch returned to day planning. Saw himself in the office. Lash the Barstew file together. Pretty it up with a few links. Season with vidclips. Fold in whatever Yaz had discovered. Fire it off.

Only one problem. Passion. Mitch lacked it. Cared even less than usual. Tank dry. The "Man/dy mystery," as he now thought of it. Not likely to get any worse if he skipped another day. Plus, there were pressing matters that needed attention. His blades needed re-working. And one of the straps on his elbow pads had come off. Hestitated taking it to his Korean. She didn't seem the sort to accept anything that wasn't straight clothing. He had playoff pool picks to submit. (Injury free, Mitch looked to make his entry fee back. Maybe win the big mickey.) Plus, check up on Andrea. Make sure she'd remembered her buy list. He also meant to drop in on the clubhouse. Hadn't been in a while. Slide by Billy's as well. Catch a period or two. Lots of things on the go.

While Mitch fleshed out his afternoon, Jill worked on flesh of her own. She swallowed and wallowed in wonder. Gave rein to her god-given gift for mouth milking. Tower buffing. Only wished her friends could see her. Wouldn't they want to change places in an instant, though. Most of their husbands were too weak to get Viagra down. That's assuming they weren't stopping by the 'Y' for date night. She cherished her good fortune.

Mitch had moved on to thinking about his stereo. The new anti-grav amps were out. Set them anywhere, looked superb. Concert quality sound. His bonus money easily covered it. Only dilemma. Determining which company made shit compatible with everything else? Bastards used different standards to fuck you over. Hard decisions to be made. Even that genius wheelchair time guy would struggle.

Jill disgorged the glistening tool. Caught her breath. The lip smacking brought Mitch around.

"Hey, you," he said. More sharply than he intended.

Jill pouted. Con. Mitch felt his blood rise. Then sighed. Gave in. There was a famous line for moments like this. Wished he could remember it. He rubbed his nose. Brought an imaginary com to his ear. Message sent. Move it or lose it.

"Thank you, thank you, thank you," Jill burbled. Bent back to work. Rubbed her face against the mallet head. It's silky texture drove her wild. "Who's my great, big soldier, huh? Who's my horse cock? Jilly wuves you werry werry much."

Mitch rolled his eyes. Now he remembered why he'd thrown her away. Because she was Hello Kitty crazy. That nursery school baby blather. He couldn't stand it. Sweet ass or not.

And the high maintenance/cultural thing played into it. D&G nosehair clippers? Prada toilet brushes? Hugo B. string-wart remover? Fuck off. Get some other moneyclip to unbelt for that shit.

Papa had prime seats at Roy Thomson? Didn't mean a thing to Mitch. He went once. For form's sake. Never again. He'd terrorgated a trio of bathhouse buttboys along with Anderson one session. Saw them all on stage that night. Shrieked about the same.

No, he knew now he'd made the right decision. Andrea could at least keep his place clean.

Jill stopped the worship cooing. Mitch refused to look at his com. He knew time was passing. Propped himself up on one elbow. He really couldn't fault her enthusiasm or style. He clamped a hand on her skull. Time to lend a hand. Manual control was always risky. Every mouth a den of razors. He'd left himself no other option, unfortunately. Drew her down, down, down.

After a minute of vigorous thrusting— seismic success. Volcanic rumblings. Jill registered the tremors. She looked at Mitch, pride in her eyes. He rotated his index finger. Fed her mercilessly. Happy butt wiggle. She took it in, thrilled.

Mountain aboil. Time to blow the cap. Jill beat his thighs, urging him on. Then, blessed eruption. Lava gush. Jill drank greedily. Mitch let her. It would be her last taste for some time. If not forever.

"Mmmmmm…" she sighed with satisfaction. Mitch already halfway out the bedroom. "See everything's neat before you go," he instructed her over his shoulder. "I gotta wash up." Through the door and down the hall.

When he hit the living room again he was alone. Jill a memory. Quick and clean. Just like his shower. Figured she msut have done a whorebath before going. Happy to see her. Happy to see the back of her.

Mitch felt supercharged. Whistled an earworm melody. Recognised the tune. Fucking Disney! Idiot buggy stooge's fault.

Final check. Lights off. Door locked. Downstairs. The pre-ordered taxi idled at the front steps. Glance in. Hamil the Tamil, driver du jour. What was that song his mother sang? Where have all the white guys gone? Long time passing.

Mitch could already hear it. "Pearson, sahib? Pearson?"

"Yeah," he answered. "By way of downtown. You know where that is, right? Where all the tall buildings are."

Then it hit. He winced. Decided to rip a counter attack. Sad day when you had to drop a bomb so your ride would smell better.

The RataTata pulled away. Promptly squealed to a stop. Mitch, harness half on, exhaled slowly. Patience. NC drivers. Paid for apartment. Stack of welfare chips for the extended family. Hospital beds for all six grannies. And a fresh car license.

Mitch beat on the barrier. "No goats! You go now! Hurry drive! Heap big tip get!"

That did the trick. Hamil sped away, bleater sounding. Scraped his way through traffic. Right direction towards the address Mitch only had to explain several times.

Mitch leaned back into his seat, exhausted. Checked his com. Did the math. Back in time for a late lunch. Hit the pool. Do a workout. Get the equipment shit dealt with. Might even meet with Yaz. Catchup. Clock off for the day. Bob's your uncle.

Looked out the window. Wry smile. Man was right. It was good to be the King. For however long it lasted.

ROLL CALL FOR ROUSTING

—◀○▶—

Yaz stood before the beam. LCD bar flashed green. The door slid away. Mitch speaking to the uni. Waved Yaz towards a chair.

"What's so funny out there," he asked Yaz after ending the conversation. "Wall of sound when I buzzed Murray."

"I don't know." Truthful answer. "Something to do with agent... Mankowski?"

Mitch nodded.

"He's returned from Ottawa."

"Hmmmm..." Mitch said. "Quarentined for the next couple days. No boom boom for Benny. That's why they're laughing."

Mitch lit up. Relaxed. "So, had some luck with those calls?"

Yaz nodded. "I would estimate about 70% are available. It will depend on how you need them, however."

Mitch stroked his chin. Gave Yaz a thumbs-up. "Not bad, really. I couldn't expect everyone to drop what they're doing. So, yeah...good response. Nice work."

"I started at the agencies you suggested," Yaz said. "They directed me to several other firms. When they heard it was you, they were very cooperative."

Mitch tried to look modest.

"The Raging Lothario agency offered several names."

Mitch smiled in approval. High-class outfit. He wasn't surprised.

"Ajax Companions. Several more." Mitch waved Yaz to continue. Multi-tasked. Read a terrorgation schedule update.

"Divine Service..."

"Weird," Mitch interrupted. "I heard they'd changed their name."

"They did," Yaz said. "Bold Angels." Mitch made a face. Scratched his throat. Yawned.

"The others were…hit and miss. Do you want the names I received positives from?"

Mitch paused. "Yeah, shit, why not. Give'er."

Held up his hand. "Hang on…a sec. Let me turn the tunes down. Okay, shoot."

"R. Berenson…"

"The Penetrator," Mitch finished for him. "Amateur…but very good."

Yaz looked up from his holopad.

"Nothing. Go on," Mitch said. "Just seeing if I can remember their stage names. It's been a while."

"MacPherson."

"Caber."

"Ferguson."

"Douglas Fur." Mitch concentrated. Helicoptered a pen with his fingers.

"Korzeniowski," Yaz said. Careful pronunciation.

"The Telephone Pole," Mitch said with near reverence. "A pro's pro. Speaks a bunch a languages. I heard he was back from the continent. Wonder if he's changed?"

Yaz slowed. Pursed his lips. "White."

"Randy!" Mitch enthused. "Excellent!"

"Does this sound right?" Yaz spelled the word. "S-A-T-Y-R-E?"

Mitch smiled. "Randy Satyre. Yeah, that's him. Why?"

Yaz cocked his head to the right. "I'm not sure about the spelling."

"It's Greek," Mitch explained. "That's why it looks strange. It means one of those half-deer, half-stud things."

Yaz touched his nose. "Next…"

Mitch nailed all their stage names. 'Horndog' Mason, 'The Big Bamboo' Gould, 'Amore Eel' Oliva, 'Open Ice' Glennie, 'General' Wolfe, 'Formidable' Guevremont, "Crowbar" Clifton, Joey "The Punisher," "Ramjet" Goldsworthy. Not a single miss. Yaz clapped politely.

"Still got it," Mitch laughed. "Too bad about MacArthur. There was your original good ol' boy. Calgary money. Not oil either. I forget where his folk's cash came from. Cows maybe."

Yaz sat patiently. Mitch horked up an oyster. Rang it into the receptacle. Slapped the desktop, then cursed. Bad for the electronics. Tex kept telling him that.

"Alright," Mitch declared. "Time to make like a raptor." He pocketed his butts. Powered everything down. Glanced at Yaz. "You're still good for Friday night?"

"Absolutely," Yaz replied. "Meet here?"

"Yeah," Mitch said, tight smile. "We can go over the new info in the car. You'll see why a little outside help can't hurt. Tomorrow I'll hit Queen's Park. See what's what. You want to come?"

"Please." Yaz checked his com. Contact code. Report in if possible.

Mitch stood. Stretched. Yawned. "Well, I got a game in Orangeville tonight."

"I may do some more research," Yaz said. Exited.

"Great idea. If we do ever catch anybody, I promise to give you half the credit," Mitch lied. With that, he bolted himself.

THE SOD SQUAD

—◄○►—

Friday night arrived. Mitch had been busy leading up to the presentation. A couple of terrorgations done. Took out a loan to buy a new hockey stick. Two electronic Weblets visited. Mitch only went hard shell for the final purchase. He still liked to heft what he emptied leather for.

He'd prepped Yaz on the drive over. CORE sources came through. Threads were linked. Connections made. But to cover the ground meant bringing in volunteers. Mitch nixed Yaz's description.

"Too American. And they're not being paid like deputies would be." Corrected himself. "Well, they are and they aren't. Hard to explain. There's compensation, let's put it that way. But we like to think of them as just… regular citizens helping out."

The hall was stifling when they walked in. Greek owner, Mitch explained. Kept it Mediterranean.

Yaz was still limping. Thought he'd pulled an upper thigh muscle. Nearly wiped out taking the steps into the club. Mitch watched. Laughed as Yaz tap-danced. Then did the exact same thing a few seconds later. Temperatures had dropped since the afternoon. Invisible ice the result. The brief but intense scare got the heart pumping. And now they stepped into an oven.

Sweat bloomed on Mitch's forehead. He removed his coat and muffler in one motion. A strikingly tall beauty appeared instantly. Moved like a gazelle. Black skirt that hugged everything down to the ankles. Black blouse. Coal-black hair. Kohl-dark eyes. Her perfume paralyzed Yaz. But the eyes were locked on Mitch.

"Jillian, babe," Mitch said. Flashed his pickup smile. Two Jills. One city. What were the odds? "Long time, princess. You look delicious."

"Hey, big fella," she grinned back. Flawless porcelain. "Let me take that." She nearly buckled under the weight of Mitch's leather. "Oh, my!" she grimaced.

225

"Yeah, bit heavy," Mitch said. "You handle this guy's as well?" He gestured at Yaz, waiting politely.

"Of course," Jillian groaned. "Happy to."

Yaz piled his coat on top of Mitch's. Jillian staggered along beside them to the coatcheck.

"I haven't heard from you in so long," Jillian said. Her heels tic-tacked over the tile.

"Yeah," Mitch agreed. "Christ it's warm in here." Made a show of wiping his forehead. "Hey, before I forget. Somebody should salt those steps. You're gonna lose staff." He thumbed towards the sidedoor entrance. "Nearly broke my neck getting in here."

Jillian plopped her load onto the counter. Sighed. "I'll have one of the girls take care of it, pronto," she said, mouth firm. "It's this…weather. Freezing rain one minute, snow the next. Then it melts. Freezes again. March is a never-ending battle."

"Tell me about it," Mitch commiserated. "Gus in?"

"Waiting for you," Jillian said. "Usual spot."

"Great," Mitch smiled. Winked. "Appreciate it."

Jillian spun like a top. Guided them to another door marked private. Mitch motioned to Yaz. Wait two. Entered.

Yaz stood with his back to the blonde wainscoting. Thought about hot noodles in spicy soup. Food and computers. His two great loves.

The smells wafted all around him. Mouth-watering. Sage, basil, tomatoes, lamb. He could detect fat, oven burned. Pan drippings. Doughy dumplings. Deep-fried beer batter. Nothing since lunch. Some near-burger from a sidewalk stall. Almost seven hours ago. Weak-kneed now.

The door opened. Mitch walked out. Smile of success. They backtracked three metres. Pushed through large wooden doors. Inside, Yaz was brought up short. The dining area was enormous. Like a basketball court. Cathedral ceiling. Yaz guessed fifteen metres from floor to skylight. Crosshatched wooden design. Wrought iron chandeliers hung from walnut-coloured hardwood beams. Blue and white urns taller than Yaz circled the room. Inside, magnificent cedars. Innumerable ferns, well-tended broadleaf plants completed the scene.

"Good enough for the sluts we go out with, eh?" Mitch said.

Yaz hesitated. Then nodded in agreement.

Mitch stopped. Stood with feet apart. Breathed in deeply. Yaz, rubbernecking, almost ran into him. Apologized. Wordlessly pointed around them. Mitch nodded.

"Yeah. Looks good, smells better." Hunger pangs attacked them both. New aromas arrived. Thick, savoury. Beef, onions, potatoes, green beans.

So many. A bouquet. Yaz had trouble distinguishing all the scents. It was a wonderful challenge.

Mitch rounded the plant wall. An opening lay before them. Grouped around tables placed in a wide semi-circle, two full hockey squads. As he predicted. Roughly fifty men, Yaz guessed. Mid-twenties to mid-thirties. All eyes focused on Mitch and his partner.

To their immediate right, a medium-length dining table. On it, pitcher of water. Glasses on a silver tray. In the middle of the table, an odd metal device. Sleek, brushed aluminum. Football-shaped, football sized.

Mitch strode forward. Nods, hands raised, smiles from the guests. Casual dress, despite the style of restaurant. Jeans. Cotton shirts. Good shoes. A few sports jackets slung over chair backs.

"Good crowd," Mitch said out of the corner of his mouth. Yaz nodded politely. Happened to glance to his far right. Saw a large man standing near a potted tree. Air of calm dignity. Dark suit. Hands crossed before him. Stiff posture. Tall. Late 50's, maybe. Hard to tell from the distance. Brilliant blue-black hair, gray wings. Eyes on Mitch. Yaz guessed it was the owner. "Gus" Chelios. Mitch praised him up and down on the ride over.

Apparently rich. Started as a busboy. Owned the place fifteen years later. Add another fifteen years, owned a lot else besides. Good accountant, good lawyer, hard work. The secret to business success, Mitch relayed. Yaz once heard his uncle say the same.

And a huge CORE fundraiser. Typical story. No specifics from Mitch. Just a wrong put right. Family matter. A crime committed. Even Gus's money couldn't buy justice. Perp had parents with pull among the Arts community. Police a joke, o f course. Courts tainted. Gus's MP a battery-operated fooltool of the NPOT. Soothing words, no cavalry.

So Gus was an early purchaser of the CORE product. Contract fulfilled. Gus a happy and extremely grateful client. So grateful, that night the area's most popular restaurant was Mitch's for the asking. On short notice. Free food. Free drinks. No questions asked.

Mitch took his place at the head table. An officer addressing the men in his command. Or a prince his knights, Yaz thought.

Yaz took the chair Mitch indicated. Unloaded his satchel.

Mitch surveyed the crowd. Made crude gestures. Milked the moment. Soaked in the waves of warm approval. Yaz handed over Mitch's holopad. Pre-prepped. Mitch continued playing to the crowd. Holopad upside down. Pretended to read it. Friendly heckles.

Yaz examined the curious-looking machine in the meantime. Unique. He'd never seen one like it at the Force. Anywhere. Had no idea what the purpose might be. No visible switches, toggles, levers, buttons. Gently touched it. A musical whistle the response. Operating, clearly. Still a mystery.

Sudden speaker snap. Mitch linking his com up to the system. Brief sound check. Thumbs up from the man. Yaz knew of Mitch's general contempt for technology. Badly designed/impossible-to-use technology. Quick-to-fail technology. But he raved about his com. Incredibly, Mitch had said, made in Canada. But really good.

Mitch cleared his throat. Clean delivery. Broke through crowd chatter easily. Conversation petered out.

Yaz took in the gathering. Understood the earlier comparison. Model jocks. Or jocks who modeled. Unconventional hair styles. From beserker mop to prison business. Job cuts. They were top escorts. Yaz also thought he detected the sheen of fresh dueling scars. (The newest outlawed sport. Mitch had shown great interest when word reached CORE. No classes offered yet.)

Nearest guess, from his distance. No one under 85 kgs. Height, 184 cm and up. Shapes varied. From weightlifter broad to tri-althlete whipstrong. And Yaz could confirm Mitch's boast. No man in attendance was anything but fit and ready for duty. The way they lounged. Like hunting cats. An alert confidence. Self-belief bordering on arrogance. Old-line Ontario look. Outsiders unwelcome. They'd have rode Yaz hard in school, he knew.

Mitch began. "First off…first off, thanks for coming. I…we…really appreciate it. Especially without much lead time. I know everyone is…busy." Snorts and chuckles. March break a money month. Tons of opportunity. Dorm events, pre-exam stress fucks, home porn film festivals. Lots of work if you wanted it.

"Well, the sooner I get through this, the sooner we can jump into the grub." Cheers. Modest bow from Mitch. Held up a hand. "And the booze." Louder cheers. Mitch explained how he'd wanted them half-oiled before he got there. Made the medicine go down smoother.

"Also, if this works out? A golden handshake should be coming your way. And you know what I mean by that." Enthusiastic applause. A few wolf howls. Mitch called it in the car. Offer the average Canadian a free case of beer to help out? He's there. Offer beer AND money? Loyal friend for life. Beer, food and money at one go? Who did you want killed? And how slowly?

Mitch pulled his nose. Checked the holopad again. Stalling. No mean favour he needed.

"Essentially, nothing has changed. You should all have received the com updates. We got a kind of… manhunt going. But it's…unofficial. It's… delicate. Political, yeah?" Cleared his throat.

"So we can't hurt them if we find them?" a voice blurted out. More snickers. Yaz would learn why later.

"If it can be avoided, yes," Mitch replied, winking manner. "No, seriously. Just…get back to me ASAP. We need to…talk with the…'P…O…I'." Person of Interest. Idiot police jargon for 'spect. Always triggered laughs.

Mitch shot a look at Yaz. Meaning understood. The teamwork thing was growing. Quick survey. Saw the large metal tub. Went over, dug around in the ice. Found a frosty. Returned to place the Corona before Mitch. Grateful nod. Mitch opened it. Drank off half. Spontaneous cheer.

"Shit," Mitch said. Made a show of wiping his mouth on the sleeve of his sports coat. Crooked grin. "Nervous standing up in public." This from an all-city escort, three years running. They roared. Too funny.

Mitch took a deep breath. Spoke into his com. "There's a remote, remote possibility some of you may…know one or more of the corpses. They might have run in some of the same circles. Well, lower circles. Bottom circles, actually. What's got people upset is…the thought of a…organized trull cull. Random kills are…normal for the trade. You're always going to lose a percentage of mattressbacks every year. But the current rate of slutloss is… abnormal. Enormous. So…you know…we have to find out…what's going on. Before they're all gone. And the profiler guy seems to think our 'spect haunts these…uh, places we're asking you to visit."

"Faggo webs," someone muttered. Concerned stirring. Chair scraping. Coughs. Mitch sensed the disquiet. Took another deep refresher. Tossed the empty to Yaz. Another message sent and received.

"Anyway…" The football amped up. Lights twinkled. Mitch took a cautionary step back. Yaz was half-way to the beertub. Missed it. A holograph suddenly shimmered in the air above everyone. Hi-def overhead slab shot. Female. Maybe. Who could be sure anymore?

Excited 'o-o-o-h-h-h-hs' from the audience. Good vistech. Piggyback program pre-embedded. Yaz surmised this upon returning. State of the art. He'd never even heard of it before. Nothing in the webzines. CORE-engineered? The Force would be very interested. Not to mention worried.

Automatic CORE-linkup. Mitch had them again. Shiny, shiny. Worked every time. Swiveled to face the audience, fresh beer in hand.

"So…this one they found…somewhere. The lake or a dumpster. I forget. Kind of ripped apart, as you can see." Muffled laughter. "NFA, of course. But it's obvious she called Tramp Avenue home. So we'll have a fix on her stoop soon." Total bullshit. No one called him on it.

"Check B J Way," someone suggested. Mitch decided not to follow up.

"We got flash gear. Knockoff shit. Makeup by Max Plaster. It could be fourteen or forty."

Mitch picking up speed. Whispered into his com. A new photo appeared. Giggle trigger. Mitch joined in.

"Yeah, somebody got…uh… a little rough with this one. Not that you need arms in the afterlife." Amusement contagious. Mitch had to stop. Pretended to dry his eyes.

"Actually, turns out it wasn't the…er… killer's fault. Harbour patrol boat propellers did it. Guys were really hungover that morning. See those trenches?" To his surprise, Mitch could gesture and have it appear near the corpse's holo-figure. Exo-tech. He liked it.

"Above her hips? Gaff marks. They kept missing her. It's a wonder we got anything back to examine."

Laughter turned to hoots of scorn. D.P.'s. Glue them to a Timmy's stool. They'd still find a way to fuck up.

Several more digi-vids. Dead doxies found in a drainage ditch. Another pair in the Beaches area. One roped to a heritage legacy maple tree in Riverside. Symbolic meaning beyond the powers of anyone to guess. Or care about. Eglinton, High Park, scores more. Dozens of images.

Mitch was intrigued. He'd no idea so many sluts had been done in. The graph at the bottom. Could that number be right. Impossible to know the total gutted by the Ovarians. Anything over and above the average monthly totals seemed likely. Whatever the actual number, Mitch made no mention of it. Better if the crew were largely ignorant of any great significance to the chase.

"This has been going on for years, of course," Mitch observed. "And they can't all be the work of one guy. But whoever they are, their balls have gotten bigger. They want us to notice this. To know the skeeze pool is leaking."

Mitch fast-forwarded the rest. Novelty value had peaked. A brief laser show followed. The machine's farewell. Shut itself off to applause from the group. Mitch patted it with affection. Made a mental note to look into it further. Mother's Day coming. Do that photo album thing with it.

"Okay," Mitch said. Kicked himself. Public speaking rule number three. Don't say 'OK' too often. Grated.

"So you've got some idea of what's what. The wrap up. Someone or some group is casually offing street meat. Might be a political angle. Ask around. Be discreet. More like you're looking for a friend. Well, a friend of a friend. Any one gets suspicious, bullshit them. Anything sound strange, anything…" He held his com up for all to see. "Day or night…preferably day…afternoons are best, actually…between two, two-thirty…"

"Unless you're busy."

"Exactly," Mitch answered. Took another slug of beer. Second's reflection. Continued.

"My…firm…signed off on this plan because our regulars…were all on other missions."

"Liar," a voice yelled. Smattering of hand claps.

"Plus," Mitch rolled on, "you guys are cockstars."

Loud cheers, footstomping.

"You've got what every poofter wants," Mitch added, pouring on the oil. "What better bait could there be? You've all been around. You know how to fake gayness." Mitch watched an impromptu call and response routine.

"Not too much though, guys, yeah? Not super-gay like that shit. Every day gayness. Retail gay. OK?" Fuck! Said it again.

"Problem is, the crew I'm with now...they might...well, the wrong look, heads roll. And that might...queer things, so to...so to speak."

Groans and boos.

Mitch shook his com. Feigned glitch trouble. Waited until the noise level moderated.

"Right. We've roughed out some places. Profile guy says this dirtbag keeps to his own kind by night. Any questions?"

Three count. Mitch cleared his throat again. "Okay...fuck...roll call. Grunt if you hear your name..."

Mitch ran the list. "Python, Punisher, Carjack, Penetrator, Clubber, Hercules, Douglas Fur, Love Lance, Caver, Harry Mammoth, The Big Bamboo, Tusk, TrumpetMan, Longhorn, Ramrod, Axle, Turbo, Beaver Cleaver, Samson, The Victimizer, Torque, Dredger, Tallywhacker, Railgun, The Commander, I-Beam, Nemesis, Tunneler, Culvert Cobra, Auger, Big Country..." The rest of his old escort colleagues or rivals got named. All present and accounted for.

"Outstanding," Mitch applauded them. "Now the ugly part. Check your coms. You should have all the information in the attachment. This is just in case."

Mitch waited for everyone to get ready. Let the whining subside.

"As I said before, you guys can divvy up the places. Whoever's closest to one spot or another. That kind of thing. O...Alright. Here we go. If you don't see these on your list, stop me. Roosters, GayLords, Lula's, Pixies, Paydirt, The Malestrom, Auber Jean's, Milt Haven, Simpering Fogs..." Mitch stopped. Cocked head. "Sorry. That last one should be Simpering Fops. Repeat, Simpering Fops. If the address is missing, tell me."

"Dress code?" Tom A. Hawk with his hand up.

Mitch nodded. "Good question. The ones I've just said? As far as I know, leather is always acceptable. You could probably wear your regular work gear and no one the wiser. Shit, women like it. What's the diff, right?"

"Thanks."

"No problem. Actually, that might save time." Mitch pursed his lips. "Yeah. For example...uh...Catamite Corner, Asparagus, Tess Tickle's Dropzone...try for something university prof-ish...or churchy. Good dress shoes. Blazers. School tie, spongepants. Shit like that."

"Props okay?"

Question stumped Mitch. Cracker reply. "Ya got me. Whud'ja have in mahn'd, Silas?"

"I don't know," a dark-haired individual admitted. Glanced to his left and right. "You said church. I thought maybe…like a gown or something?"

Mitch inhaled. Pondered the idea. Scratched his nose. "Your call," he finally said. "But…the KISS principle has…something to it."

"Wish you hadn't said that," another escort mumbled. Rubbed his chin. Nervous laughter followed. For all the light-hearted banter, the unpleasant gravity of the situation clear.

"Next…" Mitch hurried on. "Ahhh…uh…this could be a little tricky. J & F area." Mitch danced his eyebrows. "Pajamaica, Buckwheats. DeBasement, AbomiNation, The OK Kraal and Rastafairy Ian's."

"Not sure we'll pass, buddy." Gibbs this time.

"Blackface is fine," Mitch said.

"What?!!" Chorus of disbelieving shouts.

"No, no," Mitch laughed. "We'll have Human Rights Commissars after you. This one's an easy shift. Just pretend to be cops."

"Shit. That's illegal, isn't it?" Goldsworthy sounded shocked.

"Not after I shoot you passes," Mitch winked. "Only good for this job. Expires end of the month. So don't be getting any ideas."

"You really don't have anyone who could do this?"

Mitch put his hands out. "Woodpile" Jones and "Affirmative" Kwaame usually took those calls. Both were on training assignment in Montreal. Studying Haitian.

"Not available," Mitch explained."

"Okay." Goldsworthy content.

"I still don't know," Ferguson interrupted. "Why would they even talk to us?"

"Because you're going as turd burglars like everyone else," Mitch said. Matter-of-fact tone. "That's what's important. From what we got told, this sick fuck moves around. He's of that world. Splits his time between Moronto and Blahblahblottawa. NPOT staffer, possibly. Lawyer, lobbyist, treasury leech. Even a full-time pol. Don't know."

Muttering.

"Details are hard to come by," Mitch threw in. Remembered other crap from the prep sheet. "Behaviour analysis suggests he's your garden variety socprogger. Lives to help people. With your money. Then take credit for it. And a multiculti vulture. Every NC should get a pavilion along with his rent-free apartment. That sort."

"A radical queer dickhead serial killer?"

Mitch shook his head in agreement. "Just what we need."

"Now…" Mitch paused. Waited for silence. "The District."

Groans. Mitch expected it. Grim smile.

"I know, I know. Look, anything you can get is more than we have, okay? I don't…we're…flying blind here. Whatever you can think of to…loosen tongues…"

A chorus of boos drowned the rest out.

"I didn't say that!" Mitch in damage control. "I didn't say that. Skip over that. That was…that just came out wrong."

"I reserve the right to smash face in the event things go left," a voice insisted. Invoking "Kichuk Rules." Mitch had to accept them. Everyone did.

"Absolutely," Mitch assured everyone. "Goes without saying." The grousing petered out. Mitch bored on.

"Here we go." Winced as he read the first name. "'MinceMeet', 'Blicero's', 'The Bloodshed!'" Hard sell. No buyers. Just whistles and heckling. Mostly what Mitch thought would happen.

"Kickass party if we get this guy," Mitch promised. Fake ingratiating smile. Chuckles for chutzpah. Mitch looked for the quick finish. Win them over with the feast.

"Need someone to…drop in on…'The Sewer Pipe', 'Supple Muscle', 'Chocolate Stars' and 'Bottoms Up'."

Quiet room. People digested the dispiriting info.

"Is that muscle like bicep or mussel like bivalve?" someone asked.

Mitch looked like he'd been drilled between the eyes. Wet dog head shake. Looked down at his com. "The first one," he answered. "Maybe. It's on Yonge. You can check the spelling when you get there."

"Oh, yeah," Mitch added. "Some of these…businesses are hidden in the 'burbs. We cover mileage. So keep gas receipts." Smattering of applause.

"'Pelts', 'Prancers and Vixens', 'PandaMonium', 'Flambe Bambi'. Should be straightforward. No grief from that quarter, I don't think. And after…"

"Woah, woah, hold up…" Brown speaking. "These aren't…"

Caught out, Mitch surrendered. "Yeah."

"Furries?"

"Yeah."

"Oh, fuck. I hate that shit."

"Who doesn't?" Mitch countered. "But really. It might be a hoot. Think about it."

"You mean wear a fucking bunny suit?"

"Change when you get there."

"Can you do that?"

"I don't know."

"Ahhhh….shit."

"It's not bodymods, at least," Mitch reminded him.

"Or nullos," another added. "That stuff is beyond creepy."

"Yeah," Mitch concurred. "Just everyday sicko perversion. In Vaughn."

"Beautiful Vaughn."

"And I've just gotten the sign," Mitch said, amped. "We are go for grub."

Roar of approval. Feet stamped. Bottles banged.

"Wait, wait!!" Mitch heard chairs being overturned. "Just a few more… few more."

He picked up his bottle. Empty. Sighed. Waved Yaz off another run.

"Diddler Ditch," he read, monotone voice. "I know. Can't be helped. Draw straws, if you have to. Anyway, here goes. 'The Velvet Plum'. 'Scuttle Butts'. 'Buoys Ahoy!' And, 'Romper Room'. You'll probably hear some terrible, terrible shit. Whatever you do, don't dummy anyone there. Do it somewhere else. My luck, the cops show up…you've got your hand stuck in somebody's skull…well, hard to explain you were there on CORE business, yeah?"

"Last but not least, the Brit bit. 'Flan…something French…'e-u-r'…. et Cox…combs'. Not sure about the pronunciation there. Also, 'Cheerios'. 'Wilde at Heart'. 'Welcome Back, Kottagers', and 'My Man Chester'. The last for Toronto's large ultra-gay soccer fan community."

"Which means all of them," someone said to growls of approval.

"Hey, I like soccer," James protested. Shunning silence.

"Then you'll love 'My Man Chester'," Mitch said to laughter.

"Moving on…Hah!" Mitch spit out. "Ah, sorry. Lumberjack shirts? Who's got'em?"

Mitch brought a hand up to shield his eyes. "Oh, right. Fucking nobody has one. Liars!" Mitch feigned disappointment. Sighed. Tried to low ball it.

"Too bad. Dream assignment. 'The Vertical Trough', 'Gone Fishing', 'Beeves', 'Mingo Gully' and 'Seaman's Reef'."

"This guy works dyko bars, too?" White asked. Voice strained in disbelief.

"No," Mitch said. "I just threw that in to see if there'd be any takers."

"Prick!"

"Thank you," Mitch bowed. "And on that note, let me…oh, fuck, there is one more. 'Tableaux'. Late addition."

"Everyone's full up." Thibodeau. Challenge on. Cue picked up immediately.

"Fuckin' A," another voice growled. "This looks like a job for Mr. fifteen-inch himself."

Spontaneous cheers. "Fifteen-inch! Fifteen-inch!" came the famous chant.

Mitch held up his hands. Videvangelist blessing. Theatrical wave.

"Agreed. No leading from the rear. Why should you have all the fun?"

More spirited booing. Unkind comments. The lights flickered. Perfect timing. Mitch had a growl on.

Com held high, Mitch hushed everyone.

"Ding, ding, ding, boys," he yelled. "Roast beast!"

Pointed at the back of the hall. The planters had been quietly rolled away. Long tables in evidence. Goods being piled high. Already a delicious smell overwhelmed the evergreen. Gus's kitchen crew pushed out the best. Real moms turning out real food. Home food. No wonder the man did a roaring trade.

"It's a food for all!" Mitch proclaimed. "Pile in, piglets!"

He didn't have to tell anyone twice. Immediate rush.

Mitch saw Gus near the kitchen doors. A general marshalling the troops. River of passing staff bearing platters. Mitch knew they'd return empty-handed in a matter of minutes. The boys could put it away. He wandered over. Shook hands. Their benefactor looked Christmas morning happy. Barrel build. Tight-trimmed goatee. Snow white toothy smile. The sharp eyes of a wise and wary entrepreneur.

"Mr….Gus…what can I say? Looks fantastic. Outstanding."

Mitch patted the man's stomach. Impertinent hand promptly brushed away. Man was the picture of success. Glowing with pride and satisfaction. Still, he pooh-poohed the praise.

He and Mitch chatted as the men lined up, faces beaming. Mitch did a little stroking. The man would be seriously out of pocket for the event. Claimed not, but Mitch knew otherwise. Final handshake. Sincere pump. Then Mitch joined the throng, rolling in behind Yaz.

Yaz clutched his plate like an African waiting for the UN truck to unload. His eyes remained glued to the only tray he could see. The men before him were attacking it. He feared nothing would be left before he got there. And then it was his turn. A solid row of pinapple-glazed Black Forest ham slabs remained. Lean. Rich purple rind. He salivated so hard his eyes watered.

Mitch poked Yaz in the back. Chuckled. "Looks good, eh?"

Yaz nodded agreement. Much was new to him. No tofu. Or specially prepared lotus roots, burdock, white radish. But it smelled wonderful all the same.

"Well…" Mitch said, grabbing the tongs. "Time to buckle down."

Work of a moment for him to spear a shank of dead swine. Chunk of kielbasa to follow. Warm. Juices trickled onto the China. Mitch inhaled. Held it in for a five-count. Could have cried then for sheer happiness.

Step, fork. Step, fork. Roast beef. Deli-sliced. Flesh red and tender as Andrea's baltimores. Rotisserie chicken and turkey slices appeared. Were Mitch's eyes wider than his stomach? No, they weren't. Half a pullet magically appeared on his plate.

Quarter turn. Pulled into the next table. A touch of Italy. The leaning tower of pizza. Every variety known to humankind. Some still bubbled hot from the oven. Mitch grabbed a meat supremo triangle. Never change horses in mid-stream.

Entree dealt with. Mitch moved on to the veggies. Balanced meal. All that shit they went on about. Dutifully speared a celery stick. Snared the smallest broccoli sprig available. Hid it out of sight under some salami. Left the rest for Yaz. Mitch was done with the garden greens.

He straightened up. There it was. Why did it attract so many? Because it was there. Olympus. A mammoth mountain of potato salad. Secret family recipe. Mitch couldn't think of a greater contribution to local cuisine. A meal in it's own right. Cucs, carrots, summer sausage, onions, green peppers, oven-roasted bacon bits, banana peppers, and on and on. Mitch stood before it in respectful silence.

Sadly, Gus's masterpiece was already well known. Revered among his regular customers. Mitch's circle knew it mainly by rep. No standing on ceremony, though. The salad's lunar surface looked to have been shelled. Great gouges and pockmarks everywhere. Mitch moved closer. More spadework coming.

Above the glorious concoction, two more mounds moved. Both connected to a heavenly body. Mitch winked. The recipient blushed. Dessert on legs. Seventeen. Maybe. Pert nose lightly dusted with flour. Honey-sweet smile. Full-bloom pheromone generator. Mitch's nostrils widened. His unit also sensed fresh fruit cup. Bestirred itself. Fire alarm. Now wasn't the time. Tore his eyes away from the exquisite cleavage. Went to the memory vault. Pulled out an image of Modge on the charge. Those lizard eyes and public toilet breath. Cured the urge.

"Ready?" the cock-chafer asked, spoon salute. Mitch gave imperial assent. The Venus bent over. Her luscious bouncers mere inches away. In other circumstances he'd have buried both in the spud Sierras. Then tongued them spotless. Bloody Gus. He must have gone to the same school as Ahmed, the fast food magnate. Corporate rule. Only the juiciest lookers worked his rooms. Born marketers, the pair of them.

Brought to mind a banker Mitch met once. Some charity event he'd squired a cooz to. Guy had done the exact same shit. Only hired babe tellers. Paid them double the going rate. Dressed them like hookers. Acres of visible flesh. Retired the lobby ATM's after awhile. No one used them.

Lunchtime line-ups out the door. Not a single delay complaint. Students, truckers, dentists, geriatrics, fruit stall peddlers, cops, bus drivers. Guys hustling to open an account. Deposit money. Borrow money. Close their account and open a new one. Any excuse to drool over those luscious stunners.

Had to extend their hours. All transactions timed. Three minute minimum, five minute maximum. Regardless. House rules. Did triple the business of nearby competitors. Upper management asshats couldn't figure out why that one store's numbers were so phenomenal. Finally credited the new poster campaign. Starring an animated movie character. Guy looked at Mitch. Said, "Upper management." They both laughed.

Elbow in the back. Mitch turned to find the offender. Recognized Dredgerman. Full graze mode. Stopped to shoot the shit, savour the flavour.

Dredger got his salad fix. Joined Mitch on the way to the side dishes. A perfectly underclad wait-tasty slipped past them. Topped up the French fry pan from a large tray. Three kinds—spicy, battered, home-style. All mouth-watering. Hot and crispy. Sea-salted to excellence.

Beside them, half-empty hamper of onion rings. Mitch snagged one. Ate it. Nearly wept. Goodness off the scale. Thanked God he'd inherited a machine metabolism. Knew he was going to be absorbing some big kcal numbers. Might text Andrea. Tell her to keep the motor running. He'd need to burn off some of the excess.

He and Dredger found a table semi-occupied. Dumped their plates. Headed back to the crockery line. Re-stocked. This time, the vinegar venue. Devilled eggs, four-bean salad, cole slaw, monster dills. Done and done.

Cheese board up. Maker out of Tavistock, according to the sign. Mitch thought he recognized the name. Two 8-year old white cheddar chunks. Big as glacier calves. A medium one for contrast. One hot pepper slice, and a smoked one for after. Good with beer.

Dredger wiped away a tear. Pointed at the eight-year old. "Oooh," he said. "Sharp."

"Just the way I like'em," Mitch replied.

Chew festival next. Mitch nodded to the men sitting. No conversation. That would come later. None of that slow-food bullshit. Get it in and get drinking. Two hours of eating? He remembered Lindsay's comment. Last thing his relatives needed—more time at the trough.

A beer babe wandered by. Mitch held up a finger. She wiggled over. Waited until he swallowed. Took his order as he ran an approving hand over her ass. Firm as firewood.

Checked out the nearby action as the bunny tuft giggled off. His aunts would have been pleased. They liked men with appetites. No holding back with this group. Like being in a lumber mill. Chippers and shredders going full bore. Reminded him of a Hungry Planet doc. One of those "Watch Locusts Eat Africa" specials. Similar tearing and grinding sounds.

The beer arrived. Icy cold. Two. Clever minx. Mitch, eating hard, pointed at his com. Meaning cellsex money transaction. Broad wink, then tongue dance. Joke. Also, tip hint. The pert bird's nest displayed dazzling ivory. Bustled away.

Another, Mitch thought. He was picking up fuck invites right and left this evening. He'd already texted Andrea about coming home early. Hoped he hadn't been over-hasty.

Mitch bent back to his plate. The bread wench sashayed near. Mitch joined the others in corralling a couple Portugese rolls. Split one open. Seduction. Steam rose in silky ribbons. Two butter bales sacrificed. Mitch watched in fascination as they liquefied. Soaked into the soft flesh. He closed the roll. Flipped it on its back. Let the butter saturate the wheat meat. Idly thought about pocketing two more. Freeze later. Good for emerg. famine attacks. Better still. Slide by the kitchen after. Have them box up a dozen.

Another voluptuous crumpet glided near. Shot him a look. Gave the next to Dredger. Double her pleasure. Dredger stopped the jaw action. Joined Mitch in following her out. Either the world's biggest cocktease or horny as hell, Dredger murmered. At sixteen, probably both, Mitch responded.

A third wave of willing diners swept over the remains. Vultures scouring the carcass. Frantic scraping of bowls, trays, platters, containers. Potato salad history to judge from the cursing.

Noise volume rose. Banquet base put down. Booze time.

Mitch was stuffed. The last swallow of beer got no further than his tonsils. The bowl of muscat grapes looked superb. He just couldn't manage one. Lit a smoke instead. Best tasting one all day.

Guys started to drift by. Catch up on the news. Same stories, different jobs. Some clubs close. New ones open. A couple of credit chip ripoffs. Two guys moved back East where the jobs were. Another got married. Working it in Redmonton from last November.

Nobody pried too deeply about his new career. Him turning borderline official struck some as odd. Especially considering his previous badboy image. Just checking. See if he'd changed. Or still the anything-for-a-laugh/we-don't-need-no-stinkin'-badges guy they used to know.

Turned out, Yaz had to drive him home. First the feast, then the fray. Mitch got right into the whiskey. Wasn't long, he was in the 'closing-time? Fuck-that!' state everybody loved him for. This was long after they'd exited the Olympus. He remembered thanking Gus. More than once. Got pulled off the snooch flirt. They all piled out.

Group debate. Hit Ackroyd's? Why not? In the mood for blues. Had fun. Drank vodka. Abused the house band. Mitch kept calling them the Down's Syndrome Blues Band. Argument ensued. Bottles thrown. People upset. Beat it before the D.P.'s got there.

After that…blurry. Crashed some weird retro techno grotto. Fake castle walls inside. Waterspouts. Live vines wrapped around exposed ducts. Full of actual Huns. Mitch introduced himself to everyone. Couldn't remember any names. Just enjoyed saying them over and over. Had no idea Germans were so fucking tall. Especially the women. Said so. Repeatedly. To everyone he met.

Also couldn't stop laughing. Or drinking. Or falling down. On the floor now. Spazz dancing. The fit upon him. Claimed later he was trying to charm some Bavarian skin canoe. Nobody but Mitch saw her. Finally rolled him out. Kept apologizing to everyone for the war. Regretted winning. Wished they'd joined forces. Rubbled Moscow. No PC shit. Wasted opportunity.

Last place. Caver knew where to go. A genuine dance club. They bought off the doorguard. Entered en masse. Trouble right from the start. Drinks denied. Unacceptable. Threw the fire alarms. Figured to get better service if the place emptied out. No harm meant. Just wanted a drink. Or three. Watching dance wankers panic almost as much fun.

Again, objections from the bartenders, bouncers, clientele. Mitch shoved the DJ aside. Mixed up some savage beats. Fell over the electronics board. Crawled past an amp. Fell off the stage riser. Got up. Started veering about. Very drunk-looking.

Those Bev's that hadn't fled cowered in a corner. Surrounded by escorts sporting prominent prongs. Fake rape scenario. Hilarious. Mitch tried to join them but the room kept moving away from him. One step forward, two back. Introduced himself to everyone. Couldn't remember any names.

Four bouncers made to rescue the Bev's. Charged the tightening circle of Mitch's buddies. Fight on. Adrenaline brought Mitch around. Threw a body block at a wrong-headed Walter. Took a punch to his ear. Slipped out of a dangerous headlock. Kicked his way clear of the brawl. Fists and elbows flew. Mitch felt nothing. Being hammered meant getting hammered didn't register.

Rest of night, memory snippets. Running down some side street. Turtled some ridiculous EuroVelope they came across. Left it wheels up and helpless. Contest to see who could tip one by himself. D.P.'s caught up to them. They knew him even if he couldn't see them. Flashed his CORE card. Everyone got a pass. Told to go home ASAP. Complaints coming in from all over.

Blank after. Yaz straining to lift him. Falling into the back seat of… something. Then…the feel of cold tile. Morning. Face half in a hiking boot. Seeking warmth. He could barely move for cold. And his head felt like a pumpkin. Great time, though. Find out the details later.

TABLEAUX

—◆○◆—

They parked the armoured Grinder. Secured it next to a spotlessly white 9000 series Tijuana Benz. Mitch knew it was the owner's. Fifth floor intel. Useful info. Always good to know shit before you need it. Instead of after the fact, which was usually the way.

Mitch and Yaz got out. Behind them, Agent Ben Alderson, RevDiv. Tagging along for laughs. Headed for the nightclub's entrance. Empty parking lot. As it would be Sunday morning.

"Everyone gone to church," Alderson said. Mitch would have chuckled but for his hangover. Dropped in at Billy's for one drink. Hadn't had one all day. That one tasted like another. Then another. He never learned.

A tip from The Saber led to their visit. A week after the Olympus feedbag extravaganza. Seven worthwhile leads. The Commissioner pleased. Mitch stunned.

Follow it up, they said. Sunday morning best time. Surprise the 'spect. That's when he worked the books. Mitch had agreed to check the place out anyway. This meant he wouldn't have to do it when it was open. Lucky break. Except for his head.

"Fucking raw wind," Mitch observed. You'd never know April was just around the corner. Snow forecast for later in the day. Climate fickleness. The new bullshit term. Hard to keep up. They changed it every other week.

He drew his shoulders in. Should have brought his scarf.

Yaz said something. Wind carved it up before Mitch could hear it. Looked around anyway. Normal Yaz get up. Ready for sledding. In the Arctic. Black, inflatable brand-jacket thing. Ski hat. Big ass furry muffler. Marmelade orange. Khaki drill trousers. Glazed shades. Porcupine lid. Mitch liked the man's style. Had to admit it. Exurb with a dash of slumtown. But not flash. Traveling with a fashion plate. Reflected taste. Almost made him look good.

240

Alderson favoured a different look. Gestapo. Very cool. Very intimidating. Nazi's had flair. Knee-length, retro-leather overcoat. Beltless. (Because he'd lost it. Plus several loops were broken anyway.) Black Acton cowhide. Worth the trip, he used to joke. Whatever that meant. Red-coal ripped denim stovepipes. Amish barn-builder boots, unlaced. Black-ish, but spotted with white paint. No scarf or hat. Bastard was impervious to the cold. Never bothered to button up.

Mitch himself was downmarket Beretta. Hunting camo's, top to bottom. Leafs cap. Snap-over jump boots. No gloves. Buttoned up tight. But that fucking wind. It had eyes.

Debated bringing the Gulf War I surplus night vision goggles. Just for psyops. Owned a pair in decent shape. Bong night entertainment. Sometimes he disabled the breaker in his condo. Scare the shit out of some yoni visiting the can. She comes out, pitch darkness. Just Mitch seeing green. Spread against the kitchen partition. Waiting until she passed to spring out. Great yuks. Old tech now. Bit goofy looking. And he didn't feel in prank mode that morning.

Bloor dead. No traffic.

Mitch glanced at Alderson, who shrugged. "Not even eleven." Meaning they'd be nice and early.

Yaz pointed at the large windows as they rounded the corner. Neared the entrance. Mitch sneered. "Frosted for a reason. From what I've heard."

Alderson hitched his jeans. Reached inside his jacket. Mitch saw him touch his holster. Mentally counting off weapon choices. Pre-op routine. Like a batter tightening his gloves before each pitch. After the incident on Yonge a year ago, Alderson went octopus everywhere. Any incident could be handled if you were well armed. Mitch guessed he was packing two Tak tasers. A sack of popcorn—new mini-grenades for close work. Closet inspection. Crowd control. Plus MilMace. A few knives. The Glock. Not to mention he was an expert neck-snapper whan all else failed.

Mitch wasn't prepped for widespread insurrection. He had his Ros, of course. Secured in its sweetly tooled scabbard. Weapons had just returned it. Put a laser edge on the thing.

"Circumcise a flea with it," the technican boasted. "Peel an egg. Shave a kiwi. Both kinds."

Comforting claims. Mitch figured he was covered. All they were doing was rousting latrine queens. He didn't expect any sharp sliders from those kind of pitchers. What did happen was totally unpredictable anyway. A loaded SAW and a crate of ammo wouldn't have helped.

Mitch and Yaz took the steps cautiously. Both remembered their near headers at Olympus. Sun may have shone for a minute. Wind still a mean lash. Just right for secret ice.

Alderson paused on the landing. Pointed at the wine-coloured awning. The edges snapped and curled with each gust. Alderson mimed the posture of the painted pansy. Mitch laughed in spite of his headache. Hammered on the door. Solid timber. Carbon fibre finish. Expecting a SWAT assault maybe? Suspicious.

Alderson peered through the orangey bubble-glass portholes. Negative. Mitch gave the occupants a minute to respond.

"Moderne," Alderson commented, examining the restaurant front. Climbing vines. Highball stitching. Not cheap.

Mitch snorted. Beat on the door again with feeling. "Hurry the fuck up," he muttered.

"Fumigating the place," Alderson suggested. Peered over the railing into a window. No movement.

"We should be so lucky," Mitch said. Let his breath out slowly. The hangover demons twisted a fresh blade in his brain. He knew he'd feel better if he ate something. That and a beer would have him belting out the CORE anthem in no time. Get in, get out, get some grub. That was the key to feeling human again. Not to mention his bowels were sending dark hints. A dump on the move. Audible gut gurgling. Alderson had already noticed. Mitch figured another twenty minutes. Then something nasty would try for the big breakout. Dropping a load at this place was unappealing, however. Christ only knew what you'd catch in the can. Or who.

Now Mitch was annoyed. "They know we're coming, the knob-gobblers. Dispatch warned them. Twice."

"Today?" Alderson asked.

Mitch glanced over. "Tecnically, no. But…they're aware we're coming by at some point. Intelligent 'spects would guess today."

"I could check around the back," Yaz offered.

Mitch started. He'd forgotten Yaz was with them for a second. Quietest guy at CORE. Ever. Mitch not the only one to think that either."

"Nah," he said, "They open this door inside a thirty seconds. Otherwise, I shoot the fucking lock off. Or Ben does."

The words were no sooner out of his mouth. A whirring sound heard. SecuriBolts. Titanium. Thick as Mitch's dick. What banks used.

"Guy didn't cheap out on security," Alderson observed. "What's he hiding, he needs this kind of pricey tech?"

Mitch shrugged. He'd think about that later. Clenched buttcheeks. Gritted his teeth. Right then, he wanted in out of the wind. And to park his ass over porcelain. Pull the chain. Feel the joy.

The door swung open a millimetre. Mitch could see an eye. Plus an inch-thick anchor chain leading from the jamb.

"Police," Mitch said brusquely. "Sort of." Glared at the single eye. Made up. Nice.

"We're closed," came the poofter squeak. The door slammed shut. Mitch looked at Alderson in disbelief. Return grin. Alderson just there for a lark.

"Jesus, just the kind of shit I don't need this morning," Mitch said. Took a calming breath. Turned back to the door. Launched two solid kicks at it. More for appearance sake. The door hardly shuddered. Second kick removed paint, though. That was pleasing.

The door opened again. "What do you want?" Same femme voice. "We're closed!"

"I can read the fucking sign, Frodo," Mitch snarled, "I don't care. We have a meeting with the owner. So open the fucking door right now! Or I kick it off its fucking hinges!" Bold threat, Mitch knew. Wasn't altogether sure he could even dent it. Thing was GM'd ironwood or something. "Then I tear you a new..." Mitch paused. Decided he didn't want to go there. All things considered.

"You don't look like police," the voice quailed. "I'm the manager. I need to see I.D."

Mitch held up his right hand. He made a fist. Pointed at the ring insignia. Mitch had tattooed the CORE logo onto a few foreheads, cheeks, backs. Grape-coloured eyebrows shot skyward. Sharp intake of breath. CORE had that kind of rep in depraved circles.

The door closed again. Mitch stared at it. Sighed. He hated stupidity. It was boring.

"Guess we should'a brought an axe," Alderson drawled.

"Didn't think we'd need one," Mitch confessed. Yawned. Sighed once more. Why did people persist in making things difficult for themselves? He stepped back. In the old days, they'd have thrown rocks through a window. Or butaned the door. See if a fire got anyone's attention. Couldn't do that with the new safety lazers. Another giggle denied. Planet no-fun.

The door opened again. Mitch couldn't see the chain this time. He lowered his shoulder. Bulled over the threshold. The manager took the brunt. Reeled onto the boards. Mitch thought to put a boot into the bottom-bandit's face. On general principles. Held back. No kicking hobbits. Even faggo ones. CORE standards.

Yaz and Alderson followed inside. As one, nose wrinkling. Closet gym socks rank. Mitch started to feel bad about laying such a nasty assignment on his old buds. He'd have to come up with something heavy to make up for it. Caribbean cruise? Golds at the ACC for the next Cup tilt? Even money didn't make up for everything.

Overlaying the general stench, something peculiar. It took Mitch a second to put his finger on it. Evergreeny. Pine or cedar. Not that machine aroma shit, either. Real.

"I believe you must show me some identification," the manager pouted, having nimbly attained his feet. He smoothed a furry, purple jacket. Rubbed his elbow. Adopted a weary, put-upon pose.

Mitch ignored him. Panned the area. The main bar sat directly in front. Good-sized. Maybe 30-feet long. Dining area to the left. Straight ahead, through furry planked batwing doors, a long mirror. Stand-up bar, probably. Building schematics showed stage and a dance floor. Couldn't see it from the entrance. Second floor had rooms. That kind of business. Mitch had no intention of exploring further.

Something caught his eye. He looked up at the ceiling. Head gestured to Alderson. The agent was already leaning back. Had been almost from the beginning. Expression of wonder. Above them, row upon row. Canoes. Hulls down. Fixed to the ceiling. Old wooden ones, rib impressions visible. Battered aluminum. New fiber varieties. Some antiques. Camp beaters. Others, perfect condition.

Mitch let his eyes wander to the walls. There, fishing gear—rods, reels, nets, tackle boxes. Hadn't noticed them at first. Some good-sized trout mounted above the windows. Five…maybe six pounders. There was even an old-timey stove. Firewood stacked in the corner. No moosehead. Only thing missing. Must be in another room.

Alderson could have caught flies in his mouth. This was not your typical BVDeviant décor. "Wow," he finally said. "It's like…Canadian Tire in here."

Yaz smiled. Mitch missed the gag.

"Very camp," Yaz said, acknowledging Alderson's joke.

Mitch still none the wiser.

"It's…" Alderson hesitated. Shrugged. "It's a queer thing. I don't get it either. Gays pretending to be…like men, maybe. Don't know."

For Mitch, the conversation mercifully ended. The manager had sneakily retreated. Slithered over to stand against the bar.

"You!" Mitch snapped his fingers. Pointed at the floor a metre in front of him. "Get back here, now. Not too close, though. Stand there."

The manager slinked back. Even in heels he barely came up to Mitch's sternum. Wafer-thin. Pencil-neck. Perma-sneer on a chipmunk face. Retail industry escapee. Mitch regretted not kicking him earlier. Easy to see the wretch wanted and got regular beatings.

The blued Pomp flip grated on Mitch as well. He could feel his father's disgusted look. Letting the little wanker breath the same air was unforgiveable. Dignity meter redlining.

"Okay, spoke," Mitch said. Gave him the no-shit-from-weasels stare. "First thing. Get your boss out here, pronto. We have to talk. After that, open some windows. Air out the stink."

"He's not here today," the young man lisped. Tilted his head back. Heavy-lidded disdain for Mitch. Trying for attitude. Mitch couldn't believe it.

"Don't!" Alderson said. Mitch growling. "Let me, let me." Leaned down. Read the nametag. Smiled. "Tristan...Tapette? That's a...that's a nice name. Listen. Why don't you come over here for a second, okay? Away from my big, bad buddy. Can you do that?"

"We know your boss is here," Mitch barked. "That's his 9000 out there. No way you've sucked enough cock to afford that. Yet."

Alderson maneuvered the manager away. They whispered together. Mitch monitored his bowels in the meantime. Valves under pressure. Venting required. Very soon.

Yaz thought about his next report. What to enter? What to leave out? He'd been walking a fine line the last few submissions. Much about CORE attracted him. The Force was not unlike the FBI. Famous But Incompetent. CORE was about action, not reaction. Butt-kicking, as they said, not butt-covering. Cultural security as well as national security. No more pandering to towelhead assholes, Mitch had declared. Yaz's loyalty no longer fixed to the Force. Their mission had ceased to inspire him. It was a problem. One he hadn't anticipated before his assignment.

Alderson returned, manager in tow. The slimster avoided Mitch's poisonous glare. Said, "Mr. Bavin is upstairs. He's very busy at the moment. The kitchen's in absolute turmoil now. The chef has been..." Tristan rolled his eyes.

Alderson nodded sympathetically. "But...he's coming down, right?"

"Soon," Tristan promised. Alderson patted the manager on the shoulder. Tristan flinched. Mitch gave a harsh laugh. Alderson changed tack.

"Say," he pointed to a table nearby. "Isn't that a Kelly's kettle?"

Tristan looked over. Followed Alderson. "Oh, I have no idea. I suppose it's possible. These are all legimate props."

Alderson rubbed his gnarly hands together. Danced his eyebrows. Made his eyes merry. "Need one. Mine's so beaten up it looks...like shit. Wanna sell it?"

"Oh, well...I don't..." Tristan stammered. "It's part of the whole setting. I don't think we can break it up. We're acquired everything you need for the backwoods experience," came the proud announcement.

"Looks like your guide has plenty of his own backwoods experience,"

Mitch joked for Alderson't benefit. Chucked Yaz on the shoulder. Hangover had slowed his thinking. Now got the locale. A parody bar. Gayworld humour. Seen a news flashlet. Dressed up faggos gathered in groups. Pretended to be real men meeting in real bars. Themes changed. Sometimes construction. Sometimes sports. This case, outdoor guys. Hetero trap. Tourists. Unwary burbsters. Conventioneers. Suck them into a normal-looking bar. Then try and wide-stance them in the can.

Worked often enough they kept doing it. But mostly the usual story. They all dreamed of sleeping with a real man. What they ended up with was just another gay. Funny. Pathetic...but funny.

Even with the mother of all hangovers, the canoes got to Mitch. Not to mention the bar did look familiar. The Neon beer signs. Molsons, Labatts, Old Veranda. Spiceracked bottles of booze. Slidetop coolers. The dartboard. Even the fridge magnets brought back memories.

An antique 12" television didn't. It was wedged into the corner of the bar, halfway up the wall. Jutted out over a triangle shelf. Mitch searched for the word he wanted. Antennas! It probably had one. Green screen. Jagged lightning crack in the beige plastic housing. He moved closer. Motorola. Mitch had heard of the company. Something to do with the space station. Didn't know they used to make tv's.

You also needed a half-full jar of pickled eggs. Yukon toe floating in the mix. Maybe a Planter's Peanuts stand. Peanut packs with faded Best Before dates. Pool table. No nap on the felt. Sides scored with burned down cigarette trenches. The little things that made a place look and feel comfortable, real.

Of course, a true Northern bar wouldn't accept the likes of Tristan anyway. No bartender worthy of the name would serve him. An image of Sam "Bear" Bartlett came to Mitch. Helmet-round dome. Face like a collapsed overpass. Full walrus, uncombed. Healthy smoker's cough. Beachball tucked under his tee. Peek-a-boo belly button when he reached for the fly gun. End of the night. Guys tried to drain a loonie into it. Whoever scored got last round free. Great times. Sam didn't care. You missed? He kept the coin.

Mitch wandered over to where Alderson and Tristan talked. Yaz had vanished somewhere. Mitch hoped it was to visit the can. He might have to go back on his vow. A pre-dump recon would help dampen the worry.

Alderson, it turned out, was being treated to a lecture. An animated Tristan described a large papier-mache display. Several of them graced the wall.

"And this is the village," Tristan pointed with pride. Three waves of tiny yellow teepees radiated out in different directions. A nuclear warning sign. Clever.

Lots of crayon-y bold shades. Pipecleaner forests spraypainted green.

Shredded paper meadows, lighter green. Somebody'd commissioned a public school class project. You make it, we'll display it. Keep it quiet where, though.

Mitch liked the complete lack of proportion. The play-doh elk same size as the tree it stood beside. And he especially enjoyed the generous use of colour. A thing needed brown, it got brown. Lots of it. The mountains looked like 3-D chocolate pyramids. Whipped cream topping of snow.

"The glaciers are melting," Tristan explained. Alderson's question as close to sincere as the earth to the moon.

"These were crafted," Tristan gently corrected Alderson. "U. of T. geography department graduate students. The attention to historical detail is remarkable, isn't it?"

Mitch was stunned. The artwork was unimaginably bad. Drunk, he could do better. Drunk and using his feet, he could do better.

Alderson couldn't have cared less. Bored, actually. Goofing on Tristan for cheap chuckles. Were it not for Mitch, he'd have exited already. Nothing to see here. Move along.

"The designers were tasked with creating an all-natural, visual representation of pre-Canadian West Coast natives—the 'Haida,'" Tristan informed them. "This is a diorama...or 'pictorial' of first contact."

Another pronounced Mitch eye roll.

"What's this one doing?" Alderson pointed at a figurine. It had been inserted in the river. Upstream from the village.

"Sweet tooth," Mitch offered. "Wants to chew on big rock candy."

Critical huff from Tristan. "That's a Haida caregiver in the middle of a ritual cleansing."

"Shit. She naked?" Mitch asked without thinking. Pushed past Alderson to squint. Got an elbow for his trouble.

"What?" he looked at Alderson. "You can't ask that?"

Tristan wore a face. Tongue darted over glossed lips. Mitch still struck by the overall lameness of the effort. The totem poles were straightened paper clips. Glued on post-it note wings. Ineptly-drawn animal faces. Disturbing to think adults had done it.

"Look how the children are playing in the marsh, Mitch." Alderson baiting him. Prick.

"Mmmm..." Mitch murmured. Bit his lip. Gestured at the treeline.

"Those are lumberjacks," Tristan informed them. "They are about to attack. Haida oral history reveals the white men would first slaughter the children. When Haida artists raced over to discuss peace, they would be tortured and murdered in turn. Genocide was offical Hudson Bay Company policy for centuries."

Tristan rubbed a Tinkerbell nose. Mitch would have enjoyed pulverizing it. And might have if he wasn't preoccupied with the monster dump now hammering at the last hatch.

"That must be what the chainsaws are for," Alderson mused. Mitch bent closer. No question. The lurking forest dwarfs had tiny little mock-up saws. No-talent dickheads had put in some serious glueing time.

"Well, this is…something, alright," Mitch declared. "Yep."

"And more," Alderson tilted his head to the side and back. The wall sported several other crafted wonders.

"Genuine Canadian atrocities," Tristan confirmed. "What our history textbooks are still reluctant to explore fully."

Mitch nearly asked if the little creep had done any time at Sheridan. That was the kind of empty-headed, myth-spinning shit he'd heard before. Mitch suddenly pictured dragging him up a hill behind the ATV. Erase the little prick's superior air. Happy thought.

Yaz appeared.

"Where the hell'd you go?" Mitch asked.

"I thought I heard…something."

Mitch's trouble radar engaged. He turned to the manager. "Ok, Triscuit. Shut up and listen. Find Kemo Sabe. Now. No bossman? Me smash doll boards to shit." Mitch kicked a near table leg for emphasis.

"Chop, chop, twinkletoes," Alderson dropped the act. Threatening edge to his voice. Delayed response. Mitch raised his fist. The manager backpedaled three steps. Pivoted. A voice from the back of the room froze him in position.

"Thank you Tristan. I'll handle it from here."

"But they're not really…" Tristan began. The man approaching held up his hand. Radiated delight. Dali Lama serenity.

"I know. It's fine." Stepped up on the landing.

A moist wave of perfume gagged Mitch. His eyes watered. Alderson also dabbed at a tear. Mitch shot him a quick look. Same disbelief. Standing a metre away was the tallest queer Mitch had ever encountered. Or even read about. Basketball tall. Except white. 6' 11" at least. Maybe more. The man's head nearly brushed against the canoe bottoms overhead. A story for Billy's developing before their eyes.

The face was sculpted. Erected by professionals. Razored eyebrows. Scalloped cheeks. Trowel jaw. Bone china skin, pike belly white. Or dead trull. First hue Mitch was reminded of. Best of all, a pencil mustache. Mitch had never seen one on a live human before. But why not? Intent on self-beclowning? No sense settling for half-measures.

Not content with the cruising vampire look. Creature had draped itself with a fruit drink tropical shirt. Beige beach-bar slacks completed the ensemble. Unbelievable sight. Mitch couldn't imagine appearing like this in daylight. A badly colourized movie set freak. Ordinarily, Mitch would have stood and howled. Right then, he just wanted to get it over with. Other, more pressing matters at hand.

"I'm Tab Bavin," the beanpole said. Over-welcoming smile. "This is my nightclub. How can I help you?"

Tristan chose that moment to bolt. Through the batwings in an instant. Gone. Mitch remained rooted. Had trouble registering what just occurred.

"Did that little canker just beat it outta here?" he asked. Rhetorical question in the face of the obvious.

"Looks that way," a bemused Alderson replied.

"Should I go out and check?" Yaz offered. Took a step towards the front door.

Mitch shook his head. "Fuck it," he snorted. "Where's the little bag-biter gonna hide?"

Mitch stared at Tab. "Besides, what do we tell dispatch? 'All units downtown. Apprehend runaway wheat treat'."

Alderson allowed himself a chuckle. Casually circled until he was behind Bavin. Right hand lodged in his coat.

Mitch put both his hands in his pockets. Looked directly up at the tower. "Any idea why your manager just went ghost on us?"

Blank smile his answer. Mitch suspicious. Light sheen of upper lip perspiration. Room wasn't that warm. Mitch hadn't even taken off his coat. The hormone disaster seemed only half present. Eyes unfocused. Stance uncertain.

"Shit," Mitch blurted out. "He's goofed on something!"

Mitch took three steps closer. Promptly retraced his steps. Looked for Alderson. Laughed. "Wait'll you see him up close."

Alderson nodded. But his eyes never left a spot in the middle of Bavin's back. Mitch read the caution. Unsure what had triggered Alderson's concern.

Mitch gestured at the bar. "Park it, CN."

Took a deep breath. Considered the options. Excuse himself? Walk into the dining room? Release a roadkill fart? Have it follow him like a pet back to the bar? Or just slide it out next to the Tabber. Melt his face off.

Decision reached. Gave Alderson the sign. The vet rubbed the scar over his left eye. Motioned for Yaz to join him. They disappeared into the back of the club.

Mitch took up position. He could almost hear Tab's heart beat. The man looked fragile. A sharp sound might shatter him. The hair pomp less extreme than Triscuit's. Dyed, though. Gunbarrel blue. A cowlick tricked into place.

Something about that face reminded Mitch of black and white movies. His grandfather had a store of them. Guy's name on the tip of his tongue. Famous. Long ago. Same look. Frank somebody.

A sweat bead hung from the manufactured nose. Even a metre away Mitch could tell. The Tabster was on something. Window mannikens looked healthier. More real. Mitch checked the nostrils for crystal. Uncorked the sulphur. Just the thing to clear the film from Bavin's eyes.

Tab on the floor weeping when Alderson and Yaz returned. Exactly fifteen minutes had passed. As telegraphed. Alderson always punctual.

"I knew it," he said. "You and burritos. We can smell it in the back."

Mitch heading to the door. "Not just that. We're wasting time here. Light pole doesn't know anything. As for…Jack Rabbit fuck-face…?"

Alderson nodded. Held up a red digiclip. "Found this. Or…" Credited Yaz. "You should…uh…see this."

Mitch tried to read Alderson's face. Curious look. Gag coming? Didn't fit the moment. "Take long?" he asked. "I need quality time with a roll of Abitibi's best."

Wink from Alderson. "Shouldn't take more than a minute. You'll see."

Mitch kicked Tab in the ribs. "Listen, sis. Cry all you like. But don't move from that fucking spot until I get back. You do, you're dead. Okay?"

A muffled moan. Mitch's favourite answer.

"This way." Alderson led off. Mitch tried to catch Yaz's attention. No luck, no hint.

"Uni's primed," Alderson said after they entered the office. Mitch squinted at the hovering image. Alderson slipped the clip in. Image changed instantly. Mitch agog. He watched in silence. One minute, two. Then he broke. Pounded Alderson on the back. Kicked the wall. Loosed great, shuddering yowls of helpless laughter. Alderson joined in. Even Yaz understood the humour of total self-debasement.

"I can't be…am I seeing…?" Mitch couldn't finish. Alderson held onto the uni stand. Choked back screams. Looked ready to throw something. Anything for release. And so it went for another ten minutes.

Yaz kept an eye on the door. Remained vigilant until Mitch returned. Then outside via the rear exit. Mitch started in giggling again. Alderson caught it. Staggered forward holding his sides until they reached their transpo.

Yaz noted the Braslia's grillwork on the way past. Unique. New model. Spotless condition. Thought of Mitch threatening to key the CORE symbol somewhere. Same time mulling what he'd seen. He really didn't know what to make of it. It was like nothing he'd ever heard about it.

"There's wildlife docs...and then there's other wildlife docs," Mitch wheezed. Collapsed against the Grinder's driverside door. Alderson began to hiccup. Which put both into hysterics. Yaz waited patient, quiet.

Mitch had both hands wrapped around the mirror guard. "Okay, stop," he pleaded with Alderson. "Jesus, I'm going to drop another load if I'm not careful. Don't think about it. Seriously."

"Can't help it," Alderson squeaked.

The sound of his voice. Mitch openly weeping now. "Never seen anything so..." Couldn't get the rest out. Kicked the front tire. Again. Head down. Held onto the radar post. Hammered the armoured hood.

Blind, Mitch still managed to disable the alarms. The cage swung wide. He hopped in. Buzzed Yaz into the back. Started the engine. Almost didn't need the heater. Everyone warm from the best medicine.

Alderson got in. Wiped his face. Controlled his breathing. "Holy Christ," he got out. "Haven't laughed like that since...fuck me, I don't know when."

Mitch punched engine idle. Turned to look back at Yaz. "How'd you find something like that? No way they left it out in the open."

Yaz nodded. Paused. "I stepped on it. Accident."

"Better to be lucky than good, I always say," Mitch grinned. "Fortunately, I'm both."

Mitch looked away. Thought of their little runner. Fell back in his seat. Exhausted. "Jesus...feel like I've just run a marathon."

"I think I pulled a rib muscle," Alderson groaned.

"Me too," Mitch said. "That Triscuit..." Relapse danger. Images still very fresh.

Alderson prayer gestured. Pleading look.

"I know, I know," Mitch acknowledged. "No wonder he ran." Mitch thumbed at the clip Yaz held. "This stuff...have you ever seen anything like it before? Where you're from?"

Negative shake from Yaz.

Alderson held up an index finger. "Heard about it during training. Nothing that fucked up, though. No way."

"The Force?" Mitch asked Yaz.

Yaz stared at the thumbnail-sized drive. It felt toxic. "Never. I had...no idea."

"Is this even legal?" Mitch threw out the question. Alderson mumbled something. Gap in the law. Gray areas. Common pursuit of lawyers, judges. So the rumours went. Successful prosecution unlikely.

"Turn the other cheek?" Mitch joked. Panicked expression from Alderson. Eyes still shiny damp. Mitch stared out the safety glass. Tableaux's great yellow wall before them.

"I'm not kidding," he admitted. "I've never seen…or dreamed anything like that was possible. I mean…I know animals can't testify against you but… shit. I always thought that old Eminem song was just a joke."

"Officially, it's called fletching. Or filching. Or maybe it's fisting?" Alderson said.

"I thought fisting was with your…?" Mitch let the sentence trail off. Arm motion sufficed.

"Oh, yeah," Alderson agreed.

"An 'official' name?" Mitch repeated in disbelief. "C'mon."

"Yeah, I'm sure of it. The nickname's better, though."

Mitch waited.

"Gerbil rockets."

Mitch shook his hand after they recovered from the next laugh jag. Hurt it from beating it on the metal dash.

"It's been around for years, apparently," Alderson explained. "My brother-in-law…well…ex-brother-in-law, used to work in emerg. Sunnyside. Saturday nights? Unbelievable. Fagg-o-rama."

Mitch couldn't steady his hand to light a smoke. Alderson playing him like a silverback. Feed him line. Watch him struggle. Reel him in.

"You wouldn't belie-e-e-eve the things interns have to pull out…or cut out…of some stump-pumper's butt. You name it, Jeremy and his bunghole will give it a shot." Alderson failed to stifle more choking hilarity.

"Example," Mitch said. Chewed on the word. Coughed up smoke. Very much like using a vegetable peeler on his vocal cords.

"Coke bottles, curtain rods, baseball bats…the business end," Alderson said. Arched an eyebrow. Mitch grit his teeth. Nasty thought.

"Cue balls, maple syrup containers, lightbulbs…"

Mitch looked out the window. Saw Alderson's reflection. Couldn't tell if he was taking the piss. "No way!" he managed. "No fucking way!"

"Microphones, umbrella handles…" Alderson continued.

"An umbrella?" Mitch interjected. "You almost had me until that one."

"18 inches. Right up to the handle. I remember that story. I didn't believe it either." Mitch grimaced. Shook his head. Tears cascading down his cheeks. "Fucking o-w-w-w-w!"

"Eggbeaters," Alderson drove on. "Whisks…that thing you use for turkeys, check if they're cooked. Forget what it's called"

Mitch snorted. "Fuck if I know." Glanced back at Yaz. Head shake. Mitch threw his arm over the padded mounting. "Don't believe a word of this shit, man. It can't be real."

"I kid you not," Alderson protested.

"C'mon," Mitch argued. "Something that gross? People would complain. Tax dollars wasted. Right?"

Alderson laughed. "Are you crazy? They don't want that to get out. Wrong message, guru. And you think that's bad? Fucking New York is, like…worse. Ten times worse. He heard stories that would…brain drano." Alderson dead serious now. "Faggo apex down there. Get'em from all over the country. They don't…you know…they don't…they skip the fucking kitchen altogether. Too tame. They head right for the garage. Heavy hitting hardware. Rake handles, steam cleaning nozzles, solar batteries…"

Mitch teared up again. Pounded the steering unit.

"No shit," Alderson said. "Those big industrial fuckers. The six-volt ones. I seen the pictures. Chicago, too. Cook county. Horrible."

Mitch was shaking quietly in his seat. He had to look out the window or start crying again.

"Hard-core, eh? Makes pushing a rat up there seem almost…polite."

"Please, stop," Mitch begged. "I'm going to hurt something."

"How much lube would you need for that, I wonder?" Alderson mused. No mercy.

"Lot." Mitch whispered.

"Oh, yeah. Shit, save time. Swing round to Jiffy's. Bend over. Have'em grease you up."

Mitch buried his half-smoked cigarette in the vaporizer. Clamped his jaws shut. Change subject. Bowl of maggots. Bowl of wriggling maggots. Poured on his Johnson.

"Isn't it cruelty to animals or something?" Mitch slid out through his teeth. "Where are those fucking…pet people…or whatever they're called? Never seem to be around when you need them. I mean, holy Christ! Strapping a harness onto some greased weasel? Pointing him up your bum-buddy's chute? They're good with that?"

Now it was Alderson's turn to lose it.

"I'm serious," Mitch pressed his advantage. "You can't tell me there isn't a law against hamsters hiking the chocolate highway? There's a fucking law against everything else these days."

Alderson dug about in his pocket for a tissue. Leather waterproof.

"Maybe that's why they needed the mic. They wanted to interview the gerbil after. Hotel Rectum. Find how the view was?"

Mitch paused. Watched Alderson gasp for air. At risk of engaging the airbag. Pounded it so violently.

"Rectum? Damn near killed him!"

Alderson, red-faced, tried to hold it in. Made the throat-slitting gesture. Mitch not stopping. Comedy kill coming up.

"I wonder what the animal world limit is? Like, what rodent is too big to bury? Woodchuck? Beaver? Wolverine? Man, picture that last up there. I think you'd wanna medicate it some first. It's not gonna be happy when it figures out where it is."

Alderson hit the panel switch. Fell out of the vehicle.

"Guess that'll learn'im," Mitch drawled to Yaz. Back of Alderson's head visible. Shaking side to side. Did a postman. Looked at the sky for relief.

Mitch victorious. Quick moisture wipe of his own face. Bunch of kids. Caught sight of Yaz in the rearview. Bemused, as far as Mitch could tell. Hoped the whole episode hadn't put the zap on his head. Seeing white people degrade themselves that way. Degrade the species that way. Had to be unsettling. Although he thought he'd heard the Chinese could be equally filthy. Old days. Or maybe that was India.

Tap on the window. Alderson seeking a timeout. Mitch waved him in. Alderson climbed back inside. Gust of unwelcome chill joined him. Tempered the craziness.

"Jesus," he groaned. "I think I have to go back to the shop. Change. I pissed myself."

"You don't wanna eat?" Mitch alarmed.

Alderson shot Mitch a look. "I'm serious. Good thing these seats are 3M-ed. I'm sittin' in urine."

Mitch thought for second. "Hey! Just go back in and use the can here. Tabber's probably still on the floor." Laughed. "I forgot to tell him it was okay to get up."

Alderson snorted. "Are you nuts? I know what you did in there. Ten bucks says you didn't flush either."

Prank anticipated. What a rep does.

"Little thank you present," Mitch admitted. "Cut through the skunk downstairs maybe."

"I can't believe you took the chance." Alderson hunted in a side pocket. Retrieved several spearmint sticks. Offered it around the interior. Mitch pocketed his for later.

"No choice," Mitch said around a freshly lit cigarette. "Especially seeing that first episode. I nearly filled the shorts then."

"Interesting shitter?"

"Didn't look at anything. Papered the seat up good. Last thing I need is a SPID death sentence. Ejected ass baggage. Exit, stage left. Pursued by stink."

"Well, me for the showers. I'm all gluey."

Mitch shrugged. Ten minutes out of his way. Dump over, he felt more amenable to plan disruption.

"Nothing about our case?" Yaz still with them.

"No," Mitch said. Grim reminder. Empty hands. Bulled the Grinder out of the lot, mood heavier. No resistance. Traffic still light. Deep in thought. What now? Could check in with the funny doctor. See if she'd found anything important about Man/dy. Like her identity. Get Yaz on his com. Call people. Could even hit some low spots. Pass around hardcopy photos. Seemed like work, though. Plus, he hated rubbing shoulders with skids.

Hit the binders. The Dolfin in front fishtailed. Ice patch. Mitch tapped his brakes again. Traction okay. For now. Motioned for Alderson to check out the rear window. Glass smeared with shithawk greetings. Mitch laughed at the sight. Pulled up close. Rode the cheap ecobox's bumper. Whole vehicle made from pressed, recycled bumwad. Rolling barbecue. Cereal box coffin on wheels.

Mitch goosed the Grinder. Whipped around it. Veered in, then slowed. Satisfying tire yip as the toymobile screeched to avoid rear-ending him. Thing would crumple like a ciggy pack if it did. Whatever was left, Mitch knew he could back over without noticing it. Hated seeing the shit disgrace on the road. Ruined the driving experience.

Alderson chuckled. Mitch and cars. Man liked to throw his weight around. And the Grinder perfect in that role. The Skankwagon a full-size transpo. Held ten punchboards at a go. Up to eight Dreadies. Three tons total, cargo bay loaded. Warn't nimble, as P.B. would joke. Maneuvering room it got, though. Moronto drivers. Big on bluster. But insurance rates they understood. A Grinder carving up their trunks they didn't need.

Mitch picked up the thread Yaz left. "The Tabber's into some pretty weird shit, but it's just queerio crap. It was obvious he didn't know what I was talking about. Barstew's name he recognized. The rest. Nothing. Ovarians didn't register. Guy is too dipshit disorganized to work a trull dump." Mitch vaporized another heart racer. "Tall fucker. I'll give him that."

"And the manager?"

Mitch thought about it. "I guess. Yeah. Shit, one more hole in my sched. But it'll have to wait until later. Right now, I need food. I'm hungry enough to eat a horse. Chase the rider."

"Were you thinking that new place. The one Lou Sullus opened?"

Mitch nodded. Pushed the beast past a dawdling scum hauler.

"Get in and order for me. My wallet. I'll get someone to drive me back when I've changed. Join you ASAP."

"Deal, brother." Mitch said.

Shop ahead. Drop made, they trundled on. Alderson rolled in soon after, hair still wet. Glasses fogged. Perfect timing. The busty wait-trollop delivering their meal. Inch-thick 500 gr. ribeyes grilled to perfection. Garlic/

basil butter wheel melting into the hash black. Crinkle fries, liberal spray of malt vinegar. Ketchup pool on the side. Carrot for colour. Pitcher of draft. Cherry cheesecake for dessert. Hit the spot. Mitch felt human again. Ready for the afternoon. Yaz had stuffed himself. Couldn't speak. No one at the Force ate so well. Decided to keep that news out of his next report as well.

"Wonder what the poor are having for lunch?" Alderson laughed. Pushed a spotless plate away. Lit up. Several elderly diners sitting nearby overheard him. Mouth-covered titters. Must not be from Toronto if they found that funny, Mitch thought. Half envied them. Fucking last-wave Boomers. They'd lived better that any generation in earth's history. And if it was spent outside of Toronto, they could consider themselves among the luckiest people ever born.

Death was their only concern now. The PC machine couldn't touch them. Unless it was to have their doctors try and turn them into zombies. Mitch had that angle already covered. He'd be fucked if he was going to let a bunch of fag commie losers tell him when he could die. Not on, Lenin-loving hippie shitbag.

The bill appeared on the monitor. Alderson waved everyone off. Deposited his chip. Waited for the thank you melody. Didn't recognize it. No discount prize.

They departed into a sudden sleet fest. Mitch led the way, cursing as they ran. Fucking weather gods must die.

FORE! LOVE OF COUNTRY

⟶⟨◇⟩⟵

A gent Delvecchio laced his shoes. Turned to Mitch. "This really is a brilliant idea. I can't believe no one came up with it sooner."

Mitch waved off the praise. "Not mine. Read about it online. Popular in Florida. Texas. Or maybe it's Arizona. Some hardcore sheriff in the States invented it. Get your info. Have a few laughs doing it. Win-win."

Delvecchio stood, stretched. "And the brass signed off on it?"

"Yeah, well…they want to see progress. Or something. It's starting to get media notice. Stupid sluts."

Delvecchio nodded. Toronto surfing on dead sexbots. He hated turning on the holo any more. Could put you right off dinner.

To Mitch's surprise, Yaz's make-work research had been valuable. Turned out the Tableaux visit hadn't been a wasted trip after all. Triscuit go-boy had a secret. Or another secret. Different from I-hide-rats-in-my-ass. Which is why he legged it. Fortunately, the little uphill gardener couldn't resist his old haunts. A Carlton street holomonitor caught him curb-trolling. The D.P.'s were only too happy to deliver him up to CORE. Mitch made arrangements minutes after the spark arrived.

Deep breath. Shoulder rotation. Lat flex. Neck flex. Ready. Mitch launched himself upright. Grabbed his gloves. Tagged after Delvecchio. The new shoes felt good. Traction. Springy. Worth the money.

They'd just picked up their buckets when a CORE Minion ran up. Skidded to a stop.

"Sirs," the beardless intern said. Slightly winded.

"What is it?" Delvecchio answered. Brusque. Man hated interruptions.

"The…d-d-d…detainee," the Minion deliberately stuttered. Mitch grinned. CORE in-joke.

"What about him?"

"He's offered to talk."

257

"What?" Mitch burst out. Anguish.

"He said he's…he'll tell you everything." The young man gazed at the two legends with open awe. They didn't come any fresher-scrubbed, Mitch thought. Blond lid, high and tight. For size, more tailback than guard. Military bearing. Only thing missing, tail wag.

Delvecchio turned to Mitch. "What do you think?"

"Well, fuck!" Mitch said, annoyed. "We just got here. I'm not driving all the way to fucking Markham just to turn around again. He had his chance before, the little shit."

Delvecchio nodded. "Good argument." Plus, they all needed the practice. In case spring came.

"Right, right, okay" he said to the Minion. "Too late for confessions. Stake him."

The Minion saluted. RMC recruits. Mitch loved them. Well-trained. Well mannered. Keen.

"Rope, sir?" the youngster asked, half-spinning back on his heel. "How long?"

Delvecchio scrunched up his face. Rolled a fleshy beak back and forth. Deliberated a four-count. Exhaled. Shrugged. "First time I've done this. Mitch?"

"Shit, me too." Mitch's turn to weigh options. "I don't know. Thirty? No, twenty. Twenty. Don't want to make it too easy for him."

"Twenty it is," Delvecchio told the Minion. The man stiffened. Wheeled and vanished, quick time. The two men watched him hustle away.

"Like when they do that shit," Delvecchio admitted.

"Yeah. How often you have to charge his fuel cell?"

"Once a day. He's good for sixteen hours."

"Each new model, better than the last."

Mitch found his three-wood where he'd left it. They clomped up the stairs. Nuclear white sky at the top. Dome Alone. The Markham Monstrosity. A hardened carbon shell sheet painted white. Pocked like a Titleist. When empty, as now, grave quiet. You could just hear the roof Ridleys rotate. Air exchangers. Eerie.

Mitch glanced again at his com. He'd booked the facility for as long as needed. Figured to be eating lunch back in the CORE cafeteria. Told told Yaz to meet him there. Ribs, baked spuds, fresh corn on the cob. How Anatole did it was a mystery. Not a feast Mitch planned on missing.

Delvecchio raised his hand. Gestured. "They're here."

Mitch squinted. To their left large shapes approached. Their contacts. A Fed ferret and a court tic, Delvecchio said earlier. Mitch's hackles rose as they neared. The urge to swing on anyone with the government, especially a lawyer, was ever present.

"Look at what he's carrying," Delvecchio whispered.

"What?" Mitch whispered back out the side of his mouth.

"That new Calloway."

"Shit." Mitch recognized the distinctive colouring. Sure enough.

"Two K, minimum."

"Prick."

"Gentlemen," the lead man said. Same height as Mitch. Roughly the same build. The fed, he guessed. Hand out. Shook with Delvecchio. Then Mitch.

"Cliff Andrews. Another agency." Nudge, nudge. Which meant the big guy carefully placing his club against the stand had to be the widow-raper.

Mitch and Delvecchio exchanged names. Did the small talk. The wheel finally sauntered over. A head taller again than everyone present. Didn't look to miss many meals. Mitch noticed the sleek skin tone. The firm jowls. That weird shine. Like buffed steel. Professional handling. Typical of the breed.

As for the eyes. Grey, mirthless, vulpine. Somewhere north, a blind wolf wept.

"I'd like to traduce Clint Bowfin," Andrews said.

"Never heard that before," the human traffic barrier said. Carelessly extended a paw. Firm grip. One pump. Done. Mitch tried his insolent stare. Man wasn't interested. Looked to Andrews. "I've got a two-0 downtown."

Andrews nodded. "Right. What say we warm up? Get things underway."

"Sounds good," Delvecchio agreed.

"Bowfin? That Jewish?" Mitch whispered to Delvecchio on the way.

Pause. "Don't...think so."

"Maybe it's French," Mitch mused. "We had a goalie with that name once. Nope. I'm wrong. It was Boivin."

They hit the ridge. Mitch hefted his club. He did like his three-wood. Rarely betrayed him. Different story, his fickle bitch slut of a nine-iron.

Andrews and Bowfin stretched. Mitch found a pad upwind. Loosened up quick. Felt the juices flow. Good to be out, even inside. He was trying to think. Last time on the links? November? Fucking chilly. He remembered that.

Mitch watched Delvecchio take several practice swings. Mitch's liason for the day. Mitch knew him to say hello. That was it. But the man was famous in security circles.

"Holy shit," he exclaimed. "You're a righty!"

"Yeah," Delvecchio grinned. "Means I have to bring my own clubs to these places. The ones they keep for us freaks are worthless."

They spent the next several minutes taking practice swings. After, Mitch slid his account chip into the machine. Cheery cheep and swallow. Transaction registered. A ball hovered on the tee seconds later. Mitch stopped. Savoured the moment.

"But we have balls, and we can golf," he said, solemnly. "And say the Lord bethankit."

Delvecchio swung. Hooked his drive way right. Laughed. "That one's for the gods."

The crack of a well-struck ball reached their ears. Bowfin. Mitch watched the flight. Dead straight. Maybe 250 yards. Not bad for warmup. Caught Delvecchio's eye. Arched his eyebrows. Player present.

"Yeah," Delvecchio said. "Hope you brought your game today." Grunted, swung, swore.

"Hit'er fat. Shit!" Wide right again. Bounded towards the machine sheds.

Mitch's turn. Addressed the ball. Waggled the head. Let fly. "Under it," he muttered. The ball disappeared into the glare. Bounced just before the 100-yard marker. Still, felt good to swing. They had time for a dozen more. Then a siren blared. Andrews walked over.

Mitch watched the prep action out on the fairway. Waved. "Triscuit! Yo, Triscuit! Over here, little buddy!" Wondered if the bone smuggler recognized him from that distance.

Delvecchio looked worried. "How far off is he?"

Andrews pulled his cap lower to block the light. "Looks to be…150, maybe 170."

"Should have brought an iron," Delvecchio said.

Mitch shook his head. "According to the article, you don't want loft. Flat and straight is best. Two-iron, maybe. Two-wood better. Three best."

Delvecchio didn't look convinced.

"It's good practice, actually," Mitch said. "Keeps your elbow from flying out."

Demonstrated. Short, but in the right direction. "Relax. Watch your follow-through. We're not shooting for distance. Accuracy is king today."

Andrews and Delvecchio shared a glance. Made sense.

The big fed pointed at the sheds. "See the third one…with the green stripe?"

"Yep," Mitch said.

"Watch for the sensor flash. Then the buzzer. Once your intern is safe inside, Bob's your uncle. Swing away."

"Roger that," Mitch nodded. Adrenaline ramping up.

"Oh, fuck!" Gesture at Triscuit for Delvecchio's benefit. "Buttboy's fucking starkers. Too much!"

The big agent gawked out onto the barren field. Pulled at his jersey. "Jesus," he chuckled. "I think you're right. Hard to tell from here, though."

"Those aren't flesh-coloured undies, paisan." Mitch ribbed.

"Then again, if he's anything like you described him, who knows?" Delvecchio countered. "Whatever. Guess we'll find out if he's hiding a weasel soon enough."

"True, true," Mitch agreed. Repeating green light from the shed. Debate over. Their man bolted for shelter. Seconds later, siren scream. The best of sounds.

"Yee-haw!" Mitch shouted. Gut thrill of anticipation. "Puck's dropped. Sticks up, boys!"

Bowfin's solid strike snapped into the windless. Everyone followed suit. Mitch took note of the first barrage. Bowfin's flew well over the frozen Tapette. Andrew's was also off-line. Right height, though. Delvecchio delivered the best of the lot. His attempt skipped a few yards to Tapette's left. Wouldn't have hurt much if it connected. Mitch's effort. Textbook worm-burner. Weak start.

Reload. Another assault. Another mixed bag. On the strength of his first few drives, Bowfin clearly the cream of the group. Mitch skipped a hit to judge his form. Flawless. Full backswing, knees bent, sweet spot contact, PGA arc. Ball left the tee like it was under jet power.

Mitch's swing was pure sandlot in comparison. Other agents compared it to a door with broken hinges. Arnie redux. Mitch didn't care. His was the Drunken Master school of golf. He never played cards except for stakes. And he only ever golfed half-cut. That way, the day wasn't wasted. Now was different, though. Business and pleasure mixed together. The way it should be.

Five minutes in, Triscuit untouched. He had moved as far back from the stake as his rope allowed. Of course, with everyone using woods, he'd have been safer moving closer. Nothing a faggo would know. And no one hitting was gonna clue him in.

"We're looking bad, boys," Andrews yelled. "We'd better find the range. How long we got this thing for anyway?"

"As long as we want," Mitch assured everyone. He wasn't joking. Say the word. The owner would hang up a new sign. "Closed until further notice."

Andrews shanked a ball that dribbled in front of them.

"Good one, Tiger!" Delvecchio jabbed. "Clinic later?"

"Fuck you!" came the response. Mitch smiled. Golfing repartee. You had to like it.

He drilled a missile mere metres over Tapette's head. Glared at his club. "You can be replaced," he muttered. Mitch demanded consistent performance from his clubs. No excuses.

Bowfin continued to launch darts down the field. Mitch could tell he was finding the distance. He'd closed his stance. Shortened the backstroke. The ball's trajectory was frozen rope-like now. Paydirt loomed. Mitch clenched his jaw. Time to buckle down.

The men found their natural rhythm, their zone. An almost musical staccato beat developed. Balls were tattooed, one after another. Drew closer and closer to the dancing Tapette. Mitch was only mis-hitting one in five now. Delvecchio improving rapidly. He just needed to dial back on the power. Andrews had corrected his fade. Bowfin a machine. They had Tapette on the run. Twice he fell when the rope yanked his legs out from under him. Everyone cheered. But it was a hollow triumph. The goal far from accomplished.

Tapette suddenly leaped in the air. "I get him?" Andrews shouted. "I think I might a got him."

"No." Bowfin summarily rejected the claim.

"Didn't see it," Delvecchio chimed in. Mitch wasn't sure. He thought Tapette should be limping more if he'd taken a direct hit. But it was clear wagering had popped up as an idea.

"First one to nail him drinks free tonight," Mitch proposed.

"Done!" the rest said as one. Not so hard to find agreement with the right prize.

"You lucky bastard!" First time Mitch heard Bowfin speak with passion. Near miss again. They poured it on, stroke after stroke. Mitch decided to try bouncing a ball in for the kill. Sound reasoning. As luck would have it, a closer shot startled Tapette. He jumped aside just as Mitch's bounder was set to nail him. And in so doing, Andrew's ball plunked boytoy square in the ribs. Mitch watched it unfold from the beginning. He slumped the same time Tapette dropped.

"Alright, baby!!" Andrews whooped. Pumped his fist in the air. Turned for the gloat moment.

"I should get an assist for that," Mitch croaked.

Delvecchio snorted. Then ripped a shot Mitch had to pause and admire. Even more so when it dipped at exactly the right time to land on Tapette's helmet. The 'ping' echoed all the way to their platform. The ball rocketed into the sky. Tapette remained down.

"What the fuck?" Delvecchio said, bewildered.

"Nice shot," Bowfin said over his shoulder. Not entirely gracious, Mitch thought. A bit of the bluebottle there. Made Mitch happy. He watched Bowfin straighten up. Clear his throat. Sound of wet cement stirred. Discreet hork. Returned to his ball. Released a mighty 'ooff'. Pasted it. The gerbil scourge never saw it coming. Andrew's bullet had range at the same time. Weasel eyes followed the wrong ball. Bowfin's unerring wire-guided effort homed in. Mitch exulted at the sound of impact. Tapette screamed, fell. Rolled about on the artificial turf. Clutched his knee. Banshee wails bounced around the dome.

"Yeah. Helmet. Good idea," Mitch said. "Shit, if that thing had hit him in the head…obit time."

Bowfin rested his gloved hand on the top of his club handle. Barest hint of a smile. "Who's last?" he asked.

Mitch sighed. Man knew when to put in the knife. Fucking lawyers. Took a deep breath. Focused on the ball. Head still. See the club make contact. Don't overswing. The dog knows what to do. Stay within yourself. Ignore the crowd. Bring it back and…

Mental meltdown. Mitch imagined driving the ball through the twit's front teeth. The visual picture broke his concentration. All the clubface caught was air. The ball squirted off the tee, rolled down the incline. He'd barely nicked it. Whisker away from a whiff. He almost fell down himself, laughing. Delvecchio joined in.

"That's showin' him," he cracked.

"Tour on the phone," Andrews joked from afar. Guessed the cause.

"Really," Mitch replied, ear-to-ear grin. "What's my excuse? Nursin' a hangover?"

"Or hangin' over a nurse," Delvecchio said. "Har!"

Andrews joined in. Even Bowfin cracked a genuine grin. With all the bantering, everyone forgot Tapette. Andrews alerted them a few seconds later.

"Hey, boys! I think our twinkie's makin' a break for it."

Tapette remained on the ground. His knees were drawn up. He looked to be working on his ankle strap. If he got loose…? Mitch set his jaw. Not if he had anything to say about it.

"Stand back," he warned Delvecchio. "I mean to catch me a wabbit." His first three attempts were struck perfectly. Two were long. The third was the exact right distance. A little wide left. Still, he'd made Tapette leave off fooling with the rope for a bit.

Andrews applauded.

Delvecchio whistled through his teeth. "Game on."

"Damn straight," Mitch said through clamped teeth. He was determined to earn some bragging rights. Two more shots, they were his.

"Oh, righteous, brother," Delvecchio said in praise. Mitch had caught it a trifle on the toe. Put a nice little spin on it. When it landed, it kicked back towards Tapette. The toad hopped. Too late. No eluding it. Torpedo strike, amidships. It spun Tapette around. He jigged and reeled. The rope went taut, nearly taking his legs out again.

"About time!" Mitch breathed out in relief. "Fuck me."

"Well done," Delvecchio saluted him. Positive feedback from everyone.

Goose egg averted. That hurdle vaulted, the men settled down. An unspoken resolve manifested itself. Be professional. Complete the task. Then celebrate.

Heads bent. Polished balls sat on invisible cushions. Four swings. Four white bomblets addressed to Tapette. One found meat. Andrew's drive winged in. Smashed Tapette's ankle. They all heard it hit. Tapette collapsed like he'd taken a bullet. Quick round of applause. Then resumption of work. For Tapette, no rest for the wicked.

Mitch skulled his next one. Gave up on it at first. The ball hugged the ground like it was avoiding radar. But it had legs and will. It angled in on the distracted Tristan. "C'mon, baby," Mitch quietly encouraged it. "C'mon, c'mon!"

Two bounces. Then, "Nutsack!" Mitch exploded with joy. From Tapette, a soprano howl. Groin clutched, he rolled about on the carpet. Mitch was beside himself. Couldn't have asked for a better result.

"Still want a raccoon up your ass, creep?" Delvecchio yelled.

"Well-placed," Bowfin turned to congratulate Mitch. "The squirrel community will be pleased."

Perp down and damaged. Guys carefully lined up their shots. Delvecchio put a curving screamer into Tapette's back. Mitch followed suit with his own laser. And then it seemed they couldn't miss. Like a baseball team coming out of a collective slump. Success was contagious. Every ball seemed to find a piece of the wretch. Shoulder, kidneys, knee again, thigh, elbow, gut. Helmet strikes like sonar pings. A refreshing rain of pain.

"Repent, shit-stabber!" Mitch yelled out suddenly. Off the top of his head. Delvecchio almost dropped his club. Held onto the partition. Silently shook with laughter for a few seconds.

"Jesus, I'm starting to flag." Andrews said. This after topping his ball well short of Tapette.

Mitch duffed his next shot also. Killer slice making a delayed return. The sheds looked tempting. Ring one off the roof. Keep the boys inside on their toes. Triscuit had ceased to hold his interest.

"You guys had enough?" Andrews asked.

Mitch popped a thumbs-up. Delevecchio had already removed his gloves. Bowfin took a couple more half-hearted swings. Lay his club against the guard.

They all retrieved their chips from the machine. Andrews got on his com to the shed. A Minion cautiously put his head out. Andrews gave the all-clear wave. Several others joined the young intern. They all jogged out to assess the damage. Mitch and Delvecchio headed back to the clubhouse.

"It's not bad," Mitch was saying. "Crunchy. Real cheddar. Tomato sauce. A little salami. Pop it in the Dutch for three minutes. Crack a beer and… voila. A perfect late-nighter."

Delvecchio yawned. "Yeah, I've bought'em before. They're alright. Just too salty for me. I gotta watch it now. My doctor's a fascist. He doesn't even like me to eat mozzarella. You believe that? Me! My people are from Firenze, for Christ's sake."

Mitch shook his head. The unfairness of it all.

Word came to Andrews in the clubhouse. Tapette was alive. Foetal. Weeping copiously. Goth bruising. Lots of injuries. But alive. On the positive side, he'd coughed up names as promised. The confession was being uploaded to interested parties as they spoke. Very toxic material. Heads would roll once word got around.

To his surprise, Mitch got scads of credit for the catch. Tapette's intel proved vital. Not so much in solving his trull case. That would take far more time and effort than Mitch had devoted to it. Or felt like giving. But Tapette supergrassed on some heavyweights. Fully exposed the top end social rot everyone knew existed.

Better still, proof obtained. The buttslug had digiclips. Incriminating, lost to shame acts all over them. Serious public embarrassment for all the right kind of people. The coming bonuses reflected the scale of the find. For which Mitch also earned gratitude from fellow agents. His star, already bright, went supernova.

Bowfin excused himself. Appointment elsewhere. Nodded politely to everyone. Departed. As they all had other duties, it was agreed they'd meet at Billy's that evening. Do a post-mortem. Mitch and Delvecchio exchanged opinions during the walk to their cars. Andrews got the okay. Seemed genuine. That orange hair was something different. Looked like somebody'd glued a sink scrubber to his head.

As for Bowfin. Didn't come off so well. Mitch wasn't shocked. U. of T. nose-in-the-air-super-prick type. That sort always rubbed northerners like Mitch and Frank the wrong way. If he'd had the time, Mitch might have come up with a plan to put a weed up the guy's ass. But he had other matters to attend to. Another day, perhaps.

Speak of the devil. A golden vision purred past. Royal wave. Throaty rumble as Bowfin's metal horse lunged up the drive. First time Mitch had seen the new Chicom Chariot. Sleek styling. Not his kind of dragon, but impressive all the same. Delvecchio had the stats. Top speed—250/kph. Four passengers, air on. Doubleplus outlay. A level or three up from his gift Gringolet. Next life, maybe.

High-pitched farewell chirp at the gates. Bowfin's machine eating a little blacktop biscuit. Growled away.

Mitch nodded to Delvecchio. Found his pet. Climbed in. Patted the dash. Apologized for his wandering eyes. Pledged undying love.

Gutteral bark. The twelve-cylinder powerplant woke up. Happy power rumble. Apology accepted.

Mitch slipped in a music mint. Perfect random selection. Oldie but a goodie. Updated cover. Original tune by Hamilton's best-ever punk band. 'Elton is dead! Elton is dead! The big fat fag is dead, dead, dead.' Great song. He belted out the chorus rest of the drive back. Gave the finger to the over-curious at lights. Fucking critics.

Mitch sped out of the lot in high spirits. Great morning's work. Deep satisfaction. An afternoon terrorgation would put icing on the cake. Tried to remember if CORE had rounded up any idiot agitators lately. He was in the mood for a little anti-whatever smack around.

Not to be. Excellent lunch, as anticipated. Routine afternoon. Cursory check on any breaking trull news. Yaz back following more research. Had nothing. Primary 'spects remained the Ovarians. Slaughter purpose still a head-scratcher. Mitch agreed with Yaz. Slow but sure the way to success.

So…measured steps the game plan. No Tank drills on tap. Fucked around the office. Walked brisk to the can. Looked busy. Fired off a fake fan letter to Whitey. Promised big boom boom. Put down Chemo's com number. Loafed around Juicy's work station for ten. Pretended to chat. Mostly stared down her top when he could. An hour of Velikovsky's Revenge on the holo. Planet wide destruction. Day's best score. Then quittin' time. Packed it in. Did a workout. Headed for Billy's for the fish 'n chip special. That's where the earth-shaking news would arrive. He planned to be there, beer in hand.

Bowfin showed up that night. Everyone surprised. Carried shocking intel. As Andrews and Delvecchio were just turf reps, they sauntered off. Drink. Throw some darts. Just as well. The more the lawyer revealed, the angrier Mitch grew. Triscuit had delivered. A subsequent raid on Tableaux had unearthed a shoebox worth of incriminating shit. Microdiscs with all manner of nauseating imagery. Monstrous acts. Confessions forthcoming, Bowfin assured Mitch. His offer to tear them out, organ by organ? Noted and appreciated.

In a sense, the discovery simply confirmed the obvious. Anyone with eyes to see knew it already. Generation-stupid-hippie. Pioneered sex, mind-altering drug consumption and rhythm. But that wasn't enough. Had to destroy Western civilization as well. Treacherous fuckwits. Zombie devotees of a despicable Cause. Morons.

Bowfin shared Mitch's contempt. That the man couldn't abide fools was clear. Mitch watched him throw back his Scotch. Two-fisted drinker. Mitch admired that.

He gazed over at Andrews. Man joshing with spectators. Right at home minutes into the place. That hair. Instant topic of conversation. The check bowling check shirt also drawing abuse.

"Canada," Bowfin was saying. Back to the Ovarian connection. "Harpy haven. Why are so many completely fucking insane?"

Mitch had no idea. Not the first time he'd heard the question. And long before he'd heard of the Ovarians. Fucked-in-the-head feminists. Fact of life. Might as well rage against glaciers. Mosquitos. That fucking crow that ruled the tennis courts near his condo. Gun laws or no, Mitch was taking it out if the chance arose. Goddamn pre-dawn screeching. Scraped his nerves raw.

Bowfin took his time. Painted the big picture. Put names to faces to deeds. Mitch was ready to cut witch by then. Bowfin argued against it. The ground was being prepped. Had been for some time. CORE knew more of the puzzle than Mitch realized. Wondered if his was the "lurp" role. A long-range recon guy. Map terrain. Hunt, pursue, draw fire.

Whatever. He was in the loop now. Bowfin assured him of that. When the shit-rain came down on the Ovarians, Mitch would get a front row seat. And his own shit cannon. All Mitch wanted to hear. Eagerly followed Bowfin's summary. War declared. Ovarians had the high ground. Old media totally compromised. Universities owned. Supporters salted everywhere. Lickspittle bureaucrats in the bag. Those sack-suckers would agree to anything as long as their pensions were guaranteed. Oh, it was a ripe mess all right.

CORE and other agencies slow off the mark. But making up for lost time. Marshalling troops. Gaming scenarios. Stockpiling weapons. They'd have normal citizens behind them when they played Garry Owen. That was a known known. For now, the phony peace. Low-level action. Sniping from afar. Except for all the dead trulls. Even Bowfin couldn't hazard a guess as to the strategy.

By evening's end, Mitch and Bowfin best buds. Hard to believe. Mitch's "What's-black-and-brown-and-looks-good-on-a-lawyer? A: Dobermans" joke broke the ice. Bowfin's thousand-yard stare? An act. Man knew a half-dozen thigh-slappers himself. Wallaceburg, the briefcase snake's home stomping grounds. Mitch knew people nearby. Bowfin even had family on Walpole Island. One-eighth Chippewa. Or so he claimed. Mitch nodded and smiled. Heard that before. Hunky blondes. Bog Colleens. Platinum job fine arts majors. Same thing. Great-great-grandma was a Plains Indian. Right. Okay. Mitch knew how to keep their wigwam. With wampum. Because women were women everywhere. So shuck off the buckskins, Pauline. Grey Owl needs Native nookie.

Anyway, true or not, doors opened. Grants, bursaries, scholarship to U. of T. Next up, reading the law. The rest, history. Osgoode. Creative shading of the truth taught. Ho, ho, ho. Rapid rise to Crown prosecutor.

Star rep developed. Became an inter-agency gun for hire. Ruthless, deadly—courtroom or boardroom. The trail of vanquished caught CORE's attention. Legal replanted him in government. Had him run interference for CORE. Targeted symps and sap activists. Mastered his brief. Anticipate problems. Bury embarrassments. Hence, his presence at the driving range. In the event of an accident, Bowfin knew where to hide the body. Literally. Invaluable man to have on your team.

Mitch shared a highlight reel of his life in return. Possible pro-hockey career interrupted by blown knee. Two year stretch at Sheridan college after. Talent for illustration, especially caricature. Fish out of water. Hated the Che curriculum. Hated the Che teachers. Hated the Che students. And they hated testosterone. Sayonara and fuck you, commie fag wankers.

"Entertainment" work, then. Mitch skipped over the details. CORE on a trial basis. For institutional reasons, no patch. Same ice time as the regulars, though. As a parting gesture, Mitch penned a napkin portrait of Bowfin. Bowfin liked it enough, framed it. Pride of place on his office wall. Friends for life. And Mitch had a lawyer he could call anytime, day or night. Suddenly, that was a comforting thought. Better to have a lawyer and not need one, Bowfin had argued. Mitch realized that made sense. Unsavoury though lawyers were. As a subgroup of the species.

An hour later, they were rooting on Delvecchio and Andrews. Both had ruled the darts board since they started throwing. One of those nights. They couldn't miss, either one. Mitch sucked at the game. So he was delighted to see his tormentors crushed and humiliated by outsiders. Made faces. Mocked and scorned. Great fun.

Between bouts, Bowfin regaled him with pisstank relative stories. Darwin Award candidates, all. The cousin who ran over another cousin late one night. One driving, one lying on the road. Both hammered. Another relative held up the bar all day at the local hole. Decided to swim home after closing time. Funeral later. Cremation impossible. A cousin who fell out of a tree. Trying to retrieve a two-dollar fishing lure. Broke his neck. Drowned an inch from shore. In an inch of water. Funny.

The only negative note for the night. Tapette survived the surgery. After what they'd learned about his extra-curricular activities, it seemed a shame.

Otherwise, a productive day. Mitch stretched out on his bed. Alone. Still musing on intel Bowfin mentioned. "Project 89." Related to their Ovarian case. Tapette had moaned it into a mic as well. Turned up on material they found in his closet. Whispers of it elsewhere. No one knew what it meant, Bowfin said. But it gave Mitch a start. He just then remembered the first time he'd seen it. On the digiclip someone had deposited in his smokes that night at Billy's. Project 89. Too tired to make any sense of it. Mitch went down. Slept like the dead.

WENDY KENSILLA GOES SOUTH

—◄◇►—

Miami was hot. Filthy. The cabin readout flashed 99F/36C. Ugly, twisted numbers.

Arrivals Terminal passed by. Special plane. Special passengers. Special cargo. It taxied on for anther 500 metres. Hard jerking stop.

"More practice," Stewart muttered, picking peanuts off his pants.

Order given. The men gathered their gear. Jokes and jostling. Spirits high. Like a road trip for the younger guys. Mitch also pumped. Not because everything was hush-hush secret. Over-mysterious shit bored him. And everyone knew the mission was huge. Mitch just liked being out of rainbow town.

True, though. The identity of their package remained unknown. Bets were laid. Who flew freight? Captured terrorist? Found traitor? Major thief? Toilet trader? The pot got returned. All answers right.

Outside, a bright Disney sun swung at them. Milky blue skies to either side. Industrial strength humidity lapped up the escalator. March break in FLA. Welcome…students. With money. Gash Gone Grrrilla. Too late, actually. Might still be a few head catchers on the loose. Be a shame not to bag any. Travel all the way down from the Great White North. Miss out on the brown bouncers parade? Cosmic wrong.

"Moose" Vasco checked his com. "Shit," he complained. "Fucking glare."

They were last off the plane. The tarmac felt gluey. "My old man would croak down here," Vasco said. Breathed in with distaste.

"Pretty close," Mitch agreed. "Didn't realize it got this muggy. Worse than Stinkytown in August."

"Oh, yeah," Vasco said, pulling out his blockers. "This is your first time. Forgot."

"Dominica and Jamaica. That's it." Mitch donned his shades as well. Joined the rest of the crew.

A trio of men walked towards them. Mitch had seen them from the plane window. All wore baseball caps. Different colours. Different lettering. HomeSec. Mitch guessed. Dressed for the weather. Short-sleeved camo tops, various shades. Combat shorts. Ranger boots.

"Very Southern," Jenkins side-mouthed. "A black, a Mex, and the KKK."

A catcher's mitt shot out from the husky A frame. Oval face, beacon red. "Earl Thigpen," the mouth said. "HS liaison, Florida branch."

CORE lead Archie Stone shook hands. Introduced himself.

The American gestured to his companions. "Chick Hernandez, Art Baker."

"Team Canada," Stone joked. Thumbed at the twenty plus herd gathered behind him. A semi-circle of hot and sweaty bulkmeat. The oppressive heat shocked no one but Mitch. Florida a sauna in late March. Everyone ready for a swim. And a beer. Or ten. This was vacationland. Mixing work with R&R expected. CORE agents were accomplished party fiends.

Mitch's foreams prickled. Perspiration tunneled under his shirt. Raced down his crack. Not pleasant. Pothole City had been overcast when they left. The usual shitty miserable. His body used to crap weather. He'd taken more heat units in five minutes than all winter in Canada. Cursed himself. Packed his cap. Somewhere difficult to find, he knew.

Mitch panned the lamps around. Fixed on the covered conveyor.. A wave from the lead American. CORE converged under the canopy. Brief ride. Mitch watched rising heat shimmer. Like traveling underwater.

A gated area appeared. They cornered near it. Quick sprint through the link fence barrier. A sweating security stooge watched them troop past. Refridgerated air surged around them as they entered the building. Group relief. Mitch stopped kicking himself about absent headgear.

Customs a breeze. The recently installed JCS (Joint Coding System) speeded the process. CORE agreed to the surgery. Reluctantly. Determined to keep matters smooth, frictionless. The RISO chip data uploaded as they entered the building. Unknown to the Yanks, CORE engineers jury-rigged a kill-pulse device. Once the team was back on the plane for home, the units would be disabled. Good-natured middle-finger to their Yank friends. You never knew about the black bag boys. Clever lads. They did like their gizmos, the Americans. Try for a little special ops. long-distance peeping. The friendly rivalry continued.

Two new reps met them in a conference room. Both black. Both large. Skull cuts. Tatt-free. Green fatigues, ramrod posture, HS smiles. Ousiders present. Wary, even if they weren't sword-of-Allah types.

Greetings. Welcome. Hands across the border intro. Something,

something, something else. Mitch examined the meeting room. Every building in the world had the exact same one. Must be a rule.

Try not to kill anyone, the man continued. Or burn anything down. At least without express permission of the American government. That seemed the nub of the talk.

"Your package has been escorted to our transport vehicle and secured," the larger of the speakers, announced. Sargent Preston. Mitch overheard later that was his real name. Not his rank. His partner's name was Bubba. Bubba James. Super-sized. Not far removed from the gridiron. Biceps the diameter of manhole covers. Mitch didn't picture the name being popular among the oppressed set. But it was way better than Kwingi, Kwamala, Kwanzaa or some of the other made up names he'd heard. You know what you're getting with a Bubba.

"No problems, I hope," co-leader Powers spoke up. Mitch didn't know the man. Both leaders were upstairs guys. Royal Canadian Army links. Pentagon contacts. Mitch didn't care. He was happy just being invited to the party. In the meantime, wagons, ho! James made a needle jabbing motion at his forearm. So they'd put the 'spect down for a nap. That lent weight to the baddie jihadi theory.

Prescott goosed things. "Okay, guys," he said, slapping his hands together. "Motion to the ocean. Let's move."

Verspank grinned in excitement. Ran his hand over a spade face. Long, narrow and hard. Caught Mitch's eye. Core signal. Mitch laughed at the message. You could dress the man up but...

Guys drifted after James and Prescott. Dreamed of cool pools, tall glasses, naked babes.

Thigpen brought up the rear. Chuckled to hear complaints about the humidity.

"You Northern boys always say that. But we keep see'n y'all down here again when you retire."

"We're just redneck NASCAR retards at heart," Baldwin said to mocking laughter. Turned. "Anybody got family down here?"

Several men raised their hands.

"Uncle," Jenkins said.

"Grandparents," Wilson admitted. "Naples."

"Every winter my folks pack up and..." Weir began. A com buzz cut him off. Prescott held up his hand. Answered it. Listened. No talking. Signed off. Mitch noticed the camo design. Wondered if you could order it online.

"Everything's set, gentlemen. Follow Captain James." Prescott and Towers moved in behind the man. CORE did likewise. They strolled down a standard corridor. Then passed through a non-standard sensor web. Light tingle. Not unpleasant. Out into a vast underground parking area. Several armoured transpo's sat, idling. Everyone piled in. On the road in five. Where to? Speculation rampant. The beach? A photo shoot with nudies? Invading Cuba? No one even close.

The rest of the morning a blur. The flight wiped Mitch. Not to mention having partied hard the night before they left. He got comfortable. Nothing to see outside anyway. Strapped himself in. Dropped off immediately. Fitful sleep. Great fuck dream ended by speed bumps. Terrible timing. Took him a second to orient himself. No snow. No hot tub. No mermaid pumping the milk handle. So-so air conditioned troop carrier didn't compare.

The vehicle slowed. Rocked to a stop. Back hatch open. Guys humped out. Punched upright by the heat. Rubbed eyes against the harsh light.

A squad of soldiers faced them. Tenth Mountain pool cleaners for all Mitch knew. Or cared. They didn't look pissed or anal. Mostly bored. Garden-variety escort team.

Their leader engaged Stone and James in a brief conversation. Mitch breathed deep. Salt water. Great smell. Eyes adjusted, he looked around. They were on some kind of mammoth pier. Derricks and container donkeys dotted the near shoreline. Cruiser hulls rose tens of metres above them. Shadowed water only. Egg yolk sun blazing above. Mitch wasn't sure he'd missed anything not visiting. Like being in an oven.

Sound of chains bouncing in chutes. Hammering. Welding flares. Aroma of scorched metal. Repair area.

The men drifted away from the troop buggy. Mitch ran his fingers across the vehicle's side plating on his way past. Hummer Mark XX. Looked impenetrable. Solid state. Seamless. He'd read about them. Carbon-fibre blend. Poured from a mold. Grenade proof. Rocket proof. Cool to own one. Mileage would be a cunt, though. Even with the L-ion battery. Traffic? Fuck off. Even the Gringolet would have to yield to this sucker. As for that new Hangzhou Heavenly Fart? Roadkill. Grill matter. Hose off what remained of the passengers. Plead ignorance. Plausible deniability.

He joined Wilson. "Where are the rides?" he joked. "I wanna see Mickey. I wanna fuck Minnie. While he watches!"

Wilson shook his head. "You have a sick mind, Milligan." Scanned the area. "What are we doing here? I haven't heard squat."

"We zip in, we zip out," Mitch murmured. "Like Czechoslovakia."

"Where?" Wilson asked. Then, ""Hey, look!" Pointed up and left.

Mitch squinted. "Oh, yeah. There you go." A pelican arced past a ship's antenna tower. Graceful and stupid-looking at the same time. "You hungry?"

"Famished."

"Me too," Mitch said. "Let's see if we can't score some snack-ola. Must be a vendor around here somewhere. We seem to be in hurry-up-and-wait mode now."

Wilson flanked him. "Sounds like a plan, man."

No sooner had they slid past the carrier than a whistle blast pierced air. Prescott appeared from nowhere. Waved for attention. Explained the itinerary. Said food had been laid out. Let the cheering die down.

"What a great day!" a gap-toothed Clark exulted near Mitch. "And it's just beginning!"

A giant trundler pulled up. The men threw their kit on the platform. Pulled themselves up onto the flatbed. The escort team spun. Marched off.

"Back to the barracks, boys!" a high-spirited Weir yelled. "They got paid for that?" he added to group chortles.

Prescott and a portion of the HS honour guard rode the caboose. Bright orange eight-wheeler. The convoy rolled away. A short jaunt around the jetty, they were told. Major port from Mitch's perspective. Menacing bluewater cruisers sat silently at berth. Ramps speared the concrete deck. Cranes in action far above. At anchor on the other side, a selection of spectacular yachts.

"Christ," Mitch heard someone behind him say. "This must be where Gates and that kind keep their toys. Look at the size a these fuckers."

Mitch was equally drop-jawed. The scale, otherworldly. Nothing he'd seen on Georgian Bay came close. He turned to Jenkins, bouncing beside him. Shook his head. "Fucking America, eh?"

Jenkins pointed at a space between the dock and the prow of a gleaming white bay beauty. "Just room enough there for my 16-footer. What do you think the day rates are for bass boats?"

Mitch just snorted. "I think they'd sink it on sight. With you in it." He stretched. Shirt clung to him like plastic wrap. Breeze off the ocean helped. A little. And then…a wave of joy swept over him. "Motherfucker!" he exclaimed to no one. "Ya gotta like this job."

"No shit, eh?" Jenkins agreed. "Wonder what they're doin' in…" Bit it off. Close. Forgot about the driver. Wouldn't likely get the joke.

"Not this. I'll guarentee you," Mitch said, finishing the thread.

Five more minutes. Left turn. New pier. Prescott and group pulled alongside.

"This is it, boys. Grab your stuff. Hit the deck."

The Canadians jumped down. Twenty pairs of eyes gazed up. Disappointment. They stood in front of what looked like a derelict. Some old freighter, scrap yard ready. Paint flaked portholes. Shit-haloed rivets. Seams bleeding rust. Up close, worse. Several coats of cement gray held things together. Mitch took a deep breath.

"Are we here?" someone whispered.

"Figures," another added bitterly.

Mitch noticed Prescott's face working. Seemed to be enjoying their reaction. Prick.

"Hope it doesn't go down while we're on it," Mills said over his shoulder to Mitch as they entered the hoist.

"Everyone here can swim, right?" Mitch asked.

"We're probably here to fix it," Henderson grumped. "Or paint it."

"Jesus, don't say that," Mitch winced. He'd scraped and painted boats one summer. Never again.

Everyone assembled on the top deck. Prescott spoke.

"Welcome aboard the Wild Rose. The Captain sends his regrets. He will see you later at the banquet. He's preparing for departure at present."

"Party!" came a jubilant whisper. "Y-e-e-e-s-s-s!"

Joy replaced despair. The promise of food and booze trumped all. It was an abiding CORE characteristic. Get handed a shit sandwich? Crack the vodka. Get shit-faced.

Mitch heard Billington describe a wild rose.

"Don't look anything like this tub, I'll tell you that much. Back home, if this was a horse, we'd shoot it." Motormouth gibes from others. Billington's old man was a surgeon in Edmonton. Guys doubted he'd ever been near a horse. Which wasn't true. The family had property outside the city. Bred Arabians. Mitch had seen the pics. Horses did nothing for him.

As the banter flew, Mitch contented himself taking in the view from the deck. Not many Edmund F's dropped anchor at the Kap. To the side of the bridge, a scrap of horizon. Liquid sky met water. Flat blue lips pressed together. Mitch felt the giddy surge. Marble face. Resisted rubbing his hands together. Not easy.

"Short meeting, then lunch," Prescott said with amplified voice. "Follow me, please."

The men entered a shaded, open corridor running along the main bridge side. Mitch pulled himself along the railing. No fear of heights. At the same time, it looked to be a solid fall to concrete. Parachute-roll all you like. Bye-bye fib and tib.

Gasps from ahead. Prairie dog alertness from those bringing up the rear. Guys filed through a hatchway inside. Mitch steeled himself for the worst. The "Holy fuck!" outburst from Poole didn't calm anyone.

And then Mitch was in. Two steps down, one to the side. Eyes wide, mouth slack. Same as everyone else.

"Are we dead?" an agent whispered.

"If we are, I'm all for it," somebody replied.

Mitch glanced around. Nothing to hang on to. Knees gone weak. Prescott waited. Hatch seal. He flashed a mind-reading smirk.

"The Red Deer Room." Swept his hand to encompass the vista. Breathtaking. Before them lay the grandest banquet hall Mitch had ever seen. Even in picture books. Dark panelled walls surrounded them. Stretched away for thirty metres or more. Giant mirrors, bookshelves. Cabinets lined the length of the room. Everything glittered from dazzling chandelier light. Mitch had trouble taking it all in. Too much, too soon.

Several leather chesterfields. Clumped near one of several fireplaces. Why a fireplace in Florida, Mitch would wonder later? A scrum of armchairs and footstools lay hard left. Inset bar down the wall. Mitch's heart jumped. Had to be after six somewhere.

Off in the middle, a phalanx of serving tables. Snow-white linen lapped down the sides. Silver glinting everywhere. Platters and…goblets, Mitch guessed, arrayed in ranks. Candle flames guttered in the air conditioning jetstream.

Women in spray-painted costumes bustled about. Reflective black leggings. Red vests cinched in place with thick leather belts. The ruffed blouses barely able to restrain the top-heavy treats within. Topped off with round little monkey grinder hats. Red straps. Sort of cute. All looked fresh-faced, alert, eager to serve.

None of CORE had strayed far from the entrance. Uncomfortable shuffling. Side to side movement. Up and down the steps. Like a rock slide that ran out of momentum.

"Anyone else feel underdressed?" Jenkins captured the general feeling.

"I'm waiting for someone to tell us there's been a mistake," Wilson offered. "Give us brooms or something."

"I'm not polishing silver," Poole said to laughter. "Forget that shit."

Cutlery and crockery appeared. Jenkins found Mitch's eyes. Bending elbow gesture. Looked to his right. Fist pump from Mitch. The drinks tray!

"This…is more what I had in mind," Anderson breathed.

"It's like Hooters," Jenkins agreed, "only for rich people."

"Better than Buffalo Creek."

"Better than my apartment."

"Which isn't saying much."

"At least I don't live with my mother."

"You would if she fucked like mine does."

"Guys, guys," Anderson shushed everyone. "We're guests. Let's not scare the whores."

"Look at all the knight's shit," MacDonald said. Then they noticed. Gold and purple banners fell from the great ceiling beams. Brass flutes jutted from wall posts. Billings pointed out the crossed swords and shields.

"Yeah, there's other castle stuff over in the corner," Poole said. Mitch looked. Blinked. Suit of armor standing against the far wall. Missed it before. Or brain couldn't accept it. Real? Why not? The whole room had that wonderful smell of too much money.

Prescott returned from talking with the maitre'd. Or whoever the funeral-looking guy was. Chuckled to see them milling about, nervous and awkward. "No standing on ceremony here, guys. C'mon in. Make yourselves at home."

Anderson looked back at everyone. Shrugged. "Fuck it. You heard him. Their fault. They invited us in."

With that, everyone relaxed. Spread out to explore. Mitch gravitated to the furniture. Others did likewise. A lot of CORE guys handy with tools. One agent had his cabinetmaker papers. Mitch couldn't remember who.

Looking at it, it was clear the stuff was quality. Great finish. Heavy. Solid. Mitch lusted after the sideboard. His grandmother had antique shit. Bureaus. End tables. Dressers. Cherry, mahogany…something else. Walnut maybe. Too bad none of it would look good in his condo. Modern shit didn't mix with traditional. Also didn't last. Or look half as good. The best thing? No particleboard crap. On the other side. If the bookshelf across from him fell on you? Kiss your ass goodbye.

"Some nice crap in here." Wilson said.

"No lie," Mitch agreed. Ran his fingers over an ornate end table. Way out of his salary range.

The crumpets circulated. Arranged dishes on the tables. Mitch blazed a smile at one napkin nymphet. Return grin, sexy pregnant. Dimples you could slot playing cards in. Eyes that said ready, willing, free. His heart skipped. Things just kept getting better…and better.

"Jesus, clear all the furniture out. Lay down a sheet of ice. You could do four on four, no problem," Jenkins boomed. Faked a slap shot at Mitch, who shot his left hand out to glove the puck.

The room wasn't quite that large. Not for a rink. A few tennis courts laid end to end, though. Mitch had seen money while he was an escort. This was a different level of rich again. What…the…fuck were they doing there?

Wilson whistled. Wet bars were wheeled in. Happy hour! Hoo-ah!

"Refreshments, gentlemen!" Prescott again. Broke from his conversation with some military guy. Navy, maybe. Burned-in tan. Middle-aged, like Prescott. Half the size. Leaned against a woodclad support beam like he owned the place. As luck would have it, they'd meet later. After the craziness. He wasn't the owner. Did congratulate Mitch, of whom he knew thanks to Stone. Lauded CORE. Saluted the sponsor. Got around to offering Mitch a job, if he wanted one. Mitch quite drunk. Never even remembered the discussion until days later. Back in TO. And he'd lost the guy's business chip by then. Shit happens. No way he was living in that kind of swamp atmosphere anyway. But what a day. Anything could and did happen.

"Order whatever you want," Prescott advised. Must have anticipated the deep thirst they'd feel. "On the house, of course. But save some room for lunch."

Feet found pile. Agents filed forward. Prescott doing a joke Mengele impression. Finger-waved men right and left. Chatted up a storm. Mr. Congenial.

Like everyone else, Mitch was parched. Nothing tasted better than a beer when you've been hard at it. Unless it was the trussed pineapples bobbing before him. The tender trap pulling taps looked barely into her twenties. Sleek, shiny pelt. Hair spun southern style. Lush flesh. American look, top to tush. You just knew her shit didn't stink. Place in oven. Toast until brown. Slather with butter. Part and enjoy.

She eyed Mitch. Read his mind. Ran an alligator over her lips.

Mitch mouthed 'Do you fuck?' at her. She giggled. Made the sign. Mitch's turn to laugh. Beer before boom-boom. His motto also. Ordered something called Pabst. Got it down in one long swallow. Tried something from Milwaukee. Also absorbed it in seconds. Dry wasn't the word. Cactus. His third was some draft-in-a-can thing. Which didn't make sense. Decided to slow down a bit. Day was young.

"From B.C," Panzer said to listeners. "You can get it in Alberta, though. Weird seeing it here." Agents scrambled for the remaining stock. Hadn't expected to find anything Canadian. Even if most had never heard of Kokanee brand suds. Home was home. Maybe the water was a little cleaner.

The men drifted around. Shared looks. One joke and the place would break out in crazed chuckling. Anything too good to be true always was.

Jenkins drifted near again. Conspiratorial look.

"What's going on? You heard anything?" Like the rumour mill ever put out anything accurate.

Jenkins ran his fingers through platinum hair. Rubbed the Roman. Blinked the black lamps. "You know what I know. Fuck all. Show up at the island. Bring your travel kit. We're taking a trip. That's it."

Mitch reached over. Fingered the wall hanging material. Thick. And the fringe was threaded with some silky shit. Released it. All around the room. Official-looking provincial crests. What he overheard Older say, anyway. Wondered where you ordered shit like this? Not cheap. No store he'd ever been in. Meaning?

A bell rang. Clearest tone he'd ever heard.

"Penny drops?" Jenkins said. Mitch cocked his head. Hunched his shoulders.

Nothing so serious. Prescott again. He clapped his hands. Smiled. World's friendliest host.

"Gentlemen, festivities are about to begin. Sorry to keep you waiting. Lunch is served on the upper deck. If you'll follow me."

They assembled again up top. Breeze was better. Sun still on full broil.

Stone cleared his throat. All eyes swiveled to find him. "This might interest some of you. We're on a Canadian Vickers Pocket Cruiser. Commissioned in 1968, decommissioned…" Stone paused. "Not sure. Anyway, as you can see, it's undergone some…redecorating." Appreciative chuckles. Dry humour. "More on that later."

Two hours would pass before the big ship reached its destination. During that time Mitch and Team CORE got the rest of the refurbishing tale. They also wolfed down a cow, several pigs and a whack a chickens. All sacrificed for the greater good. The best subs and sandwiches they'd ever eaten. All the fixings, fresh as day. To wash it down, orange juice so good Mitch felt ten percent healthier in an instant. Then beer. Energy drinks, sodas, anything you wanted. Variety was the word.

A tour followed. Chance to stow gear in their staterooms. Rub up against the maids. Undo their belts and buttons. Make them laugh.

"You know the best thing about a beer and beef feed?" Anderson said. Threw himself into a deck chair next to Mitch. "Having one fixed for you when you really want it."

"No Corona." Mitch feigned reproach.

"I didn't see any garlic salt either. Shoddy operation. We should dash and not pay."

Mitch shaded his eyes. "Not sure about the dashing. Diving, maybe. I don't see shore anywhere." To all sides, glycerine green ocean. Aqua gel. Nothing like the hard cobalt blue of Superior or Huron. Pure invitation for fun.

Cotton ball clouds drifted with them. Tailing wind. Enough to snap flags. Take some of the heaviness out of the air.

Shithawks snaked and wheeled above the wake. Mitch yearned for his rifle. What better place for some sport shooting? Middle of the ocean. Total safety. No butt clumsy sound hunters within a hundred klicks. Caught himself breathing deep again. That tangy sea air. Loved it.

The ship churned through light swells. Almost no motion. Like being on a ferry, James said earlier. Any fears about being in open water on a wreck faded away after the tour. The bridge rigged out like a spacecraft. State-of-the-art navigation, propulsion. Comsat links. More. Or so the guide claimed. Piracy rampant in some parts of the world. Better to appear a junker. No jewels, no interest.

Any piracy attempt would get an ugly surprise, though. Long before a grappling hook found purchase villains would be doing the Somalian crawl. Face down. Motionless. For days at a time. The ship was a floating weapon. 120 mm cannons concealed everywhere. Aegis quality intel. Mine-laying capability. Torpdeo bay. Could actually go hovercraft for short, high-speed bursts. The guide joked it could have cleaned house at Jutland. Which meant bugger all to Mitch. He'd never even heard of the country. Still, he felt way better about his chances of surviving the trip in one ever-lovable piece.

The deck chair complained a bit as Mitch leaned back. Closed his eyes. Let another wave of contentment roll over him. He was almost asleep when another whistle sounded. Extreme high-pitch. Anderson rattled a lengthy fart response. Got everyone laughing.

"Showtime, ya' think?" Eyes darted around.

"Must be," Mitch said. Pulled himself out of his chair. Stretch, yawn, scratch ass. Time to meet the Pope.

A line of men waiting. Heads bobbing down the spiral ladder to the deck below. Mitch laughed. Verspank and Vasco in front of him. At it again.

"Said it before. You ain't much if you ain't Dutch."

"Wooden shoes, wooden head, wouldn't listen."

Badgering, jawing, needling. CORE was back. Found their sea legs. Full stomachs. Beers and Bev's. Beautiful ocean. Throttle up. Fun time comin'. You could feel it.

They converged on the lower deck, stern. Larger than expected. Shaped like an inflated arrowhead. Room to toss a football. Short passing game. Going long could be risky.

Air electric with purpose. Men in uniforms. White shorts, light blue short-sleeved shirts, rig runners. Most tech prepping. Curious-looking shit. Navy grey. Composites. Bubble domes, erect tubing, antenna stacks. None of it Mitch had ever seen before. Not even in Holly holo's.

Mitch saw several team members grouped near the ship's end. He, Jenkins and a few others joined them.

"We've dropped anchor," Mills said as they approached. "Something's up."

Johnson's watchful eyes followed the crewmen. Half-scrambling with cable-thick ropes. Sweat stains creeping over beltloops. Laddering down fronts. No surprise. Mitch was ready to jump into the ocean. Plead accident.

"Beer?" Mitch asked. Light a candle. Deal with the heat or whinge about it.

McIntryre nodded. The red-faced giant lofted an index finger. Threw his arm forward. "Why we're standing here. All the beer in the world. There."

Mitch and posse saw an aluminum rain barrel to McIntyre's immediate left.

"Saw it on tour. Before it got filled. Guessed. There's like…1000 cans in it. Every variety known to man. Punch in what you want. The Lab-bot finds it."

Johnson brightened immediately. "I love the future. Who wants one?" A dozen hands shot up.

"Your fuckin' legs broke?" He walked over. Mitch and contingent bounced after. Quips and queries. Shoving, messing around. Good cheer atmosphere.

Back and relaxing. Mitch, elbows on the railing. Coloured triangle banners flapped from numerous guy-wires. Very festive. Still no idea what was on tap…apart from beer. Whatever it was drew closer. To judge by the shouts, bleats, whistles and chunking machinery sounds.

Out on the ocean, tiny whitecaps appeared and vanished as quickly. Unlike how Mitch pictured it. No roller coaster rogue waves. Trawlers capsizing. Going under. He'd been in kiddie pools with more turbulence.

The horizon, flat and featureless. Unsettling, in a way. Thought of the old story his grandpa told. About the candidate for mayor in Toronto. His platform? Change the city's name to Miami. So the weather would improve. The 905 horror all dream gauzy. Distant. Imagined. Bye bye brown snow. Hello paradise on the boil.

Mills handed him a beer. They clinked cans.

"Wish we could send the shop some vid of this," Mills said. "Guys'd rip their lungs out."

"I heard they were lifting the com blanket," Beecham said. "Not sure what the security danger is. Fucking ocean everywhere." Launched an oyster over the side to underline the point. Rubbed a pinking nose. "Anybody bring their sunblock with them?"

A chorus of regretful no's. Mills' cheeks tomatoed. Even huddling in the semi-shade of spurs and support posts. Mitch's forehead crisping. Never did find his stupid cap. And he absolutely fucking packed it.

"At least everyone'll know we were in Florida," Big Phil smiled. Big Phil. A sunnier outlook was hard to imagine. Mitch had heard about him. Laughing during brawls. Having the time of his life. Couldn't imagine being anywhere else but in the middle of a punch-up. Toe-to-toe, dead crazy fighter. Have to throw a net over him when it's done. Wait till he comes down from the adreno heights. Mitch looked forward to meeting more of the inner circle.

"Tell you this…" Mitch said. Stopped to drain his drink. Fourth dead soldier. Fifth, maybe. Beer sponge today. "I didn't know what to expect. Still don't, actually. But so far…" He held up his empty. Salute to the monkey god, fortune, whoever pulled the strings. Sometimes they didn't fuck up. Others joined him.

"Carpe the diem." Jenkins joked. Important reminder. Mark the moment. Acknowledge the good times. Who knew when they'd come again?

Mills gave a knowing chuckle. "Uh…not to give anything away…"

All eyes turned. Mills looked smug.

"Don't be a fag," Mitch said. "What?"

"Too late," Mills waggled his eyebrows. "It's starting."

Heads spun towards a fresh grinding sound. From beneath the deck. Ship engines kicked in. Novel propulsion system. Mitch had overheard Prescott explaining to Stone. Pulse technology. The horizon swung past, counter-clockwise.

"Holy shit!" someone to Mitch's far left shouted out. "Look!"

"Oh, for Christ sake!" Jenkins groaned. "Hooray! Another fucking pelican! Jesus! What are you? Ten?"

"Sorry." An agent Mitch didn't know gazed down at his shoes.

"I love pelicans." Heads swiveled in the opposite direction. No mistaking that baritone. Political Bob!

Mitch jumped forward to greet him. The others gathered, grinning. Reunion time. The gang all here. Deluge of questions.

"What's with the Miami pimp look? You runnin' a string already?"

"How'd you get aboard?"

"Where's the package?"

"And what is the package?"

"Yeah, what's going on?"

Political waved them quiet. "One at a time, guys, okay?"

Mitch stood back. Marveled. Creamy Panama hat, cummerbund band. Not Political. Nothing else he was wearing fit the image either. Some kind of rainbow-coloured…African thing. A walking fireworks display. Black beach trunks. Hemp surf-slippers. Mickey rat shades. A chameleon. Mitch got how he could go Pashtun. Just a knack for disappearing into character.

"You're in disguise!" Mitch blurted out.

"Or chew here for some coke, eh?" Johnson mocked. "Spic'a da lingo?"

The square bull stood before them. Impassive. Amused. Listened to the gibes and stories. Five minutes later, the kids finished describing their day. Political's turn. He waved the men in closer. The story came quick. He fleshed out the trip's purpose. Revealed the identity of their cargo. Half looked stunned. The rest, younger, had no idea who he was talking about.

"Fuck me," Anderson said softly. Speaking for everyone who understood. A smile creased his face. "Fuck-ing A! I can't believe it!"

Elation. The news was too good to believe. Captured. In the hold. Wendell Kensilla. The most odious, bag-biting, shithead lawyer in Canada. CORE code name—"Potter Pirbright." AKA, "Warfarin Wendell," "Wendell the

Weasel," and "Dick Waud." Man was utter filth. The kind of asshole assholes avoided. Long a top operative, National Party of Toronto. Part of the job description. Wendell a pioneer. Explored new territory. Went where no ratbag had gone before.

Political described their reluctant guest. As miserable a prick in person as predicted. Mitch's snitch, Triscuit, fingered him. Plenty of jokes followed.

"He's actually here? On board?" 'Baldy' Bergman, astonished. Agent had a pre-CORE history with Kensilla. Couldn't abide the cockgobbler as a result. The rest kept an eye on him. Unperturbed, placid as a lake at sunrise. Provoked? Vikings were hairdressers by comparison. A Baldy berserk? Bet on casualties. And property insurance reps phoning the next day.

"Absolutely," Political assured everyone. "Saw him into the brig myself. He's going nowhere. He's convinced we're some merc outfit from the States. Blackwater. Michigan Militia. KKK."

"Self-important moron," Billings sneered. "Mercs. I like that, actually." General agreement. Mercs were straight. Mercs had cachet. Mercs governed.

"Forget Blackwater," Political joked. "CORE pays better, believe me. And we have cooler toys."

"Tank," Mitch said reverently.

"Tank, tank, tank," the agents chorused.

Political checked his com. Slapped his hands together. "Okay, guys. Pitter, patter, time to scatter. This way."

Commotion on the bridge. Stone appeared. Several other uniforms. None Mitch had seen before. Ballcaps pulled from hip pockets. Shades slid into place.

The Canadians lined themselves around the stern. Serviettes showed up. Ready to take orders. Hot and topless. Finally. The long deck trek for refills wasn't appealing.

Cuban swabbies rolled in as they walked past. Winching and rope work ensued. Mock encouragement from Mitch's mates. Mitch always enjoyed watching imports put their backs into it. How it should be.

Warning horn. A garage door-sized section of the deck disappeared. Another scissored in behind it. Two more. All eyes on the large infield hole before them. What next? Danger? Fun? Work?

Horn again. From the depths appeared a brutish head. Stump with ears. Shovel jaw, shaved skull. Insolent pan of the forward audience. Wave from the bridge. Man tapped his earpeas. Saluted. Dropped from sight. Shrugs and smiles from the circle of witnesses. America. Never a dull moment.

Speaker snap. Direction, bridge. The men looked up. Slender figure standing forward. Motionless. Hands clasping the hip-high barrier. Flanked by a dozen military types, both sides. Reviewing line, Mitch guessed. Finished off his beer. Belched politely. No Bev in sight. Wedged the empty behind him between two hull struts. Second thoughts when he spotted a herd of Americans coming their way. Had they seen that? Might have committed some breach-of-protocol thing. Deny it. Or blame Jenkins.

"Hope they don't do the anthem thing," Mitch heard a voice whisper. "I can never remember the fucking words."

"Oh, say, can you see..." came the response. "Fake the rest."

"I meant our anthem," the agent said in exasperation. "Fuck if I know the American anthem. Except the 'bombs bursting in air' part. I always liked that."

"Here it comes," Anderson said. Conversation trailed away.

Sunflash prevented Mitch from seeing the speaker. It was like the air was on the point of combustion. Hold a fresh smoke up. Watch it flame alive. He didn't think he could ever live near the equator. Way too fucking hot.

The Captain guy was talking now. Sounded official. Trim build. Looked in good shape for someone in his fifties. From what he could scope out. Interesting. Not all Americans were landwhales by thirty.

Several minutes of boilerplate. Three sentences in, Mitch tuned it out. Longest, hardly-patrolled border...SSP working as well as...mutual sharing of critical...no more 9/11's, Newport Melts, San Diego craters...assistance appreciated...and so on, and so forth. Boring. Mitch dug at his crotch.

A drink doxie drifted near. She stopped to listen to the speech. Mitch tried to catch her eye. Desperate for another barley cocktail. He could see three cold ones on her tray. Their perspiration glistened in the early afternoon sunlight.

Mitch hestitated to act. No one else was moving. He was still a bit low on the totem pole, rank-wise. Was it worth drawing negative attention over a beer swipe? Pussy. He was a pussy. Decided to give the speaker another minute. Then he was going for it, regardless. Screw the career. His beer glow was fading.

"Fuck," Anderson said out of the corner of his mouth. "Why do they keep peddling that bullshit? Not all Islamic terrorists come from Canada."

Mitch shrugged. "Enough do, I guess," he whispered back. "Don't ask what you can do for your terrorist. Canada's immigration policy. If that's what you call it when absolutely anyone can enter the country."

"Provided they've got fifteen sick relatives, no money, and hate us," Anderson corrected. "We need a 'fuck-off, we're not interested in you' immigration policy instead."

"No argument there," Mitch nodded. Snapped his fingers. Nothing. The juicy little crumpet would not look his way. The can was sweating. He was sweating. They could help each other. It wasn't right.

Another speaker took the mic. When the third one stepped up, Mitch broke. Buzz had wilted in the heat. He bolted for the boozebabe. Snaffled two away from her before she could react. Figured to argue he was doing a run on behalf of the team. Fake-smiled an apology. Forgiving wink in return. Many a slip twixt tit and lip, as the saying went. Mitch considered himself supremely lucky.

"Best beer I've had for twenty minutes," he winked to Bergman. The man eyed the Heineken Mitch clutched with obvious envy. Before he could mimic Mitch, two other CORE soldiers had followed his example with other stationary attendants.

"Ya' snooze, ya' lose," Bergman cursed his own hesitation. "Fuck!"

Mitch handed over his find. Grateful clap on the shoulder.

Applause broke out. Mitch patted his can. Never cost you anything to be polite. They'd hardly begun celebrating when a loud, grinding noise interrupted things. From inside the hole. The bridge emptied. Sweeties started rotating with their cold refreshers. The grinding gave way to rumbling. Earthquake sensations. Teeth-chattering deck vibrations. Once again, nervous looks among CORE reps. A follow-up 'whump' had people clutching posts and rail.

"What the fuck?" Mitch heard a voice ask. His feelings exactly. Pictured giant magnets colliding.

Older beside Mitch. Blue eyes in an ocean of white. Eyebrows at forty-five degree angles. The two of them leaned forward in tandem. Curiosity overcame common sense. Something was rising out of the hole.

"Okay..." Jenkins said. Took a brave step ahead. Promptly reversed himself when a silvery ball came thrusting out. A flagpole was attached beneath it. Finger-thick wires rang and slapped. The mystery object rose two metres into the air. Then a putty-gray umbrella-shaped platform rolled into view. Under that, a brightly polished aluminum cocoon.

"Somewhere a playground is missing this," Weir muttered under his breath. Mitch snorted. It was a peculiar item, no argument. Plumbing protusions jutted out at odd angles. Rubbery fabric-covered hoses flared out from the base of the metal egg. Except for the colour, it looked a bit like a big dock spider. With a skewer through it. Mitch had no idea what to make of it. From the general comments, no one else did either.

Four "mesquite runners," as a Yank called them, raced up. Grabbed hold. Attached the spider legs to an undercarriage rigged to the deck. Finished in less than a minute. Skipped off like they'd seen border patrol.

Anderson looked at Mitch, who shook his head.

"Maybe it's some kind of ball toss game," came a suggestion.

"Lot of excitement for a satellite dish."

"I got it!" Mills said. "I know what it is! It's one of those…shit…fuck, I don't know what they're called. One of those deep ocean…science capsule things."

"Submersibles."

"Yeah, yeah! They drop them in and you…go down…to the bottom. Fuck around. Look for crabs."

"You don't have to go that far to get crabs." Billings the wise-ass.

"Those things are fucking bigger, though, aren't they?"

"Yeah. This thing…shit. Two people? Somebody's pitchin', somebody's catchin'."

"Public art?" That one got laughs. A few claps. There was something just ugly enough about the contraption. In a park, somewhere it could offend the eye, sure.

"Sci-fi drugs, whatever it is," Cole said.

No shit, Mitch quietly agreed. Between the roping, clamps, nozzles, swiss cheese metalwork. An alien showed up? Claimed it? No one would have been all that surprised.

"I give up. Time for another beer," Wilson said, voice raised. General relief. Wisdom response. Attention turned to waving over the serviettes. Orders placed.

No sooner had the next round arrived than new sounds erupted from the hold. Old-style machine chatter. Tappet clatter, chains running, generator thrum, turbine hum.

Mitch felt the urge. Others as well. Fuck guessing. Look in the hole. Face the monster.

The egg quivered ever so slightly. Exploration postponed. Billings backed onto Mitch's toe. Took a rib jab for his trouble.

All eyes glued to the device. It began to telescope into itself. Now a voice heard. Loud, indignant. Political smiled. Waved everyone closer. The circle of men collapsed around the steel-shiny hammock.

"It's okay. We're good," he yelled. "You'll want to see this." Something rocked the basket.

"Gotta be Kensilla, right?" Mitch said.

"If it isn't that cocksmoker, I'll be disappointed." Billings with a hard-eyed glare.

The mount tilted back. Oiled racheting racket. Then a solid, locked-in-place "ka-chunk." The hoist disengaged. Reversed back into the hold. More hydrolic whirring and hissing. The deck slivered close up against the device base. Mitch and the rest stepped forward.

"Sorry," Political said. "Now it's done."

"Flying blind here," Jenkins reminded him.

Commander Stone strolled up. Brace of Americans by his side. Explained the moment. They gathered to peer in at a trussed and raging Wendell Kensilla. The drugs had worn off. No governors on the man's mouth now. Full dickhead tantrum mode. Screamed about his rights. Demanded a lawyer. Vowed terrible revenge. Name-dropped.. Com numbers. Spark addresses. Who his friends were. Who'd miss him when he didn't turn up for meetings. Old Media interviews. On and on. Utterly wasted. Half his listeners barely knew who he was. Those who did couldn't wait to see what humiliations were planned.

"I don't think he fully appreciates his current position." Deadpan delivery, Stone. Mitch did like that. Held off laughing. Would look kiss-ass. But everyone wore smiles.

The Commander turned. Signaled the bridge. Older and Bergman started wrestling with each other. One pushing the other closer to the basket. Guys gave them room. Heckled freely. Stone finally whistled it finished. Pointed to their rear. Older wheezed what everyone was thinking.

"Who's the nearly dead guy?"

Stone heard. Fixed Older with 'the look'. "That would be the man paying for this."

Older managed a weak smile. "He looks like my grandfather."

"Liar!" Anderson spouted behind him. "He's an orphan, sir."

"I am not," Older replied with heat. "Honest, sir, I have par…"

Stone held up his hands. "Never mind. You've got two minutes with the subject." He and his honour guard marched off.

Mitch looked around. "Well, shit. PAL-time, boys!"

"Point and laugh," Anderson explained to a puzzled Yank nearby.

Mitch looked inside. Sure enough, recognized him. Wendell the weasel lay bound within. Mitch grunted with pleasure. The rest of CORE crowded around. Scattered cheers when it was confirmed. Kensilla. Live and unhappy. Excellent.

Several Americans returned. Room made. They knew of Kensilla for different reasons, it was discovered. Among then IntelSec community, he was thought to be disordered. Another deranged anti-American. Except that he had the ear of the powerful in Ottawa. A cause for concern. Earned him a spot on the watch list. Subsequent investigation turned up links to various radical Left organizations. Including the Ovarians. Man was less an enemy of the state than an enemy of all thinking people.

PB snorted at the sight. Politics mostly bored Mitch. To him, Kensilla was just another holovid tongue-wagger. What the Sage said. A Party of Toronto suck-up lawyers. Nothing new. Toronto had a million of'em.

Billings, some of the others, filled in the blanks. How Kensilla was the perfect Party hack. Public loudmouth. Inner circle jerk. Brown envelope shifter. Keyhole listener. Washroom skulker. His Party attracted that kind. Stalinist, shut-up-and-pay-your-taxes types. BigGov leeches and looters. And they had a slimey, shameless spokesman in Kensilla.

Mitch's usual fantasy for dealing with dorks. Bury them in a pit. Feed a hose down. Bleed off the methane. Heat the garage forever. Turned out, someone came up with an even better idea. Take him on a cruise. Invite friends. Have a party. Mitch bowed to the clever reasoning.

The figure strapped inside the shell continued to sputter and croak. Wrenched at his restraints. The chanting mockery infuriated him. He blustered. Cursed in fury. Everyone laughed. Cheap entertainment.

Mitch followed the lead of other agents. Horked a lugie. Joined others dripping from Kensilla's chin. Onto his spotted shirt. The CORE treatment. Soften them up. What the dickhead deserved at a minimum.

Jenkins lifted his head. Sandy eyebrows narrowed down. "Jesus! What's with all the fucking horns? That's starting to annoy me."

"Our two must be up," Mitch replied. Looked for confirmation. General movement evident. The Americans, agents and sailors, pulled away. CORE did the same.

A brown boat-stooge played with levers. The basket lurched back to a horizontal position. Even with the deck. Kensilla just visible. An insect trapped. Perfect expression. Camera smug superiority long gone. Dispirited now. Uncertain. Mouth slack between bouts of shouting. Overall colour, that of drying cement. Weak strands of combover glued to his forehead. Buggy eyes set well apart. The skull out of proportion to the jaw. As though the doctor had a real grip on the birth tongs.

Kensilla shifted looks from face to face. Typical of the captured crim. Hoping to find an ally among his accusers. Someone to plead his case. No Fonda here, Mitch thought with satisfaction. Happy trails, you self-admiring fudpucker.

The egg rotated slightly. Dropped another 20 degrees. Kensilla now a billiard ball in an end pocket. Mitch looked up just then. The ancient shuffled towards them. Guy from the bridge, Older whispered the obvious. Several worthies followed in his wake. They approached the undercarriage lip. Looked into Kensilla's web.

"What's going on with the Gerrie?" Jenkins whispered.

"How the fuck would I know?" Mitch answered.

The buffer removed his Panama. Eyes slid to Political. Mitch tried to think of a good one to nail him with after. Some "you guys shop at the same place?" gag. At the same time, wondered if those lids came in black. Mitch wasn't a fedora man. Ball caps were it for headgear. But it wasn't a bad look. Might draw women, worn well. Cream wasn't his favourite shade, though.

The breeze played with the feathery old-man hair. Mitch was close enough to see the liver spots on his face and hands. Loose, patterned cotton shirt. White trousers. Open-toe sandals. With socks. Mitch never understood that. Must have ugly feet. Gray guy gear for sure.

The men with him caught Mitch's notice. All wore Navy monkey suits. Officer collars. But they looked hard. Alert eyes. Ready-for-shit bearing.

A final keening outburst from Kensilla. High-pitched wheedling, begging, guilt denial. The man waited patiently until Wendy stopped spewing. Mitch just far enough away. Couldn't hear what Moses said. The oldie never raised his voice. Lasted a minute, no more. Hat replaced, steps retraced. Man and entourage departed.

"Anybody know what that was about?" someone murmured. Mitch didn't. Triggered a reaction from Kensilla. Suddenly the air was filled with frantic roaring. CORE and others returned to stand, stare, gloat. Pour on the abuse.

"You can't do this!" Kensilla snarled.

"Why not?" Mills asked, perfectly serious.

"Yeah, shit-for-brains," Peterson echoed. Curled his lip. Showed his teeth. Gestured whacking off. Ran out of ideas after that.

"Yeah!" Billings added with emphasis. Previous summer's blockbuster tagline. Never got old. Looked around. "Now what?"

"S-s-something…w-w-wonderful," Kay Dullea stuttered. Because he already knew what was coming.

Mitch sniffed the air. Anderson did likewise.

"What is that?" he asked. They'd smelled BBQ earlier. This was different. Burned electricity. Melted rubber. Sound of gear click and mesh. Heavy rumble. Bowling balls thrown down an escalator. Sharp yell from below decks. Then quiet. Nothing. Seconds later, something heavy scraped over concrete. Dead silence again.

"Yeah," Vanasseldonk mused. Straw-blond mini-Mohawk bristling in the wind. "Like…after a lightning storm. And a fire. I can smell it, too.

"Pulse power," a Yank enjoying their discomfort said. There was enough free-floating static electicity to make arm hairs stand on end. Lockstep retreat from the cage area. Mom hadn't raised up no morons. Things that snap, crackle and pop without milk? Probably trouble.

Mitch never forgot his last look at Kensilla. Screamhead's face still glistened from spit. Man jabbering senselessly. The jaw working. Making demands. Explaining. Ferret eyebrows like Venetian blinds in a hurricane. Ruin sat in his eyes. Curtain time. The man was done. Exposed, charged, sentence carried out.

Mitch figured another couple hours out in the sun, he'd be properly cooked. Like that bikinied babe back a few years ago. Fell asleep on the beach. Laid out in the sun all afternoon. Felt unwell that night. Went to emerg. Diagnosed as having broiled her own intestines. Human haggis, the gag around the shop. No remedy. Shipped the corpse north two days later. Darwin Award nominee. If that was what lay in wait for Wendell, Mitch good with that.

As if in response, stooges appeared. The great grey device shook like a wet dog. Panel lights winked on and off. Humming again. No jets of steam. No squeal of metal on metal. Mitch reminded of his uncle's home-built frankenmower. An immoral melding of rototiller and first generation jet-ski. Perfect for his uncle's rock garden of a lawn. Worked. In a fashion. More fun operated when drunk. In front of stone-dodging drunks. Finished after his cousin drove it into the river chasing down a long fly. Last game of frog baseball that summer.

More dworks circled the apparatus.

"BBQ sauce?" Mitch speculated. No rebuttal. Made sense. Still, a lot of activity for a celebrity bake-off with only one contestant. Elastic ropes snapped taut under the basket. Looks of wonder among the CORE constituency. Agents redoubled their verbal taunting.

"Kensilla, you pathetic pile a donkey shit! You're history, you sick motherfucker!" Jenkins in top form.

The rest joined in. A profanity-laced shitstorm of commentary. Even men who couldn't have picked him from a line-up earlier jockeyed forward to unleash insults. Any Kensilla replies were drowned out by a cascade of good-natured hoots and laughter.

Mitch lit a smoke. Half-noticed something odd out on the water. Forgot it when he glanced at his forearms. They'd taken ray damage. Knew he'd be feeling it in the morning.

The egg cage jerked again. Rolled back still more. Kensilla yelling. Hard to make out. No one cared anyway.

A crane creaked and swiveled overhead. Back on deck, wire cables slithered into grooved channels. Snugged up into base eyelets. Louder engine thrum. The horizon slowly moved left to right.

Billings wondered if some old-time keelhauling might be on the menu. Explained it. "You hook 'im up," he said, pointing at the crane overhead. "Toss him in. Run him under the hull for a bit. They did it on old sailing ships. Somebody got outta line."

Had to be it. Propwash the bastard's ass. Guys were looking forward to seeing it happen. Time for some cool nautical shit. Now all the prep made sense.

Stone appeared near the cage. The Commander raised his arm. Chatter fell off.

"Five minutes, gentlemen." Eyes bright. That sent a message.

Mitch looked at Anderson. "Beer?"

"Twist my arm." Anderson pointed to a cache hidden against the hull. "Way ahead of you. Got four stored. Still cold. Find the one with your name on it."

"Oh, baby. Me love you long time," Mitch said. Waggled his tongue. Returned with two. Cracked one. Satisfying slug. Noticed an old salt nearby. Crewmember, obviously. But with rank. Uniform casual. Faded tennis shoes. Worn cargo shorts. Muscled up for an older guy. Legs weren't all varicose veiny. White tee, sleeves rolled up. No anchor tat on the pipes. Disappointing. Cancer pack in his back pocket. Half-turned to watch the Kensilla follies. Saw Mitch looking at him. Chuckled. Beckoned him over. Mitch chucked Anderson on the arm. Head-gestured to follow.

"Hey," Mitch smiled. "What's up?"

The man nodded a greeting. Pointed at a distant patch of churning water Same thing Mitch had spotted earlier.

"Yeah, I kind a saw that," Mitch nodded. "All the birds. What is it? A reef? Something sunk?"

The man shook his head. Explained. The news rocked Mitch and Anderson both.

"An hour they've been chumming that spot," the man confided. Pulled a pipe from his shirt. Scratched at the face frosting. Mitch couldn't believe what he was seeing. Pipes were illegal in Canada. Like almost everything else.

"Slow release bait," he continued. Tamped leaf into bowl. "Disposable raft. You can just see the flag there." Placed a lazer over the rim. Blue jet. Blue smoke. Just like that. Mitch caught a whiff before the spray took it. Beautiful. And then the guy glided away.

"They've been chumming for an hour," Mitch repeated the line to Anderson.

"So he said." Anderson took a reflective pull on his bottle. Ran a beefy hand over a reddening slab of neck. Peered out at the foamy excitement. Eighty or so metres from the boat. "Wha'dya think that means? Being friendly?"

"Fuck if I know," Mitch said. A clap on his shoulder spun him around. Political Bob. Large as life, twice as happy.

"Looking at the entertainment?"

"Yeah. Some great chumming goin' on out there."

Political gave Mitch the quizzical eye. "Feeding frenzy. Yeah! Only ever seen one on vid."

Blank expression on Mitch. Anderson scratched his nose. Grimaced in sudden pain.

"Sharks, for fuck sakes!" Political Bob exploded in laughter. Eased back. Only one amused. "Guess you don't see many up where you're from."

"Not compared to Buffalo, no," Mitch shot back. Anderson grinned.

"Point," Political conceded. "Anyway, it's great. There's a...whole herd a sharks out there now. They've been feeding them for..."

"An hour," Mitch nodded. "We know. They anchored a...raft or something out there."

Political squinted at the horizon. Motioned for a smoke from Mitch.

"Shark food," Anderson mused. "What the hell would that be?"

"Lot of retirement communities in Florida," Billings said, joining the conversation.

"Ohhhh...two minutes, unsportsmanlike," Mitch laughed.

"So why are they feeding sharks now?" Billings asked. "Is it for us? Maybe we get to shoot them or something. That would be cool."

The light flashed for Mitch. "You don't...think..."

He never had a chance to finish. Engine surge. The stern began to swing around. Towards the ocean action. Political slapped his hands together in delight. Blew a cloud out. Bounced away. Anderson went for another beer. Staggered slightly as the ship rocked.

Mitch and the others jostled for the best sightlines. "Looks like you were right," Mitch shouted to Billings. "We're probably going to catch a Great White. Wonder what we can do with it after?" That for Kensilla's benefit. Let his imagination play with the idea.

Mitch had just the right glow on. He breathed deep. Held it. Let it rejuvenate his lungs. Probably canceled out a year's smoking right there. Practiced flick. Launched the finished cigarette out over the side. A shithawk appeared as if by magic. Swooped low. Snapped up the still smoking end. Bolted. Strangled screech. Corksrew plunge into the surf. Mitch slapped the rail. Roared with laughter. Terminal error. Teachable moment for bird world. All that glitters....don't be gulled.

A greasy hydraulic spurt spun his attention back to the deck. Men fell silent. Easier to hear Kensilla bellering. Near the opening, a sun-blackened crew stooge finger-pecked a holopad. Kensilla's chamber rose into the air. Invisible inside the giant scoop. Denunciations poured out. Mitch grinned with pleasure. Wait till the brine bath. Be singing a different tune after.

The crane rotated parallel with the the side of the ship. The hoist jumped on its base. Cables thrashed and whipped. A piercing scream. Legs kicking, arms tearing at emptiness, Wendell Kensilla disappeared into the sky.

"Holy shit!" Cole exploded as Americans threw their caps in the air. "It's a fucking catapult!"

"Unbelievable!" Mitch yelled, face rapt with delight.

CORE agents hugged the railing, wonder on every face. No trouble finding Kensilla. Just follow the screech trail.

"He's gotta be, what…sixty…seventy-feet in the air?" Older guessed. Hand shielded his eyes. Neck craned back.

"Oh, yeah, anyway," Anderson agreed.

"Man, he's headin' for orbit," Poole observed. Others kicked in.

"Houston, we have no problems here."

"Look at him bicycle!"

"Call in your markers now, you faggot!"

"Eighty-eight, eighty-eight, eighty- eight! Woo-hoo!"

Jenkins howled. Kensilla's great looping ride looked set to end.

"Three…two…one…yes!!" Anderson yelled. "And we have splashdown!!"

And then it all came together. The ship had brought them to within thirty metres of impact. Cheers greeted the geyser foam. Menacing glint of sunlit shark fins. Closing. The deck erupted again. Men shook their fists. Praised God.

Mitch, too, felt a glow of triumph. Around him, CORE agents shook hands. Raised beers. Saluted their victory. With Kensilla safely off ship many of the Americans turned away. Cole's shout brought them back in a hurry.

"Tell me I'm wrong," he exclaimed to nearby scoffers. "Look. A hand!"

Sure enough, Mitch saw something. A wave, though the waters roiled.

"What's out there again," he said to anyone who might know. It was obvious from the commotion something had excited the locals. Just then, a giant, squared off chunk of shiny brown leather leapt into view.

. "Okay," Thompson said with deliberate slowness. "What…the fuck… was that?"

The salt was ready. Pulled the dead pipe from his mouth.

"Hammerhead." Cold smile. Smacked ashes out. Reached over the railing to release them. "They breed around here this time of year. That's one reason the captain picked this location."

Mitch wanted to laugh. "There's another reason?"

"Deep sea eels. Lamprey family. They never come to the surface like this. They prefer colder water. But if properly tempted…" he winked. "And we've got other surprises in the mix. Sea snakes. Poisonous, of course. Barracuda. Some black-tip beauties. Portugese man o' wars. More. You'll see."

A full-throated bellow of pain and terror reached them. Applause from the deck.

"Swim, Wendell, swim!" somebody shouted. Everyone laughed.

Warning heeded. Kensilla breached the surface like a sub blowing ballast. Clapping, more laughter met the sight. A lowlife pugknuckler got introduced to a party of sharks. Who said prayer was ineffectual, Mitch wanted to know? The essence of faith realized. Expect the impossible. Make it so.

"Head's up!" Vader yelled. Granite face showing concern. "He's coming this way!"

Incredible but true. Kensilla remained alive. Afloat. And making a bid for the boat.

"Spears!" someone screamed. "Guns! Anything!"

"Throw beer at him!"

"No!!" Jenkins blared out. "Don't be insane!"

"Joking."

Jenkins, exasperated sigh. Gestured removing the hook from his mouth.

"Evil gives him strength!" another voice cried out. Mitch looked around. Only an American would say that. Kensilla was the lowest form of life imaginable. But genuinely evil? Satan had more class.

Fortunately, the sharks weren't having any of it. Kensilla's attempted escape aborted. His fifth free-style lunge his last. A leaping shark sawed his arm off. A single chomp brought Kensilla up short. Hoots of joy reverberated around the Wild Rose. The sight of lawyer boy gushing blood restored spirits. Toasts were offered to the heroic hammerhead. Nameless but not forgotten.

"Party can't help you now, ha ha!" Political yelled out. Attention returned to Kensilla.

"Follow the blood and arrive in ill humour!" Anderson encouraged unseen sea creatures. A foot-tall dorsal fin razored through the gentle blue. Viewer approval. More thrashing. Plumes of water jetted up. The ocean seemed to shake with excitement. Suddenly, a mammoth tentacle arced up. Awed agents watched it slam down. A wave-wall obscured the scene. Chorus of boos. The giant squid had missed. Kensilla lived.

"Try again, Sid, you losair!" Cournoyer belted out. Big laughs. The name stuck. From then on, doing a "Sid the Squid." Shorthand for unexpected failure.

Sharks massed. Dozens of other indistinct forms converged.

"Snakes!" a cry went up. "Hundreds of'em!" Mitch looked over. Cursed his stupidity. Of course. The com zoom. Zero in on ze exciting conclusion.

A school of barracuda knifed in for the feast. Surged towards Kensilla, who still found breath to object.

"What balls!" Political said in amazement. "Now I wish we'd got him in the Tank first."

"I hear that," Mitch nodded. Some people never knew when to shut up.

"Like National Geographics!" Billings enthused, "Only better." The broad careworn Newfie face radiated extreme happiness. Billings hated liberals with a deep and abiding passion. Winked at Mitch and Political as he pocketed his winnings. Frantic wagering. All manner of bets taken, odds given. What time would Kensilla go under and not come up? Which animal would deliver the coup de grace? Who would get to inform his family of the joyous news? Mitch imagined the moment. Hammering the knocker. The blue-haired biddy opens the door. Mitch hiding his delight. "Mrs. Kensilla. You remember your son, Wen-dell? Well, he's been eaten by sharks. Real ones. So sorry. Ha, ha, ha." If only.

Every time Kensilla slide from sight, boots stamped the deck with satisfaction. When a gasping Weasel pinwheeled into visibility, groans and curses. So much fun it was probably illegal, Mitch thought.

"Holo!" a voice barked. The urgent tone cut through Kensilla's entertaining yowls. Mitch knew the voice. Spun to his left. Political slumped. Holding his head in his hands. The meaning of his cry finally registered. Mitch clutched his own skull. Waste! Everyone watching. No one preserving this one time, ultra-quality event. A viewing treasure lost forever. It didn't bear thinking on.

"Covered, gentlemen," the salt reassured them. Tapped his finger against a boxer's twisted beak. Pointed to the tower. Elsewhere. Mitch spotted several black, unblinking eyes. "Numerous angles. Bow to stern. Worry not."

Mitch relieved. But for his own shelves, a personal record would be good. Held up his com. The old man nodded permission. Mitch spread the word. Save what you could.

Everyone immediately into it. For the savvy users, live uplinks initiated. Buddies back home would go batshit for this. Who didn't like revenge vids?

"More splashing!" somebody yelled.

"Stop doggin' it, ya' fag!" a different wit urged.

Time slowed. Mitch howled to hear men rooting on the sharks. As the guy said, you'd need a heart of stone not to laugh at Kensilla's dismemberment. Mitch sent up a prayer of gratitude. He couldn't think of a better way to spend a day at sea.

Something hurled itself out of the water. Kensilla? Still? Sudden intake of breath. Yes, Kensilla! Bleeding and squealing like the proverbial stuck pig. It streamed off his entire body. Several vipers hung from his neck. A length of intestine dragged like a rudder. Wriggling shapes burrowed into a wicked abdominal gash. Slime eels was Mitch's first hope. Laying eggs in one of their own. Poetic justice if ever there was such.

He was about to yell something cruel but funny when a hammerhead leaped. Mitch stopped. Admired it's form. Magnificent animals. Well worth shooting.

And then a miracle. Mitch watched it unfold with joyous disbelief. The nimble fish deftly removed Kensilla's other arm at the shoulder. Mitch pounded his thigh. Brilliant! Hoped the holoshots weren't jerky. They'd sell like candy at a kindergarten.

Hard on the hammerhead's heels, a lamprey exploded out of the water. Sinewy viciousness. Pride of the Sargasso Sea. A live torpedo fired from the ocean floor. Airborne now. Wire-guided to its target. Giant eyes beamed livid, raw hatred. The sight electrified everyone. Few white men had ever seen one. Outside of a holodoc, that is.

The Weasel sensed it. Turned. Opened his mouth for one last abject scream of terror. Too late. His wretched, undignified life promptly ended. The final view—a mouthful of prehistoric daggers. The ancient razors filleted his fear-frozen gob. Tables turned. Fresh human sashimi.

SatMics recorded a mighty roar of triumph. Congratulations extended to all. Kudos especially to the eel. More cheering. A a passing black tip idly tore off and ate what remained of Kensilla's head. Magic moment. Mitch relished it. Those fish had served society well. Whether they knew it or not. Probably not.

Still pumped from the show. Mitch took in the group. Faces animated. Exuberant sharing of joy. Punching in another beer request. "Big Dave" Porchak. Mitch only knew him by rep. Crazy Sarnia dude. Winter surfer. Scuba diver. Triathlete. Ultra fit. A legend. Rumours he'd saved over a dozen divers from drowning. Pre-CORE career. At some oil company. Now he was the in–house dive pro. Nicer person you'd never meet.

Right behind him, throat working on a brown pop—"Steady Eddie" White. Chili master. The only guy Mitch knew who really was part status-Indian. Family lived on reserve land near Huron. Claimed his grandfather was related to Chuvalo. Which explained why he was an excellent scrapper. Style like Mitch. More dangerous as time went on. Sneaky quick counter-puncher. Take three to give two. But the two would put you down. And then he could kick you into the hospital.

"Zombie" Poole. Deep in conversation with some American. 6'9"/260lbs. Short fuse. Safer to goad a grizzly.

Half-step to his right, Benny "BB" Boudreau. Laughing hearty about something. Only 5' 8". Massive upper body. Could do pull-ups until told to stop.

Paul Thornton. Holding his com above his head. Still screaming advice to Kensilla. Martial arts/MMA brute.

"Uncle Joe" Kosinski. Piercing gray eyes, bad 'stache. Also knew a hundred lawyer jokes. Each better than the last.

Peter Scott, one foot on a strut. Looked ready to leap into the froth. Help the sharks. Quim wizard. Could enter any bar. Five minutes circulation. Corral the best-looking bearded taco in the place. Mitch's only real rival for pulling punash.

Spread around the deck, the rest of the CORE pantheon. Some he knew well. Some would become brothers. Robson, Vine, McCorqedale, Hartgers, Bidini, Carruthers, James, Woods, Mazza, Vanderspank, Williams, Sutherland, Gordon, Miller. Top flight guys in every way. Hard, focused, fun-loving. Every area of the country represented. Except the new parts up north. And B.C. Mitch was pretty sure Boudreau was from Swift Current. So maybe nobody from Quebec either. No matter. Mitch was proud to know them. Felt privileged to be asked to contribute here and there. Had their respect, just as he had theirs. Mitch could walk it alone. Had done so. But to know they had his back. Always. Forever. Whatever the problem, the team was there. No questions asked. A good feeling.

Something else he'd noticed from this trip. The growing sense CORE might just win in the end. Fate and circumstances seemed to be turning their way. The last of the Boomers finally expiring. Three cheers for Death! Those with more money than brains became Gerribots. The rest surrendered to the everlasting flames of Hell. Or the eternal bottomless Void plunge. Graveyards across the country. Flooded with dried-up 60's crypt fodder. Well-seasoned beefy jerks. Stacked like flapjacks in spare corners. Hidden in utility sheds. Squeezed into recycle bins. Idiot pricks had near bankrupted the place. But what cancer (wonderful cancer!) hadn't beaten back, CORE might yet. And in time to salvage something of the country.

And the good news traveled. Nearly destroyed by leftists, green shoots appeared within Canada's old-line culture. New, encouraging signs of revival. Meeting secretly. In church basements. Curling rinks. People recounted, celebrated their disparaged legacy. Grown weary of being politely enraged. Backlash action brewing. The current existed. It just needed direction. Organization. Some figure or group willing to lead them. Help them kick over the whole rotten structure. Stick it to the pantywaist, cocksmoking, pinky hippo social engineering fuckwits running things into the ground. Lop off some heads. Roll them down the street. The revolution will not be temporized.

Calling CORE. Its very reason for being. Got a problem with bad legislation? Bad legislators? Burn down the legislature. No rathole? No rats.

So lancing boils the likes of Vermann, Barstew, Kensilla? That was achievable. They'd proven it. What next? Appropriate targets as numberless as the stars. First they'd take Scarborough. Then they'd take North York. Take it back from the undeserving little troughlickers fellating their way to power.

A fresh beer appeared. Interrupted Mitch's reverie. Jenkins shoved in beside him. "Isn't this fucking great?" he yelled. Faked a punch into Mitch's midriff.

Late afternoon light sparkled off the water. The temperature had dropped some. Banners riffed in the breeze. A fish jumped. Gone before they could get a good look. They stood and smoked. Stared out to where Kensilla met justice. Luxuriated in the moment. And then the word arrived. Next event. Banqueting, sluicing, dancing. The whole nine yards. Life was a slice of cherry pie.

They turned to go. Mitch shot a last look at the hallowed spot. Gulls continued to circle the dump zone. Scrap hunt. Mitch wished them good eating.

On the deck, wet backs were bent. Hoses coiled. Springs unhooked. Metal plates broomed clean. Ship shape in under an hour. Toxic cargo? What toxic cargo?

The amazing catapult had already been retracted. Jenkins read Mitch's mind. Asked the question. Wild guesses from both parties. Great to have one at CORE. Think of the fun you could have. Serious money maybe. And twinning it with the Tank wouldn't be easy. See what Santa Sage said.

From food for thought to thoughts of food. Cooking smells saturated the air. Mitch smacked his lips. Caught bacon. Jenkins lifted his head. About to mention it when they came abreast of Billings. Chatting with one of the Americans. Billings shaking his head with vigor. Overheard him ask, "So… you do this on a regular basis?"

"No, no. I wish," the man said. Bandaged paw rasped over five o'clock shadow. Blue jowls. "This tour is the luxury special. Just for you boys. Your Mr McIntyre rigged this ship out for us. Lets the department use it whenever. And we sure do appreciate it."

The statement took a second to register. Billings was fixated on the concept itself. He'd already mentioned it to Mitch earlier in the afternoon. No lake sharks in Superior or Huron. No deep-sea Sidney the squidney either. Pike was about the ugliest thing you'd find. Apart from some of the women. But blackfly season had potential. Ask any moose. Run a crim trundler up. Stake'em all outside. Near the water.

Billings' said his folks had a cottage near Tobermory. Make it a day of it. Beers and a barbie. Boating for the kids. Everyone gorges on steaks and burgers. The local bug population dines out as well. Win-win. Billings just blue-skying. But Mitch liked it. Jenkins on board. Proposal had merit. Bring it up at the next meeting.

It was then the American's statement sank in. Mitch looked at Billings. Then back at the swabbie captain. "This boat is owned by…a…Canadian?"

The man looked at each of them in surprise. Sun-ravaged face. Badland wrinkling. Nose red as a marker buoy. "Yeah. One a yours. Some rich guy from…shit, I forget where now. You didn't know that?"

"No!" Mitch and Billings said, same time.

The American shrugged. You-just-never-know chuckle. Took the ladder down. Ducked through a hatchway, Mitch and the others close behind. As they entered the main corridor Mitch paused. The chilled air was sweet. Less so, his own smell. Long day. Hellish sun. He was greasy in all the wrong places. Cold shower time.

Their companion waved. Broke off for his own destination. A ship staffer passed near. Mitch hijacked him. Described their needs. Man found them their staterooms. Grinned as he deposited them in front of their doors. Refused the offer of a tip. Cheery salute and gone.

Billings flashed a grateful thumbs up to Mitch. Disappeared inside his room.

Mitch's sanctuary three doors down. Solid entry click as card devoured. Quick scan. Nicely-appointed place. Cadillac lawyer sofa. Flanked by heavy end tables. Nature prints on the walls. Wolves and eagles. Batemen's, he wondered?. His Sheridan art teachers hated Bateman. Too obvious. Too successful. Not nearly gay enough.

No windows. Oak motif, tables and chairs. Huge holovid on the wall opposite the sofa. Wet bar. What more could you want?

Mitch stripped down. Went to find the shower. Opposite the bedroom. Glanced in. Reclining on the four-poster, a Norse morsel he'd eyed earlier. Wearing a big smile. Nothing else. Blond ringlets strategically wrapped around her bunker busters. Mitch waved. Said hello. Pointed at the bathroom.

"Me smell. Take shower. Back soon."

In and lathered up. Water smelled odd. Metallic. Wet, though. Most important. Tan lines already. Neck prickly. Sensitive to touch. Burned, baby, burned. Couldn't help whistling though. What a day.

Ten minutes later. Taking the I-95 into Savannah. Business moniker, Mitch guessed. Woman looked more Tammy-ish. Maybe Lurleen. Genuine applause when she finished him off, though. Strumpet knew how to strop razor. Raspberry tongue darted out. Flicked up missed juice. Smiled. Eyes dilated from dark work. First thing she thought when she laid them on Mitch's marvel. Navel-gazing time.

"Top…thirty," Mitch assured her when she asked. "No doubt."

"Really?" the possibly blonde bomber asked. Stood up. Water cascaded down seal-shiny skin. "Mean it?"

"Absolutely," Mitch confirmed. All he could do to keep his eyes open. "Outstanding. No teeth. Good lubing. Relaxed but thorough action. Solid follow-through. Nine point eight from this judge."

"I'm so glad," she beamed. "You'll tell management? We get extra credit for happy customers."

"You got it," Mitch said. Climbed out of the marble tub. Allowed the surf serf to towel him dry. Savannah patted and chatted away. A fount of personal info Mitch couldn't care less about. Lingered over his slumping lumber.

"The girls say y'all are from Canada."

"Yep." Mitch loved her accent. Exactly like in the movies. Fake.

"Is everyone built like this in Canada?"

"Nope."

"It's just...your cock. It's so...it makes me think of a..."

"Let me guess," Mitch interjected. "An armadillo?"

"Yeah! Exactly!" Savannah gazed at it with obvious affection. Ran her hand along the smooth expanse of blood-engorged skin. "I've never seen anything like it. You're so lucky."

"Some people are born great. Others have greatness thrust into them."

"That's good," Savannah acknowledged. "Who said that?"

"I did. Just now," Mitch snorted. But his thoughts had already moved on. Something was niggling at him. Something other than Savannah. She'd taken to buffing his scrotum. He'd forgotten to do...what? Hated that suspicion. Work? His trull case? Yaz? The Commissioner? He was overlooking something. Couldn't dredge it up though. Especially with "Savannah" scraping her tastebuds over his balls. Finger-flicked her skull.

"Thanks, eh?" Pointed at the door.

She bounced up. Watched him reel in the leather. Pulled on the bright yellow one-piece. No panties. Mitch reached for his moneyclip. Removed an American fifty. Waved the peso in front of her.

"You don't have to do this," Savannah protested, spearing the note. "Everything's already covered."

Mitch leaned forward. Cupped a suspect tit. Botboob? Rotated it. Pushed the nipple in. No warning bells, smoke.

"Consider it a scholarship top up," he said. "Keep practicing that mouth. You could be President someday. It's worked before."

"You're sweet," Savannah glowed. Grabbed her bag from the chair. Turned on her heels. Blew him a kiss. "See you at the dance tonight?"

"Count on it," Mitch lied. Threw himself onto the bed. Spent two more seconds wondering what he was supposed to be doing. Fell asleep.

A loud banging brought him to. He rolled off the bed. Looked for his shorts. His clothes gone. Shook his head. Made a toga from the top sheet.

"What?" he yelled.

"Open up!" a voice he recognized. Mitch took several unsteady steps to the door. Found his balance as he keyed the lock.

"It's open," he grunted. Outside, Anderson, Jenkins, half-dozen others. Everyone looking at him. He stared back. "What?"

"Are you coming?" Billings asked.

Mitch still fogged from sleep. "Yeah, yeah, of course," he said. "Where?"

"The party, guy!" Anderson barked, "Holy shit! It's in our honour!"

Mitch rubbed his eyes. "Fuck, yeah, I'm coming. Jesus, what time is it?"

"Time to put on the red dress, Mags," Jenkins said. Banged his fist on the opened door. "Fuck this. He knows the way. I'm dry. Let's go!"

Mitch was on the trail five minutes later. His clothes, flash-washed and dried. Somebody'd stayed alert. Clean and sweet.

Grateful the boys had dropped by. He'd have killed himself to miss the party of the century. The stories on the plane back to Canada. More outrageous with each re-telling. Wild drinking. Wilder fucking. Midnight feast after. Big chunk of reward money. First, though, the answer to Mitch's questions. Courtesy of the host himself.

Ship staff intercepted Mitch wandering the corridor, looking for the banquet room. Led him to the captain's quarters.. The rest of TeamCORE already there.

Commander Stone stood up, front of the room. Conversation petered out. Some American next to him also standing. Whitest set of teeth Mitch had ever seen. Hollywood jaw. Full head of silver. Dark blue, perfectly-tailored uniform. Brass clasps. Yellow-braided shoulder bar thingys. The whole military package.

Man spoke straight. Mister business. Complete story outlined in five minutes. When he finished, everyone stood and applauded. It seemed the least they could do.

And then the day's benefactor got the call. James Harold McIntyre. Not Hall, Mitch realized. Steward who told him that confused. Same guy who'd talked to Kensilla at the last. No Panama. Looked less fragile without it, for some reason.

Originally out of Airdrie, Alta. Mr. Moneybags. Or so Anderson explained. He'd heard Stone talking on the flight down. Put two and two together. Owned the party barn they were on. Also had a bunch of paper mills. Farm equipment dealerships. Part-owner of a WHL team. Some oil thing with the Chinese. Player, large. Bank balance with more zero's than Mitch had empties in his closet.

Short, too. Mitch guessed 5' 7", 5' 8", tops. Old guy Dumbo ears. Corn silk hair that waved in the air conditioning jet stream. Grandfatherly look. If your grandfather was Rommel.

Pin drop silence as he spoke. Gravely voice. Ex-smoker, Mitch wondered. Direct, like the officer before him. Explained the who, why and what. When he'd finished, a current of rage ran through the room. Kensilla's toilet lurking habit was inexcusable, of course. But normal behaviour for HRC types. Deliberate self-beclowning. The political treachery? Also par for the course. Same for his political party. What he'd helped cover up regarding McIntryre's grandson? Beyond despicable. The connection between Ovarians and the NPOT was now clear. Even so, Mitch wasn't the only one in the room who regretted nothing of the Weasel remained. Had they known, they might have salvaged a part of him. Sun-dried it. Torched what they had. Ground the ashes into his parent's doorstep as a pointed rebuke.

Gut gurgle. Older looked at Mitch. Smirked. Mitch pointed at Anderson, sitting in front of him. Guilty as charged, however. Florida. The state had sabotaged his plumbing. He was desperate to open the valves. Release the evil. Unfortunately, unleashing those fumes might trigger fire alarms. Or a riot.

"Time, boys." Stone shifted his chair back. Took the floor. Thanked McIntryre for his generosity. Accepted congratulations on behalf of CORE. Found Mitch in the crowd. Recognition for the breakthrough that outed Kensilla. And then the almost imperceptible smile. Agents held their breaths. Famous signal. Sure enough, Stone the prize-giver.

"As you know," he said, "CORE is…very pleased with what we've…you've all accomplished recently. So…in keeping with tradition, and the successful conclusion to this mission, I hereby declare…blowjobs for everyone!"

The room exploded. Canadians and Americans alike jumped to their feet. Fists in the air. Orangutan bellows of approval. Mitch led a congo line to the exit. Giddy knowing more to come, so to speak. Headlocked a passing room porter. Demanded to know where the porcelain pisser was kept. Strangled directions provided. Tossed the man aside. Raced for the stairs. Up two flights. Never a more welcome sight than the tophatted dandy sign.

Ten minutes later. Emergence. Smile of intense satisfaction. Several agents waiting, lips curled.

Mitch shook his head. "You wanna be real desperate. Know what I'm saying?"

"We heard," Randalls said, "How bad?"

"Remember that dead cat we found near the guard's shack last summer?"

Randalls rolled his eyes.

"Oh, man!" Mills complained. Wiped his eyes. "It followed you."

"Yeah, she's pretty toxic in there," Mitch chuckled. "What? There's only one can on this wreck?"

Query fell on departing ears. The cloying stench drove everyone out. Exploration on for distant shitters. Mitch indifferent. His bowels bare. A load off his shoulders. And not into his pants. Like he'd feared. Something about Florida. Anyway, bounced down the hall. Bring on the banquet.

Several failed attempts later, he found White and Bergman in conference. Having a pre-feed ciggy. Event space around the corner. Mitch joined them. Old days, the topic of c. First year, recruit school. The psych evaluations. All new to Mitch. He'd bypassed the intro. Ears wide as White explained a famous test. Two guys grow up alone. Other ends of a desert island. They meet each other for the first time as adults. What should their reaction be? Instant combat? Instant friendship? Pretend it's not happening. Walk away? For Mitch, the answer was obvious.

"Throw down. Challenge him. Or at least find out what his intentions are real quick. I don't know him. That makes him a threat. If he bolts, he wasn't. No loss. If he is, we duke it out. Better man cooks up the loser. Darwin, baby."

Two heads nodded knowingly. "Exactly," Bergman said. "Doesn't have to be a fight to the death, of course. In fact, if you can establish he's on the same wavelength, then you've met a possible ally. But thinking he's a reasonable, intelligent being…like yourself…is foolhardy. Always smarter to assume he's a fruitbat in need of correction. See danger. Address danger. Right then."

"Misread the moment. Deny reality…" White trailed off. "Well, let's just say CORE isn't what you're looking for. Off you go to the CBC, young freckle-puncher. Step and fetch for faggos."

Hearty laughter followed. Bluff buccaneers chortling over a treasured jest. Happy note complete. Popped dying cigs into the vent vacuum. Sauntered to the hall doors. Let the busty bimb usher them inside.

Mitch, pulling up the rear, remarked on the impressive doors. Lots of excellent scrollwork. His father was good with a lathe. Grandfather too. This was a step above spindles and dowel work. Almost church-like. Serious skill. Somebody'd got a nice day's pay out of it.

He nearly stepped on Bergman. Both agents at a complete stop. The whole day had been one shock after another. Now they'd had entered fantasyland. Spread out to the far wall. Table after table laden with food. A steaming smorgasbord. Every colour under God. From corncob yellow to bean green. Mitch teared up. It was the most beautiful thing he'd ever seen.

CORE was there, in force. Plates in hand. Eyes round. Mitch hurried to join up. Dozens of semi-nude serviettes stood ready. A rigid line of forkers, spooners and stabbers behind every table. Many he recognized. Beerbabes from up top. Different duds donned now. Bikinis swapped for sporty sailor skirts. Beautifully bronzed legs exited one end. The other—tapered waists leading up to full milkers, proudly displayed. Mitch knew what he wanted for dessert. First things first, though. Time for all good trenchermen to tie it on.

"And I'd a been happy with a half-dozen pigs in a blanket," Stevens said to Mitch, slipping in behind him.

"Don't wake me up," Mitch replied.

More musical notes sounded.

"Again with the fucking gongs." Stevens shook his head. "I don't think I could last in the Navy. That shit would fuck me up."

Mitch snorted with amusement. "Dinner…?" Stopped. A delicious nymph was beckoning them down to her aisle. Billings stepped forward. A chorus of abuse drove him back in line.

"Can't you bastards smell that? Ribs! Oh, man! I gotta get in there before they're all gone!" He inhaled deeply. "I'm coming, you gorgeous slut. Save it all for me, yeah?"

"Don't listen to him," an objector shouted. "He's a vegetarian."

"I love you," said another.

Slippery smacked his lips. "What else smells like…?"

Mitch didn't care. They were surrounded by heavenly aromas. Lunch had been years ago. He was starving.

Hammer met metal. The entire company stood straight. Watched silver lids lifted away. Now giant trays lay exposed. Steam rose from dishes of every description. Mitch salivated violently. Grew light-headed. Wobbled on his feet.

Elsewhere eyes rolled back into heads. The smells were intoxicating. More moaning. Others joined in. Mitch nearly bolted himself. Didn't think he could wait. Billings' ribs were getting to him.

"This isn't some tease, right?" Porchak in a loud whisper. Ever suspicious of good fortune. "They're not going to show us all this and then…send us off to the basement to eat tubesteak?"

"Not the basement, you idiot," Mills chided him. "We're on a boat. It's called the uh…shit…I forget."

"Whatever the fuck it is, I don't wanna to go there. I wanna stay here and…eat my way through the table."

Finally, an announcement. Open season. First come, first stuffed. Hungry agents flooded the zone. Mitch took another look-see. A world's-greatest-buffet spectacle. He'd worked some monied weddings during his escort days. What he saw stretched out before. Whole different league of excess.

A new boobie detachment rolled in from the kitchen. Piloting self-propelled beer kegs. Mitch was torn. A beer would be perfect right then. Decided to come back for the ribs. Fateful decision. On his way to suds alley, Mitch passed great metal racks. Mammoth King crabs pinned like butterflys. Steamed, grilled, boiled. An oily-rich plume rose into the air. Tickled Mitch's nose. He teared up again. Never ate crab in real life. Too expensive. Here he knew could have all he wanted. Put out his plate. Scored three thick tubes. Candycane crustacean. Popped the fourth directly into his mouth. Flavour explosion. Wanted to fall to the floor. Go foetal.

The tong doxie's eyes danced. She giggled. Frantic eyelid batting. Mitch caught the hint. Directed his eyes down to her boulders. Smiled in approval. Mouthed 'labia' after he swallowed. Lip-read her reply. Instant trouser seam stress.

Next up, hot pot lobsters. Cracked and whole. The little ladle labia sized him up as well.

"Fresh from Nova Scotia," she purred. "Butter or lime?"

"Both." Mitch flashed enamel.

"That's next to Canada! Nova Scotia."

"It is so," Mitch agreed. "Beautiful AND clever? What's your name, mammal hole?"

"Mindy. I'm a a student at the U of F." Proud burble. "Computers."

"Wow," Mitch said. Surprised. "Writing software or something?"

"Cleaning. Keyboards, monitors. Everything," she replied. "You'd be surprised how dusty they get."

Mitch found her a delight. Moreso after the petit scholar lodged her erect nipple into the crook of a lobster's open claw. He goggled. The baldly erotic sight staggered him.

"Mindy," he said. "That's my second favourite word, all-time."

"What's your first?" Mindy asked.

"Head," Mitch grinned. The perfect porcelain wall. Few could resist. "How about it? After this is over?"

Mindy crinkled her nose. Made her eyes sparkle. "I'll be at the dance tonight."

"Bring your appetite," Mitch joked. Grabbed half a tail by the foil end. Double-dipped. Moved on.

And so continued the grand tour of a moving feast. Table after table groaning with goods for grazing. Fish of every description. Baked, grilled, pan-fried, deep-fried. Mitch ate with abandon. At the end of each row, a keg stand. All doing heavy business.

Mitch bellied up. Pointed at a freshly poured stein. "Gimme the Kitchener."

Took it. Drained it. Turned it. Slammed it onto the counter. Keg quim quake. Mitch licked foam from his lips. Pink spigots proffered. Nixed.

"Loose tits sink Mitch," he said by way of explanation. Belched thanks.

Heel turn. Room scan. Happy diners feeding hard. Thought of the sharks going after Kensilla. Finally got Political's reference.

Saw Jenkins again. Headed for bread alley. Shook his head when they found it. "Looks like a truck overturned."

"No shit," Mitch agreed. "It's fucking…everything." Overwhelming variety. Hard rolls, lightly-floured Scotch baps, scones, muffins, croissants, sesame seed table buns, mini-baguettes, rye loafs, twelve grains, hoecakes, and on and on. They tumbled from brown wicker hampers. Spilled out of picnic baskets. Littered the chintz. Mitch wiped away drool with the back of his hand. Waded in.

A sourdough biscuit hid behind the butter bowl. Eagle-eyed Mitch. Cornered it. Cracked it. Still warm. Rubbed it. Slowly, delicately worked a thumb inside. Felt it surrender. Spread the tender flesh. Stabbed in a butter pat. Watched it soak into the dough. Pause, then gobble. Glorious.

Up ahead, a Southern peach explained the cuisine. Mitch nodded with the others. Like them, his eyes never left her magnificent, pearly jugs. Heavy, yet dignified. Perfectly aware of their brilliant perfection. Both baltimores artistically etched. Snowflake design. Special effort. Laudable.

Mitch thumbed Savard in the back. Pointed at the twin glories.

Return nod. "Yeah. Already mentioned them."

"What'd she say?"

"She'd see me at the dance."

"Oh, yeah? Hunh." Same answer Mitch had got. Rote or genuine? Oh, well. Find out soon enough.

"Some fucking kitchen, this boat...." Mitch began. Too late. Savard saw something he wanted. Spinarama move. Around Mitch, legs working.

Mitch tossed a smile to the sulty snail-tracker. No salad yet. Chewed over what next to try. Cole the rookie rolled up. Trailed by a tasty fuckable tartlette. Mitch said so. Forty-five kgs, tops. Evenly tanned columns. Hourglass curves. Balcony you could entertain a Broadway cast party on. Nips done nice. Patriotic balties. Dyed red and blue. Silos snowy white. Above those wonders, cupid bow mouth. Dimples. Blue eyes of a goddess. Milkweed fine blond hair. Straight fall. Framing the painting. Trust Americans. When they do something, they do it all the way.

He reached over. Gave the closest bub an affectionate pinball pull. "Boing!" Chuckled. "Swell guns, honey. Tickle your cunt with a feather?"

Bobblehead grin. Then knitted brow. "I'm sorry?"

"Typical country weather," Mitch said. Shit-eating grin. Old joke. But worth trotting out to see Cole's alarmed expression. Like he wouldn't get laid that night. Paranoid child.

"Oh, yes, it certainly is," the choice little cud-chewer replied.

"You must be another college student. Let me guess your major." Mitch pretended to ponder. "Systems analyst? Graphics designer? NASA engineer?" The last from a holodoc he'd just seen about...something hard. Mitch hated physics.

Noochie giggles. "No."

"Ape history?"

Deliberate pout. Preened her pajama fillers. "Hint, hint."

"Women's...studies?" Mitch groaned. Rolled his eyes.

"No! God!" Frantic head shake. "I'm in kinesia...kinisio..sports science!"

"I knew it!" Mitch exclaimed. "What do you play? Volleyball?"

"Rhythmic gmnastics."

Mitch arched an eyebrow at Cole. "That bendy shit? On a mat?"

"Ribbons and balls," she added. Raised her arms in the air. Majorette pose. Mitch applauded. Head gestured at Cole so the idiot would follow suit. Glanced out of the corner of his eye. Fresh goodies poured into a pan.

"Tell him," Cole urged the cupcake.

"No," she quivered, mock embarrassment.

"They practice in the nude," Cole blurted out, clock eyes.

Mitch waited for a sign they were shitting him. Nothing. Just Cole's shining face. Innocent as Adam before the Fall.

"Bullshit," Mitch said, bluffing.

"No, no, we really do," the white delight swore, balloons bouncing. "You can come if you want."

"I already have," Mitch laughed. Mussed Coles' hair to see him blush.

"She's serious," Cole said, ducking away. "We have to go. I mean...we have to."

"Why would they let us in?"

"She can get us passes. They let in, like, boyfriends and..."

"Total strangers. Beautiful. Colour me there...except...we go home tomorrow. No time."

Beagle eyes plead. Stevens had been teaching somebody. Mitch shrugged. "Not my call. Good luck. Run it past the Commander. You got me on board." Winked at the glowing love glove. Knob spin. Satisfying squeal of pleasure.

"You should rent those towers out as transmitters," Mitch said, half-joking. "Seriously, though, you two kids should have what fun you can tonight. Live for the day, as they say. No telling when we'll be back."

Wisdom given, Mitch leaned to his left. Found what he'd been looking for. Opened his mouth. Popped a hot battered scallop in. Abruptly closed his eyes. Ecstatic smile.

"Good?" Cole asked.

Mitch nodded. "Unbelievable," he finally managed. Cole twitching again. Mitch did his duty?

"What?"

"Have you seen it?"

"Uh...I don't know. Seen what?" Mitch glanced around. Nothing but wolverines laying waste.

"The roast pig!"

"Oh, yeah?"

"I mean the whole thing," Cole said breathless. "70 or 80 pounds! With, like, an apple in its mouth and…everything. It's…excellent!. You gotta see it!"

Mitch nearly choked. Laughing and swallowing at the same time. He was about to follow Cole and his plaything when Slippery rolled up. Mitch relayed the pig bit.

Slippery rolled his eyes. "I know, I know. It's even got a fucking apple in its mouth. Big deal." Gestured at Cole. "You! Give me the tourgash for a minute."

Cole's shoulders briefly sagged. Slippery glared. "No argument, rook." Motioned the nymphet and Mitch after him.

"We need her," he explained on the way. "Don't worry. They been trained." Left banquet table. Right banquet table. Left again. Slippery covering ground. Mitch trying to walk and window shop at the same time. They roared past some interesting looking dishes.

"I've died and gone to heaven," Slippery gushed in an aside. "You seen the fish?"

"Yeah, I came this way already," Mitch answered. Let a touch of annoyance creep in.

He kind of did want to see the pig. Brought back fond memories. Except for that one that caught on fire. Stu Baker charged with tending it. Got drunk. Fell asleep. A frightening sight when everyone got back from the beer store. Baker on the ground. Surrounded by empties. Face red. Snoring. One-hundred-and-fifty-pound porker in flames. They still had enough for a feed. Barely. Baker got salad for his troubles.

"Freshwater and saltwater," Slippery said with fervour. "Trout, rock bass, walleyes, swordfish, grilled tuna, flounder, grouper. Even got Jewfish."

Mitch gound to a halt. "What?"

"Yeah, I know," Slippery laughed. Caterpillar eyebrows bowed up. Fish names.

Mitch surprised Slip knew more than church perch frys. Hailed from Norwich. Some spot on the map south of Hogtown. Admitted the family grew up victims of Captain Hindgrinder. Those famous floor-sweeping fish fingers. From the freezer to the nuker. Paired up with creamed corn. Something you ended up eating when you couldn't think of a good excuse to escape.

Mitch's mother, to the contrary, did battered bass on a griddle you'd give up an organ for. But even his mother's eyes would go vinyl at this layout.

They drew up on Billings. Still with his American sherpa. Both busy sampling the steak selection. Half a herd's worth. Recently unloaded. Row upon row of perfectly grilled sirloins. Flash seared. Seal in the syrup. Beautiful marbling. Noses up all over. Mitch speared a still sizzling beauty. Avoided the swarm. Found a side table. Attention must be paid.

"Juicy as any I've had all day," Slippery said, jaws grinding.

"Muchas flavour, muchacho," Mitch seconded. Five bites. Battle over. Second helping time. A New York strip for variety. Have it any way you wanted it. Long as that meant bloody. Hesitated by the stack of T-bones next table. Tempting. Decided not. Maybe later. After he purged to make room.

"More, more," Jenkins garbled.

"Get in there," Mitch encouraged him.

The carved statue pushed in beside Mitch. Stabbing another steak. Pointed at tables reaching on to the end of the room. "Recognize any of it?"

Mitch peered at bowls and pans. Round, square, rectangular. Blue, yellow, green and red. Some painted, others plain. Inside, nothing familiar. Glanced at Slippery.

"That's why we have 'Guns 'R Us'." Slippery smiled. Jerked his thumb at the selections. "Hit it, helmet hider."

They tumbled after the giggling guide. Mitch launched a sad eye at the departing beef. Promised to return before the night was over.

The hot pocket started in. "Okay. This here, on my right, is a Southern specialty. It's called Spanish Style Chicken and Rice. Very popular."

Mitch's brow clouded in doubt. He lowered a nostril. Deep breath. Scooped a spoonful. Slippery did likewise.

"This is Lobster Ceviche," Lucy continued. Cole had returned from his brood at the bar. Mitch shot him a 'worry not' wink.

"Don't think so." Mitch slapped his belly. "Enough Spanish food for one day."

"Buttercup squash and butternut squash, here." Smile and point.

Questioning looks. Mitch led in. "I'll bite. What's the difference?" No one wiser after the answer.

"Next, tomatoes stuffed with crabmeat."

"Me for that," Slippery said eagerly.

"Yeah," Mitch agreed, "Yeah, I'm there."

"Kraut salad."

"Really?" Mitch laughed. "I'm surprised they'd be able to say that. Isn't that, like, racist or something?"

"It's okay. The Jewfish are over in a different aisle." Billings observed.

"Should've brought Heisz along for the trip. He'd have something to say about it," Jenkins said.

"Steak fajitas, there."

"Oh, shit, that we should know." Mitch took the tongs. Liberal helping. Laughed to think of that description. Meaning taking more than your share. Appropriate.

"Blackened Sea Scallops are here."

"Recommend them?" Mitch asked. Winked at Slippery.

"Absolutely," the youngster replied. Mitch tried the items. Pretty good.

"Okay, we have Shrimp Orzo in this bowl. It's a famous dish."

"Hmmm…." Mitch winced. "Not where I'm from. Maybe later. Maybe never."

"Some Smokey Chicken Chile."

"Mmmm…now we're talkin'." The hot trot tittered.

Slippery paused. Forked in a mouthful. "Oh, man," he sighed. "Try it."

Mitch did. Went saucer-eyed. "Jesus, that is good. Smokey chicken…?"

"Chili," the furby finished, boobs bobbing. "Everybody likes it."

"So they should! It's fantastic."

"We're eating better than those poor fucking sharks, I'll say that." Slippery observed between chews.

"No question," Mitch nodded. "Probably regretting it now. Christ only knows what horrible diseases they picked up from him. You just know the guy was a carrier. Anybody who prowls washrooms gotta be contagious."

And on they strolled. Stopped every now and again to top up. The pan-seared salmon with pineapple jalapeno relish got a look-in. Respect paid to the grilled Brats-in-a-Blanket with Mango Salsa. The roast chicken wheels tray suffered losses. Mitch popped two onto his plate. Ate one. Almost collapsed from overjoy. Succulent and savoury. Stuffed with sage-seasoned dressing. Mitch offered up yet another prayer of thanks.

"Superb," Billings said, meeting them. Mitch snorted agreement. But he wasn't to be diverted. The main business remained. Punching food into his face. Do one thing at a time. Do it well. The old man knew what he was talking about.

Others would be encountered on their roundabout travels. Yanks and Canucks shared security stories. Between devouring great slabs of tenderloin. Country-fried ham. Breaded cutlets. Ribs done every which way, all delicious. Spicy mesquite barbecued chicken in a mouth-watering onion sauce. The entrees stretched to the horizon. After an hour of ceaseless eating Mitch felt woozy.

The dessert compound remained. Billing's cupped Mindy's melon buttocks. Steered her forward. Mitch and the others plodded behind.

He couldn't imagine being enticed by anything. Felt swelled. Wrong. The glories present scalded his eyes. Everyone fell silent before a rainbow of beautiful confections. Chocolate shone. Glazes glistened. Sugar in all its glory. Spun, smeared, slathered and sprinkled wherever possible. Mitch nearly fell to his knees. What bounty.

Their cupcake companion continued reciting the menu. Mitch stopped counting the cakes they saw after hitting fifteen. The three story chocolate layer version led the parade. Cream, lemon and regular fillings. Angel food up next. The Bundt he recognized from home. Ernie Bloch's mother used to slice one up regularly after hockey practice. Technically, cheesecakes probably didn't count. But there were a half-dozen he managed to try anyway. No way he was passing on a cherry cheesecake. And the almond whipped cream... what could you do but stuff it in? Pray you didn't blow a lining.

An adjacent table buckled under the weight of pies—cherry, apple, raspberry, blueberry, strawberry-rhubarb, lemon. Others with names he'd never heard. Like Key Lime. The no baking angle was new. As was the honour given it.

"Get outta here," Jenkins said, shocked. "You have a State pie? An official Florida pie? Fuck. No way!"

"Swear to God," the princess said. Liquid sincerity. Mitch couldn't help picturing her on his prong. That perfect, shrink-wrapped figure. Dairy cannons driven into the duvet. Nappy dugout in the air. Bit of hickory lashing for laughs. This was the dessert section, after all. Hotcross buns fit right in.

"Does Ontario have a provincial pie?" Slippery said. Remains of a strawberry éclair on his chin and cheeks.

"I think we'd have heard of it by now," Mitch replied. Let his eyes linger on the goods.

"Try the cherry cobbler!" the minx advised. "We also have peach cobbler, peach crumble, and peach Betty!"

"Bet it doesn't top your peach, Betty," Slippery said. Stuck his tongue out. Coyote panting.

Mitch feigned a jab. "That kind a candour'll get you married, you're not careful," he warned. "Besides, I'm sure some big old...Gatorback lineman is already dining out on her crotch waffle. That's right, isn't it?"

"You guys," the siren blushed. No church virgin could have acted more coy. "They told us to look out for you. I don't know what a quimhound is. But they said that's what you all were."

Slippery snorted. "Slander! No man in Toronto like that."

Crumpet confusion. "But they said...I thought you...aren't you from Toronto? Up in Canada?"

"Yes," Billings confirmed.

"No," Mitch contradicted him.

"We are from Canada," Billings leapt in. "But no one's actually from Toronto. We just work there."

"Right," Mitch added. "Guys here are all straight. Choose anybody. Take the test. Your ol' wizard sleeve'll need a week to recover."

"But if you're actually from Toronto," Billings muttered, "...well, let's just say..."

"You ever hear of that movie Brokebutt Mountain?" Slippery interrupted. The girl shook her head. "No."

"Wait a minute?" Billings threw in again. "Wasn't it called 'The Silence of The Sheep' or something?"

"No!" Mitch said. "You're thinking of that other one. With that other guy."

Billings paused to think. "Oh, yeah. Maybe you're right."

"It's called Blowback Mountain," Cole jumped in. "I know 'cause we just watched it in school a year ago. It's mandatory now."

Collective 'E-w-w-w-w'.

"Anyway," Mitch said, "T.O. is fairyboy heaven. Saves time if you know that going in.

"Oh, I see." Scornful laugh. "One of the those. We have them here, too. There's even a club on campus. The Clamhaters. It's so funny."

Billings checked his com. "Guys. Interesting. But we got a party waiting for us up top. Last call for food."

Words to the wise. Everyone scattered. Mitch watched Cole whisper into his pump's ear. She nodded with enthusiasm. He grabbed a glad tit. Pulled her after him. They exited at a run. Mitch pleased for the rookie. Boy meets girl. Boy cleaves beef curtains. Girl grateful. The natural order of things.

Mitch took a last tour of the room. Had yet to weary of the amazing aromas, stellar array of dishes. Serviette come-ons. Tongs and ladles waved. Just patted his stomach. Shook his head. No mas, baby. Not now anyway. Felt again the joy of being totally satisfied.

Mitch still on a high when he reached the forward deck. The gang gathering. Retro lanterns strung from wires. Biologic hues—venery red, particle green, vitamin yellow. Early evening stars faintly visible. Above the horizon, a pastel sandwich. Soft shades of colour Mitch never even knew existed.

People drifted past, digesting dinner. Muffled voices. Agents paired up with the uni poon. Their afternoon work as beer Bev's over. Jigging and jiving to the live band. Or teaching southern sky astronomy. Cut-out moon rising. Put Mitch in mind of some 'tang himself.

Reg Swain signaling. Snicked a beer from an idle tray. Joined him looking over the railing. Dolphins! Three. Four, maybe. Slipstreaming in the wake. Making great time. Wherever they were going, they'd get there early. Surprise the other dolphins.

"Good luck," Swain said. Exhaled a cloud of Virginia's best. Looked out on the placid water. Mitch playfully tattooed him on the arm. Asked the older agent if he needed a beer? All clear given. Man kicked a small bag at his feet. Tinkle of ice. Brought his own stash with him.

"Can you fucking believe this boat?" he said. "Outside, it looks like…it should be sold for scrap." He tapped his fingers on their light standard. "But inside…shit. Fucking rich people. What are they worried about? Smalians?" Dropped the 'o'. Mitch wondered if it was on purpose?"

"You wouldn't trade places?" Slippery said, coming up from behind.

"In a second. Y'all cud come down. Visit me anytahm," Swain lied. Spot on impression of their bartender. Everyone laughed.

Mitch had no complaints. Top-flight service, start to finish. The rich expected no less. There had to be some reward for the inconvenience of obscene wealth.

Beer gone. Mitch ordered up the porter. Tall lad approached. Nearly saluted. Mitch quick-checked the money he waved. American bills all looked the same in twilight. Between rampant inflation and the exchange rate, the currency was like monopoly money. But he still didn't want to throw it around.

Gave instructions. Find the dining room pocket pie he'd played with earlier. Mitch couldn't remember the name. Gave a description. Promised a healthy tip for success. Returned to shooting the shit.

Incentive in action. The porter marched Mitch's titbit up ten minutes later. Kid's eyes lit up when Mitch paid him. Bounced away. Tip must have been credible. Mitch had no idea what he'd given him in real Canadian money.

"Hi, again," from the queef quarter. Toss of golden hair. Trollop blaze of teeth.

"You ask me? Commies and zombies, same solution. Cut off their heads or destroy their brains. What they have of'em. Only option. Can't live with'em. Can't reason'em either. But never mind that," he said. The Yank turned away to leer at Mitch's catch. "Fuck Cuba. It's party time."

"I can't wait," the Furby purred. Ran both hands down her thighs. Mitch promptly steered her away from the hanging tongue troupe. Let'em get their own. They brought money.

He introduced himself once more. Something to say. The lead guitarist went hard on a solo just as she spoke. He missed her name. Called her 'Bindy' for the next hour or so. 'Bendy' once, by accident. Thinking of someone else.

A moment's chit chat. Praise for the cool-ish evening breeze. Praise for the blues band. Mitch steered her to the railing. Right hand gestured at the moon. Left hand cracked her safe. Mindy turned. Leaned back against a safety float. Thrust her twin towers towards Mitch. He accepted the invite. Latched on. Worked the nips like ham radio dials. Reception fine.

The pop tart bubbled with delight. Relaxed into position, legs spread. Mitch knew she was talking. Hadn't heard a word. The band was jumping. Straight-ahead, bottomland boogie. He could hear Older doing his whoop coyote. Few more beers the boys would be showing ankle. Mitch had no fear of the dance floor. But the business of banging Mindy came first. Mitch a man of his word.

He looked deep into her eyes. Pulled her close. Drew her chin forward. She got the message. Shut up.

Mitch found an ear. Whispered, "You're about to take the ride a your life." Felt her melt in anticipation. Waited a two-count. Then gave her the full Labrador. Cheek and nose. Laughed to see her reaction. The scramble to wipe away saliva.

Doing it always tickled him. Was just funny. Didn't know why.

Fake apology concluded, Mitch returned to priming his pump. Mindy parted her lips. Then her legs. Mitch watched her eyes roll back. Room lights harder to turn on.

Click clack of approaching clogs. He whipped around. Snagged a beer from the passing Latin. Held it up to the moonlight. Throat gravy.

"What's so funny?" Mindy asked, face flushed.

Mitch shook his head. "Nothing. Just…this beer. Canada Pale Ale. Ever heard of it?"

"No."

"Probably something rich guy owns." Took a tentative sip. "Good," he declared. "Try it. No, seriously. It's tasty."

Mitch and Mindy shared the rest of the bottle. He ordered another when Miss Menudo announced her return. The dusky jewel salsa-ed away. A surgical grope refocused his attention. He grinned as the truth hit Mindy. Her hand jerked back in shock. Mitch closed immediately. Fingered away her beer 'stache. Buried his tongue in her ear.

When her knees gave way, Mitch was ready. Caught her before she fell. Threw her over his shoulder. Area scan. Agents milled about on the dance floor. Arms draped around or inside dates. Many looked unfamiliar. Somebody must have sent for more. Or they'd been kept on ice in the hold. Mitch cursed himself. He'd overpayed the porter. Prick knew supply was going to exceed demand. No matter. Probably losing it in craps with some Castro raftugees.

Tempest in a sexpot time. Mitch humped Mindy three steps away. An alcove presented itself. Dark. No-entry 'X' emblazoned on the door. He could just make out the screaming yellow seal. Heavy handle. Perfect. Mitch had no intention of going any further. As long as no one exited, they'd be fine.

Moist darkness closed them in. Mindy squeaked in delight. Mitch had smoothly removed her shortlets and panties. Began massaging mooseknuckle. Pastrami flaps sprang open. Sound of ripping zipper. Cheek flush against the steel wall, Mindy reached under to help. For the third time she gasped.

"Oh, my God!" She felt it again. Her heartrate redlined. "It is…it's…real. I wasn't sure..to believe it."

"Don't be telling scrimmage boy, okay?" Mitch said, loosing the swamp monster. "It'll put the zap on his head. Bad trouble."

"Don't worry," Mindy wheezed. "No one…no one will..ever believe me."

Mitch snorted. Heard that before. Mindy'd be telling fish tales to her friends soon enough. They all did. Only this time she couldn't exaggerate. Told her not to worry. He was an old hand at prospecting. Never hit a dry hole. Never would.

Mindy found a water pipe running the length of the wall. Latched on with her right hand. Shuddered. Squealed Sighed. Arched her back. Well-trained thresher, Mitch thought. She was right there and ready. The surroundings unmatchable. Calm ocean, heavy moon, Tex-Mex bootstomp-and-jump filtering down to them. Prime moment for mitten filling.

Mitch in the saddle now, full gallop. Hands on Mind's hips. Riding hard for the border. Flesh jack on cruise control. Mitch passed the time flicking through memory panels. So much had happened. Seemed like a week's activities crammed into one day.

Arrived from Canada in the morning. Filthy heat. Met Prescott, the NSC spooks. Buggy to the wharf. Thrill and disappointment together. Relief upon seeing the ultra-lux interior. Great lunch. Many near-naked sex objects providing comfort. Seeing Kensilla off. Back to the trough for an even better feed. Getting the shaft buffed. What was that torqued-tongued tramp's name? Gloria? Glinda? Like he cared. Power nap. Nosh again. Then more nookie! If every day was like today…he'd be a corpse before the month was out. But a what a way to go. Sure beat the treatment you'd get from some indifferent nurse biddy working night shift at the local death emporium.

Wrestler tap on his forearm. Mindy in joyous agony. Ever the gentleman, Mitch obliged. She reared back, nearly blown. He slapped her flanks for fun.

"My…my…" Mindy moaned.

"Take a break," Mitch commanded. Winced. Hamperlids pinched. Sap trapped. Each heartbeat, another wrenching spasm. He reached behind him. Felt along the ledge. Found it! The half-full beer. Just what the doctor wanted. He tipped it back. Drank deep. Beautiful.

Mindy's breathing slowed. Mitch went back to work with a will. Locked in. Ninja boot probe re-engaged. Surging forward. Braced his left foot against the wall. Right hand anchored above her hipbone. Pale Ale cradled in his left. Set sail for the isle of Morgasm.

And so it went. Mitch nursed his drink. Savoured the breeze. Casually ground Mindy to mush. The night curled around them like a cat. Splash of a fish jumping. He glanced over. Creamy white light skated over the waves. Another fish jumped. Heavier. Made you want to drop line. He wondered what that would be like. Fucking and fishing at the same time? And drinking? One-handed hook-baiting a challenge. X-treme multi-tasking. Something to consider for the future. Knew he could interest a few CORE guys in the prospect.

Sound and movement in the corridor. Mitch parked his beer. Crab-fucked Mindy near the edge for a look-see. Colourful Chinese lantern swirls on the walkway mats. In the murky gloom, familiar-looking headgear. Kangol beret. Mitch knew it had to be Jenkins. Four legs became visible. Familiar groan of animal pleasure. A local grail getting gaffed.

Mitch whistled. CORE signal. Pause and a look back. Rear assault slowed.

"Yo, Jenks?"

"Mitch?"

"Howdy, sailor," Mitch laughed. "Not catching you in the middle of anyone, am I?"

"Now that you mention it..." Jenkins gruffed.

Mitch grabbed a handful of Mindy's hair. "Jesus. Stop for a second. I'm trying to talk."

"Sorry," Mindy said. "Please. I'm so close...again."

"Okay, okay," Mitch sighed. "Just...work alone for a minute. Quietly."

American tobacco smell. Mitch inhaled. Something he'd forgotten.

"Hey, Jenks! Shit, man," he stage whispered. "I could use a smoke. Got any handy?"

Answer delay. Then, "Yeah, hang on." Another delay. "Careful. It's one of those weakass American packages."

"I know," Mitch answered. Saw a flash of reflected light. Speared the object at the last second. Stunned by his own luck.

"Lazer inside," Jenkins added.

"Beautiful." Mitch put the box in his mouth. Lifted Mindy up without missing a stroke. Disappeared back into shadow. Retrieved a cigarette.

Checked he wasn't sparking the filter. Lit it. Draw in a satisfying breath of fresh air. Slug of semi-warm brown pop chaser. Couldn't think of a single thing missing. Except colder beer. Maybe a toke. Game on the holoscreen up in the corner. Otherwise, pretty close to perfection.

"Need it back?" Mitch stage-whispered.

"No, keep it," Jenkins advised. "I got anther pack."

"Roger that." Back to Mindy, now weeping openly from joy and exhaustion. Mitch relaxed against the cool wall. Like the man said. A woman was a woman. But a cigar was a smoke. Great having your cake and eating it too.

Ocean sounds. Waves lapping gently as they slid away from the hull. Driving bass line bouncing in from the deck. Regular grunts as Jenkins filled pothole. Slamming ass like he was angry at it. Mad as hell. Not going to take it anymore.

Mind wandering. Wondered what they were doing in ol' Currytown. Any more trulls wash up on the beach? Discovered in gutters? Squashed into recycle bins? What pranks were being pulled? How'd the Leafs do? Chicago into the Hangar. Nice rivalry rekindled. Whatever they were doing, it probably involved scraping slush off their boots. Dry chuckle. He couldn't wait to tell this story. Good thing there were witnesses. Wouldn't get a listen without them. Nobody'd believe it.

Mitch drilled his cigarette against the wall. Thought about burying it in Mindy's quivering butt cheek. Sado laughs. And cinch the whisker biscuit closed in a hurry.

Another splash audible. Swordfish? Did they surface like that?

Mystery explained in a moment. A pantless Jenkins, silhouetted in the alcove opening. Rapid fire delivery.

"Holy, shit! I think I just fucked my slut into the drink."

Mitch spit-spewed his last swig of beer over Mindy's bouncing ass. "What?! Are you serious? What do you mean think?"

"Ok. I did it," Jenkins admitted.

"How?"

"I don't know. Not on purpose. You didn't see her. She's…pretty top heavy. I was really giving it, you know, when…I looked away for a second. Next thing I know, she just kind of…slid over…the side." Dark giggle. "Fucking med students. They're not very stable. Didn't you hear her hit the water?"

"Thought it was…something else."

"What should we do?"

"What do you mean, 'we'?" Mitch replied. "She's your whore. Jump in and get her."

"I'm not going in there!," Jenkins protested. "Could be sharks!"

Mitch cleared his throat. Good point. "Take a paddle with you. They're afraid of wood. Besides, they're probably not interested. They ate earlier."

"Shit! You're no help." Jenkins spun. Grabbed the top bar. Looked out. "Oh! There she is. I can see her."

"What's going on?" Mindy breathed.

"Shut up!" Mitch ordered. Threw her an extra four inches. Take her mind off the disturbance.

"What's she doing?" he whispered to Jenkins. Not sure why he was keeping his voice down. He hadn't done anything.

"Fucking splashing up a storm, that's what. Hey!" he yelled. "Stop that shit! You'll attract...things. Just...float! We're comin' to get ya'."

"What'd she say?" Mitch finished his beer. Things were getting interesting.

"Who knows? She's Cuban, I think. Or Mexican. It's hard to make out when they get jabbering.

"Try this," Mitch said. "Donde esta sharkola que pasa."

A pause. Then Jenkins shouted down the instructions. Waited. Turned back to Mitch.

"Worked. What's it mean? "

"Don't splash. You'll attract sharks."

"No shit. I didn't know you could speak Spanish."

"Just that line," Mitch said. Voice neutral. Glad it was dark. Jenkins couldn't see him.

Mindy was going mental on the meat hitch. Blitzkrieging the bone. Both hands pressed flat against the opposite wall. Launching herself along the pole again and again.

Jenkins still leaning over the rail, demanding she not drown until help arrived. Mitch was keen to watch the fun. Whistled to Jenkins.

"Deal with this, will you?" he asked. Tossed over the empty. "Don't worry. It's biodegradable glass." Shushed Mindy. Grabbed love bars. Bore down.

A sharp wail of pain reached them.

"What was that?" Mitch asked. Mild alarm.

"What are the fucking odds?" Jenkins moaned. "An entire ocean and I still hit the stupid twat. Unbelievable."

Mitch continued to hole seal. Or seal hole. Trying to think of a solution to Jenkin's problem.

"Christ, I suppose I should find a...a raft or something, " Jenkins finally said. "Where do you think they'd be?"

"The raft room," Mitch grunted. "Where else?"

"Yeah. Yeah, you're right. Okay. Shit."

Then he was gone. Mitch's sixth sense told him entertainment knocked.

Time to finish off Mindy. Mitch ramped up the tempo. Full throttle. Concentrated, deliberate fucking now. Sweat dripped from his nose as he focused on really nailing her beehive. Mindy could do nothing but note each plunge with a tiny gasp.

"Whore overboard! Whore overboard!" Mitch knew that wasn't Jenkins yelling. An emergency siren wailed. The ship lurched. He could hear the pulse engine working in reverse. Perfect. Jenkins had them all in stitches the next day, describing events. "You believe it? They even got a special 'slut in the suds' horn. Now that's Boy Scouts prep."

"Goddamn it" Mitch cursed himself. "Hurry up, hurry up. C'mon! Let's go!" he urged on his joybar. "Why must I always take so long? I'm going to miss everything."

"Sorry," Mitch apologized. In his haste, he'd had driven Mindy's face into the wall. She threw a hand up. Apology accepted. On rolled the porking, savage but satisfying.

And then, the arresting sense of closure. Gutteral cries from Mindy. Wild bucking. Rabid wall pounding. Drool pool growing.

Mitch grizzlied upright. Mindy's feet dangled above the deck. She took his scrotal explosion with a warbling scream of success. The baby vault Pollacked. The red canvas coated with creamed DNA. The best kind of artistic expression.

Masterpiece complete, she eased off his easel. Knee wobble. Spent. Dropped. Down and out.

Mitch had no towel. Found her shorts. Buffed love lube off the brush. Tossed the sticky onto the unconscious choot.

"Sayonara, sweetmeat," he said. Pulled on his gear. "Gotta go. Have to provide emergency assistance." A good joke. Bolted out into the walkway. Listened for where the action was.

Ship a madhouse. Word had spread. Men crowded the rail. Orgy postponed. Operation Save Our Slut took precedence. Searchbeams scoured the ocean surface. Several roborafts were launched. Sped off in all directions. Useless. Crewmembers lowered a rope ladder. Lifejackets got thrown over. Drunks helping.

"Jesus, you'd think the Titanic just went down," Mitch heard a voice say. "It's just one harlot. Twenty bucks says she's probably fucking the anchor right now. Pull it up. Let's see."

Mitch found Jenkins. Still pantless. Giving directions to the deck captain. Fighting off a cock-hungry sociology major at the same time.

Orders relayed. Rescue boom extended. Safety net winched down. CORE agents loudly offering suspect advice. No drones nearby. Bombing the ocean? What was the point? Booze reasoning.

Then came the false shark sightings. Another giggle. Beerspouts cascaded into the brine. Typical, high-spirited carousing. Mitch hallooed a Bev. Cracked a fresh can of foreign shit. Spontaneous wolf howl. Great climax to his climax.

Missed what happened next. Billings filled him in between laughing fits later. Some comic looking for cheap laughs. CORE or Yank, no one knew. Whoever, guy happened across a spare flare. Threw it at the mattress back as she clambered up the ladder. Portable spot illuminated everything. Target found. Hit her in the kisser. Stunned look. Blood trail. Hands to face. Blurts of staccato jabber. Roundheels Rebecca abandoned hull. Re-entered the wet and frothy.

"Blonde in the pond!" a voice near Mitch yelled. "I'm outta here!" The old Chappaquiddick gag always got a laugh. Even if the wand waxer was a brunette.

Cascade of good-natured abuse. Each comment funnier than the last. Burnt-faced agents collapsed. Pounded railing. Stamped the deck. Web-ready gold material.

Agents regrouped. Her clumsiness forgiven, they hurled down encouragement. The flailing tart took heart. Stabbed out wildly. Found a rung. Began the ascent. Third of the way up, another flare landed. Lit. Spewing smoke and flame. Bounced off her ample rack. Pinwheeled up. Last revolution set her hair on fire. Roar went up from elated viewers. Com's out and filming.

Once again, the undergrad simpleton lost focus. Dangling above a proven fire retardant, tried to beat the flames out with her free hand. Mitch erased his recording attempt. Roller coaster cam work. Lesson learned. Never do digi while reduced to hysterics.

Bent over, clutching a support pipe, Mitch failed to see the assbackward cannonball. Gill had it on his com. Mitch able to argue the merits of her attempt. Credit for the geyser. Points lost on form. So no moving onto the final round. Older laughed so hard he threw up into a cooler.

And that was all it took. Seemed obvious. Jenkins' dinner roll was joined by another soon after. Mitch recognized her from the feast. Starchuk had partnered up with some Yank. Sent the slit over the side. Spreadeagled and screaming. Another fountain of spray. More incomprehensible talk. Jenkins threw up his hands. He'd done what he could. Looked to find his pants before the hovering sluts ate all the meat off his joint.

"Pool party!" Sinclair's baritone bellow. The race was on. Guys throwing pussy into space "like bales of pot off a speedboat," O'Brien said, telling it at Billy's. "For awhile, you couldn't see the stars. That much ass going past."

An impromptu contest developed. CORE regulars competing. Who could throw a tramp from the steamer so she hit water most awkward? Some spectacular splashlandings the result. Butt first. Neck and shoulders. Legs akimbo, windmilling chute runners. Mitch was done for again. Rolling on the floor. From fucks to yuks. Even after a gruelling day, the boys maintained that stylish sense of humour. You had to admire it.

Precedent established. Even so, Mitch didn't have the heart to dump Mindy in. Not with a fresh keepsake in her pearl hotel. He let Jenkins do it instead. Premium face plant. Wave swamped several nearby. Mitch saw an American SecStooge drop a fire extinguisher on his foot. Muscles gave way.

Even old guys were wiping away tears. And you'd think they'd seen it all before. Funny just didn't come any faster.

But good times end. "The drunk little d-d-d-dork," Mills mocked, telling it later for listeners. "Nobody even noticed the idiot up on the railing."

"What was he doing up there," Sanders wondered.

"Taking a fucking whiz on'em, that's what, the rook." Mills shook his head. That was a memory. "Lost his balance. You can guess the rest."

Mitch didn't have to. He watched Cole go in. Horns, klaxons, whistles, bells, sirens...the whole alarm orchestra blared at once. Danishes hit the water. Giant, six-person glow-in-the-dark rafts. Bridge operators remote-steered them away from the thrashing blow holes. Made for Cole at speed.

Clanking chains cut through the shouts and hooting. Wild Rose crew lowered the main lifeboat. Rigged-out rescuers stood ready. Agents closed ranks along the ship's side. Various states of undress. Waiting for the call. One man in jeopardy, all in jeopardy. Sharks and other deep water nasties— FOAD. CORE ready to spill blood in defense of their own.

An official-sounding bellow warned everyone off.

"Pros here," an agent observed. Special ops divers waddled into view. Fully prepped. Teksuits and flashguns. Not needed, unfortunately. Cole was topside and safe a minute later. Soaked, slightly embarrassed. Otherwise, none the worse for his impromptu dip.

And the Americans couldn't stop praising him. They loved the way Cole had kicked his way free of clinging cooz. Drowners were always desperate, determined. Cole treated them like so much seaweed. Crawled over them, elbows swinging, into the safety raft. Scramble from there to the net the work of a moment. Not an ounce of cheap sentimentality evident. Composure in the presence of possible harm. Widespread respect garnered.

"Show's over," Stone announced. No-contradiction-accepted voice. The crew, he said, would fish out all the papaya smiles in due time. "They've put on another feed down below. Everyone expected."

Nobody need their arms twisted. CORE agents and their American hosts scattered. Gathered up their clothes. Made for the exits. Corraling the fur herd someone else's job. The party of heroes raced to the mess hall.

The Castle of Hautdesert, Stone called it. Mitch was a believer. He'd never seen so many sweets. Booze flowed. Wenches glowed. And agents stowed it away like it was holy. Roast beef subs, thick and filling. Extra-spicy Buffalo wings. Mini-burgers, hot and juicy. Perfectly grilled Italian sausages lazing in fresh, chewy buns. Bacon-fried steaksticks in honey-garlic sauce. Breaded cutlets, chicken and pork. Crunchy good. More homemade pizzas. Onionated, melty mozzarella, summer sausage, salami, hot banana peppers, jalapenos, green pepper, pineapples. And no fucking olives. Great nacho bins. Buckets of tangy salsa. Gallons of ice-cold draft to chase it. A long, glorious feed. A long, glorious day. Cultural exchange. Septic songs sung with relish. Serviette ass slapped. More international bonding promised. For those with the strength. If ever a day warranted it, they were living it. Mitch delirious. And getting a little drunk.

While CORE indulged, the tit brigade trudged back into the hold. Job done. Loving and laughs provided. Not a single slut lost to sharks. The Wild Rose crew knew their business. Hoisted up their soiled southern cousins. Deposited them on deck. Hosed them down.

"They smelled about as fishy going in," a wit noted. Two more circulated with re-engineered leaf blowers. Dried the briny banana portals. After, hustled all below. Where they were paid off. And advised to keep the day's activities private. Nothing viral on the web. No twitting. No assbook.

No need for concern. The college Calcuttas all good sports. Never complain, never explain. The black hole code. Half the girls, Mindy in the lead, lobbied hard to be considered for the next conference. CORE cocksmen made themselves memorable.

Back in the Captain's quarters. Cigars, strippers and kegs. McIntryre retired early. Left word the men were to be taken care of. No request denied. Guys off their heads at the news. Like Halloween, Christmas and Barbarrosa all rolled into one.

By first bell the party was well-ramped. Between Bad Brains and group karaoke the din blew out portholes. New naked women, legs splayed, draped themselves everywhere. Rubbed up against spectators. Purred. Licked furniture. Anderson moaned that you couldn't sit down without getting a rim job. Mitch, too, found it almost too much. Not so put out he didn't sample some front bottom himself. Agents were slipping in and out of the master cabins. Giggling strippers in tow. Mitch did likewise. Or so they told him later. Didn't recall it. Cock on automatic.

The casino corner sparkled with shining faces. Joyous cries erupted every few minutes. The roulette wheel seemed to only spin winners. Mitch himself pocketed eight-hundred of the best playing blackjack. Described how later. His "skill" came from being hammered. He thought he was playing 31. Kept asking for more cards. Dealer a magician.

The bartender a buxom beauty. Took a shine to Mitch. Right after he buried his face between her butterbags. Went "brrrrrrr." She roared with pleasure. Shot him specials from then on. Lowballs. Name changed after Mitch dropped his pants to make a point. Cadillac Margaritas. Tequila mixed with unpronounceable shit. He lost all track of reality after the fifth snifter.

Mills fell into the karaoke machine at one point. Broke it. Much cheering. Stripper walked past, Dirty Sanchez on display. Hilarious. A stunt with balloons. Cutler's Last Charge of the Light Sabers. A Patpong pro timed her queef jets. Kept several ping pong balls aloft simultaneously. Another smoked cigarettes from every orifice in her body. Spectacular. Guys right on the floor laughing their asses off.

Then an agent burst into the room screaming, "Hallelujah Akbar! Let the bells ring and the banners fly. It's too good to be true, but I'm Bashir!"

Hadfield, wasted. Found cartridge belt across barrel chest. Bathtowel burqa. Brandished candles, duct tape bundled. Ran around the room. Threatened death to all infidels. Demanded a Jew to persecute. Or the Hindu selling photos of Mohammed. Blow the joint if they didn't give him a drink. Missed when reaching for it. Hit his head on a bar stool as it passed by. Terror alert over.

Mitch got provocative. Joked they were all heading to New York after. See the new Muslim Not-a-MegaMosque. 9/11 celebrations on tap. A couple Americans got shirty. Words exchanged. Ratelle talked everyone down. Explained Mitch was just putting the needle in. He was sure a memorial to the Twin Tower victims would get built. One day. No rush.

"Like for a fucking mosque," someone piped up. Tempers flared again. Mitch had already drifted away. Seeing double. Searched for his car keys. Panicked. Couldn't find them. Have to phone Andrea. Come get him. Wherever he was.

Three o'clock. Mitch on all fours in the corridor. Babywander. Drooling. Thought he knew a convenience store nearby. Needed one more beer.

Four o'clock. Same goal, different corrridor. Tried to triangulate position from the sound of singing. Standing not an option. Up too far away. Rounded the corner. Pile of sluts gently snoring. One, his trusty, busty tarbender. Gave her exposed snuggle pups a fond squeeze on the way past. Heard later guys grabbed her. Gagged her. Dragged her up top. Roped her to the main mast. The Tippi Treatment. Drunken knotting. She escaped. A lesson there.

Mitch woke up in his room. Alarm. Checked under the blanket. Relief. Only a dream. Hadn't shit himself while accepting his award.

Asked for light. Blinked back pain. Morning. Maybe. Afternoon more likely. Someone had been in his room. Shirt and jeans, pressed and clean. On the dresser. Coffee maker plugged in. Smell must have woke him up.What a great hotel.

Ran through the night's events. All in all, felt as he should. Ruined. Same story for the rest. Instant CORE classic. A night to be spoken of with reverence. Viewtube and VoxVid sales cemented the tale. Set the bar for all future blowouts. A few came close. None topped it. Legions would later claimed to have been there. The boast, "I was on the Wild Rose the night…" worked on more than a few brakepads. Mitch never used the line. Too easy.

Mitch punched the airplane pillow. Took a last look at Florida pavement out the porthole. Take off in ten.

"Good thing there's evidence," he said to no one. "Hard sell otherwise."

Thump of luggage being gently squished into place. Flashing light of the departing robohandler. Motoring home. Shed an oven, Mitch figured. You need to be a machine to stay there.

Gassed up, ready. The jet taxied forward.

"Fucking slush waiting," Jenkins groused. Face glum. TO info flashed across the cabin holoscreen. Weather, shitty. Next day's forecast, shittier. Traveling sigh of despair. Seasoned with hangover grief. And the realization warm and water were going away. What was to come, unappealing.

Mitch knew he looked like he felt. A bucket of used and broken. Wasn't in synch with anything. Agents moved up and down the aisle as though fighting river current. Idiot pilot's needless announcements. Made no sense. Three times he'd brushed his teeth. Moss mouth remained.

Fuck curing the common cold. Or cancer. Concentrate on what was important. Hangover remedies were what required serious investigation. Useless research 'spurts. Cancel their grants!"

Tequila. Rhymed with Sheila. Which didn't sound like Andrea. Who he'd promised to phone. Who he hadn't bought anything for. Or told they'd be a day late into Pearson. So don't go.

In a perfect world, he'd simply order something stupid online. The YYZ duty-free shop would have it wrapped and ready when they landed. Tech barrier. Can't get there from here. Fell asleep inventing painful digithead revenge scenarios.

Woke up totally fucked. Rattled and confused. Dry as dirt. Raised a hand. Bev appeared beside him. Wrapped his fingers around a frosty Corona. Lime inserted. Bubbles dancing. How had she known? Brought it to his lips…

Woke up for real. Pissed off again. Fucking dreams. Peeled the pillow off his face. Raised his hand. Bev brought him his icy Corona. He launched it upwards. Let that delicious amber fluid kick the top off his hangover.

Truth was, Mitch hated them. Hangovers. The best thing to do with them, he'd learned, was postpone the pain. And the way you did that was to keep drinking. Max probably knew this. One of the secrets to a successful career. Master the hangover. All it was…alcohol withdrawal. No alcohol withdrawal, no hangover. Bob's your uncle…with a shot liver. So it goes.

A good thing, though. He'd slept through most of the flight. They were already circling Toronto Island airport. Quiet plane. No one spoke. Overheads emptied. Minions would pick up the heavy shit. Time to get home, take a long shower. Pour a triple Crown. Get Andrea to make him something. Catch up on the sports news. Then hit the mattress for some sweet, sweet sleep. He'd earned it.

The private party post-mortem at Billy's a week later. Everyone convulsed. Packed bar to watch the premiere vid. The ship pics, exquisite. Kensilla on Zeiss zoom. The righteous chomping. Brought all the good times back. Everyone competed to paint the picture. The Weasel trapped. His face hate-twisted, spittle-flecked, demon indignant. Scrabbling in the net. Math prof. hair. Hork bath. Gradual understanding. The pasty-faced penis-puffer finally grasping his fate. Too late.

The Cape Canaveral send off. Man shrieking like a dyke on fire. In the soup seconds later. Excellent digicam work. Bird's eye angle got 'ahhh's'. Agents pointing out their favourite predator. 'Hip hip hooray's' for the hammerheads. Magnificent, machine-like maneaters. Tearing an asshole a new asshole. The way they joined forces. "Gleichschaltung" the Germans called it. (Or so the Sage said. And had everyone doing Hunspeak for the next twenty minutes.)

Cheers for the snakes. Cheers for the 'cuda. Scorn for Sid. The hapless, near-sighted giant squid. His clumsy efforts a stain upon his kind. So unlike the lampreys. When that glistening torpedo latched onto Kensilla's skull. Ripped it wide. Well, Billy's reverberated. The rafters rattled. Then the great Robert Shaw finish. Roll credits. Count your money.

"Blockbuster," a knowing critic cried out. Mitch was a believer. He figured they should twin it with the banquet. Make a killing in Third World countries. Impoverished villagers could gather in the king's hut. Marvel at the food whitey got to eat. Then enjoy a bit of exciting true-life violence for dessert. Toss in the sorority dunking as an extra feature…let's see Hollywood top it.

Mitch felt a shoulder tap. Bev gestured across the room. Jameson applauding. Mitch gave the we're-number-one finger salute. Another nod to the smirking Max nearby. Glass in hand. Rumpled as ever. Like he slept in a laundry basket. Some day, Mitch figured. Hunched over on a park bench. Hungry sparrows and chickadees looking on. Overdue suicide successful.

Then listeners heard about the mystery moneybags. Mister Wild Rose. Hawk nosed, take-no-shit-shove-your-idiot-gun-registry-up-your-ass country boy done good. Snaps told the tale. Weathered as barnboard. Barb wiry. Still sharp, Stone claimed. Even if he did have old guy symptoms, Mitch thought to himself. Nobody ever tells them to mow the nose hair?

But all that came later. Meanwhile, Mitch and a weary away team were whisked through immigration. Another perk of CORE employment. Lineups, patdowns, suspicious looks? Reserved for the innocent. Mitch flew out of Pearson rarely. When he did, he always made a point of praising staff for giving the elderly grief. Loudly demanded their walkers be checked for explosives. Corrective shoes probed for poisons. Depends searched. White retirees a known security threat, he'd declare to the circle of onlooking passengers. Nothing better than a LUB with a fume on. For Mitch, humiliating lazy union bastards was every citizen's duty. Today the exception, though. Too zapped.

Chinese eyes on the drive home. Didn't remember hitting any thing. Parked. Found elevator, door. Flashed chip. Threw his bag in the closet. Andrea could wash everything later. Andrea. Shit! Wondered if she was still at the airport. They'd skipped right through to the shuttle transpo. Never went near the lounge.

Went into the bedroom. Looked around. Didn't see her bag. She might have forgot. Gone shopping. He lay down on the bed, trying to think of what to do. He wasn't sure he had the energy to work his com. GPS her location. Drifted off thinking of fried rice, egg rolls, chicken balls, the soup with the plump doughy shit in it, spring rolls…

MORNING IS BROKEN

—◄○►—

Sunlight poured through the bedroom window.

"You brought it back from Florida," Andrea joked. Snuggled against him.

"Holy shit," Mitch said, blinking. "How long I been out?"

"You slept round the clock. Must have been some trip."

"You don't know the half of it," Mitch smiled. He took a deep breath. Rubbed his eyes. Stretched until his muscles creaked. Stomach rumble.

"I'm not surprised," Andrea said. "You must be starving. I hope you remembered to eat something."

"Here and there," Mitch replied. He grimaced.

"What's wrong?"

"Nothing," Mitch said. Suddenly threw the coverlet over Andrea's head. Held her down. She giggled. Mistook his intention. He unleashed a bubble fart so heavy and poisonous he feared for a second he'd shit himself. Andrea screamed. Fought to surface. Futile. Mitch was too strong. Gave her the full treatment. Buried her head in his crotch. Always made him laugh. Finally let her up before she passed out.

"Present from Walt," he said. Backed away himself as the fumes hit. Laughed. "Oh, man! Fucking rank or what. Holy shit!"

Andrea slapped his shoulder. Mock-glared at him. "That was terrible!"

"Sorry. Good to be home, I guess. Body getting rid of all that crap Panhandle air."

Andrea shivered. Pulled the coverlet back up under her chin. Mitch debated. Then realized there was no choice. Bolted for the can. Returned slapping his hands. Jumped into warmth. Squished up against Andrea. Sniffed the air for residual stink.

"Fuck me! It's colder in here than outside."

"You said keep it at 10C." Andrea protested.

326

"When no one's here!" Mitch rejoined. "When I'm here...12C is okay." His old man would have hooked him one for wasting money. If you couldn't see your breath in the morning, you were a wuss.

"What day is it?" Mitch asked. Voice muffled.

"Monday."

"Don't you have work?"

"Floating holiday. I wanted to see you when you came back."

"That's wonder..." Mitch said. Garbled it. "I think I'm falling in..." Chewed the rest of the phrase up. Andrea tried to box his ear.

"Do you work?" she asked.

A grunt from Mitch. "Technically. Yeah. I guess."

Groan of disappointment from Andrea. "But you worked all weekend. They can't make you work every day. You're not a machine."

"Crime doesn't take a break," Mitch said. It sounded like Andrea's right tit was talking. She giggled.

"What?" Mitch feeling playful.

"Oh, I don't know. I just thought that...you know. All weekend. Slaving away catching bad guys. My own James Bond. I wanted to sap your maple as a reward."

Mitch sighed, thinking. If he was out as long as she said, the tank should be back to near full. Still. "Listen," he said. "I appreciate the offer but..." Too late. Andrea had eeled down beside him. Plunged her hands deep into his hemp Flexers.

"Oh," she began to moan, "I was so hoping."

Mitch could feel his resolve melting. "Okay," he said, a little more gruffly than he intended. "But...let's not dally. I really do...I should show my face in the office this morning. Sometime. I must have...shit to do."

"Miff Capan Thithathelli?" Andrea whinnied, her tongue jockeying around Mitch's braced razor.

Mitch shook his head. "What did your Mom always say?" he admonished. "Don't talk with your mouth full."

He hiked himself up. Leaned against the icy headboard. Folded his arms. Checked the night table digi. Could still make work by lunchtime. Third floor café had some kind of special menu the whole week. Steak sandwiches, if he remembered right. Salivated at the thought. Anatole's steaks were famous. Garlic toast bed. Everything done just the way he liked it.

Having thought it, Mitch was now determined to make it happen. He wondered how many others would make it in. Knew Jensen wouldn't. Anderson? Probably not. Older. Yeah. Cole? Didn't count. Maybe half the others. He'd look like a keener. Plus, he needed a good workout. The living had been a little rich in Fla.

Andrea drew breath. "Whoo-eee!" she trilled. "Still delish! Like smoked salmon."

Mitch patted her on the head. Urged her on. Now thinking about the DVP. Monday. Maybe not ugly. But you never knew. Plan on it and you'd fuck yourself. Some tanker truck overturns. Fireball backs traffic up to Pickering. You'd get to work in time to punch out.

Mitch threw the coverlet half off. He'd warmed up. Also, he liked to watch. Offer technique pointers where necessary. Flashed suddenly on the quality tonsil work performed by that dusky Wild Rose tub turtle. Her name escaped him. He hadn't over-praised her, though. The scholarship bint blew with the best.

Not that Andrea was second-rate. But her sword-swallowing skills were commonplace. No lack of enthusiasm. Just nothing in the way of theatrics. Workmanlike, robotic bob and gulp. Showmanship? Vegas theatrics? Lacking.

Mitch watched Andrea hoover away. Eyes closed. Face serene. Demeanor as meek and mild as the Madonna's. Lips distended, ghostly white. Maximum elasticity. Like a mason jar seal wrapped around a natural gas pipeline.

Sudden lust alert. Animalistic huffing. Mitch recognized the signals. Reached behind him. Secured a handhold on the headboard. A precaution in the event of oversuck vapour lock. Experience the great teacher. He'd never live down another Jaws-of-Life incident. The last episode had gone viral. Paramedics couldn't stop laughing. Lots of T-shirts sold. Mitch never saw a penny of revenue.

He'd only been gone a couple of days. You wouldn't know it to judge from Andrea's famished attack. It was like feeding a North Korean. Eyebrows narrowed in concentration. Train tunnel nostrils. The creamy cheeks billowed and snapped. Mitch cleared his throat. Fun and games, yes. But time pressure remained. Tapped his wrist. Retro joke.

Andrea cleared her throat as well. Disgorged the totemic pole.

"I'm so sorry," she apologized. "I really am. It's just…" She sighed. More words unnecessary. If she even knew them. Mitch couldn't be too angry or impatient.

"Yeah, yeah," Mitch said. "Look…they don't call you 'Maytag' for nothing. But seriously. I gotta go to work. Finish up, eh?"

Andrea nodded, ever-compliant. It was a quality Mitch did appreciate. She beheld the bulbous beet. Stroked its golden shaft. Mitch's centrepost. The axis around which her world revolved. With what throbbing majesty did it stand erect. Aloof ruler of all it surveyed. Something about its bearing, its native intelligence, spoke to Andrea like no other cock she'd sucked. She often pictured herself astride it. Racing aross verdant meadows of azure green. Her tresses free and flowing. A dream only. Mitch would never permit it. Too bad. It would make a great movie.

She returned with a will to pleasing it. Teased it. Eased her mouth along the mighty musculature. Surrendered to pure carnality. Her questing tongue discovered the hidden grove of wonders. Mitch's magnificent moghuls. The heavenly orbs of glory.

Andrea offered up a silent prayer of thanks. Unhinged her bottom jaw. Popped the entire grapefruit in. Tongue-buffed it with serious love. Set it free, sparkling clean. Eyed the partner. Grasped the iron stanchion for balance. Inhaled Mitch's manly musk. Bore in. Tastebuds rewarded. A banquet of sea salty flavours greeted her. On she explored. Darted over serrated flesh dunes. Polished the silky soft sac. In her heart, a song. She couldn't wait to tell the girls in accounting.

Leagues away again, Mitch revisiting a missed chance. Open net an armless 'tard could find. Bouncing puck. Three swats. Last put it over the crossbar. Hat trick for the game. Always the bungled one that haunts you after, though. At least they won. Took the season series from Metro DP. Bragging rights again.

Andrea had moved on. Began to root and snuffle about the deeper recesses of Mitch's groin. The rabbit nuzzling drew Mitch back from daydreaming.

"Jesus H. Christ!" he complained. "What the hell are you doing down there? The business end is the opposite direction!"

"Mime meemming more malls." Incredibly, Mitch deciphered the meaning. Exhaled slowly. Maytag. The perfectionist.

"Okay, okay," he said. "I'm not saying stop, just...you don't smoke a pipe from the bowl. If you catch my drift."

"Aye, aye, Captain," Andrea said. Eyes shone with gratitude. She shuffled back into position. Impaled her face. Beavered away on Mitch's pulsing lance. He telegraphed his eruption in the customary manner. Grabbed Andrea by the neck. Held her in place. Uttered his legendary crow's nest cry. One bellowed for centuries by sharp-eyed whalers. Andrea rocked on her heels Orca quantity discharge. Total Gillespie for Andrea. Eyes round as dinner plates. Tears of happiness leaked down bulging cheeks. She'd served her man in the classic fashion.

Emptied, Mitch relaxed his grip. Andrea fell back on the sheets, gurgling like a plugged drain. She recovered quickly. Reached out. Tried to cuddle. Mitch flinched, repulsed. Moved upwind. What was she thinking? He knew where her mouth had just been.

Offered her five more minutes of his presence. He'd already recalibrated his day. Lunch was a non-starter. Hit the gym right off. Slide into the kitchen after. Shoot the lads a twelve pack from his stash of freebies. Try and score some takeout. Push it in over the uni. Scratch out a summary of Florida. Be visible. Then deke. Head to the arena. Find the practice pad. Get some drills in, especially with an open net. Back to Billy's in time for the puck drop. Call Mitch when you needed a path charted. He was the 'spurt on that score.

Meanwhile, Andrea chattered on about this and that. Always interested in his family. Yes, Mitch said, the old man was also hung. Nicknamed "Three Legs" when he played with the Marlies. Mitch shared the family story. A Sunday morning. Dad rolls out of bed with the world's largest, hardest piss woodie. On the way to the can gets asked by the wife how he'd slept. Turns around to answer. Clears breakfast from the table. Those old guys. They didn't talk in inches.

"Oh, Mitch," Andrea purred. "Your Mom must have been in heaven."

Mitch nodded. "Yeah, she looked pretty happy most days. They finally had to rip out her guts, though. Surgeon said her uterus looked like it'd been run over by a truck. I guess you can have too much of a good thing."

He checked the wall digi. Triple-S time. Bounced off the bed. Bathroom duty.

Shit, shave and shower completed, Mitch rolled into the living room. Andrea sat scrunched up on the sofa. Grinned over as he toweled dry. Mitch returned it. Hid his annoyance. What he really wanted was her absence. ASAP. Flung the damp and pungent at her.

"Hey, if you plan on hanging around, hang this. I gotta vanish soon."

Andrea peeled the flannel from off her face. "Sure thing, horny. I mean honey."

"Har, har," Mitch mock-laughed. Checked the holovid. "What's on?"

"Not sure. It's the news, I think. Or a documentary. Or sports. Some guy is doing an obstacle course. Only he's riding on one of those…two-wheeled things. The ones you stand up on."

"A Segway," Mitch explained.

"What's a Segway?"

Mitch laughed. "About 40 kgs, you empty-headed dit." Strolled up behind her. Bounced his unit off her head. Always made her laugh. Reached down. Latched onto the love bubbles. Expertly kneaded her nipples rigid.

"Are you sure you have to go right now," she moaned. Arched her back. Unbundled her legs.

"Yeah," Mitch said. Slapped her sandbags about with honest affection. Sudden business flash. Titballs! All those mastectomy things were wasted. Once they got sliced off, suck out the muck. Seam the two halves together. Bingo. A soft, durable, waterproof ball. Rugby. The beach. Schools. How could that not sell?

Mitch was pumped. Call Doc Robbins when he got to the shop. Find out if the trull had given up any leads. Maybe the whole Ovarian thing got solved while he slept. He could hope. Then feel her out, so to speak, about his idea. Offer her shares in the company if she knew where she could lay her hands on any chopped off product. Should be cheap. Pay somebody to dumpster dive outside the guilty clinic. He knew a guy up north who'd prep them, cheap. Mounted fish all the time. Did nice work. Slip the halves to Mrs. pay-cash/register-always-closed/never-a-receipt Korean pants-fixer. Just to see the expression on her face. Shoot her some folding paper with high numbers. She was the type to get over any initial concerns.

"Look," Mitch said. Serious now. "I'm gone as of already. That means you've got time to make sure this place is spotless before you do anything else. You know where the central vac is. Pitter patter, butter butt."

Without waiting for a response, Mitch grabbed a handful of hair. Jammed Andrea's face into the old throw pillow. Held her down as she struggled for air. Finally released her. Gave her semi-gentle cuff on the ear. "Mind me, now," he said. "All my travel shit is in the closet. Wash clothes, clean up, clear out. Got it?"

Andrea leapt up from the sofa. Saluted. Scampered to the closet. Mitch turned off the holovid. Remembered the weather. Turned it on again. Groaned when the channel appeared. Perfect timing. Update right then. Andrea'd already shared the wonderful news. Sleet two nights earlier. Inch of snow after. April in a day's time.

"Rain, rain, go away, all this freezing shit is gay," he muttered to himself. Told Andrea to relax. He was talking to himself.

A last quick check. Hit the bedroom. Jeans, Fighting Haddocks pullover. Grabbed his com. Smiled into the mirror. Scar blaze always whiter after a binge. The rest. Not bad for what he'd been through. Vaulted for the door. Leather jacket, homemade wool muffler, Leaf's lid. Showing it's age. Didn't remember so many hanging threads. Wondered if that pizza box had swapped hers for his. Shifty minx. Put it on. Felt right. Fuck it. Smokes, lazer, money card, car chip. Hit the locks. Outside. Vroooom.

FADE TO BLOOD RED

~~⊰⟨◇⟩⊱~~

"Wow! No shit!" Mitch's first reaction. Grins around the table. Ciccarrelli, Jameson, the Sage (Mitch still didn't know his real name), Mort, Peters from StratDiv. Even Max got an invite. Which confirmed Mitch's earlier suspicions. Looking frumpled and frowzy as always. Asteroid face pocks. Dry riverbed skin. Squinch wrinkles. Actually blended with the brown tie and winey corduroy jacket. Which looked made from the skin of a beat up porch sofa.

News was big. No question. Turned out, the trulls were missing more than limbs, heads and whatnot. Mort the award-winner. It was true the major organs were intact in all the found corpses. So no one faulted the coroners for not digging deeper. Mort happened upon the discovery by chance. Demo for some students. Opened a slut up for for study purposes. Dice and slice texture test. It was then he noticed she didn't have a baby crate. Her ovaries were gone.

Lights and bells. Com call. Iced down python siphons got wheeled out on trays. Hacked open. Echoes down below. Of reproductive organs, there were none. Eyebrows raised all over top floor. Speculative threads woven together. Bombshell theory. The Ovarians were trying to create a frankenfemme. Maybe that was Project 89. It fit with intel coming in from faculty room listening posts. Bio lab break-in's might also be explained. Grave robbing next. Or already.

Too weird for Mitch. Bad enough his vic got whacked for nothing. Small comfort considering the time he'd wasted thinking about the case. And that trip to Hospital of the Living Dead. An afternoon he'd never get back. Though he liked the Doc. Have to get her outside where it was safe to breath. Mitch hated to see a prime rack of beef go unsampled.

Anyway, it meant his dead slot was but one off-colour in a rainbow of slayings. Only important in the sense Man/dy might be the twisted offspring of money. CORE could stand to profit if the killers were discovered. Better still, eliminated. Mitch wasn't sure how things would turn. But the mood at the table seemed upbeat. It had been a good month, March. Except for the fucking weather.

Mitch had already been brought up to date before he saw Yaz. Wasted no time in congratulating him. Yaz, shy grin as his hand got pumped. Back slapped.

"Shit, I'll probably be taking orders from you this time next year," Mitch joked. Threw a punch at Yaz's midriff.

"I'll have to take the exams first." Yaz flinched away. Smiled.

Mitch waved the thought off. "Like that'll cause you grief. You'll blow through them. No fear." He stepped back. "Seriously, though. Good news. So how'd the Force take it?"

Yaz looked at the floor. "Not, uh...Comissioner Ciccarrelli suggested they...don't need to know just yet."

Mitch reared back. Roared. "You're a double agent. You're a double agent," he teased. "Royal Canadian Mental Pygmies. Anal retentive, incompetent PR fuckups. Serves'em right."

"There's something else I should...confess," Yaz said. Eyes failed to set anywhere for long.

"The secret message shit? Don't bother," Mitch interrupted. "Already know."

Yaz was taken aback. "But...and you're not...?"

"Fuck no," Mitch chuckled. "We figured that was the story right from the start. I don't care. And I had an idea that once you saw how we operate..." Mitch shrugged. "Let's just say...your joining the team? No surprise. Cause we're gonna win. Eventually."

Mitch waved off the uni. Then the lights. "Shit," he breathed a heavy sigh. "Enough. Finish the report tomorrow. No fucking rush. There'll be, like, fifty of'em. Don't know why I should even have to write one. It'll be the same as everybody else's."

"About the...?"

"Yeah," Mitch nodded, leaning towards the door. "Yeah, what a...story. Tell you what. Help me pick out a souvenir for the ol' mossy jaw. First round's on me after practice tonight. You gotta come to Billy's. Celebrate your joining the white hats. What do you say? Give you all the shit on Florida. Probably watch some of it. Big event in a couple of days. Amazing stuff. No lie."

Yaz patted his pocket. "I should stop at an ATM. I'm..."

"Forget about it," Mitch said, sailing out the door. "After the bonuses we got handed, I'm so flush it's dangerous. If we got time, I wouldn't mind stopping off at that electronics shop out on…" And they were in the corridor and gone.

They stopped in the lobby for a second. Mitch liked to flirt with the all-female Muzz-bomber-decoy SecTeam. Remind them they were still women, unisex uniforms or not.

Mitch had a running routine with the supervisor, Nanci. With an 'I'. So it was Nanci who was able to answer both Yaz's questions. Fake lobby guard and info queen. Well-prepped professor. Mitch himself hadn't a clue. In fact, he'd never even looked at the CORE shield that close. He knew "Eat, Shit, Fight and Fuck" was not the real motto. But it suited. So when Nanci translated the inscription, he was as surprised as Yaz. Also impressed with Yaz's pronunciation.

"Jesus, that's pretty good. Say it again."

Yaz did so. "Christus dominatus restituo passim."

Mitch applauded, sincere. "Sounds like something the pope would say. I'd have never known the meaning if you hadn't asked. So there you go. Learn something new everyday." Looked at Nanci with admiration as well.

"Beautiful and brainy. No wonder the guys are all half-a'sceert a ya'," he drawled.

"You're not," Nanci said, eyes flashing.

"That's because I'm also beautiful and brainy," Mitch replied. Grabbed his crotch. Nanci licked her lips. So bad. The other guards shared smiles with each other. They'd all fantasized about a sex sandwich with Mitch. What a delicious and satisfying centre.

Yaz wasn't sure what to make of Nanci's answer to his second question. Mitch was clearly entertained. Nanci wore a knowing look as well.

"That's true? Why your nickname is Magnet?"

"Absolutely," Mitch said, winking at Nanci. He turned to the exit. "'Cause I'm so fucking attractive. Isn't that right, ladies?"

"Some day, Mitch Milligan," the rusty-haired bear trap winked.

"And the happiest day of our lives it'll be, darlin'," Mitch rejoined. His infectious laugh filled the foyer. The good mood carried them through a chill wind. Above ground parking lot reached. The Gringolet sat, pre-warmed. They got in. Mitch mulled his answer to Yaz's next question.

"Yeah," he said. "I mean, technically, we haven't charged anyone for the crimes. We've cut off a few heads, but the tentacles…? Still out there. Slaughtering whores. Operating without any restraint. Beyond the pale. It might mean pocket filler, we find out who," Mitch chuckled. "And we're still the main detectives. Until told otherwise. I was kinda hopin' we'd get the hook today. No such luck. So…that's our agenda. Manyana. Keep up the hunt. But not let it overwhelm everything else. Life's too short. And stress'll kill you. Who needs it, right?" Laughed.

"No lead from…?"

"N-o-o-o," Mitch shook his head. Lit a smoke. Passed the pack to Yaz. "Or…I don't know. Never came up. With me anyway. Fucking…well, shit, I guess I can say his name. Fucking Kensilla was just a…National Party of Moronto assboy. Errand-runner. Professional sneak. Liar. Well-poisoner. Typical Party shithead. But not enough balls to murder. Not even women. Just a grocery clerk. Dinner dancer. Nothing more."

Mitch held his finger to his lips. Winked. "Now you're on the inside, it's okay. But some things should stay close to the vest. Know what I'm saying? You'll see why on the weekend."

Yaz lowered his window. Blew smoke into the crisp early evening air. Described his week. One day in particular. When he'd finished, Mitch's happy state had evaporated. He slammed the Gringolet into gear.

"Fuck the present," he snarled. "You say this happened on Carlton?"

Yaz nodded.

"They yelled that driving by?"

"Yes. I didn't…I was simply walking around. Learn more of the city."

"Cunts must have recognized you. You remember their car?"

"A Ford. Late model. Eco-style."

Mitch rolled his eyes. "Jesus. Colour?"

"Taupe."

Mitch shot a disapproving sidelong look at his passenger.

"Grayish brown."

"Thank you." Mitch stared out the windshield. Pulpy sky. Almost dark. Weighed options. Nobody ambushed a CORE man. Scandalous. Way outta line Thought of his other CORE code name. Appropriate when dealing with cobras. Argue it was a Project 89 takedown. Plus, a juicy payback would give him another angle for the Friday night Florida storyboard at Billy's. The chance to see Yaz pull some more of his gymno shit sealed it for Mitch.

Carcom addressed. Three numbers appeared. Mitch okayed contact. Replies would come quick, he knew. All outsiders. Two cement workers. The other guy worked door at a club downtown. Northerners. Excellent toe-to-toe scrappers. Untraceable to the shop. Case of beer. They'd be ready to go whenever he wanted. Mitch was primed now. He could use the workout.

"This gets dealt with," Mitch growled. "And I mean now. Battle declared. Battle engaged. Fucking dykos. We'll go pay'em a little visit. Heh, heh, heh…" He looked over at Yaz. Smiled. "You need to do any stretching for that… stuff?"

"The gymno?"

"Yeah."

"No. Not really. Why?"

Mitch dropped the clutch. Chirped away. Waved to the guard on the way through the gates.

"We might have to move fast, is all," he explained. A menacing grin appeared. "Eat, shit, fight and fuck," he said to the windshield. Always tickled him. As did the tag line. "But not always in that order." The night was shaping up to be proof of that.

Diamond-shaped taillights winked out in the gathering gloom. Must have kicked the turbo's on, the guard figured. Glanced at the monitor. Mitch's departure time registered. Another early night. Wondered what devilment the kid had lined up for himself. As if that Florida thing had everybody talking wasn't enough. Hear about it in the morning, he guessed. Wished he was young again for the millionth time. The new gen had all the fun.